The Bearer of the Sign

A Continuation of Uncaged

By

Deeva Denez

Cover design by Toshia Fomby.

First published in 1999 by The Literary Connection, 2794 Stardust Court, Decatur, GA 30034

ISBN: 0-7596-6551-6

This book is printed on acid free paper.

1stBooks - rev. 11/27/01

ACKNOWLEDGMENTS

I would like to thank Melanie Duncan, a good friend, who helped me edit this work for almost nothing.

I would also like to thank Sandy Mitchell, my daughter and assistant, who helped me complete this work.

DEDICATION

This book is dedicated to my beloved husband, who is the bearer of the sign, Robert Earl Mitchell.

THE BEARER OF THE SIGN

Dear Lord, only You know who the next man will be in my life. My divorce from Carl marked the end of one life and the beginning of another. I prayed to You before my divorce for a sign—the confirmation of the next man in my life. We decided, Father, that this was the sign I had chosen to identify the next man in my life. The man I hope to spend my last days with until I die. The man who will treat me like I want to be treated. The man who will cherish me. The man who will build me up instead of tearing me down. The man who will love my mind and my body. The man who will be faithful and devoted to me until death do us part. The man who fears You and walks in Your ways. As long as I am single, I will never ask a man for money. But the next man in my life will give me fifty or more dollars voluntarily. When he gives me the money, I'll ask him, "What is this for?" He will reply, "This is for you because I am your man." And indeed he will be from that day on until I die.

ONE

Lord, I am so adamant about my sign that even if Carl gives it to me, I will remarry him. As disgusting as that sounds, I will do it because I know it is Your Will for me. However, I hope You have someone else in mind. The thought of living with Carl again makes me ill. At any rate, my life is in Your hands to do with as You please, regardless of how I feel, think or puke. Let everything I do from this day forward praise You. Amen.

Just as I finished my prayer, the telephone rang. I stood from my kneeling position to answer the phone. The clock by the phone glowed 5:33 p.m.

"Hello?"

"Hello, Vanessa, this is Bryson. I called to see how the divorce went today. I wanted to call earlier, but I knew you were asleep."

"Oh, it was a piece of cake. You are talking to a woman who is uncaged and unleashed!"

"Great! Let me come over to help celebrate your freedom."

"No. I don't want company. I need to spend the evening with the boys. Besides, it's too early to introduce them to another man."

"What about tomorrow? They'll have a whole day to adjust."

"Bryson, you're impossible! Tomorrow is also too soon."

"Vanessa, I want to see you. I've been waiting for your divorce for over a month."

"It's only been thirty-two days."

"I know how long it's been. I've been counting off each day. Now, you're telling me I have to wait until the boys adjust. How much time are we talking about? A day, a week, or a damn lifetime? I think twenty-four hours is long enough."

"Bryson, I know you want to see me, but you have to wait until the right time. I'll let you know when that time comes."

"For Christ-sakes, Vanessa! Can't you see the time is now, this evening?"

"No, Bryson, the time is not this evening. We'll talk about it more at work. I have to go now, to spend time with Little Carl and Carlos. Good-bye."

"All right, have it your way. We'll discuss it tonight. Good-bye."

1

As I hung up the phone, I thought about Mike Taylor, the car serviceman who wanted to take me out to dinner after my divorce. Although, I wasn't ready for dinner, I wanted to spread the good news that I was finally a free woman. I looked his number up in my phone book and dialed. He picked up on the second ring.

"Hello?"

"Hello, Mike, this is Vanessa Lewis."

"Vanessa, it's good to hear from you! I think of you every day. I've told everyone at the dealership that you'll be my next wife."

"Mike, I called to tell you I'm a free woman. My divorce was final today. This is the day we've both been waiting for."

"When can I take you out for dinner? I have to work late Friday and go in early Saturday. How does Saturday evening sound? Is that okay?"

"Mike, I need more time. I'm not ready to date yet. I'll call you when I am."

"Are you ready to receive calls?"

"Sure."

"I have your number. I'll call you every day. Hurry up, though. I can't wait much longer to make you may fiancee, then wife."

"Slow down, Mike! Let's take it one step at a time, okay?"

"Okay. I'll step from my house, to my car, to your house, to take you as my wife."

"No, Mike. That's not what I had in mind. I'll call you later when I'm ready for my dinner."

"Okay, have it your way. But my way is better."

"Bye, Mike. I need to get off the phone, so I can spend time with the boys."

"Good-bye, the future Mrs. Taylor."

I slowly put the receiver back. I haven't been divorced eight hours and I already have a two-man dilemma on my hands, I thought, as I went downstairs to the boys.

"Mama, what's for dinner?" Carlos, my eight year old, asked reaching for the two liter Coke bottle from the refrigerator as I entered the kitchen.

"Leftover spaghetti or leftover leftovers."

"I'll take spaghetti."

"Okay, spaghetti coming up," I said, going to the sink to wash my hands.

"Mama, can I get a dog?" Carlos asked.

"No. You know how I feel about pets, especially dogs. Dogs are too destructive and shitty. Besides, we don't have a fenced yard to contain it. Although I don't like dogs, I think chains around their necks are inhumane. And you know, no dog will live in my house," I said putting my hands on my hips to emphasize my point.

"But, Mama...we need a dog to eat the leftover leftovers! It's inhumane to feed that stuff to your kids," he whined.

"You eat what the Good Lord provides, leftovers and all!"

"Gary's dog eats his spinach and broccoli straight from his plate. He feeds him everything he don't want. That's what I need. A spinach, broccoli, leftover, eating dog."

"No, what you need is to be more thankful. Hand me the spaghetti, please, so I can heat it up." Carlos reached inside the refrigerator to retrieve the spaghetti. "I'll ask Dad for a dog. I'll bet he'll say yes," he said, handing me the spaghetti.

"He can say whatever he wants. I won't have to live with it. We're divorced now, so whatever he does doesn't affect me."

"Are you glad you divorced Dad?"

"Yes, I am. How do you feel?"

"Sad...real sad," he said as he left the kitchen.

I watched him leave, not knowing what else to say. Heating up the spaghetti, I thought about Carlos. What have I done to my son?

As the spaghetti simmered so did my thoughts. My happiness wouldn't be at the expense of my sons. Somehow this divorce must work for all of us. I'll consider their feelings in things that directly affect them. Their mental, emotional, spiritual, and physical well-being will be my number one priority.

Little Carl, my six-foot two, two hundred thirty pound, thirteen-year-old came into the kitchen as the spaghetti was ready to be served.

"Ready to eat?" I asked, reaching for the black, plastic, plates in the cabinet next to the sink.

"What are we having?" he asked, opening the refrigerator.

"Spaghetti."

"We had that yesterday at Dad's. What else do we have?"

"Leftover barbecue chicken..."

"We had that twice last week," Little Carl complained.

"I know, but we still have some left over for this week."

"Take me to McDonald's. I'm tired of eating the same thing."

"Do you have money for McDonald's?"

"No, but you do."

"No, I don't. I need to really watch my spending now because I can't rely on your dad for child support."

"This divorce thing really sucks. One day we can eat out and the next day we can't. I'm calling Dad to see if he'll stop by McDonald's and bring me something to eat."

"Carl, I'm going to do everything in my power to make our lives as normal as possible, but I need your cooperation. Stop acting like a spoiled brat and start acting like a responsible young man!"

"Mama, I am a responsible young man. That's why I'm going to page Dad now." He left the kitchen and went upstairs to use the phone in my room.

I hope today is no indication of what it'll be like from now on, I thought as I called Carlos to dinner. Carlos and I ate our spaghetti. Little Carl joined us and ate a sandwich because his father didn't have any money. We played UNO for an hour after dinner then I took a short nap before work.

During my nap, I rested my eyes but not my mind. I kept thinking of my sons' happiness, feelings, and loss. I could never replace their dad, but I could make them as happy as possible in his absence.

Apparently, I managed to fall asleep because Carlos woke me up to answer the phone.

"Mama, the telephone's for you."

"Who is it? I'm asleep."

"He has a funny name. I think he said, 'Ykey'."

"I don't know a Ykey."

"He knows you. He asked to speak to Mrs. Vanessa Lewis."

"Okay. I'll take the call."

"I'll go hang up the other phone," he said as he left the room.

I picked up the receiver by my bed. "Hello," I said sleepily.

"Hello, Vanessa, this is Zakee."

I shot straight up in bed. "Zakee! What a surprise to hear from you!"

"I was thinking of our last conversation, my last day at Grady. You said you were getting a divorce soon. I believe you mentioned today. As a matter of fact, I know you did because I wrote the date down with your number."

"You did?"

"Yes, I did. This day is important to me."

"It is?"

"Yes, it is."

"Why?"

"Because I want us to get together."

"You do? When?"

"As soon as you are ready."

"I'm ready now, but I feel it's too soon for my sons. They worship their father. Introducing another man in my life may make them upset or something. I don't think they can handle it for awhile."

"I understand. In Islam, we have to wait three months before we can start a new relationship. You have my number. Call me when you think they're ready."

"Okay, I will."

4

"Good-bye, Vanessa. I hope to hear from you soon."

"Good-bye, Zakee. You will."

As I hung up the phone, I remembered the "Price Tag Prophecy", "Before you take the last price tag off, something will happen for the two of you to get together."

I decided to pray. "Lord, I know You work in mysterious ways. Are You telling me Zakee will finally be mine? But what about Bryson and Mike? How do they fit into my life? How can I have three men in my life at one time? Will one or all of them give me my sign?" Now, I just have to wait.

TWO

I gazed at the clock that displayed 9:27 p.m.. Realizing I still had forty-five minutes to sleep before work, I turned over and dozed off. As I slept, thoughts kept churning in my head.

In my dream, I awaken from my sleep when the doorbell rang. I quickly grabbed my long, ivory housecoat from the closet and securing the sash snugly around my waist answered the door. Zakee stood on the porch holding a dozen long-stemmed red roses. His six-foot four, perfectly proportioned physique looked marvelous in his red, black, and white, shirt and black slacks.

"Zakee! What a pleasant surprise!"

"I hope you don't mind me dropping by without calling first."

"No, not at all. You're welcomed to come by anytime."

"May I come inside?"

"Oh, forgive me. Please do," I said, unlocking the screened door.

Once inside, we gazed into each other's eyes. A crescent smile appeared on his face as his eyes scanned my face.

"These are for you," he said, giving me the roses.

"Oh, thank you. They are lovely," I said, smelling one near the center.

"Not as lovely as you. You are the personification of the perfect woman."

"Thank you," I said, blushing. I was probably as red as the roses. "Have a seat while I find a nice home for my roses." I went into the kitchen and opened the cabinet under the sink where I kept my only vase. Carefully, I removed the plastic casing and placed the roses in the clear glass vase. When I turned to go into the living room, Zakee was standing at the threshold, admiring me. Both excited and nervous, I walked toward him.

"I've been waiting a long time for this moment," he said, with his eyes inviting me to come closer. I immediately thought about his ex-non-wife/wife whom he married last year but was not legally married to although they had a wedding ceremony. I didn't realize he was thinking about me since he was with her. Unless he meant the time since their final separation in January. Nevertheless, this was not the time to bring her up. I simply accepted what he said at face value. "So have I."

He pulled me close to him, looked me in the eye, and said, "I want to be your man."

This was no time to tell Zakee my next man must give me a sign. Forgive me Lord, but for Zakee I might have to make an exception, I thought. "How can I know you're sincere?"

"By this," he said, as his lips kissed mine. "Do you need any more proof?" he asked as our bodies clung together.

"Yes, but God must reveal it to you."

"He already has."

"What do you mean?"

"Here is your proof," he said, reaching into his back pocket for his wallet. He opened it and pulled out a crisp fifty dollar bill.

"What is that for?" I asked, grinning. But before he answered the doorbell rang and Zakee disappeared.

Very upset, I answered the door. Mike Taylor was on the porch dressed in a navy, double-breasted suit with a blue and white flowered tie. A wide grin covered his plain, medium brown face. His hands were behind his back.

"Mike, what are you doing here?" I grumbled.

"I couldn't wait any longer to see you. I dropped by to see if you're ready for our dinner date?"

"Not tonight, I have to go to work soon. But please, come inside."

"Thank you. I thought you'd never ask. These are for you," he said, handing me a large box of Russell Stover chocolates, a bouquet of white, peach, violet and yellow flowers, and a small wrapped box.

"Thank you. The flowers are beautiful."

"Sweets for my sweetheart and flowers for my orchid," he recited.

"What's in the box?"

"You have to open it to find out," he said, taking the candy and flowers back to free both my hands.

I opened the box. Inside was a large, oval-shaped diamond engagement ring. "Mike, this ring is lovely, but I can't accept it. We don't even know each other yet!"

"That doesn't matter. You can find out all about me after we're married. I'm an ordinary guy. What you see is what you get."

"Mike, I know you are a very nice man. You are caring, sincere, honest, a hard worker, witty, and charming, but...."

"But, what else do you want if I'm all that? Vanessa, those qualities you named for me, I see in you. That is why I want you to be my wife. We're a perfect match! A match made from heaven, I might add."

"Why do you say that?"

"I know what you are looking for, and I have the answer."

"You do? What is it?"

He laid the candy and flowers on the loveseat next to the door. "Here is your answer, your sign," he said, reaching into his suit pocket pulling out his wallet. He opened it and removed a new one hundred dollar bill.

"What's that for?"

"This is for you because...."

In mid-sentence, a horn blew outside, and Mike disappeared. I heard footsteps on the porch then the doorbell rang. When I opened it, Bryson was outside, sucking a blow-pop. He was dressed in his dark blue uniform, and his dark face made it hard to distinguish where the uniform ended and his skin began. He looked like one blue-black blob.

"Are you going to let me in, or do I have to break the damn door down?"

"Come on in," I said, as I opened the door. "Why did you blow your horn?"

"I wanted my presence to be known. I didn't want nobody to shoot my ass at the door. If any shooting was going to be done, do it while I was in the driveway. That way, I could get the hell out of here."

"Are you always so crazy?" I asked.

"I'm crazy about you. Here's a blow-pop to show my love," he said, handing me a blow-pop from his shirt pocket.

"Is this all you have to give me to show your love, a blow-pop?" I demanded.

"No, I have something else, but your sons are home. Maybe, before the evening is over, we can go back downstairs," he said, locking me into his arms, kissing me.

"Bryson, you're full of shit. You came over here to screw!"

"No, I came to see you, then screw. But if you want to screw first, I'm here to oblige," he said, waving his arms.

"Have a seat, Bryson. Let me get you some cold water to cool your hot ass down."

"I don't need water to cool off! I need you!"

"Bryson, if you keep talking like that, I'll ask you to leave."

"Okay, okay, don't be so mean. That housecoat shows your figure," he said, admiringly.

"Bryson, you think I'm kidding. One more remark and your visit is over."

"Let me rephrase my comment. Your ass looks just as nice in that housecoat as it does without clothes."

"Bryson, out! Your visit is over," I said, showing him the door.

"Wait a damn minute before you throw my ass out the door!"

"What?" I snapped.

"I have something to give you before I go."

"What?" I asked again.

He reached in his front pants pocket and pulled out a wrinkled five dollar bill then handed it to me.

"What's that for?"

"I want you to take this money and buy you some flowers, tomorrow. I meant to buy you some but didn't have time. And to show how much I love you, you can keep the change."

"Out, Bryson. Get out of my house, right now!"

"Okay, okay," he said, putting the five back into his pocket. "No sense letting a perfectly good five dollar bill go to waste."

My alarm went off as I closed the door in his face.

THREE

I woke up pissed off with Bryson. How dare he interrupt Mike from giving me my sign? I wasn't upset with Mike for cutting Zakee off because maybe he was going to be my next man instead of Zakee. Only God knew for sure. But Bryson, on the other hand, was obviously a total waste of my time. The dream clearly revealed that to me.

Bryson was waiting for me in the parking lot, at Grady, dressed in his black and white security uniform. When I opened my car door, he kissed me.

"I thought you would never get here," he said, smiling. "I couldn't wait to see you, to kiss your lips."

"Bryson, you're full of surprises. I never know what to expect from you from one minute to the next."

"Good. I'll try to keep it that way."

"I don't have time to talk. I need to clock in."

"I know. I'm out of my area anyway, but I just had to see you. I'll call or come by later."

"Okay," I said, as I hurried away.

Bryson went in the opposite direction. He was out of sight before I reached the parking stairwell. I thought about him as I walked to the lab. Bryson had a way with me. I couldn't deny it, and I couldn't shake it either.

At 3:10 a.m., Bryson came to the lab window. I was putting blood specimens in the centrifuge when he stopped by.

"Give me a minute to finish," I said, closing the hood. He shook his head as if to say, "okay". I walked toward the door, pressed the green exit button, then went outside the lab to talk.

"You look good tonight," he said, giving me the once over. "Divorce agrees with you."

"Thank you," I said, glancing at my white Reeboks, white pants, and white lab coat. "You've seen me wearing this a hundred times."

"That's true, and you look good every time."

"Bryson, you're making me blush," I said, as I felt blood rush to my face.

"I'm off tomorrow night. Can I come by?"

"No. I told you over the phone, it's too soon!"

"Why?"

"How do I explain to my sons that I'm seeing another man when I've only been divorced one day?"

"Easy. Tell them the damn truth."

"Which is?"

"Tell them you met me the day you got your divorce papers, at work. We've been talking since then and have become very close to one another. You understand they still love their father, and hope they always will, but you have a life and a new man to share your life with. You'd like for them to meet me and get to know me as soon as possible."

"Do you really think they'll understand their mother being with a man other than their dad?"

"Yes, I do," he stated.

"I don't think so."

"Okay. Then prove me wrong. Tell them what I just told you and see for yourself. Tell them. I know I'm right."

"Let me pray about it first. I'll let the Lord guide me. I don't want to do anything to hurt them. They've been through enough."

"So have I! It's time to move forward, to go on with our lives. Vanessa, I care a great deal about you, more than you realize."

"I can't just think about me. I have to consider their feelings, too."

"And mine. I'm in this with you and them. And don't ever forget it either. We're in this shit together."

"Okay. Let me see how God leads me. Then I'll let you know."

"That's fair enough."

"I've been talking long enough. My specimens should be ready."

"Not as ready as I am to be with you."

"Bye, Bryson. Call me later if you get a chance."

"You got it," he said as he walked off.

I entered the lab and thought of our conversation for the remainder of the night. Bryson must have been busy because he never called.

I prayed before I went to sleep.

Dear Heavenly Father, Great Creator of the universe. The Great Omniscient, Omnipresent, and Omnipotent One, Who knows all things. Please direct my steps and fill my mouth with Your Words to speak to my sons concerning my new life. I'm now free to be with another man. I'm ready to move forward. But only You know if my sons are ready. I don't want to hurt them or act hastily. Their mental and emotional well-being are very important to me. I don't want to do anything that will hurt them. I love them, not as much as You, but as much as I can in this clay vessel. I ask this in the name of Your Son, Jesus Christ. Amen.

Carl called that evening to see if it was okay for him to come by to see the boys. He would be at the house in thirty minutes. The boys were excited when I told them their dad was on his way. They both hugged my neck at the news.

Carl's horn blew thirty-five minutes later. I motioned for him to come inside. I watched him as his long legs swerved from his new burgundy Ford Tempo onto the driveway. Covering his body were a pair of faded jeans and a beige pullover sweater. Butterflies filled my stomach as he approached. For some reason, he seemed like a stranger. It was hard to believe we had spent the last twenty-five years together. We'd only been divorced for one day, but already the distance between us seemed like eternity.

"What you want?" he asked, coldly, as he reached the door.

"To talk with you a few minutes if you don't mind."

"All right."

When he set foot in the house, the boys greeted him.

"Hi Dad," Little Carl said, hugging Carl.

They exchanged high-fives before Carl gave him a bear hug.

"Where's Carlos?"

"Right here, Dad," Carlos said, standing behind the door.

Instantly, Carl hugged him, too.

"Where're we going Dad?" Little Carl asked.

"To my place. Now, what do you want to talk about?" he asked me.

"Have a seat first. Boys, sit down, too." We all sat down before I continued. "Carl, I want you to know that you're welcome to get the boys anytime you want. There are no visitation stipulations in our divorce decree. You can see your sons seven days a week if you choose. No matter what happens, I'll never keep you from seeing Carlos and Carl. I know I would hurt them if I did. Feel free to call them as often as you wish. Holidays are open. We'll play them by ear. Whatever the four of us decide, that's what we'll do," I finished.

"Suppose we want to live with Dad?" Little Carl asked.

"I have legal custody of you and Carlos. You can visit your dad as often as you like, but this is your home."

"Can we stay with Dad for the weekends?" Carlos asked.

"Sure."

"What about your men? Have you told your sons about your other men? That's why you divorced my ass!" Carl yelled.

"Carl, that's not true. I didn't divorce you because of another man," I replied calmly.

"That's a damned lie! Tell the truth. Tell them about your men!"

"Okay. Last year, I fell in love with a Muslim named Zakee."

"That's who called you last night," Carlos added.

"Yes. We only talked for several months before he married in September. We never kissed or did anything else."

"Did he give you any bean pies?" Carlos asked.

"No."

"Tell them about your other man. The one you're seeing now."

"I met a man at work, the night I received my divorce papers, in February. He stopped by my work window and started talking. During our conversation, I discovered he was a repair man. I asked him if he could do the repairs I wanted on the house. He said he could. So he agreed to work for me the week of Spring Break. He also is divorced. We found we had a lot in common and enjoyed each other's company. His name is Bryson Collier."

"What kind of car does he drive?" Carlos asked.

"A van."

"How much money does he make?" Little Carl asked.

"I don't know."

"Does he have any money?" Carlos asked.

"I don't know."

"You don't know if your man have any dough, bread, cheese, bills, presidents, cash? Why not?" Carlos asked.

"Because we never talked about money. Besides, I'm not interested in him or anybody else for how much money they have."

"Yeah, we know that. That's why you married Dad," retorted Little Carl.

"Your mother is more interested in what he has in his pants, not what's in his pockets," said Carl jumping up. "Let's go! I've had enough of this shit!" The boys followed him. "Bye, Mom," they both said as they left. Carlos turned back around and asked me, "Mama, what do you know about him?"

"I don't know."

"Gee Mom, you need to get mo' info."

I sat dumbfounded but glad the boys knew of Bryson. I had no idea they would find out this way. God sometimes has a strange way of answering prayers.

After they left, I called Bryson. His recording picked up on the first ring. "Bryson, this is Vanessa. I just told the boys about you. Call me so we can discuss you coming over. Bye."

A few minutes later, the phone rang. Bryson wanted to know what was said. I told him everything. We decided Friday would be a good day for him to come over since we were both off.

Wednesday evening, I told the boys Bryson would be coming over Friday. They said, they wanted to meet him, and I told him he wanted to meet them, too.

At eight o'clock Friday evening, I nervously waited for Bryson to arrive. Dressed in a calf-length, baby-blue, clinging skirt with a split in the front, a white, lace-collared blouse, black belt and black, open-toed shoes. My hair was swept to the left side with a full bang to give me a very sexy look. The boys kept peeping out the window waiting for Bryson to come.

Finally, Carlos shouted, "He's here!"

I stood up and they pulled the curtains completely back to get a good view.

"Look at his car!" Carlos exclaimed. "Mama, you can marry him!" he said, turning his head toward me for a second.

I smiled. Obviously, Bryson had made a good impression before he even entered the house.

"That's a black Mazda MX6 LS," reported Little Carl. "Mama, I thought you said he drove a van."

"He does. At least, that's what I saw him drive one day."

"I can tell he's smooth and has lots of cash in his pockets. Mama you did all right for yourself this time," Carlos said, turning around. "I was beginning to think you only liked broke men," "Maybe he'll let me take it for a spin sometimes. Mama put in a good word for me. Tell him I've been driving since I was eight," Little Carl said, as the doorbell rang.

"Let him in and tell him yourself."

Both Carl and Carlos opened the door. Bryson's full chest stood out in his brown-orange buttonless shirt and dark brown pants.

Bryson said, "Good evening," as he entered. "So-oo. You must be Carl," he said to Little Carl. "And you must be Carlos," he said to Carlos. "Your mother has told me a lot about you. How 'bout it," he said, lowering his hand for a low-five.

They looked at him as if he had just arrived from another planet. Neither gave him a low-five.

"We'll leave y'all alone," Little Carl said, pulling Carlos up the steps.

Bryson wiped his low-five hand on his shirt as if it was dirty. "I just love warm greetings."

"If you had two five dollar bills in your hand instead of five fingers, you would have gotten a different response. I have your warm greeting," I said, walking to him to give him a kiss.

"That's more like it. Now, I feel welcomed."

"Actually, you made a good first impression. When Carlos saw your car, he told me I could marry you."

Bryson laughed. "See, even he knows a good man when he sees one. What did Carl say?"

"He wanted me to ask you if he could drive your car?"

"I'll let him drive when he gets his license."

"Would you like something to eat or drink?" I asked, embracing him again.

"What do you have?"

"Pepsi, Sprite, rum, grape juice, wine, chips and dip, fried chicken wings, grapes, cheese and crackers."

"Um, I'll take rum with Sprite, chicken wings, grapes, and cheese and crackers."

"Okay. Let's get everything you want from the kitchen. Then we'll go downstairs and listen to the radio while we eat and talk."

"Oh, that sounds good."

Bryson fixed us both a strong rum and Sprite drink. We sipped several while listening and dancing to the music.

Two hours later, the rum was beginning to kick in. We kissed more than we danced or talked. His kisses became demanding. My body responded accordingly.

"I'll close the door," Bryson said, after our last kiss.

"Keep the door open. We can't do anything with the boys in the house," I said.

"Yes we can after I lock the door."

"That door doesn't lock."

"We'll just have to take our chances with it being closed," he said, closing the door.

"I can't do that. Suppose they walk in on us?"

"Say what? Relax and enjoy this," he said, kissing me on my neck, moving his hands on my hips.

"No Bryson, stop," I moaned, softly.

"I can't stop what is meant to happen," he said, unbuttoning my blouse, putting his erection between the split of my skirt.

We took a few short steps to the sofa that faced the door. He laid me down, took my blouse off and lifted up my skirt then we made love like two machines. Bryson sucked my breast tenderly while his penis thrust inside of me. His sweat covered our bodies. Before we finished, I heard the boys at the door. He said he was too close to stop. Seconds later, Bryson came. We straighten our clothes and hair then opened the door.

Little Carl and Carlos were sitting on the steps facing the door. "What were y'all doing? Carlos asked.

"Talking," both Bryson and I said together.

"Yeah, right," Little Carl replied.

We walked passed the boys with our dirty dishes, headed for the kitchen. Then I walked Bryson to the door. We kissed good night. When I turned around, the boys were facing me.

"Mama, you told us, no sex before marriage," said Little Carl standing by the door.

"That's true, and I meant it."

"Mama, tell us what really happened downstairs. We weren't born yesterday," Carlos queried.

"Magic, son. Magic," was all I could say.

FOUR

Bryson called early Saturday morning.

"Good morning, my love. How is my angel?"

"I'm fine, Bryson. How are you?"

"Better than good. I feel sweeter than honey. I really enjoyed myself last night."

"I did, too."

"I thought about you all night long."

"I bet it was all X-rated."

He laughed. "No some of it was actually PG."

"As in Pussy-Grinding?"

"No. As in Pleasantly Good."

"There's something I need to tell you about me."

"Don't tell me you have AIDS!" he screeched.

"No, silly! We both had HIV tests, remember?"

"That don't mean shit! You can have a false negative test if you test before antibodies are produced."

"That's correct. But that's not what I wanted to tell you."

"What is it? Since you don't have AIDS, it couldn't be too bad."

"It's not bad at all. I want you to know I'm looking for a sign to identify the next man in my life. After last night, I thought you needed to know."

"What the hell is a damn sign? What does a sign have to do with anything?"

"A sign is my confirmation that I have the man God has chosen for me to spend the rest of my life with."

"Look, Van...you've already gotten your sign. There was a reason I stopped and talked with you the day you got your divorce papers. Something made me stop that night, and you and I both know what that something was—God."

"That's true. But if God made you stop at my window, He will also give you the sign."

"Okay, Van, you have your sign, and I have mine. I've never felt the way I feel about you with anyone else before. Do my feelings count for anything?"

"Yes, and so do my feelings. You know, I've been close to you ever since the day we met."

"See, you already have your sign. Our relationship had God's intervention from the beginning."

"I still want my sign. Just to be sure."

"Have it your way, my love. I've got to go. I wanted to call you before I started a job this morning."

"I'm glad you did. Good-bye."

"Good-bye."

I hung up the phone, turned over and was fast asleep until the telephone woke me up at 9:33 a.m.. "Hello," I said, low and sleepy.

"Hi, Vanessa, this is Mike Taylor. I have been, unsuccessfully, trying to reach you for four days."

"I've been here. My sons never told me you called."

"They said either you were not there or you were asleep. I even called last night around 9:30 and your son said you couldn't come to the phone."

"You must have spoken to my oldest son. He's constantly on the phone. He probably didn't want to get off the line. I was here. I had company."

"Male or female?"

"Male."

"That was fast. What about us?"

"There is no us. I like the person I was with last night. I met him the day I got my divorce papers in February. That was the same day I left the dealership with my car after you repaired the front axle."

"I see you don't waste any time. I thought you were going to be mine, but I see you have someone else."

"That's true. I wasn't looking for him when we met. It just happened."

"All right then. I guess there's nothing else for me to say, except, congratulations, Ms. Lewis, for finding your man. Good-bye."

"Thanks, Mike. Good-bye."

Well, I guess, I can kiss his dinner invitation good-bye also. I thought as I got out of bed. Mike's conversation eradicated both my desire to sleep and to get to know him better. Bryson was my man, hands-down.

Carl came by for the boys as we finished breakfast. I was cleaning the kitchen when he arrived. He handed me a letter as he entered the kitchen.

"What's this?" I asked, as he shoved the envelope in my hand.

"It's a letter. I had a few things on my mind I wanted to say."

"Okay, I'll read it," I said, placing it on the counter by the sink. "Is there anything you want to say to my face?"

"Yeah," he said, pausing. "Your man is married."

"What are you talking about?"

"He's married. That's why he drives a van."

"You're crazy! Driving a van doesn't make you married. He's divorced with two sons. Anybody can drive a van, Carl."

"Maybe after you read my letter, you'll come to your senses," he said, as he walked towards the door. "You'll see I'm the man for you. You're wasting your time with Bryson. Wake up and smell the coffee!"

"Bye, Mama," both Carlos and Little Carl said as they walked out the door with Carl.

"Do I get a hug and kiss before you leave?"

They both hugged and kissed me.

"I love you," I said, during the hugging.

"I love you, too," they each said.

I ripped open the letter as the door closed.

Vanessa, I'm writing this letter to clear my mind. I'm trying very hard to accept our divorce and move on with my life, but I find it harder and harder to deal with each day. My friends are telling me to forget you and find someone else. They've even introduced me to several of their single friends. But I'm not interested because my heart is still with you. I can't seem to erase twenty-five years of my life overnight, although you have. It still hurts me to know that you are with someone else. How can you be with someone else so soon? I tell myself, maybe you never really loved me. But I know you did. Didn't you love me twenty-five years ago when we were teenagers? Didn't you love me when little Carl and Carlos were born? Didn't you love me when we got back together after breaking up and almost divorcing twice? Didn't you love me through the good times and the bad? Didn't you love me when we celebrated our twentieth wedding anniversary this January? If the answers are yes, then when did you stop loving me and why? When, Vanessa, when? And what can I do to turn your love around?

Heartbroken,
Carl

I threw the letter in the trash when I finished, envelope and all. "Carl, our relationship is over forever," I said aloud. "I stopped loving you when I started loving myself. I stopped loving you when I fell in love with Zakee." With that said, I finished cleaning the kitchen, I thought about the letter and Carl's conversation. Was Bryson married? No way. He told me himself about Helen, his friend. A friend and a wife are two different things, and the difference makes him mine.

Since the boys would be gone for the remainder of the weekend, I used the time to clean and read.

The telephone rang during my Bible study that evening. "Hello?"

"Hi, Van, this is Bryson."

"I know."

"My MARTA lines are clear. I was wondering if you wanted any company?"

"I'm having my Bible study right now. Your company will be nice later."

"Are the boys home?"

"No. They're gone for the weekend."

"When will you finish your Bible study?"

"Probably in the next thirty to forty-five minutes."

"I'll be over in an hour."

"Carl gave me a letter when he came by."

"He did? What did it say?"

"Basically it said, he still loved me and he wanted to know when I stopped loving him."

"Did you tell him he could kiss your ass and go to hell? That he could take his sorry ass somewhere else?"

"No. I didn't tell him anything. I didn't read the letter until after he left."

"What do you plan to tell him?"

"Nothing. I threw it away. Our relationship is over. There is nothing else left to say."

"Tell him to kiss your ass for the road."

"Carl thinks you're married because you drive a van."

"Tell Carl, he can kiss my ass. Van, he really is a jerk. How did you put up with him for all these years? I bought the van for my business. I totaled my pick-up truck two months before I bought the van. I needed something to carry equipment and supplies in. I'd been wanting some more transportation anyway. I like to keep the Mazda looking good. With kids, they have paper and shit everywhere. I try to keep them out of the Mazda. So, I bought the van for my business and my sons," Bryson explained.

"I told Carl just because you drove a van didn't mean you were married. I also told him he was crazy for thinking such a stupid thing!"

"I second that. Stupid should be his middle name, Carl "Stupid Ass" Lewis. He was stupid for letting you go. But his loss is my gain."

"Bryson, where do I stand with you? I know, I'm number two, but you treat me like I'm number one."

"You are number one, and don't you ever forget it."

"Okay, I won't. I'll see you in an hour. I need to finish my Bible study."

"Good-bye, my love."

It was hard concentrating on the Scriptures because I kept thinking of Bryson. Somehow, I managed to read for another thirty minutes. I then prayed and sang praises to God before Bryson arrived.

We had a wonderful evening together. We danced, ate, talked, drank and made love.

I enjoyed making love to Bryson because he explored different parts of my body to find my erogenous zones. One zone, at the base of my neck, was very responsive to his lips. His kisses drove me crazy whenever he stimulated that area.

Being with Bryson, however, made me feel guilty. Having sex outside of marriage was against my Christian beliefs. It was wrong in the sight of God. I felt like Paul in Romans 7:15-25: *"I do not understand my own actions. For I do not do what I want, but I do the very thing I hate...So then it is no longer I that do it, but sin which dwells in me. For I do not do the good I want, but the evil I do not want is what I do...for I delight in the law of God, in my inmost self, but I see in my members another law at war with the law of my mind and making me captive to the law of sin which dwells in my members. Wretched man that I am! Who will deliver me from this body of death? Thanks be to God through Jesus Christ our Lord! So then, I of myself serve the law of God with my mind, but with my flesh I serve the law of sin."*

After each sexual encounter with Bryson, I prayed.

Dear Heavenly Father, please forgive my trespass against You and Your Son, Jesus Christ. Father, I struggle with my flesh just as Paul did in Romans 7. Remove my sexual desire because I am not able to control it. I do not wish to disobey you, but I find myself doing the very thing I do not want to do. Father, please help me because I am unable to help myself. Do not cast me away or take Your Holy Spirit from me. I come to You as Your child not for wrath but for love, forgiveness, understanding, mercy and correction. I ask this in the name of Your Son and my Savior, Jesus Christ. Amen.

Prayer did not remove my guilt. It simply gave me an opportunity to voice my guilt, the struggle with my flesh, to God. I knew He understood. He could help me. He would keep me on the right path.

21

FIVE

Bryson and I talked every night at work, every morning after work, and every evening before work. Often he came over on his dinner break from MARTA to eat with me.

The boys, however, weren't receptive to Bryson when he came by. They exchanged their hellos and moved on. Carlos told me Bryson was my company. He didn't come over to see them. That was a true statement, so I didn't argue the point. Bryson said he was giving them time to get used to him. He knew how much they loved their father. He also knew that, although he was my friend, he was not theirs.

We planned a big date for Saturday, April 1, the weekend before Spring Break when Bryson was scheduled to work on my house. Our big date included going to the Fox Theater to see the Broadway Musical, "Raisin," based on Lorraine Hansberry's, "A Raisin in the Sun." We also planned to eat out and go dancing. I discovered Bryson loved dancing just as much as I did.

Even bigger than the big date was today, March 25, when I would attend my first I.B.W.A., International Black Writers and Artists, Inc., meeting. Since I planned to start writing "Uncaged" at the end of April or the beginning of May, the association would be very helpful.

I arrived early. Several people were sitting outside the conference room of the downtown Federal Building, waiting for the meeting to begin. Edna Crutchfield, the original founder, an elderly, white- haired, cocoa-brown woman, was among those gathered. When I introduced myself, she remembered talking to me.

The meeting started late because there was a mix-up concerning the room reservation. At the beginning of the meeting, we introduced ourselves and stated what our writing or artistic experiences were. Amazingly, the talents ranged from beginners, like myself, to educators, an actor, poets, screenplay writers, TV personnel, published authors, radio personnel, play writers, short story writers, song writers, and regular business people. Next, we discussed upcoming events before Robert Jackson, the president, a published author, lecturer, and successful computer businessman, gave a forty-five minute presentation on "The How-To's of Effective Writing." A question and answer period followed his presentation. We adjourned shortly after several people read their works.

I felt good about the meeting, especially being in the presence of such a diverse group of people. Instinctively, I knew I was in the right place. Maisha, the person who told me about the meeting, was truly God-sent. With the help of this organization, I knew the prophecy concerning "Uncaged" would come to pass: This book would be written and published.

The writing of "Uncaged" would take place after my house was repaired. Unfortunately, the divorce made me feel broken inside, mentally, physically, spiritually, and emotionally. I knew, my physical house had to be mended before my physical body could be healed of its brokenness. Therefore, God sent me a repairman, Bryson, because he was what I needed. I didn't need Mike, a service consultant, or Zakee, a corrections officer. I needed repairing from the inside out.

Bryson arrived early Saturday morning on April 1. He went through the house taking measurements. Carl came fifteen minutes later to pick up the boys. This was Bryson's and Carl's first face-to-face encounter. Bryson was at the base of the living room steps when Carl rang the bell. I was standing beside Bryson as Carlos let his dad inside.

"I couldn't wait for you to get here. I've been looking out my window for fifteen minutes," Carlos said, exchanging high-fives with Carl.

"Go get your things and tell Carl to come on," commanded Carl, stepping inside.

"All my stuff's ready. But I need some help to bring it down."

"Carl," I interrupted, "this is Bryson Collier. Bryson, this is Carl," I said, introducing them.

"Hi, man," Carl said, walking passed Bryson to get to Carlos's room.

Bryson didn't reply. He watched Carl climb the steps.

"So, that's Carl. He looks like a punk. I was expecting you to have a different type man."

Before I could respond, Carl, Little Carl, and Carlos came down the steps.

"Mama, I need some money," Little Carl said with his hand extended.

"Me, too," Carlos echoed.

"Go get my purse in my room, Carl. I'll give you five dollars apiece because I need my money to pay Bryson for working on the house and buy supplies."

Carl laughed. "Ha, ha, Vanessa! You're a fool. You have to pay your man to work for you? Aren't you putting out for him?"

"It's none of your damn business what she does," Bryson snapped at Carl.

"Let's go boys before I have to put this black gorilla in his place!"

"I am in my place, thank you. With your punk a...."

"Bryson, stop! That's not necessary. Here boys, here's ten dollars. Go! I'll see you later." We kissed before they ran out the door to catch up with Carl.

"Bryson, you're acting like an imbecile," I said, turning to him.

"Your ex is the imbecile. His IQ is the same as his shoe size—12."

"That's enough. Now, stop. Go back to taking measurements or something. You know we have to go to Home Depot to purchase supplies before we go to the musical."

Bryson pulled me close. "I'd rather take your measurements and supply your needs," he said softly, putting his lips on mine.

"Not now, Bryson. Work first. Pleasure later."

"You got that all wrong. Pleasure is now and later. My battery needs charging before I can work."

"You're full of it, Bryson. Now, get your horny butt to work, or there will be no pleasure later."

"Okay, Madame Boss. But I have one question to ask you before I start working."

"What is it?"

"Who's the best? Me or Carl."

"I'm not going to answer that."

"Let me ask you another question? Who can send you to the third heaven without wings?"

"Christ. Question and answer period is over. Get back to work!"

When Bryson finished, we went to Home Depot to buy three inside doors, paint and other supplies. He wanted to have as much as possible at the house, so he wouldn't have to waste time next week buying supplies. Since the musical started at two o'clock, he called it a day at noon, showered and dressed. The remainder of the day was simply marvelous!

Surprisingly, the remainder of the weekend passed quickly, and the big day finally arrived. Bryson came over early Monday morning, clad in his dark-blue work overalls. His first order of business was to paint Carlos's room a lighter, softer blue. Carl had painted it a horrifying dark-dark blue. Bryson said that blue was so ugly it brought tears to his eyes every time he went into Carlos's room. It also made him think of his ex-wife's Honda. Any reminders of his ex made him ballistic. Sometimes thinking of her made him kick his own ass. Next, Bryson painted the great room, kitchen, and hallways, an eggshell white. The hall bathroom was painted the same color as Carlos's room. Last, he painted my bedroom and bathroom a dark pink.

Day two, Bryson hung ceiling fans in the kitchen and my bedroom. He installed blinds on four windows. He took out the medicine cabinets in both bathrooms and replaced them with large vanity mirrors that had four light bulbs. The towel racks were replaced with two towel rings.

Together we carried the broken sofa and soiled loveseat to the curb. Only the kitchen table and matching china cabinet remained in the great room and kitchen. Looking at my empty great room, void of the broken, worn furniture, was a source of healing. Now, I was forced to buy new furniture to fill the void. The kitchen table and cabinet I would give away because they were too nice to discard. I didn't want to keep them, however, because they didn't have the original chairs, and I wanted all things new in my life.

Day three, Bryson worked outside. He installed new gutters, painted the porch and overhang, and planted grass seeds.

Day four, we cleaned windows and hung new curtains. My Uncle Mark sold me a four piece bedroom suite for Carlos for one hundred dollars. Bryson carried the old suite to the curb and put up the new one. We cleaned the house from top to bottom. I was embarrassed by the amount of dirt I cleaned. The more I cleaned, the more dirt I found.

As the house began to take on a different appearance, so did my mind, my emotional state, my happiness and my self-esteem. Repairing the house was therapy, a source of healing and solace.

On day five, Bryson installed two inside metal doors, an inside wooden door with a glass center, and three outside, burglar-bar doors. He also fixed my ice maker.

"Well, I'm all done here," Bryson said from the kitchen sink, as he washed his hands.

"This place looks good! Thanks for its face-lift," I replied from the kitchen entrance, walking toward him.

He pulled me close to him by the sink. "Is that all I get, a thanks?"

"No. I paid you last Saturday, but I have something else I want you to have."

"What, some kitty?" he said, placing his hands between my legs.

"No. Some keys. I have a set of keys to the house I want you to have since you are the man in my life. That makes you the man of the house."

"Does the man of the house get unlimited kitty?" he asked, grinning.

"That depends."

"On what?"

"If he pays the mortgage, car note, utility bills, buys the groceries, cooks, cleans, spends time with the kids, and keeps me happy."

"Damn, Van. You want a slave. You don't want a man. As your man, I can do all those things, not because you expect it, but because I chose to do them out of love for you. That's the kind of man I am. I believe in taking care of home."

"Good. I'm glad we have an understanding of your responsibilities."

"Tell me something, Van. If I'm doing all of that, then what are you responsible for?"

"Satisfying my man. That's a full-time job, especially with your horny butt."

He smiled. "You can start now, meeting your responsibility."

"Not so fast. My obligation starts when you put a ring on this finger," I said, lifting my marriage finger.

"Is that so? That's too bad."

I looked at him perplexed. "What do you mean?"

"I can't save all this good loving until we get married. I guess, I'll have to find me someone else."

"But you already have someone else, Helen."

"Helen thinks sex is only for having children. She's still on this baby kick."

"Why don't you kick her to the curb since you can't have children?"

"It's not that easy. She was there for me when I needed somebody. She's helped me through a lot of rough spots since my divorce three years ago."

"Maybe I need to kick your ass to the curb so you and Helen can enjoy each other's misery."

"You wouldn't do that, would you?" he asked softly, kissing me on the ear.

"Stop, Bryson," I moaned. "I don't know why I put up with you."

"I know why."

"Why?"

"Because we were meant to be together. Even you can't deny it."

"No. I can't."

He kissed me passionately. His hands slipped inside my pants. My body responded with slow, rocking, motions. With one hand on my back and the other hand unzipping our pants, my pants fell to the floor, allowing his erection to enter. He pulled me close as our bodies clung together rocking synchronously. Several minutes passed before he made his Tarzan, climatic yell. Our bond was broken as he came. We separated, becoming two again.

"Damn! That was good," he said, wiping sweat from his forehead.

"Isn't all sex good to a man?"

"Yes. But the latest is always the best," he said, reaching for a paper towel to wipe his head and penis.

I reached for several tissues to wipe between my legs. Pulling our pants up, we embraced. "Bryson, you have a way with me. I seem to always do the things I don't want to do with you."

"Good. Let's keep it that way."

"Thanks again for everything. I feel a healing taking place inside, every time I look at this place. Every room also reminds me of you. When I see your work, I see you."

"That's interesting because my work is me. I give a part of myself in everything I do. It's getting late. I need to leave," he said looking at his watch.

"Before you leave, I want to give you the keys to the house," I said, handing him the keys from my pant's pocket. "You are my man and the man of this house."

"Now, I can come over late at night when the boys are asleep and get in your bed."

"Would you do that?"

"Yeah."

"I'll be waiting."

He kissed me on my cheek. "Baby, I have to go," he said, walking to the door.

"Bryson, before you leave, I have a request."

"What is it, baby?"

"I need some T.P.R., temporary premenstrual relief."

"Okay, Van. The next time, your man will give you some T.P.R. Bye, baby."

"Bye, Bryson."

After he left, I walked through my house thinking of him.

SIX

With my physical house restored, the following two weeks were a time of spiritual renewal. My church observed Passover service on Thursday evening, April 13. Although many falsely believe Passover is a "Jewish" tradition, the New Testament Passover is Christian. Christ instituted the New Testament Passover upon His death. In Luke 22:14-20, on the evening of His death, He washed the disciples' feet, broke unleavened bread representing His body, and drank wine representing His blood that would be shed on the Cross. He said, "Do this in remembrance of me." Remembering Christ's death, His pain and suffering for my sake and the sake of all humanity is sobering. It makes me examine myself and thank Christ for His unselfish sacrifice to give me life. My sins are absolved by His righteousness. There is one thing for certain: The Jews are scapegoats for Christ's death because He died for us all. We are all responsible for His death. He died so that we could live.

The First Day of Unleavened Bread, where you eat bread products without leavening agents such as yeast and baking soda, follows Passover for seven days. The leavening agents represent sin that puffs us up. To be unleavened is to be humble. Christ died so that His people could live a sinless life.

During this holy week, I reflected on my life and repented of my sins, which were many. By the Last Day of Unleavened Bread, April 21, I felt spiritually recharged. That evening I started writing "Uncaged." God knew, to accomplish such a task, I needed to be unleavened.

By the time the I.B.W.A. novel writing group met on May 19, I had written two chapters. When I read the love scene at the end of the first chapter between my parents, Xavier and Betty, I was told it was too technical. I went home and changed it to something silly. The group loved it. It was at that point I decided to make "Uncaged" a comedy. That meeting set the tone for the remainder of the manuscript.

Since I started writing "Uncaged," I had less time for Bryson. Our time together was mostly at dinner time. The Memorial Day weekend passed without sight or sound from him. I was both anxious and upset to see him. At first, I thought something dreadful had happened until I asked him why he had not called or came by. He said he had been busy and was also giving me time to write. He then said he missed me and wanted to come over. I told him to come on.

"Mama, Superman is here," Little Carl announced as Bryson pulled into the driveway.

The boys' relationship with Bryson had not changed. They thought of him as Superman since he could do all things. Bryson was the opposite of Carl, who was Sorryman because he did nothing.

"Hey," Bryson said to Little Carl as he opened the door.

"Yeah," Little Carl mumbled back, drinking a cola.

Bryson walked into the kitchen where I was standing over the stove. "Damn! You look good," he said, walking to me. "What's for dinner?"

I smiled as he approached me. I had on white shorts, and a yellow, blue and white striped, clinging blouse. "For dinner, we're having field peas, cabbage, macaroni and cheese, squash, cornbread and fried chicken."

He kissed me. "I'll start with dessert," he said, holding me so tight I passed gas.

"Excuse me," I said when we finished kissing.

"That's okay. I missed you this weekend. I thought about you all the time."

"Why didn't you call? You know I can only get your recording. I called you three times and left messages, but you never called me back."

"I went to South Carolina to see my mom this weekend. I decided to go at the last minute and forgot to call you before I left."

"When did you get back?"

"Late last night."

"Do you want dinner or more dessert?" I asked, looking into his dark brown eyes.

"I want more dessert, but I better eat dinner before it's time to leave."

"Okay. Give me a minute and I'll fix our plates."

Bryson washed his hands in the sink while I fixed our plates. He placed the blue plastic place mats on the table from the top of the refrigerator.

"What do you want to drink?" he asked when he finished placing the mats.

"Cranberry juice." Since I met Bryson, I started drinking cranberry juice and taking vitamins. He recommended them because he had both daily.

"I'll have the same."

"Dinner's ready," I said, putting his plate in front of his mat.

He placed the container of juice on the table beside his glass. "This looks good," he said, picking at his chicken. "I only eat like this on Sundays and when I go home to Mom's. You'd be damn lucky to get bread and water with most city women. Most of them don't know how to cook and the rest don't damn try."

"Maybe they don't have time to cook with their busy schedules."

"That might be true for some women, but others, like my ex, are just lazy, or have a good man like me who will do all the cooking."

"Is that so? Well I'm glad you appreciate a woman who will serve you a good, wholesome meal everyday."

"Oh yes, I do appreciate the good meals, but the desserts are what make my day."

"Bryson, you're impossible. Say grace please so we can eat."

"Good food, good meat, good bread, let's eat."

"Is that the best you can do?"

He bowed his head again and said, "Very good food, very good meat, very good bread, Dear Lord have some so we can eat."

I looked at him, shaking my head. I thought to myself, Lord, what did I do to deserve two fools? Not knowing what to say, I started eating. Bryson had already finished two pieces of chicken before I lifted my fork.

"Van, I never told you this before, but knowing you has filled an empty void in my life. Over twenty years ago, I was engaged to a very intelligent, caring, beautiful woman," he said, drinking his glass of cranberry juice and refilling it before continuing. "Two weeks before our wedding, two of my best friends came over to my apartment with three women. Eventually, the guys paired off leaving me with the third woman. We talked, had a couple of drinks and ended up in my bed. My fiancee caught us in bed together, and after she beat both our asses, she called off the wedding. She was the only woman I really loved until I met you," he said, wiping his mouth before eating his macaroni and cheese.

"If you had married her, you would probably still be married."

"Probably."

"And you would not have married the kids' mother."

"Probably."

"And you would not have met me."

"We were destined to meet. I know that for certain. I was meant to stop by your window and talk that night. I'm meant to be here now."

"So you are. Only God knows why things happen in our lives."

"He knows, I'm meant to be here with you."

Carlos came into the kitchen as Bryson completed his sentence. He walked passed me to the refrigerator.

"Y'all don't have to stop talking because of me," Carlos said, as he opened the refrigerator door.

"You're not disturbing us. Bryson was finished talking."

"Mama, fix me some ice cream."

"Can't you fix it? I'm eating my dinner."

"I can, but I want you to fix it. If Bryson wasn't here, you would fix it."

30

"Well, I'm here. You're big enough to fix your own ice cream. Your mother is eating her dinner," Bryson chimed in as he ate the last of his food.

"So?"

"Okay, I'll fix your ice cream," I said, getting up, not wanting a disturbance.

"Van, you're making a mistake. Let him fix his own ice cream. You don't have to wait on him hand and foot."

"I know I don't. But for the sake of peace, I'll do it this time."

"I'm going to the van for a minute. I'll be right back."

While Bryson was gone, I fixed the ice cream. Carlos grabbed a soda from the refrigerator.

"Mama, don't act different when Bryson is here. You know you always fix my ice cream."

"I wasn't trying to act differently, Carlos. I was trying to enjoy his company. You have me all the time. I don't spend that much time with Bryson."

"I'm your son! I come before your company."

"Only if I allow you to. Carlos, you must realize I'm more than your mama. I'm a woman, and I have a life other than being your mama. From now on, when I have company, be a big boy and fix your own ice cream."

"Mama, I'm only eight years old. You have at least ten more years to do stuff for me. You can enjoy your company, but I'm still gonna enjoy my mama for as long as I can."

"Here's your ice cream, son," I said, handing it to him. "Give me a hug."

We hugged. "I love you, Carlos."

"I love you, too."

Bryson came back inside as Carlos left the kitchen. He cleared his side of the table off and sat down.

"Come here. I have something to show you," Bryson motioned.

I walked over to his side. "What is it?"

"This is something else I never told you or anyone else about. It's a blueprint of a house I want built someday." He opened the blueprint and spread it across the table. "I saw this house in a magazine and sent off for the blueprint. One day, I'm going to have it built. Here's the entrance," he said, pointing to the paper. "It has a front foyer, with the living room to the right. The dining room is adjacent to the living room and country kitchen."

"This really looks nice. I love the way the rooms are laid out."

"The master bedroom is in its own wing of the house. The other two bedrooms are here, next to the den and kitchen. When I saw this house, I knew someday it would be mine. Just like you. One day, I will have both you and the house."

I smiled. "Bryson, I love this house. I'm glad you shared it with me. What else do you have up your sleeve?"

He looked at his sleeve. "Nothing. Just my arm."

"I'd better finish eating my food while it's still warm." I kissed him on the cheek, then sat down in front of my food. "Have you shown Helen the house?"

"I told you I haven't told anyone about the house, except you. Helen has a new house that she had built three years ago. I told her the other day she spends too much money on the house and kids. She's always spending money. And with Renekia getting her license this year, our car insurance will be sky high. She needs to reduce her spending."

An alarm went off in my head when he said "our insurance." I put the fork down. "You act like y'all live together."

"I live with Helen's brother Ryan. After my divorce, I started living with him because I couldn't afford to live on my own. That's how I met Helen. She would come over to visit, and we hit it off. She helped me financially when I needed help. So in return, I help her pay some of her bills."

"I see. Do you love her?"

"I love you."

"What does she mean to you?"

"Look Van, I know what you're getting at. I love you. Helen needs me. I can't dump her because of all she did for me. I'm sorry I can't answer anymore questions. I should have been back at work fifteen minutes ago," he said, looking at his watch. He kissed me on my cheek and walked to the door. "I'm off tonight. We'll talk later. Bye."

"Bye, Bryson."

I looked at my cold food. No longer did I have an appetite. I got up from the table and scraped what was left in my plate into the trash. I said a silent prayer as I walked to the sink.

Dear Lord, show me where I stand with Bryson. Don't leave me in the dark as he has done. Don't leave me here wondering about his relationship with Helen. Father, You know all things. Please, enlighten me. Amen.

Little Carl walked into the kitchen as I finished my prayer. "What's wrong with you? You look like you've seen a ghost."

"I'm okay. I just have some things on my mind. Make sure you wash the dishes before I leave for work."

"When are you going to get a new dishwasher?"

"Soon."

"Yeah, right. I've been hearing that for three years. Isn't it time for Carlos to start washing dishes?"

"Not yet. Washing dishes is part of your chores. It's how you earn your allowance."

"Can't you just give me an allowance without me earning it?"

"No, son. In the real world, you have to work to get paid."

"Mama, do you love Bryson?"

"I think so."

"Do you still love Dad?"

"No. I stopped loving your dad a long time ago. Our relationship is over. Can you accept that?"

"I don't know. I hope in the back of my mind that y'all will get back together, like you did so many times before."

"This time is different. We're divorced. There will be no getting back together."

"It never hurts to hope."

"You're right son, it never hurts to hope. Excuse me, I'm going to my room to read and get ready for work. I feel tired, so I will probably take a nap in another hour."

"Okay, Mama. I'll clean the kitchen while you sleep."

"Thanks, son. Now if you'll excuse me, I'm going to my room."

I went to my room, read, ironed my clothes, then took a nap. The boys were asleep, and the kitchen was clean when I went to work.

Isaiah Avery, the married security guard who had a crush on me and who visited my window regularly, stopped by the lab window while I was accessioning specimens.

"What's up, Ms. Lewis?" he asked, standing in the window with a smirky look on his face.

"Oh, nothing much. What about you?" I replied, smiling back.

"How is everything going with you and officer Collier?"

"Fine. Why do you ask?"

"Are you sure?"

"Yes, I am."

"I found out something about him, but I need to investigate one thing before I say anymore. I'll be right back."

Isaiah left as quickly as he came. I had no idea what he had on his mind, but he had piqued my curiosity. I couldn't wait for his return and kept glancing at the window every few seconds. Five minutes later, he returned. When I saw him, I dropped what I was doing and went outside the lab.

"What's this all about?" I asked, eager to know.

"I thought something was up with officer Collier, but I couldn't put my finger on it. Tonight, a couple of officers were talking about being in officer Collier's wedding. He's married. His wife works on the 4th floor, on this shift. I just went upstairs to see her name tag to verify the information. Her name tag says "Helen Lewis Collier.""

"What? Bryson's married!" I exclaimed, stunned. "And his wife works here? On this shift?"

"That's right."

"When did they get married?"

"This past December. He's a newlywed."

"I knew about Helen, but I didn't know they were married."

"Now you know."

"Thanks, Isaiah. I didn't know."

"You're welcome. Now, what are you going to do?"

"There's only one thing to do and that's to end the relationship."

He smiled. "These married men ought to be ashamed of themselves, preying on innocent females such as yourself."

I looked at Isaiah, knowing he would love to be in Bryson's shoes. "I need to finish my work. Thanks again."

"Anytime."

He walked off and I went back inside the lab. My first order of business was to call Bryson. Still fuming, I dialed his number. Of course, I only got a recording. "Bryson, I just found out you and Helen are married. She works in this hospital, on this shift! How can you be so low?" I slammed the phone down and went back to work.

SEVEN

I have to be careful what I pray for because sometimes I'm not prepared for the answer. Of course, I knew Bryson was seeing Helen, but I didn't know they were married. Now, I have committed the "Big A" sin—Adultery. How can Christ forgive me for committing adultery? How can I forgive myself for being a fool? How can I see Bryson again without kicking his ass?

I answered an outside call in the lab at 6:00 a.m. "Emergency Clinic Lab, Lewis. How..."

"Vanessa, I know you're angry with me, but I wanted to tell you myself."

"You had plenty of opportunities, Bryson! You should have told the truth from the beginning. Don't you know lies catch up with you?"

"I couldn't tell you because I know how you feel about married men. I wanted you to know and love me for me, regardless of my status. I have been infatuated with you since we first started talking. I didn't want our relationship to end; I wanted it to continue."

"Well, it can't continue! Our relationship is over. Furthermore, how dare you talk to me when your wife works in this hospital, on this shift. Suppose she saw us together?"

"That's impossible. She never leaves her area."

"There's always a first time. Who knows, I could have ended up as a patient, fooling around with you. There's nothing fiercer than a woman's wrath, especially when her man is cheating on her."

"How did you find out anyway?"

"That's not important."

"I bet Avery told you. He's just upset because he can't have you."

"And neither can you! Good-bye, Bryson. Save your small talk for Helen, your wife. And give me back my keys!" I hung up on his lying ass. Then I thought, Lord, can You send me one good, honest, single man? He quickly reminded me that He had sent me two, Mike Taylor and Zakee Abdul-Rauf, but I rejected them for Bryson. Yes, Lord, I stand corrected, I thought. Now, I must rectify my error.

For the remainder of the shift, I thought about Zakee. I hadn't heard from him since the day of my divorce. This morning, I'll give him a call to see how he's doing. Maybe, we can finally get together.

When I got home, I called Zakee. "Hello," Zakee answered, with his very masculine voice.

Hearing his voice, made me nervous.

"Hello," he said again to the silence over the phone.

"Zakee, this is Vanessa Lewis. How are you?"

"I'm tired. I just got home from work. Can you make this call brief," he said, obviously annoyed.

"I called to invite you to a reading, this Saturday. I'm with I.B.W.A., International Black Writers and Artists, Inc. Five other writers and I will be reading chapters from our novels. I'll be reading "Uncaged," the novel I'm writing about us."

"What time and where?"

"Two o'clock at The Source Bookstore near downtown Decatur, across from the Dairy Queen at the railroad tracks."

"I know where that is. It's not far from my house."

"Good. Will you be there?"

"If nothing comes up, I'll try to make it."

"That's good enough. I'll let you get some sleep. Good-bye."

I slowly put the receiver down. Thoughts filled my head of what it would be like to be with Zakee. If he was my man, I'd follow him around like a puppy-dog. I'd grant him his every command. In return, he would supply my every need. And we would be happy ever after.

Suddenly, feeling very tired, I went to my room to lie down. As soon as my head hit the pillow, I went to sleep. While sleeping, I dreamed of Zakee at the reading Saturday. I scanned the small crowd when I entered the bookstore, but he wasn't present. However, when I got up to read, I saw him sitting, isolated, in the back. He smiled, and I smiled back. He looked more handsome than ever with his shaved head, yellow-tinted glasses, gold stud earring, wine-colored, short sleeved shirt with green and wine shorts. I took my place in the reader's chair in front. Each time I looked up at the crowd, he was staring at me, smiling. I glanced into his eyes and kept reading. When everything was over, he approached me.

"Well, I'm glad you could make it. I looked for you earlier, but I didn't see you," I said, as we met face to face.

"I arrived shortly before you read. I thought you said the book was about us. You read about Big Mama, Xavier and Betty."

"The end of the book will be about us. The beginning is about my beginning, how my parents wanted to abort me but didn't. I had to start from my beginning to get the full impact of why you mean so much to me, and how you changed my life."

"You keep saying that. I still don't understand because I didn't do anything special. We only talked."

"I can't explain it now. You have to read "Uncaged" later to understand."

"What are you doing after you leave here?" he asked, looking admiringly into my eyes.

"I don't have any plans."

"Would you like to spend some time with me? Maybe we could get something to eat and talk."

"That sounds great!" I replied, excited.

"Are you ready to leave now?"

"Sure. Why not?"

"Do you mind if I hold your hand?"

"No. I'd be delighted."

Zakee and I left the bookstore, holding hands, smiling. His touch felt wonderful. As we walked outside, I hoped this day would never end. My dream continued with Zakee until Carlos woke me up as he entered my room to say, hello. He had just gotten home from school.

"Hello, son. How was your day at school?"

"It was okay, except I punched two guys out in the bathroom. I gave them my awesome upper-cut," he said, demonstrating. "Pow! Pow! Pow went my fist into Jason's gut. Then I karate kicked David who was trying to get me off Jason."

Carlos had a vivid imagination about karate and fighting. His favorite pastime was beating up imaginary victims. I knew he was just going through one of his spells, but I had to ask one question to be sure if what he was saying was real or make-believe. "Did you get suspended?"

"Psyche! I was just kidding. I know if I get suspended again, you'll whip my a—"

"Carlos, you watch your mouth!" I said, running after him as he left the room.

"Sorry, Mom. I can't help it if I'm a chip off the old block. You've always told me I was just like my dad."

"You're right. I can't argue with you there. You look and act exactly like Carl. But Carlos, unless you want to go down the same path as your father, you need to change. Start telling the truth and control your anger. Those two things alone will make a difference between you and your dad."

"I'm hungry. When are you going to cook?"

Yes, you're Carl's son, I thought. "Give me a minute, then I'll cook."

"Okay, Mama. I guess, I'll go in my room and kick some butt before dinner," he said, punching into the air.

I looked at Carlos and shook my head. He is exactly like Carl. Carl fought all the time when he was growing up. I need to do something to turn my son around. I definitely, don't want him being a replica of Carl.

I was cooking dinner when Little Carl came home. He entered the kitchen and kissed me on my cheek.

"Welcome home, son," I said, giving him a hug.

"What's for dinner?" he asked opening the lids of the pots and pans.

"Yellow rice, broccoli, and sweet `n'sour chicken."

"Mmmm, that sounds good. Call me when it's ready. I'll be in my room on the phone." Bryson had installed a new jack for his room last week.

"What about homework?"

"I don't have any. I did it at school."

"Carl, you never have homework. How do you expect to pass your classes if you never do any homework?"

"I do my homework at school, Mama, so I won't have to do it at home," he said, running upstairs to answer his ringing telephone. "Call me when dinner's ready!"

I shook my head and continued cooking. He's just like Carl too, I thought, as I stirred the chicken.

After dinner, I worked on the third chapter of "Uncaged" for the remainder of the evening before I went to work. I wanted to read it at I.B.W.A on Saturday. In the chapter, Betty and Xavier were on their way to the hospital to deliver me. While writing, God helped me remember Mama barking at my birth. I had completely forgotten it until that evening.

At 9:30 I finished writing and got ready for work. When I arrived at the lab, Gail, from the evening shift, handed me a letter.

"A man in a uniform came to the window and asked me to give this letter to you."

"Thank you," I said, looking at the letter. It was from Bryson. I opened and read it right there.

Dear Vanessa,

I'm sorry you had to discover my marital status through someone else. I really intended to tell you myself on several occasions, but couldn't get up enough nerve. Sometimes, when we were together, and I was quiet and you would ask me what was wrong? It was at those times I wanted to tell you. Remember when you told me about Rocket, the man who tried to have an affair with you, and later you found out he was married? And because of him, you detested lying, married men. Vanessa, a lump would always get in my throat whenever I wanted to tell you. I didn't want you to leave me like you did Rocket. Please forgive me for deceiving you. I love you very much and don't want our relationship to end. I understand, however, if our relationship is over. But remember, I love you with all my heart. Bryson

He has his nerve, writing me a letter with his married butt! I will not date a married man even if I am in love with him, I thought as I put on my lab coat and started my controls for my shift. I put his letter in my lab pocket.

Around 1:30 a.m., Hassin Mohammed, another security guard friend, stopped at the lab window. "Hey, Ms. V., what's happenin'?" Hassin asked, profiling with his gold-rimmed glasses and baldhead. Hassin reminded me of Zakee with his baldhead. They were also good friends.

"Hassin, did you know Bryson was married?"

"Yep."

"Didn't you know I was seeing Bryson?"

"Yep."

"Aren't you my buddy, my good friend?"

"Yep and yep."

"Why didn't you tell me he was married?"

"I thought you knew. Besides, I mind my own business."

"Some friend you are! Well, I just found out last night, he's married."

"Who told you? Avery?"

"Yes. How did you know?"

"By minding my own business, I see and hear a lot of things that's none of my business."

"I want you to read a letter Bryson wrote." I gave him the letter; he read it at the window. "What do you think?" I asked after he read it.

"I'm not one to dip into your business, but if I were you, I wouldn't have anything else to do with him. And if he calls, hang the phone up in his ear."

"That's good advice. Thanks Hassin. I guess I can forgive you for not telling me earlier."

"Sure thing Ms. V. Anytime. I have to check you later because it's time to check in with the man."

"Okay, Hassin. I'll see you later." He walked off and I continued my work.

All night long, there was no word from Bryson. If he did call, I was gong to take Hassin's advice. I refused to be involved with someone else's husband. Anybody who would two-time their present wife, would two-time me, too. I was through with Bryson, and I didn't want to see or hear from him again.

Friday, came and went, and still no Bryson. I was so busy working on chapter three, I didn't realize I hadn't heard from him until Carl mentioned his name Saturday morning. He came by to go to the reading with us. I invited him since the book was about him. He arrived just after noon.

"Is Superman going to be there?" Carl asked, referring to Bryson.

"No. I didn't invite him because he works on Saturday. Besides, we're not seeing each other anymore."

Carl smiled. "Vanessa, I have something I need to discuss with you. Can you stop working long enough for me to discuss it?"

I was at the kitchen table typing the last two pages of chapter three. "What is it? I want to finish and read this at the reading at two."

"Do you think you will read three chapters today?"

"Yes, I do. I don't need anything negative from you. Since you've been gone, my life has been positive. I hope you want to discuss paying me child support. Here it is June 3, and you've only paid me half!"

"That's exactly what I want to discuss. I want you to co-sign for me to go to school to get my CDL. It costs over two thousand dollars. When I get my license, I can get a decent job and start paying you child support payments, regularly."

I looked at him as if he was a fool, and he was. "What part of divorce don't you understand? I'm not signing any papers with you or for you. You must think I'm crazy."

"No, I don't think you're crazy. I just thought you'd help me get a better job so I can pay you child support."

"You're not thinking about me or the child support. You're thinking about your own black ass. Leave me alone! I'm almost finished with this chapter. Talk to your sons while I finish."

"I'll get my CDL with our without your help," he said, as he went downstairs.

I completed the chapter by 1:35 p.m.. We all rushed out the door to the reading at 1:40 p.m.. The Source Bookstore was twenty minutes away.

EIGHT

We arrived at The Source Bookstore by 2:05. It took another five minutes to find two parking spaces because Carl and the boys rode in his car. Luckily, we found two vacant spaces in the back of the bookstore. Entering the small crowded, bookstore, Carl and I found two seats on the front row, next to each other. The boys sat behind us.

"Vanessa, I'm glad you're here," said Barbara Faison, the coordinator. "Everybody else on the program is here. We'll begin in five minutes."

"Good. I was hoping I wasn't late. May I have a program?"

"Oh sure," she said, handing me several. "Pass some around, please."

"I'll be glad to." Distributing the programs also gave me an opportunity to scout for Zakee. I didn't see him. But, then I remembered, he wasn't present at the beginning in my dream either. Maybe, his absence was a sure sign my dream would come true.

"Ladies and gentlemen," Barbara spoke through the microphone, "We are ready to begin reading. Does everyone have a program?"

Three people raised their hands. I quickly handed them a program before taking my seat. More people came in as the first author, Nora DeLoach, read from her latest manuscript, "Mama Thwarts a Murder." Nora was writing a series of "Mama" mystery books. This book was the third of the series. She read the part when Simone, Mama's daughter, and Mama had just left a third cousin's house. On the way home, Simone, who was driving, almost hit a woman who ran in her path. Simone later visits her girlfriend, Nadine. They eat lasagna while trying to put a few missing pieces together about the woman.

Next, Andranika Gangnier, Mrs. Edna Crutchfield's daughter and author of "Breeding Has No Color," read two chapters from her manuscript. Her story was about an attractive black, interior designer named Jeri who was being coerced by a white client, Isabella, to make her son, Earl, a client. Actually, Isabella was trying to play matchmaker. Jeri knew Earl had to be a real loser. Why would a white mother want to match her white son with a black woman? Only Andranika could make this story seem real.

Barbara took the reader's seat next. Her manuscript was titled, "Easy Love." The two chapters she read centered around two black sisters, Cassandra and Elana. Cassandra was an accountant who had found a better paying job in another city. The hardest part about starting her new job, however, was leaving Elana and Cassandra's eight-year-old daughter, Kenya behind. Cassandra wanted to give herself time to settle in before sending for Kenya. The inner conflict all three faced was tough, but they were determined to make this transition easy.

Lawrence Chestnut followed Barbara. He read from his manuscript, "Boots." Boots was a tall, lanky black man who always wore tall, high-heeled boots. In this particular chapter, Boots met a sexy hussy who charmed his boots off and ended up in his bed.

Finally, it was my turn to take the hot seat. I was the last reader. Before I read, Barbara asked all the children to step outside. She informed the audience, my manuscript was not appropriate for children. All the children left except my own. Some parents went with their children. Once the room was cleared, I read "Uncaged."

In chapter one, Big Mama cusses out my parents when my dad, Xavier, informs her I am on the way. She strongly suggests an abortion. Xavier stands up to Big Mama for the first time in his life. She quickly retaliates by throwing a hammer at his head. She misses and his escape enables my parents to move out the following day.

In chapter two, Betty and Xavier plan a birthday party for Big Mama in their new apartment. The party is over, however, when the rats and roaches invite themselves.

In chapter three, time passes and it's my delivery day. Mama barks like a dog at my birth, creating a commotion in the waiting room. Xavier believes he has fathered a dog until he sees me. At the end of chapter three, he is happy about the birth of his daughter and his upcoming tennis match with Marvin.

My eyes scanned the audience as I rose from the chair. Zakee was not present. I guess something else came up. Although I was disappointed, I tried not to show it. I smiled as I sat beside Carl.

"That was good, Vanessa," Carl whispered, leaning his head to my ear.

"Thanks. I'm glad you liked it."

"Let's give all our readers a round of applause," said Douglas Williams, the owner of The Source Bookstore.

Everyone thunderously applauded.

"Nora DeLoach will be signing her latest book, "Mama Solves a Murder", at the table up front. Refreshments are in the back. Please help yourselves. Stay and mingle with each other."

"I want to thank everyone for attending I.B.W.A.'s first reading," shouted Barbara when Doug finished speaking.

Actually, it was because Barbara received a $1,000 grant to write her book that we had the reading. One of the stipulations in the grant was she had to read her work publicly. Since she had to read, Barbara invited us to read with her and make an event out of it. We, in the novel writing group, gladly accepted and appreciated her invitation. We had read among ourselves, but it would be interesting to see how the public responded to our work.

Several people came up to me and said they enjoyed "Uncaged." I also overheard someone say, "If she can write a book, anybody can." I smiled when I overheard the comment because I knew writing was harder than it appeared. Overall, the reading was a success. I heard positive comments about everyone's work.

Lawrence Chestnut approached me as I was preparing to leave. "Well, now that you have three chapters written, I want to be your agent. I have a literary company called Kinfolk, Inc. Let's get together next week. I want to send your three chapters out to publishers as soon as possible."

I was stunned. I thought about how hard I had worked to complete the third chapter for the reading. God knew the outcome. "I'd be delighted for you to be my agent. Call me Monday so we can get started."

"Monday will be perfect."

A short, dark brown woman came up to Chestnut as he finished speaking. "I love "Boots!" It's hilarious. You had me cracking up the whole time," she said, looking up into his captivating eyes.

They continued to talk and I walked off. My eyes scanned the crowd for Zakee again, but he obviously was a no-show.

"Mama, I'm ready to eat," said Little Carl, standing beside me.

"They have refreshments in the back. Go help yourself."

"I want Chinese food."

"Okay. We'll go get some Chinese food."

"Can Dad come with us?"

"Sure, he can come. Get Carlos and your dad, and we'll leave."

"They're outside waiting on you. I came inside to get you."

"Okay. I'm ready. Let's go. Wait a minute, let me thank Barbara and Doug before I leave. I want to say good-bye to the other writers, too." Little Carl went outside while I said my thank yous and good-byes. Afterwards, we went to the food court at South Dekalb Mall.

While driving alone to the mall, I kept thinking, I hope Carl doesn't make anymore out of this than what it is—a family dinner. I, definitely, was not his dessert anymore and he, definitely, was not my main course. Those days were over, forever.

When we arrived at the food court, we ordered Chinese food.

"Order what you want," Carl said, standing beside me, looking at the choices, "I'm paying for the meals."

I couldn't believe my ears. But no matter what Carl did or said today would not change anything. We are divorced, and I refuse to date my ex-husband. I would not be like some couples who marry, divorce, date, then re-marry. That's absurd. When I divorced Carl, it was until death do we stay apart. "Thank you. I want the honey chicken."

"I'll take four honey chickens with noodles," Carl instructed the server.

We ordered drinks and sat at a table near the pizza booth. Carl said grace and we ate. The boys sat next to Carl. I sat directly in front of Carl and next to the boys also. I could tell they were happy being with their dad. I was happy for them.

"Vanessa," Carl said, wiping his mouth. "I was wondering if you would like to go dancing with me tonight. I know how much you like to dance."

If you know how much I like to dance, why didn't you take me dancing when we were married, I thought. You wouldn't spend time with me because you were too busy going out with your single friends. Now that we're divorced, you want to take me out instead of being with your friends. I think you're confused. "Carl, we're divorced. I'm not dating you."

"I'm not asking you to date me. I'm asking you to go dancing."

"No."

"Mama, you love to dance," chimed Little Carl. "Dad wants to show you a good time. All you do is sit at home and work. Bryson never takes you anywhere."

"My writing is important. I don't have time to play and work. Let's hurry up and eat, so I can get back home to write. Carl are you keeping the boys?"

"No. Since you turned me down, I think I'll kick it around with Lenny."

"That's fine. I guess, I'll do something with the boys then. I've been working hard all week. I'll take a break today. Boys, what do you want to do?"

"Go to the movies," they both answered.

I felt as if I had been set up. "We'll look at the paper when we get home."

"Mama."

"What Carlos?"

"Don't you want to be with Dad?"

"Those days are over. Don't get the wrong idea because we're eating dinner together today. Your dad and I are never getting back together."

"I think you've made that very clear. Let's go boys. We're finished," Carl said, getting up.

When we got home, the boys changed their minds about going to the movies. They wanted to watch a special program on TV instead. I called Mike Taylor since I had not heard from him. Also, I was pissed off with Zakee for not showing up at the reading. How dare he not show up when I wanted to see him so badly!

I dialed Mike's number.

"Hello."

"Mike, this is Vanessa Lewis. How are you doing?"

"Ms. Lewis," he said, with an obvious attitude, "what is the nature of your call?"

"Did I call you at a bad time?"

"No. I am just surprised you called me at all since you have a male friend. You are still seeing your friend, I gather?"

"As a matter of fact, I'm not."

"Is that why you called me because you had a lover's quarrel?"

"No. I'm no longer with my friend."

"Why are you calling me?"

"Do you remember asking to take me out to dinner after my divorce?"

"Yes."

"I was hoping we could still go."

"My dinner invitation was canceled when you started seeing your friend. Why don't you call him up and ask him to take you to dinner? Sorry, I can't converse with you any longer. I'm watching a really good program on TV."

Click.

I stared at the phone. What happened to him, I thought. Boy, was he nasty! I know I'm having a bad day when Mike Taylor turns me down.

The phone rang as I put it on the receiver.

"Hello."

"Baby, I miss you. I tried not to call, but I couldn't help myself."

"Bryson, it's over between us. You have no business calling me."

"I can't help it if I love you. It may be over for you, but it will never be over for me."

"You have a wife, remember? It's wrong for us to be together."

"Look, I know right from wrong. I also know how I feel about you. You're the first person I've ever really loved. If I'm wrong for loving you, then I don't want to be right."

"You know how I feel about you. I meant everything I ever said to you."

"Vanessa, I would give anything to hold you in my arms one more time."

When he said those words, something went through me. "Bryson, I miss you very much. I wish we could get back together, but we can't, not with you being married."

"I love you, baby. Just let me hold you one more time. Please, open the door and let me in."

"Where are you?"

"In your driveway, on my cell phone."

"What are you doing in my driveway?"

"I came to see you, to hold you, to kiss you one more time."

"Go home, Bryson."

"Give me one minute to look at you before I leave, please."

"Okay, one minute. But I will not unlock the burglar door."

"Thanks, baby."

We hung up at the same time. When I opened the door, Bryson was standing on the porch in his blue uniform with a small bouquet of flowers. He was grinning from ear-to-ear.

"These are for you," he said through the door. "They are not much, but I wanted you to have them."

I unlocked the burglar door and took the flowers. "Thanks," I said smelling them. "They're beautiful!"

"Not as beautiful as you. Thanks for allowing me to see you, one more time."

I looked into Bryson's eyes. All the love I felt for him resurfaced. "Come in," I said, mesmerized by the flowers and his presence.

He came inside, took me in his arms and kissed me. "I missed you. I love you more than you'll ever know," he said after a long, passionate kiss.

"I love you, too," I heard myself say.

"Vanessa, these last few days have been pure hell without you. I don't ever want us to be separated again. Please, tell me it's not over between us."

I thought for a moment before replying. "No, Bryson. Our relationship is not over. It has only just begun," I said, closing the door.

NINE

Why didn't I heed Hassin's advice? If I had hung up on Bryson, then I wouldn't be in this adultery boat with him. It seems I left one triangle with Carl and Zakee to enter another triangle with Bryson and Helen. Two women sharing the same man is too much. One of us will have to let go. May the best woman get Bryson and eliminate this triangle.

Bryson knew I was "green" when he met me. I was ending a twenty-five year relationship with Carl. In a lot of ways, I was the same eighteen-year-old girl who had been removed from the single's scene. Although I was a thirty-eight year old woman, I felt like a young girl. I felt strange, at first, talking to grown men instead of boys. I must say, I adapted quickly. I went from the arms of my husband to the arms of another woman's husband in the same day.

Saturday evening with Bryson confirmed my worst fear—I was in love with a married man. How could I, Vanessa Lewis, be in such a sinful relationship? God, you have to get me out of this because I am too far immersed in this adultery quicksand to rescue myself. Please Lord help me. Take my hand and pull me out.

I knew the Lord heard me. I must wait patiently for Him to deliver me from the mess I'm in. Lately, my heart has gotten me into a lot trouble. It's repeatedly overruled my mind. I'm not afraid of what lies ahead. I only hope no one gets hurt, especially me.

Sunday morning, Bryson and I talked on the phone. He woke me up to tell me how much he loved me, how glad he was that I did not leave him, and how he was sorry for not telling me earlier he was married. I forgave him and told him I looked forward to seeing him that night at work. We said our good-byes, then hung up.

Sunday afternoon, I wondered what had happened to Zakee. Since he hadn't called to explain his absence at the reading, I called him.

"Hello, Zakee, this is Vanessa. What happened to you yesterday?"

"I started taking drum and dance classes on Saturdays. I was having such a good time, I forgot. When I realized what time it was, it was too late to come."

"Why didn't you call to explain why you didn't come?"

"A group of us went to get something to eat. I was having such a good time, I didn't think about it anymore. I did think about you today at the mosque when someone read poetry from their book."

"I see. I.B.W.A. is having a gathering on the seventeenth of this month. Would you like to go with me?"

"I don't think I have any plans for that day except my class."

"Good. Meet me at John White Park on Beecher Street at 2:00."

"I know where it is. Call me to remind me. I may forget."

"Write it down. I'm not calling you back."

"Okay. I can't promise you I'll be there, but I'll try to come."

"I understand. I hope to see you. We have a lot to talk about."

"Why don't you say what's on your mind now?"

"Because I want to say it to your face."

"We will talk later, but I must go now."

"Okay. Good-bye."

When Zakee hung up, I wondered why he never asked me out. Or, was I supposed to ask him over? Which was correct? I don't want him to ever think I was running after him. If he doesn't ask me out, then I won't ask him over. The ball was in your court, Zakee. What were you going to do?

For the remainder of the day, the boys and I spent a quiet time together. We rented movies, popped popcorn, ate hot wings, laughed and had a good time. Although I enjoyed our activities, I was also anxious for Monday to arrive. I was excited about meeting with Lawrence Chestnut.

Monday at noon, I arrived at Chestnut's apartment. We sat in his living room as we discussed, "Uncaged."

"Vanessa, you had the audience laughing while you read Saturday," said Chestnut sipping on a Coke. His white T-shirt and shorts contrasted his mahogany skin. He looked like his character, Boots, without boots.

"Really? I didn't hear anything. I guess I was too busy reading."

"Chapter three was your funniest chapter."

"Thank you."

"I want to edit your work and send it off to publishers."

"That's exactly what I wanted to do too. I read where publishers will review three chapters to consider for publication."

"That's correct. As your agent, I'm asking for ten percent. My job is to get it ready and send it out."

"Chestnut, you are exactly what I need. I want to concentrate on writing. You can concentrate on the business end."

"Good. Did you bring the three chapters with you?" he asked, putting his Coke down.

"Yes, here they are," I said, handing him the brown envelope from my lap.

"Would you like something to drink?" he asked, reaching for the envelope.

"No, thank you."

"I will read over these chapters and get back with you later."

"Okay."

"What good books have you read lately?"

"The Color Purple, by Alice Walker."

"She can't write. I have a book I want you to read," he said, standing up and walking to the bookcase behind him. He examined several books before taking one from his collection and handing it to me. "Here, read this. She's an excellent writer!"

I took the book, Song of Solomon, by Toni Morrison. "Thank you," I said, looking at the cover then placing it next to me. "I have never heard of Song of Solomon, but The Color Purple was a movie. "Uncaged" will be a movie, also. I won't mention it in "Uncaged," but God revealed it to me when He said, 'This book will be written and published.'

"I still want you to read the book. It'll help you as a writer."

"I'll read it. I need all the help I can get. I can always learn from others writers."

"A good writer is also a good reader. You have to read in order to write."

"I know. I read that in my writer's book."

"Do you have anything else you want to discuss?"

"How long do you think it will take you to get it ready?"

"I don't know. I have to look at it first."

"I will call you after I have read it to determine our next session."

"Okay," I said, getting up to leave.

Chestnut walked me to the door. We said our good-byes and I left. Excitement filled me as I drove home. *Lord, I can't believe what's happening. I thank you for Chestnut. I pray that you empower him with Your Holy Spirit to accomplish this task. Amen.*

For the remainder of the week, I worked feverishly on "Uncaged." It, and Bryson, consumed my every waking moment. Bryson and I were closer than ever. I tried not to think about Helen, how and when he made love to her. I pretended he only made love to me, like he said. Of course, I knew better, but I'd rather lie to myself than admit the truth, that he was screwing both of us. I was being screwed in more ways than one. But I tried not to think about it. In my mind, he was all mine.

We continued to have dinner together, almost daily. He enjoyed my cooking, and I enjoyed his company. We had a lot of laughs. He not only talked about his past and future plans, but about his home life with Helen and her three kids, Renika, Ryan, and Mario. Renika and Ryan had the same dad. They were sixteen and eight, respectively. Mario was six. His dad was by Helen's last boyfriend, Mario Sr. Bryson talked about how hard Helen had had it with her other men. How he was the best man who had come into her life. She wanted to work and let him be a house husband. He said he wasn't going for that. He didn't feel like a real man, not working. Although he did all the cooking and cleaning while she worked nights and slept days, he wasn't giving up his job. Consequently, he stayed pissed off with her because she slept all day, didn't cook for her own kids, didn't clean the house, or have sex with him. To her, sex was for conceiving. Since Bryson was sterile, she lost her desire for sex.

"Bryson, didn't you have sex with Helen, before you got married?" I asked, drinking my cranberry juice, after finishing Friday's dinner.

"Damn right. Before we got married, she wanted sex all the time. Every time I was with her she wanted to screw. Even when I didn't want to have sex, she wanted to screw.

"When did she lose her desire for sex?"

"Right after I said, 'I do'. She said, 'I do' too, but she don't do a damn thing."

"But she knew you couldn't have children before you got married?"

"Yes, she did. It didn't matter then, but it matters now. I think, she's just using my vasectomy as an excuse for not having sex," he said, eating the last of his cubed steak.

"So, what are you going to do?"

"Right now, I can't do anything. I'm not financially able to live on my own since my kids' mother gets over half of my take-home pay. I was living with Helen's brother and was in the process of getting my own apartment when we got married. She felt like I would be better off living with her than having my own place. We knew we couldn't live together without being married. So we planned to get married. Boy, was that a mistake. I feel like this marriage is another failure."

"Where do I fit into your life?"

"I love you. You make me happy."

"Our relationship is wrong. You have a wife you're sharing your life with. You sleep in her bed and reside in her house. You need to be faithful to the wife you promised to love and cherish until you die."

"I feel like the marriage has already killed me. Therefore, I'm free to be with you. I love you. I don't love Helen." He got up from the table and put our plates in the sink. "Come here," he said standing at the sink with his arms outstretched.

I took a deep breath, then went to him. "Bryson, now that I know you're married, I have a lot of guilt about our relationship."

"Look at me," he said, holding my head up. "I love you. You have nothing to feel guilty about. God put us together for a reason. I'm certain of that. One thing about God, He doesn't make mistakes."

"Why would God put me with a married man? That goes against His Word."

"I can't answer that question. That's His business. My business is to keep you happy. Am I doing my job satisfactorily?" he asked, kissing me before I replied. His embrace felt so wonderful, his status didn't matter anymore. He was mine. All mine.

TEN

Early Saturday morning, Carl picked up the boys. I ran up the steps as he entered the house. I had left something in my bedroom I did not want him to see. Since our divorce, Carl had made it his business to stay in my business. Lately, he had started a very annoying habit. On days I worked, he brought the boys home after I left for work. This gave him access to the house without my interfering with his investigation into my personal belongings. On one occasion, I found a letter in his old chest of drawers where I kept all my writings. He read an article I had submitted to a magazine. The article contained reasons why I was glad I was not married and how much I was enjoying my new man. I also noticed both leftover food and other food items were missing such as coffee, bread and eggs. Carl loved eggs. I didn't question him about the missing food, but I did keep my eyes open, observing what he did in my absence. Once, he even cooked dinner while I slept. He didn't eat anything before he left, but I noticed the next morning when I came home from work, some of the leftovers were gone. He even asked what happened to the potato salad he made, the next time I saw him? The potato salad tasted so bad, I threw it away the same day.

"Why did you run up the steps?" Carl demanded, when I came back down.

"This is my house. I don't have to explain anything to you. We're divorced, remember? What I do is my business."

"You're going to tell me why you ran up the steps before we get back together."

"Carl, I thought I made myself perfectly clear to you. We are never, ever, getting back together. It is forever over between us."

"It's not over. We'll get back together. And you'll tell me why you ran up the steps."

"I know you have a set of keys to the house, hand them over," I said with my hand out.

"I don't have any keys."

"You're lying. You come in this house after I'm gone. I've noticed food missing as well as finding a letter you wrote on top of my work in your old dresser."

"I had to use the toilet and wanted something to read."

"So you went in the dresser where I keep my writings and read my article," I added.

"I wanted something to read," he defended himself like it was a good excuse.

"Carl, give me my keys. I could have you arrested for trespassing."

"I don't have no keys."

"If you don't give me my keys, right now, I'm going to call the police and have you locked up for trespassing!" I shouted. The boys were looking at us. Little Carl started to cry. It always upset him when we argued. Carlos had a blank expression on his face. Carl saw their reactions and handed me the keys. "If I ever think you're in my house again without me being here, I'm going to file a trespassing warrant on you. I will not put up with you disrespecting me anymore."

"Come on boys, let's go! Let's get out of here!"

Little Carl and Carlos eagerly headed to the door with their stuff. "See ya, Mama," they both said.

"Before I leave, I want you to know, I enrolled into the CDL school. My training starts in two weeks. I'll be on the road a lot, traveling from city to city. I won't have any child support money to give you while I'm in training. I probably won't have any money until I get a job and get on my feet."

"It's a good thing I can support us. Otherwise, we'd be shit-out-of-luck if we depended on you. If you don't pay me when you complete your course, I'm going to turn you into the child support people for non-support."

"I see you're still trying to stick it to my ass."

"You haven't seen nothing yet. I advise you to do right about my house and the boys. Otherwise, you'll see a side of me you didn't know existed."

"Oh, I know you can be a bitch. But I'm not gonna let you bother me. It's hard to keep a good man down."

"It's also hard to get rid of leeches and parasites."

"I know I'm a good man. I don't care what you say. Just wait until I finish my training. I'll be making mo' money than I have in a long time. You'll be sorry you divorced my ass then."

"Bye, Carl. Don't keep the boys waiting any longer. I wish you well with your training and new life. I hope you're able to do everything you weren't able to do when we were married. I only ask two things from you, and you won't have any problems with me: you pay me child support and you keep your ass out of my house when I'm not here."

"I'm outta here," he said, leaving. The boys already had blown his horn twice. He hurried to the car and out of the driveway. Carl was gone. Would he abide by my two golden rules? Only time would tell. Knowing Carl, I think not.

While the boys were gone, I worked on "Uncaged." Lately, it occupied all my free time. I had completed chapter four and was working on chapter five.

Chestnut called and said he wanted us to meet after the I.B.W.A. gathering, next Saturday.

Bryson also called. We talked briefly. He stayed extremely busy working two jobs, besides working odd jobs on the side. Despite his hectic schedule, we continued eating dinner together as much as possible and seeing each other briefly on the weekend.

Knowing Bryson made the brokenness I felt before my divorce gradually disappear. It was replaced with a feeling of contentment. I was content with my life the way it was. I hoped and prayed often that, maybe, one day, the contentment would be replaced with happiness.

While thinking about the gathering Saturday, I realized July was rapidly approaching, which meant the blue carpet had to be replaced by then. Otherwise, it would be down longer than seven years. Since the depressed years were over, only God knew what the next era meant. I prayed and He directed my decision. He had shown me earlier how the color of my carpet characterized my life during each era. God revealed my previous golden and depressed eras when I had my gold and blue carpet, respectively. Now, I must rely on His guidance to select the third color or era of my life.

I instinctively knew gold was not a choice. Surely, I could only experience one golden era. Although I expected to have more children during this next era, it couldn't be golden again. Consequently, I searched the dictionary for different colors and their meanings.

I thought of green, but dismissed it quickly. My parents house was green inside and outside. My mama loved green. Since I saw green all my life growing up, I didn't want green carpet in my house. Besides, green means "easily imposed on or deceived; naive." Green was negative to me. It definitely was not a choice.

Brown was not a choice either because it was too drab. I needed an uplifting color. White, off-white and beige were out because they would be too hard to keep clean. I kept thinking until the color rose came to my mind. I looked up its definition. Rose meant pinkish-red or purplish-red. It also meant cheerful or optimistic. When I read its definition, I knew I had found my next carpet color—rose. My next era would be both cheerful and optimistic. It was the perfect color. In April, Bryson had already painted my bedroom walls magenta. A rose-colored era sounded marvelous!

When I told Bryson my next carpet color, he told me to go to Carpet City on Wesley Chapel Road. He thought they had good prices and selections. They also installed carpet at reasonable rates. He was too busy working other jobs to lay my carpet before July. Monday, I planned to give them a visit.

Sunday night, Carl brought the boys home after I left for work. When I returned home Monday morning, three of my black, sexy, lingerie pieces were sprawled across my bed. A bottle of douche sat on my bathroom counter. I fumed. I was angry with Carl. He had gone too far!

Monday after the boys came home from school, ate, and did their homework, we went to Carpet City. A short, polite, black man waited on me. The place was full of carpet rolls and other floor covers. Three aisles separated mounds of carpet.

"Welcome to Carpet City. My name is Freddie Tucker. How may I help you?" the salesman asked from behind his desk as we entered.

"I came to look at some carpet. Rose-colored in particular."

"Mama, we wanna look around some," both boys said as they walked off down the first aisle.

"Okay."

"Come this way," he said, going down the middle aisle to the second row of carpet. "Do you know what grade of carpet you're interested in?"

"No. I just want some carpet I can afford."

"What is your price range?"

"Under two thousand dollars. Way under."

"Depending on the size of your house, you'll come out cheaper putting throw rugs throughout the house. Now we have throw rugs that start from $6.99 and up. Unless, of course, you are interested in purchasing our top of the line oriental rugs on aisle one."

"No. I want wall-to-wall carpet."

"Well, this cranberry carpet here is an excellent quality. It is very durable, perfect for high traffic areas. It's dirt resistant, easy to care for, and only cost $11.99 a yard. Do you know how many yards you'll need?"

"No."

"That's no problem. We can have somebody go over to your house and get all the measurements. Do you want this color throughout the house?"

"No. I'm sure my sons want a different color in their bedrooms. Carl and Carlos come here!" I yelled. They came quickly.

"Yeah, Mama? What you want?" they both asked.

"What color carpet do you want in your rooms?"

"Black!" answered Carl, loudly.

"I don't know, Mama," Carlos replied, "What do you like?"

"I think brown will go good in your room. You don't need anything too light as nasty as you are."

"Brown is fine with me."

"Let me suggest a lower grade of carpet for their rooms," Freddie added. "Follow me. I have the perfect carpet for you." We walked to the end of the aisle. He selected a black carpet for $8.99 and a chestnut carpet for $7.99. "Of course, these are not as durable but they will not be in your high traffic areas. Do you need padding?"

"I guess so since it hasn't been replaced in fourteen years. The builders put the cheapest padding down anyway. The last time I bought carpet, seven years ago, the installers commented on how poor the padding was, and how it needed to be replaced then, but I couldn't afford to replace it."

"New padding will add life to your carpet. It won't wear out as fast."

"I also need vinyl for two bathrooms and my kitchen."

"Let's go over to the far left corner where we keep our other floor covers." We walked behind the next aisle. "Do you want me to leave you for a few minutes to decide which ones you want?"

"No, that won't be necessary. I've already decided."

"Good. What do you want?" he asked, ready to write.

"The white one here," I said, pointing directly in front of me, "and the light brown one over there, at the end."

"Those are nice choices."

"How soon will somebody be able to take the measurements?" I asked, eager to get started.

"Come to my desk and let me write everything down on a work order. I'll make a few phone calls to some independent contractors who work for us. If I can't get anybody, I'll come myself, later this evening after we close."

"Good."

"How do you plan to pay for this? All the money has to be paid before any work begins."

"I plan to charge it with my new credit card I received in the mail today. This is something that I needed done and my new credit card is the answer."

"Okay, Mrs. ...?"

"Miss, I mean, Ms. Lewis."

He looked at me and smiled. "I need you to fill out this section at the top with your full name, address and credit history."

When I completed filling out the application, I gave it back to him.

"You don't live far from here," he said, reviewing the information. "I could get to your house in five minutes. I think I'll come myself as soon as I wrap up everything here. It shouldn't take me too long to get all the measurements."

"How soon can you get started?"

"That depends on whether you want dinner," he said, smiling, leaning back in his chair.

ELEVEN

What have I gotten myself into, I thought, as I drove home from Carpet City. I know what's on Freddie's mind, but he can forget it. All I want is new carpet for my house. I don't need a new man. Bryson is enough man for me.

"Mama, when are you gonna get new living room furniture? Since you're buying new carpet, you need new furniture," Little Carl queried.

"Yeah, Mama, I'm tired of walking into an empty house," Carlos added.

"I hadn't thought about when to buy new furniture. I was only concerned with buying new carpet."

"Rhodes has a sale today. Let's go see what they have," Carl replied.

"When did you start watching furniture sales?"

"When we got rid of our furniture. I knew you'd have to buy some sooner or later."

"Okay. I guess we have time to look. Mr. Tucker is coming to the house later to take the measurements for the carpet." Luckily, I was at the I-20 intersection. I entered the ramp and drove to Rhodes on Memorial Drive. I pulled into an empty parking space, close to the door. "C'mon, on boys. Remember, I don't have a lot of time. We're only looking."

We closed the doors and hurried inside. At the door, I saw an old high school classmate, William Gilbert, who was a salesman.

"Welcome to Rhodes' One Day Sale," William said as we entered the store. "Vanessa Grant," he said recognizing me, "I haven't seen you since high school. How may I help you?"

"William Gilbert! This is really a surprise. I need some living room and kitchen furniture. These are my sons, Carl and Carlos. You know, I married Carl Lewis over twenty years ago."

"No. I didn't know since we lost touch with each other. Hello, young men. How are you doing?"

"Fine," they both answered.

"Well, Mrs. Lewis, let me show you what we have."

"William, you don't have to be so formal. Call me Vanessa. I'm not Mrs. Lewis anymore, anyway. I'm divorced."

"Certainly, Vanessa. Did you have anything in mind?"

"No. Just show me what you have."

"Certainly."

William walked me all through the store. The boys were interested in leather furniture. I had never bought leather furniture before. But there is always a first time for everything. Since the boys were bigger, leather would be feasible now. I bought a forest-green leather sofa and loveseat; a round, white, revolving coffee table; two white, glass-topped end tables; a gold picture mirror; a beige kitchen table with four matching beige and rose-colored chairs and two beige lamps. I opened a ninety-days-same-as-cash Rhodes account for my purchase. I told them to deliver it the following Monday. I wanted to make sure the carpet was down first.

We left Rhodes and went home. Freddie came ten minutes later. He took the measurements and calculated the total cost. The price was over two thousand dollars, but I didn't care. I wanted the work done at any price. Besides, I was ready to get started and I knew their prices were in line with other carpet companies. He assured me the work could be done by Wednesday or Thursday of this week. Before he left, he gave me a smirky grin. I let him know with my stone face that I was not interested in him. His involvement in my life was strictly business. And I do mean strictly!

The carpet was laid Wednesday and the vinyl was laid Thursday by two different crews. Looking at the new carpet and floors made me feel good inside. I felt completely healed and whole again.

Carl picked up the boys early Friday evening. He said it would be his last weekend with them before he started his training next week. He would be in town the first part of the week, but expected to go out of town by Wednesday or Thursday. The boys eagerly left with Carl. Being with their dad was the highlight of their week. Their faces always lit up when Carl came around. I knew one day he would try to take them from me. I saw it written all over his face.

Feeling tired from a hectic week, I went to bed early. My thoughts and prayers were of Little Carl and Carlos. I hoped and prayed they were happy, despite the divorce. From all indications, they seemed to be coping well. But only Jesus knew for sure. I prayed He would help them understand and cope with any ill feelings they may be harboring, that He would remove any stigma of being from a broken home. Jesus is always the answer. He knows how to make our wrongs right.

Saturday was the I.B.W.A. gathering at John White Park. I refused to call Zakee again to confirm if he planned to attend. If being there was important, he would have written it down and planned to come. I knew one thing. If he didn't show up, it would be my last attempt at seeing him. I would interpret his lack of attendance as his obvious lack of interest in me. Okay, Zakee. The ball is in your court. Either play ball or sit on the bench. What are you going to do?

I arrived at John White Park promptly at 2:00. I drove around looking for the tennis court, our designated location. Spotting the tennis court behind the clubhouse, I parked near its entrance. Once inside, I saw Chestnut sitting alone at a large round table reading a paper.

"Is anyone else here?" I asked, as I pulled out a chair.

"No. Just us," he said, turning another page of his newspaper.

"Uhmmmm, something smells wonderful!"

"Oh, that must be my ribs. They're next to you in the plastic bag," he said, not looking away from his paper.

"I brought whole wheat brownies and fruit salad."

"Those sound like laxative foods. You need something that will stick to your ribs and stop you up, like my ribs," he said, putting the paper down. "By the way, can you come to my place tomorrow? I'm ready to get started preparing your first three chapters for the publishers."

"Tomorrow will be fine. What time?"

"One o'clock. Have you written anymore chapters?"

"I'm on chapter five."

"Cool," he said as he picked up another section of the paper to read.

"Excuse me. I think I'll walk around and see the place. Maybe, some more of our people are here. I'll leave my food next to yours if you don't mind," I said, getting up.

"Don't worry. I won't take off with it. Just thinking about it gives me the runs."

I left Chestnut and scouted the place. I was in search of Zakee. It was 2:15, so maybe he was here looking for me, too. My search took me to the tennis court in the rear, the grassy areas on the side, and the parking lot in the front. No Zakee. No other I.B.W.A. members either. I guess they were operating on c.p., or colored people's time, being late. Not having anything else to do, I rejoined Chestnut at his table and read his paper.

Thirty minutes later most of the members and guests had arrived. Unfortunately, Zakee was not among them. We ate and shared stories. Jimmy Stroud sold and autographed his latest book, Obie. I stayed until four. Part of my mind was at the event. The other part kept wondering where Zakee was, and if he was still coming? Since he had not shown up by four, I knew he wasn't coming. When I left the park, I also left any hope of Zakee and I ever getting together. I went home disappointed and hurt.

On the way home, a voice inside started talking to me.

"Yo, Vanessa! Did you really think Zakee was going to show up?"

"Yes, I did. Who are you?"

"I'm Viva, your inner self."

"What inner self? What are you talking about?"

"Pull over, girlfriend. Let me tell you all about me."

I stopped at the entrance of the park and listened to Viva.

"Girlfriend, let me take you down memory lane. First off, I'm the opposite of your wimpy ass. You're so passive you get on my nerves. I took over when you nearly had us both killed in the bathtub. I'm your creative side. You like math, science and Carl. I like writing, Zakee and Bryson. Remember those two attractions you had? That was me. I'm attracted to both Zakee and Bryson. I like worldly men because I'm of the world. You were spiritual until I became uncaged. Yeah, you heard me right. I, your worldly self, was uncaged. Remember, your welling up experience and how you felt like a new person? Then you went downstairs and realized you didn't love Carl anymore? Well that was me. I couldn't stand his sorry ass. I was in love with him, at first, when you both were in the world. But after your conversion, all he wanted to do was use you, and you let him. I had to put an end to his madness before he used you up. By the way, I get pissed off easily. And when I do, I get sweet revenge. I protect you. From now on, anyone who loves you must meet my approval. He has to satisfy both of us, especially me. Do you understand?"

"No."

"You will. Do you remember when you first had the desire to write a book in 1980?"

"Yes."

"That was me. Those were the days you stayed stoned out of your ever loving mind. You smoked reefer, drank alcohol, went to triple X movies and did all the worldly things. Your book was about illicit sexual activities. I love illicit sex. Hell, I love sex, period. Remember, in 1981, when Sherry prayed over you, and you felt a warm sensation all over your body?"

"Yes."

"You wanted to get pregnant but couldn't until she prayed for you that day. Her prayer purged your body of me. Once I was put into submission, you were able to get pregnant. I'm selfish and don't want to be tied down with children. Shortly after that, when you became pregnant, you gave your life to Christ. I can't dwell where Jesus dwells. I'm of the flesh, He's of the Spirit. I'm crucified with Christ. But when you stopped abiding in Christ, I took over. Your love for Zakee got your mind off Christ and His Word. Zakee became your god and I became uncaged. And Vanessa, darling, I'm here to stay."

"No. Go back where you came from! You're evil!"

"Yes, I am. I, the flesh, dwells in every carnal person."

"Now, I understand why I've been doing things that are so uncharacteristic of me such as adultery, cursing, and listening to the secular radio all the time. I understand why my Bible study and prayer life are practically nonexistent. Because of you, Viva!

"No, it's because of you, Vanessa. While you were close to Jesus, you ruled. When you forsook your devotion to Jesus and let Zakee be your god, your admiration, your reason for living, I reigned. As long as you're spiritually weak, I'll rule. I'll do everything in my power to keep you from the Word. Your prayers will decrease. And I, Viva, will increase. Take five, Vanessa. I'll take us home."

TWELVE

While Viva drove, I was reminded of several Scriptures. The first was Galatians 5:17-25, *"For the desires of the flesh are against the Spirit, and the desires of the Spirit are against the flesh; for these are opposed to each other, to prevent you from doing what you would...Now the works of the flesh are plain: fornication, impurity, licentiousness, idolatry, sorcery, enmity, strife, jealousy, selfishness, dissension, party spirit, envy, drunkenness, carousing and the like. I warn you, as I warned you before, that those who do such things shall not inherit the kingdom of God. But the fruit of the Spirit is love, joy, peace, patience, kindness, goodness, faithfulness, gentleness, self-control; against such there is no law. And those who belong to Christ Jesus have crucified the flesh with its passions and desires. If we live by the Spirit, let us also walk by the Spirit."* The other Scriptures were in Romans 8:2-13. *"For the law of the Spirit of life in Christ Jesus has set me free from the law of sin and death. For God has done what the law, weakened by the flesh could not do: sending his own Son in the likeness of sinful flesh and sin, he condemned sin in the flesh, in order that the just requirement of the law might be fulfilled in us, who walk not according to the flesh but according to the Spirit. For those who live according to the flesh set their minds on the things of the flesh, but those who live according to the Spirit set their minds on things of the Spirit. To set the mind on the flesh is death, but to set the mind on the Spirit is life and peace. For the mind that is set on the flesh is hostile to God; it does not submit to God's law, indeed it cannot; and those who are in the flesh cannot please God....So then, brethren, we are debtors, not to the flesh, to live according to the flesh—for if you live according to the flesh you will die, but if by the Spirit you put to death the deeds of the body you will live."*

After I thought about these Scriptures, I prayed.

Dear Heavenly Father, please deliver me from my sinful flesh. Jesus came to crucify the flesh of all mankind by allowing His Holy Spirit to dwell in all who repent of their evil ways and believe in Him. I now see the error of my ways by idolizing man. My flesh has overtaken me because I am spiritually weak. Please strengthen me with Your indwelling Holy Spirit to conquer the sin that lies within me. Forgive me of my trespasses against You. Wash me with the blood of Your Son, Jesus Christ, then I will know my sins are forgiven. Hold not my trespasses against me, but wipe my slate clean as before. I ask this in Your Son, Jesus Christ. Amen.

Viva was gone after I prayed. I hoped she would never return. But somehow, I instinctively knew I had not seen the last of her evil self. The flesh is very hard to get rid of, especially when you are spiritually weak.

My new goal was to become as spiritually strong as before. My objective was to pray more, read the Bible more, fast and put every thought into the captivity of Jesus Christ. I needed to put off the old self and put on the new woman who was shaped and molded in Jesus Christ.

When I arrived home, Bryson's van was parked in the driveway. Since he had keys to my house, he had let himself inside. Wanting desperately to study the Bible, I regretted his company. He came to the door as I walked up the steps. He opened the door and greeted me with a passionate kiss as I stepped inside.

"I thought you would never get here," he said, holding me close.

"How long have you been waiting?"

"Thirty minutes."

"That's not too long."

"It's a long time when your penis is as hard as mine."

"Did you come over here to screw?"

"No. I came to see you. But you know every time I think about you, I have an erection. You have that effect on me."

My body felt his erect penis. I could tell he was ready twenty-nine minutes ago. "Bryson, you might as well cool off because nothing is going to happen today. I really need to have a Bible study instead of entertaining you."

"I won't be here long. Maybe, twenty more minutes. You can have your Bible study then." His hands glided up and down my hips. He kissed my lips again while his body demanded to be satisfied. And I felt Viva coming back.

"C'mon, let's go to my room," I heard Viva say. "I'll take care of you, Big Daddy. Let's just close this door first."

Bryson smiled, then scooped me up in his arms and carried me up the stairs. Within seconds, we were on my bed and the lovemaking began. Viva had triumphed again! "Oh Lord, deliver me from myself," I said, after Bryson left.

I wanted to read my Bible and pray, but I was too guilt-ridden to talk to God. I also didn't want His Word to chastise me. All I wanted to do was sleep and forget the whole thing happened, to forget how sinful I was, how far from God's truth I had strayed.

A smile covered my face as I opened my eyes the next morning. Today, I meet with Chestnut. Today, I can forget about yesterday. Today, Vanessa will rule!

"Oh, yeah?" I heard Viva say, "Not if I have anything to do with it! Your ruling days are over, sweetie. If Chestnut was my type, I might have some fun with him today. But he's not. He's too square. Square men turn me off. Bryson is still number one in my book."

"Get lost, Viva! You're not ruining this day," I said, getting out of bed.

"Ha! I'm not going nowhere. I have plans for this day, too. May the best half win, Nessa, darling."

If I could get my hands on Viva, I'd kill her. But I'm sure she's thinking the same thing about me.

I got up, dressed, ate breakfast, then worked on chapter five before leaving for Chestnut's. I prayed and rebuked Viva before I left, hoping Jesus Christ would keep her in check.

The time with Chestnut was well spent. He gave me a small, blue, 9 1/2" X 6" single subject notebook. On the front, he wrote, "Vanessa Lewis, Critique of 'Uncaged.'" I opened it and read the first page.

Vanessa, this book will serve as my critique book. Throughout the writing of your novel, I will write all my concerns in this journal. Do not call to talk about it. Write it down. To me, this is best because it forces us both to do in-depth analysis. It always takes more time to write about a problem than it does to verbalize one. When responding, date the response. Use a number system (like the one I will use to make my suggestions), so I will know what point you are responding to. After reading your response, we can sit down and talk about it and decide where we want to go.

So now let's begin. My statement. I love how this story is written. I see great potential. If I didn't, I would never have asked to represent you. The comments on the following pages represent issues that, if addressed, will make your project more marketable.

After reading the first page, I looked up at Chestnut. "Chestnut, I want to thank you again for helping me. I need someone like you to help me get 'Uncaged' published."

Save your thanks for later. We have work to do. Turn to the next page."

The next page contained:

I. General Comments.

    A) I think we need to decide who is telling the story. Is it some unidentified third person? Is it Betty or Xavier? Or is it a combination of Betty and

Xavier? From my reading, it should probably be Betty and Xavier (at least until Vanessa is old enough to tell her story). If the narrator/narrators are Betty and Xavier, we need to look at the chapters again.

B) Equally important is what tense are we speaking in? If it is present tense, we should use the present tense throughout. "Show, don't tell" applies here. Don't tell us what Xavier or Betty or Big Mama are doing. Show us.

C) The cursing is going to be a serious problem for getting this work published. Remember, we are living in a very conservative time. Books written by great artists like Mark Twain are being taken off the shelves. I have generally gone and reduced the cursing by 70%. Read the new version and tell me if it will work.

I re-read the first three chapters. The changes Chestnut made worked. We were on to something. I was very thankful God had put us together. Two heads were better than one; especially, when this one didn't know what it was doing. I simply was being led by Christ to write "Uncaged." He supplied everything. And I do mean everything.

We wrapped up the session ten minutes later then I went home. Excitement filled me as I drove. I felt good about Chestnut and his input. Christ truly put us together to accomplish this task.

The next day, the furniture arrived. My decor colors were forest green, cranberry, white, beige, gold, and pink. The combinations worked well. It looked better than what I had imagined in the store. My Ten Commandment plaque and the gold-framed mirror decorated the walls and accented the room.

I spent the remainder of the day cleaning up. The spic-n-span look made the house look even better. I felt blessed and healed as I inspected my new domain.

That night at work, around 6:00 a.m., Carl called me.

"Emergency Clinic Lab, Lewis," I said, as I picked up the phone.

"Vanessa, get a pen and piece of paper," Carl instructed hurriedly.

"Okay, I'm ready," I said, reaching for the scratch pad near the phone.

"Write this down. Get on I-20 West. Take I-285 to Bankhead Highway. Turn right. Take the first right on Harwell Road. Turn in the first complex, Willow Trace. Take a right into the complex, and then take a left."

"What are these directions to?"

"My apartment. I'm in apartment H, directly across from the clubhouse."

"Why are you giving me directions to your place? Before now, you've been keeping it a secret."

"I want to see you."

"Why?"

"I want you to go to the store first and buy some baby lotion and whipped cream."

"Why?"

"I want you to be my whipped-cream-delight."

When he said that, I burst out laughing. I laughed so loud and hard, tears streamed from my eyes. My co-worker Jenny came out of the office to see what was going on.

"What happened?" she queried.

I couldn't talk for laughing. She eventually went back into the office. When I could finally compose myself long enough to talk, I said. "You have totally lost your mind! I am not coming to your apartment."

"I don't want to lick the front. I want to stick my tongue in your ass."

"No! When did you start doing such things? When we were married, we never used baby lotion or whipped cream. Neither did you lick my ass. I'm busy Carl. You can put some whipped cream on your dick and have a popsicle delight. I've got to go, bye," I said, before he could say anything else. When I hung up the phone, I went straight to the office. "Jenny, you won't believe what Carl said."

"I heard you laughing. I thought someone was at the window."

"Listen to this. Carl gave me directions to his apartment and told me to go by the store and buy baby lotion and whipped cream."

"For what?"

"He wanted me to be his whipped-cream-delight," I said, laughing again.

"What an odd combination. I can tell he's not fully oriented," she said laughing with me.

"I told him he could put whip cream on himself and have a popsicle delight."

Jenny's face turned red. "Men and their pricks have always been a problem."

We both laughed even harder.

THIRTEEN

Monday, July 3, a letter and two postcards from Carl arrived from New York. The postcards were for the boys. I opened the letter addressed to me.

Dear Vanessa,

I'm enjoying my truck driving training, but I miss you and my sons. I'm still trying hard to adjust to being divorced. I can't believe I'm hundreds of miles away from my family. I've met several new friends but none replaces you. Being single is a lot different from what I imagined. It has its advantages, but I still miss being with my family. This is a special time for me. I go out and kick-it-around as often as I can. I like going to different cities, meeting new people, eating new foods, but none of this replaces being at home with my family. Kiss Carl and Carlos. Tell them I love them and I miss them very much. I'll be back in town soon.

Carl

I threw the letter away when I finished reading it. I left the kids' postcards on the table where they would see them when they came in from playing outside. I guess, Carl value's family life now that he's single. But when he was married, he wanted to be single. He's one confused man, I thought, as I opened my other mail.

The phone rang as I read my letter from church.

"Hello."

"Vanessa, this is Zakee."

"Zakee! What a pleasant surprise."

"I was sitting here thinking about you and decided to call."

"From your no-shows, and you not calling me, I didn't think you ever thought about me."

"I think about you sometimes. I just don't call."

"Well, why did you call today?" You must have something on your mind."

"I do. I was wondering what you're doing for the Fourth of July?"

"I don't have any plans. I'll probably be at home writing or do something with my sons. I'll decide tomorrow when I wake up. Unless you wanted us to do something together?"

"Oh, no. I don't have any plans either. I just wanted to know what you were doing."

"How are you doing in your drum classes?"

"It's funny you should mention my class. There's a sister there that reminds me of you. She wears dreadlocks. Have you ever considered wearing dreadlocks?"

"No."

"I think they look good. You'd look better in dreadlocks than you did in that wig."

"You still remember the wig?"

"How can I forget? If you saw how you looked in it, you couldn't forget either."

"I still have the wig, but I don't wear it."

"That's good. You look better without it. I liked you natural. There's something about natural hair that really turns me on."

"Well, Zakee, I'm glad you called, but I really must go."

"Okay. I was getting ready to end the conversation myself."

"Good-bye."

"Bye."

He sure is weird these days, I thought, as I hung up the phone. He's not the same Zakee I fell in love with last year. He seems to be dancing to the beat of a different drum. I hope he never calls me again, and I definitely won't call him. I do wonder why he never asked me out. Today, it seemed as if he wanted to, but he just didn't know how. What is he afraid of? Why is he dragging his feet? Is he expecting me to invite him over first? Or is he really not interested? I don't know about Zakee these days and from this last conversation, I don't care to find out.

As I was meditating on my conversation with Zakee, Carlos, Gary and Noel came in from outside. Gary and Noel were brothers who lived in the first house of our five house cul-de-sac. However, they were both younger than Carlos by one and three years, respectively. They played together well despite the difference in ages.

"Mama, we came to get something to drink," Carlos said as he entered the house.

"Hey, Miss Lewis," said Gary and Noel as they crossed the threshold.

"You can only have water."

"I know. I know," Carlos repeated. "I don't drink enough water. Water is good for me. Too much soda is not good. And when I come home with my friends, we can only have water!"

"That's right. I see you do pay attention when I talk to you."

"Mama, I hear every word you say. You just think I don't be listening."

"Here's a postcard your daddy sent," I said, waving it into the air.

Carlos took the postcard from my hand and read it aloud. *"Hi Carlos, I hope you are doing well. I'm enjoying my training because I get to see different parts of the United States. I'm sending this postcard from New York City. One day, I will bring you and Carl to this place to see the different sights, especially the Statue of Liberty. I miss you very much. I'll be home soon. I love you. Dad.* C'mon Gary, and Noel. We'll go to my room for a while," he said, holding onto the postcard, placing his empty glass down on the counter.

"Do you miss your dad?" I asked, examining his face.

"Of course I do! But I know he's away to better himself, to make more money for Carl and me, so he can buy us some of the things we ask for all the time. He explained to us, before he left, why he had to go. He said he wanted to be in a position to do more for us."

"Since you do listen to your dad and me when we talk to you. Now hear this. Go clean up your nasty room!"

"Ah, Mama, I'll clean it up when Gary and Noel leave. It's rude to clean up when you have company. Didn't you teach me that? C'mon guys. Let's go play with my Saga."

They trod up the steps to Carlos's bedroom. I shook my head as they left. That's Carl's son, all right. Every last conniving inch of him.

Little Carl came home ten minutes later. Marlon, his best friend in the neighborhood, accompanied him. They were both over six-feet tall with medium builds. Marlon's dark skin contrasted with Carl's yellow complexion. Although they looked like night and day, they got along well and had a lot of things in common, primarily not doing well in school. They both considered school boring, something they had to do for their parents, instead of what they wanted to do for themselves.

"Hi, foxy lady," Little Carl said, hugging and kissing me on my cheek as he entered the kitchen. "How is the greatest mom in the world?"

"Okay. What did you do?" I asked, giving him a quizzical glare.

"Ah, Mama! I haven't done anything. Can't I show you love without you thinking I'm into something?"

"No. I know you, son. C'mon, out with it."

"Man, I told you you weren't going to get away with it," Marlon added, looking at Little Carl.

"All right, Carl spit it out before I lose my composure and be like Cool Whip all over your ass."

"I made two C's, two D's, and two F's on my report card. I found out last week, but I didn't know how to tell you."

"You must want to be a dumb ass like your father. Those are the type grades he made throughout school. I made all A's and two B's in high school. Carl, you have the potential to make all A's and B's because you have my blood running through your veins."

"My typing teacher don't like me. That's why I didn't do well. I won't have her next year, so I'll do better. I'll make all A's and B's. You'll see."

"You know your telephone is D and F, too."

"What do you mean?"

"Your telephone will be disconnected for future use."

"Ah, Mama, you can't do that! I just got my phone three months ago."

"And you just lost it today. Having your own phone is a privilege, not a right. When you make D's and F's on your report card, you're telling me loud and clear that your priorities are wrong. You value talking on the telephone more than you value your education."

"Don't turn my phone off. Give me another chance. I promise, I'll make all A's and B's next school year," he said, hugging me again.

"No, son. Your phone will be disconnected today. Part of growing up is taking responsibility for your actions. Every action has a consequence. Good actions produce good consequences. Wrong actions result in bad ones. You reap what you sow."

"I'm sowing love now," he said, kissing my cheek.

"And you'll reap love from me. Because I love you, I'm still turning your phone off. I want you to be somebody when you grow up. Without an education, you'll struggle all your life. You'll be the tail, not the head. Here's a postcard from your dad," I said, picking it up from the table.

He took the postcard, read it and laid it back down on the table. C'mon, Marlon. Let's grab a soda and go to my room. I want to talk on my phone before it's disconnected."

"No soda. You can only drink water."

"I'll be glad when I live with Dad. This house has too many rules," Little Carl said as he poured two glasses of water and went upstairs with Marlon.

"Man, you better be glad your mama didn't light into your behind like my father did me when I showed him my three D's and three F's," Marlon said, as they left the kitchen.

I felt Carl's grades were more a reflection of being a teenager, growing up, enjoying life, and not taking education seriously, more than from the impact of the divorce. Coupled with having his own phone and friends with low self-esteem, he got off track. My goal, now, was to put both of us back on track. Removing his telephone would be a start for him. Forgetting Zakee would be a start for me. I knew I must also get rid of Viva to live a spirit-filled life again.

"So, you think you're going to get rid of me?" Viva said. "You must have lost your mind! Girlfriend, fix me a drink and turn the radio up. I feel like getting my groove on. Let's bring the Fourth of July in right now. Call Bryson so we can party."

"No! I'm going to my room to pray and have Bible study, you wicked witch!"

After calling the phone company to disconnect Carl's phone, I went to my room. I retrieved my Bible from the head of my bed and placed it in the chair near the bathroom. Since I had to use the toilet, I did that first. While washing my hands, I heard the doorbell.

"Mama, you have company!" Carl shouted.

As I came down the steps, Bryson was standing near the door. "Bryson, what a surprise."

He pulled me close to him when I reached the last step. "I couldn't wait to see you. I came by to get our Fourth started early," he said, gently kissing me. "We're both off. What do you say?"

Before I could say anything, Viva answered, "That sounds great! C'mon. Let's make a drink, grab some fruit, cheese and crackers, and go downstairs."

His mouth watered and his eyes glowed. "I see I came to the right place," he said, gliding his hands on my hips. "I'll take a rum and Coke."

"I'll have one, too."

Little Carl and Marlon came down the steps. "Mama, I'm going to South Dekalb Mall with Marlon and Jermaine."

"Okay."

Immediately after Carl left, Carlos, Gary, and Noel came down the steps also. "Mama, can I go over to their grandmother's house? They're going over there to visit."

"Sure. If Tunya doesn't mind you going."

"It's all right if he goes, Mrs. Lewis. We already asked our Mom," Gary added.

"If it's okay with your mom, then it's okay with me."

"Bye, Mama."

"Good-bye, Mrs. Lewis."

"Bye, boys," I said as they left.

"Well, well, well. We have the house to ourselves," Bryson said, grinning, locking both doors.

"Fix the drinks while I get the radio from my room. We'll get this party started," Viva announced.

"Don't take too long."

"I won't!" I ran up the steps, entered my room and unplugged the radio on the nightstand. As I rushed out the door with it, I saw my Bible in the chair. "Take five," Viva commanded. "And, thanks for allowing me to have a fantastic third of July! I'm coming, Big Daddy!" she yelled, as we ran down the steps.

FOURTEEN

The third of July was a blast with Bryson. Viva triumphed again. Her sexy, devilish ways kept Bryson stirred up since they were two of a kind. They love sex, alcohol, dancing, and good times. I must defeat her before she defeats me. I, Vanessa, must rule again!

Early the next morning, I prayed silently in bed.

Dear Heavenly Father, Please forgive me for my trespasses against You. My spirit is weak. I know I don't read Your Word like I should, pray like I should, fast like I should, do any of the spiritual things that strengthen the spirit and weaken the flesh. On the contrary, I have strengthened my flesh by listening to suggestive music on the radio and neglecting my Bible study and prayer time. As a result, my flesh has taken control. Now my spirit person is the tail, not the head. Renew Your Holy Spirit within me. Allow it to dominate and rule my life. Let me not give in to my flesh or Satan anymore. In Christ's name I pray, Amen.

While praying, I recalled several Scriptures. One was Romans 13:12-14. *"The night is far gone, the day is at hand. Let us then cast off the works of darkness and put on the armor of light; let us conduct ourselves becomingly as in the day, not in reveling and drunkenness, not in debauchery and licentiousness, not in quarreling and jealousy. But put on the Lord Jesus Christ, and make no provisions for the flesh, to gratify its desires."*

Reading the Scriptures made me realize my problem with Viva was not unique. Adam and Eve struggled with their flesh, and so has everyone else since them. That's why Jesus came, to crucify the flesh and its evil desires. Jesus gave His Holy Spirit to mankind to live a righteous life, to cast off the dark works of Satan. Jesus came as The Light of the world to overcome the darkness, and its evil ways.

My soul longed for a close relationship with Jesus Christ again, but Viva wanted to live according to the ways of this world. And I must overcome Viva through Jesus Christ, who strengthens me.

"Yeah, right," Viva said, as I rolled out of bed. "He came to strengthen you and get rid of me. But I am here to stay! You might as well get used to the idea, girlfriend, because your other half is very well and alive. How 'bout some breakfast, or are you trying to starve me to death?"

"If I could, I would," I replied, putting on my housecoat. "But it will take more than a lack of food to get rid of your evil nature."

"Yo, girlfriend! I want two eggs over easy, grits, cheese toast, bacon and coffee with French Vanilla creamer."

"Is that all, Viva, dear?"

"For now. You know today is the Fourth of July. I had a ball last night, today I plan to have a blowout! So much for small talk, girlfriend, I'm ready to eat."

My feet carried me to the bathroom to wash up. Then I went to the kitchen to fix breakfast for Viva and the boys. They woke up when it was ready. My day was spent entertaining them and keeping Viva at bay.

The rest of the week was uneventful except when Carl came back into town for the weekend. He called at six o'clock to say he was on his way to pick up the boys to keep them for the weekend. He talked to Little Carl and Carlos briefly before hanging up. Twenty minutes later, he rang the doorbell.

"Daddy's here!" shouted Carlos, running down the steps to open the door.

Little Carl was close behind. "I thought, he'd never get here," he said, reaching the door.

I was in the great room reading my Bible. Before I could move, Carlos opened the door and Carl was inside.

"What ya bring me?" Carlos asked, as Carl crossed the threshold.

"Yeah, Dad! I know you have something for us," Little Carl added.

"Wait-a-minute! Don't I get a hello first? Or, how you doing? I miss you. I'm glad you're home." Carl screeched before pulling money from his pocket and giving them each a twenty dollar bill.

"Thanks, Dad!" they each yelled, hugging his neck.

"Oh, I get a hug after I give you money! Y'all not right. Y'all should have given me a hug even if I didn't give you anything."

"We would have, Dad. But we knew you wouldn't come back empty-handed. We know you, and you know us," Little Carl said, putting his money in his pocket.

"Let's go! Get your things. I'm ready to leave."

"We're ready. Our things are right here at the door," Carlos said, picking up his bags.

As they turned to leave, I asked Carl, "Where's my money? You haven't paid child support in almost two months!"

"Why is it every time I see you, you're always asking me for damn money? I just got back, and the first thing that comes out of your damn mouth is something about money! I don't have no money for you! You don't have to keep asking me for money. When I have some for you, I'll give it to your begging ass! Come on, boys, let's go!" he said, storming out the door.

Well, so much for expecting any help from Carl, I thought, as I continued my Bible study in Psalms 146:5-10. *"Happy is he whose help is the God of Jacob, whose hope is in the Lord his God, who made heaven and earth, the sea, and all that is in them; who keeps faith forever; who executes justice for the oppressed; who gives food to the hungry. The Lord sets the prisoners free; the Lord opens the eyes of the blind. The Lord lifts up those who are bowed down; the Lord loved the righteous. The Lord watches over the sojourners, he upholds the widow and the fatherless; but the way of the wicked he brings to ruin. The Lord will reign forever, thy God, O Zion, to all generations. Praise the Lord!"*

Bryson called when I finished my Bible study. He wanted to come by that evening, but the I.B.W.A Novel Writing Group was scheduled to meet at my place at 7:00 p.m.. We met once a month in the home of a member to read our works in progress. The meeting usually ran late. We also used the time for fellowship and to eat. Constructive criticism was given to each writer after they read. Most comments were positive. The negative comments were designed to improve the clarity, content or construction of the material read. In most cases, the critiques were received favorably. In some instances' feelings were hurt, irrevocably. A writer has to have thick skin to absorb the constant criticism of his work. A revision of an old saying holds true: You can't please all the people all the time. You can please some of the people some of the time. And some people you can never please.

Early Saturday morning before I was out of bed, the phone rang.

"Hello," I whispered, sleepily.

"Baby, aren't you up yet?"

"No. Who is this?"

"The man of your life. The man who makes all your dreams come true. Did you dream about me last night?"

"Yes. I dreamed I was on a deserted island, eating a coconut under a large palm tree. I used a leaf to cover my naked body. As I lay on the warm white sand to eat, a tall handsome man in a small boat came to my rescue. He tied his boat to the tree with a long rope. I stood up as he approached me carrying a black bag and a small box. The leaf covered me from my waist down, exposing my breasts. As he drew closer, I saw it was you. You opened the black bag and took out a stethoscope to listen to my heart. Next, you held my wrist to check my pulse. `All is fine,' you said. You put the stethoscope back inside the black bag, then pushed it aside. You then reached into the box. You pulled out a small bottle with blue liquid inside. `Lie down,' you instructed me, `I want to rub this on your body.' I did as you commanded. The liquid felt warm and tingly as you massaged it into my skin. `Ahhh, that's nice,' I moaned. You put the bottle back, then pulled out a bottle of wine, two wine glasses and a thin blanket. You placed the blanket on the sand, then you opened the wine. We drank every drop. After drinking the wine, you instructed me to lie down again. Your hands glided all over my body, stopping at my breasts. You gently caressed and kissed each one. Your mouth moved up to passionately kiss my lips, then it traveled passed my breasts, to my womanhood where your tongue moved freely. Sensing my arousal, you quickly removed your clothes. As your body lay on top of mine, the telephone woke me up."

"What? The telephone woke you up! You need to go back to sleep and finish where you left off, at the good part," Bryson said, excitedly.

"Sorry. It doesn't work that way. When you woke me up, the dream ended."

"Well, I can make the last part come true in real life. I can be over there in twenty minutes."

"Sorry again, Bryson. I plan to work on my manuscript before I go to church since the kids are gone for the weekend."

"Damn, I can't win for losing! What are you doing after church?"

"Resting. I have to work tonight."

"I'll be over to rest with you. By the way, I have some motion lotion to massage you with like in your dream. I'll even provide the wine. Who says dreams don't come true?"

"But Bryson, I don't have time to see you today!"

"No 'buts' about it. I'm coming over and that's final. Go back to sleep. Maybe you'll pick up where you left off. Bye, baby, I'll see you later."

"Bye, Bryson, man of my dreams."

I called Bryson after church and told him not to come over. I was really tired and needed to rest. Entertaining him would cut into my sleep too much. He would have to make his own dreams come true.

I spent the remainder of the weekend catching up on my sleep. Monday morning, Carl called while I was at work.

"Hello, Vanessa," he said, as I finished my standard greeting. "I just want you to know I love you, and miss you, and want us to get back together. I've been thinking about it all weekend long. Our sons really need both parents under one roof. I've let you have your little time to sow wild oats. I know before we divorced I was the only man you had been with. You've had enough time to try your friend out. I forgive you. What do you say?"

"You must have lost your mind while you were gone! I'm never getting back with you unless you give me my sign."

"What are you talking about, a sign?"

"Before we divorced, I prayed to God about a specific sign, a confirmation, an act that will identify the next man in my life. I even prayed after our divorce that if you gave me the sign, I would remarry you."

"I got your sign, right here with me."

"What is it?"

"All this good loving. I have it right here at the house waiting on you to come home."

"What are you doing at the house? You're not suppose to be there when I'm not there! You made another key didn't you? I'm going to file a trespassing warrant on you today. I told you I would, if you ever were at the house when I was not there."

"I was just kidding. I'm not at the house. You don't have to get bitchy. You need this loving more than you realize. Your friend can't love you the way I can, can he? I can tell you need the real thing."

"What I need is for you to get your ass out of my house! You can look for the sheriff to serve you your warrant papers soon. In the meantime, don't come near the house to pick up the boys unless I'm there!"

A dial tone followed my last words. I was fuming when I hung up the phone. God, I pray he never gives me my sign, I thought. No way, I could ever live with him again. Between Carl and Viva, I'd be a perfect candidate for the funny farm.

When I arrived home, a letter was waiting for me on the kitchen table. The boys were in their beds asleep. My newspaper was also on the table which was unusual. The boys never brought the newspaper inside, nor did they leave me letters. If they had something to tell me, they either told me before I left to go to work, told me when I came back home, or called me at work. The combination confirmed my worst suspicions: Carl was indeed inside my house, uninvited and unwanted. I looked on the stove where I had left half a pan of meatloaf. I had told the kids to put it in the refrigerator before they went to sleep. The meatloaf was missing, but the empty pan was still on the stove. I knew the boys did not eat up all the meatloaf because they don't like it that well. But Carl loves my meatloaf. Only he would clean the pan. For some reason, I looked inside the cabinet by the stove. I noticed the two coffee jars in the front. The jar of Maxwell House was almost empty, but it had more coffee in it now than before. I reached for the unopened Mountain Blend, unscrewed the cap, and found it was opened with the seal partially removed. Obviously, Carl also made himself a cup of coffee. The Maxwell House jar had only held enough coffee for one or two more cups. He must have emptied the jar, then realized he couldn't leave an empty jar in the cabinet, or I would know he had been there. So, he opened the new jar and switched some of the coffee to deceive me. All I could think of was how could he be so sneaky? He hasn't given me child support in over two months. Now he thinks he can come in here and eat up all our food? I don't think so! I then went to the refrigerator to inspect its contents. Several eggs were missing as well as some bread. I know how Carl loves eggs. Giving Carl the benefit of doubt, I woke the boys up and asked them if they ate the meatloaf.

I knew they hadn't eaten the eggs. They both said no. Going back downstairs, I read the letter on the table.

Dear Doll,
    I know you have moved on with your life without me, but I still want us to get back together. If only you knew how much I long to hold you one more time. How much I wish I could kiss you and make love to you again. I know, I've made many mistakes in the past, but can you find it in your heart to forgive me? I've prayed to God and I know He's forgiven me. Let's let bygones be bygones. We can start over and have another happy marriage. Vanessa, I love you very much. There is no other woman for me but you. I love you more than life itself. Please let's get back together. If not for our sakes, for the boys. They love both of us. Can't you see how you're tearing them apart? I see the hurt in their eyes when I look at them. Enough is enough! For all of our sakes, Vanessa, please end this madness.

Love, your only man,
Carl

Enclosed was $86 cash. After reading Carl's letter, I could have lit a barbecue grill with my anger. I threw his letter into the trash can nearby, placed the money in my purse and headed for the door. Maybe I could file a trespassing warrant on Carl before the boys woke up, I thought, as I opened the door.

FIFTEEN

I arrived at the police station on Memorial Drive in twenty minutes and parked my car across the street in the visitor's parking lot. The courthouse was on the right; fines were paid in the building on the left. The building straight ahead issued warrants and housed police officers who gave public assistance. In the foyer were two flights of steps leading up and down. I asked a police officer where warrants were issued. He told me to go upstairs, on the right, to the first window. I thanked him. A tall, robust police officer appeared at the door that had been converted to a window. The bottom half was closed while the top half opened. When I questioned him about taking out a trespassing warrant, he gave me a form to complete and said the fee was ten dollars. I filled out the form and paid him. It would take two to five days to execute. I thanked him, then went on my merry way.

Carl called two weeks later, upset and angry. The police had been by his sister's house where he was staying concerning the warrant charges. He wasn't home when they arrived or he may have been arrested. Being scared out of his wits, he fled to his brother's house in south Georgia. Carl was so pissed off with me, I could feel his anger over the phone. His cuss words echoed in my mind several hours later. All I could think was how did I ever live with him for twenty years?

The following week I gave Carl another reason to be upset. He had to appear before a judge concerning his delinquent child support payments. The outcome was he had to pay the Child Support Office directly. I was happy with this arrangement because now I knew I would get my money.

Getting money directly from Carl was harder than getting blood from a turnip. I know it's impossible for Carl to do right, to be responsible and take care of his sons. Thank God for judges and the courts who can make deadbeat dads pay and probably can make turnips bleed!

The next day, Chestnut called to tell me he was moving to California. Consequently, he would only be in town once a month to attend the I.B.W.A. meetings. He also informed me he had the first three chapters of "Uncaged" ready for review by at least three people who could critique the grammar. He said he would be back in town Friday, September 22, to pick them up so he could send them off to publishers. I immediately thought of Wendi Harper, my English instructor at Atlanta Metropolitan College; Douglas Williams, owner of The Source Bookstore; and Jamila Fonseka, an Emory University employee who edited books as well as worked in the Emergency Clinic Laboratory part-time on the evening shift.

Wendi was good with sentence structure; Jamila with proper form; and Doug was well read and knew what sold. My dynamic trio evaluated the chapters, added their comments and returned them to me before Chestnut returned. Wendi thought it was acceptable the way it was with only a few minor changes. Jamila didn't like the contractions which are unacceptable for standard English. Doug recommended adding some Ebonics because most black people don't have a good command of the King's English, particularly people like Big Mama, Pop, Xavier and Betty. I reviewed their critiques and made the changes I felt were relevant.

Luckily, I finished my evaluation of the three chapters before Chestnut returned and the fall Holy Days began. Monday, September 25, was the Feast of Trumpets, or Rosh Hashanah, the Jewish New Year. Jesus was a Jew and celebrated the "Jewish" festivals but He also expected Christians to observed them because he was both a Jew and Christian. As a Christian, the Feast of Trumpets signifies His Second Coming that will usher in a New Year and a New World Order.

Zechariah 14:1,4-7,&9, speak of the Second Coming of Jesus. *"Behold the day of the Lord is coming... And on that day his feet shall stand on the Mount of Olives which lies before Jerusalem on the east; and the Mount of Olives shall be split in two from the east to the west by a very wide valley.... Then the Lord your God will come, and all the holy ones with Him. On that day there shall be neither cold nor frost. And there shall be continuous day, not day and night, for at evening time there shall be light.... And the Lord will become king over all the earth; on that day the Lord will be one and His name one.*

First Thessalonians 4:13-17 further explains what day Christ will return. But I would not have you ignorant, brethren, concerning those who are asleep, that you may not grieve as others do who have no hope. For since we believe that Jesus died and rose again, even so, through Jesus, God will bring with him those who have fallen asleep. For this we declare to you by the word of the Lord, that we who are alive, who are left until the coming of the Lord, shall not precede those who have fallen asleep. For the Lord himself will descend from heaven with a cry of command, with the archangel's call, and with the sound of the trumpet of God. And the dead in Christ will rise first; then we who are alive, who are left, shall be caught up together with them in the clouds to meet the Lord in the air; and so shall we always be with the Lord.

Leviticus 23:23 explains how the Holy Day of God that was given to the people of Israel, from whom Christ is descended, is indeed Rosh Hashanah or the

And the Lord said to Moses, "Say to the people of Israel, `In ҃ ᴐn the first day of the month, you shall observe a day of ᴗᴗₑᴍₙ rest, a memorial proclaimed with blast of trumpets, a holy convocation.'"
God's sacred calendar is different from the Roman calendar we presently use. God's calendar begins in the spring when new life begins, not in the winter when everything is dead. Leviticus 23:4-5 says, *"These are the appointed feasts of the Lord, the holy convocations, which you shall proclaim at the time appointed for them. In the first month on the fourteenth day of the month in the evening is the Lord's Passover."* Every Christian knows Christ died on the Passover in the spring, either in March or April, depending on the year. Furthermore, God's first month is called Abib. Deuteronomy 16:1 explains. "Observe the month of Abib, and keep the Passover to the Lord your God...."

Following the Feast of Trumpets was Yom Kippur, or the Day of Atonement, and a seven day festival, the Feast of Tabernacles. The Holy Days were always joyous occasions. They were times of rejoicing and repenting. I took this time to repent of my sins, especially my relationship with Bryson. I prayed for deliverance.

Dear Heavenly Father, the Almighty One who is worthy to be praised. Who sent Your only Son, Jesus to eradicate sin from mankind. Please cleanse me of all my iniquities. Forgive all my trespasses. Deliver me from my relationship with Bryson, a married man. Do not cast me from Your presence, or take Your Holy Spirit from me. But strengthen me because I am weak. Love me as a father loves his child, even when I am wrong. With Your love and Son, Jesus Christ, I can do all things. With your forgiveness, I am made whole. I pray this in your Son's name. Amen.

Bryson wanted to come by before I went to the Feast of Tabernacles. He knew the following week I would be busy packing, getting ready for my trip. Carlos and I were going to Myrtle Beach, South Carolina, a new feast site. Little Carl didn't want to miss school. So he stayed with my brother, Xavier and my parents. Carl was too unstable to keep his own son because he was still living from pillar to post.

Bryson came by at 7:00 p.m. sharp dressed in his blue MARTA uniform. The boys were spending the weekend with Carl. He grinned from ear-to-ear when I opened the door.

"You look ravishing," he said, as he stepped inside.

I had on a short black skirt, with a black, beige and green vest, and a black shirt. "You must be hungry," I said, closing the door.

"Hungry for your love." He smiled, then held me close.

I felt a rush of passion all over my body as Viva came forth. "What's y pleasure, Big Daddy?" she asked in an invitingly, sexy voice, luring him to the sofa.

"Have you eaten?" I asked before he replied.

"I don't want food," he said, kissing me passionately, moving his hands over my body.

Viva wanted more, but I didn't want him to go any further. I had been thinking about our relationship and wanted to talk. The upcoming Holy Days filled my mind with guilt. How could I be a born-again Christian and commit not only fornication, but adultery? How could I be so unrighteous? "Stop, Bryson!" I screeched, as his mouth moved to my neck.

"Relax, baby. I haven't seen you in two whole days. I couldn't wait to see you again," he said, kissing me a little lower. "You look so good, I can't keep my hands off you."

"Bryson, stop! We need to talk," I said, pushing him away.

"We can talk later. Let's just enjoy each other right now. You're leaving next Friday, and I won't see you for two weeks," he said, facing me, standing a foot away.

"Bryson, I want to end the relationship," I said firmly, standing like a statue.

"Why? Why end a perfectly good relationship when two people love each other?" he asked, looking into my eyes as he adjusted his glasses.

"Bryson, I can't handle the guilt of being with another woman's husband, anymore. When I'm with you, I think of Helen. I put myself in her shoes. I wouldn't want my man to be with another woman. I don't like being the other woman!"

"You're not the other woman! You're number one. Helen and I don't sleep together, don't talk, and don't go out! We don't do nothing together but live under the same roof. She goes her way, and I go mine. All she does is work and sleep. She doesn't cook, doesn't see about her kids, and doesn't try to satisfy me either. Trying to have sex with her is like trying to fuck something dead," he said, walking to the loveseat by the door.

"Bryson, I don't care what you say, our relationship is wrong. If you're not happy with Helen, why don't you divorce her?"

"Let me tell you something," he said, turning around, facing me again. "I want to leave Helen, but I can't afford to live on my own. Over half my check goes to my ex for child support for my sons. What's left over is not enough for me to support myself."

"Our relationship is wrong in the sight of God. We're both Christians. We need to repent and go our separate ways."

, to do with the way I feel about you. I love
or say can change the way I feel," he said,

s!" I said, backing away. "I can't be disobedient
His life for me so that I can live in righteousness.
profaning His shed blood for my sins."
by grace. Jesus knows we're subject to sin. But
what I tee.   1. I love you, Vanessa! God is love, and He expects
us to love one anou..   aid, grabbing my arm.

"Yes, he does," I said, shaking my arm from his grip. "But He also expects
us not to commit fornication and adultery. I can't handle the guilt anymore. You
belong to Helen. The Tenth Commandment tells us not to covet another man's
wife and here I am coveting someone else's husband. This is wrong!"

"What I feel for you will never be wrong," he said, trying to put his arms
around me. "We met for a reason. Something brought me to the lab window the
night we met, and I'm convinced that something was God."

"You and God knew you were married," I said, escaping his grasp. "I didn't
know then, but I know now. God is pure and righteous. He would never lead
you to do wrong. Good-bye, Bryson. It's over between us," I said walking to the
door to let him out. I looked at him as he slowly walked to the door.

"Do you really want our relationship to be over?"

"Yes."

He reached in his pocket for his keys. "I guess I won't need these anymore,"
he said, taking my two house keys off his key ring.

"No, you won't," I responded, taking the keys.

"I love you, Vanessa. I always will," he said, as I held the keys in my hand.

"I love you too, Big Daddy," Viva said, giving him the keys back, kissing
him passionately. "Please don't go! Don't leave me. I love you too much!" She
held him and wouldn't let him go.

I tried to defeat her, but her love for Bryson was too strong, and I was too
spiritually weak.

"Give me more time," he said, as we held each other close.

SIXTEEN

Bryson stayed until four in the morning, the longest he'd ever remained. Neither of us wanted the evening to end, but he had to go home to his empty bed and play the faithful husband while Helen worked an overtime shift. His love for me surpassed his love for her, at least, that's what I told myself when we made love. Surely, he would be mine one day. I wished, every night could be like tonight—filled with passion. Every night he would be in my bed, in my arms, in my life. If only this night would never end, then I wouldn't have to deal with another episode of guilt in the morning.

The next day, I started packing for the Holy Day trip. I needed something to occupy my mind and fill the void left by Bryson. On Sundays, he went to church with his family. His pastor wanted him to become a deacon since he repaired the church for almost nothing, and was a faithful dedicated member. Bryson loved his church. If both our pastors knew what we were doing, we would be tarred, feathered, and fried. If Helen ever found out, we'd be maimed greeters at the gates of hell.

By Friday, October 6, everything was packed and all the preparations were made. It was time for Carlos and I to leave for Myrtle Beach. My mom would pick Little Carl up from school and take him home with her. Carl said he would check in on Little Carl when he could. Xavier said he would make sure Little Carl got to school on time.

Knowing Little Carl was in good hands gave me a peace of mind. This was the second time in twelve years I had left him behind to attend the Feast of Tabernacles. The first time was for my first feast in 1983 when he was one year old. I felt strange going to the feast without him. In my mind, he was like the luggage—I couldn't leave home without him.

Bryson drove up as I packed the last item in the car. Carlos was coming out of the house with his hands full of his stuff. He entered the car while I watched Bryson approach. His smile grew wider with each step. "I didn't think I would see you before I left," I said, with a smile to match his.

"I thought about you all night. I had to see your face, hear your voice, and hold you in my arms just one more time," he said, hugging me.

I always melted in his embrace. He felt so-o-o good! "I'll call you after I check-in, and I'll leave my number on your recorder."

He tilted my head up and kissed me softly, then placed his arms back around me, rubbing my back. "I'm going to miss you," he said taking a deep breath.

"I'll miss you, too." He kissed me again, harder. Carlos blew the horn. "I guess I'd better go."

"Remember, I love you. Drive safely. I'll be here when you return," he said, as he released his hold.

Carlos blew the horn again, then opened the car door. "C'mon Mama! Let's go!" he shouted.

"Hold your horses, child! I'm coming," I shouted back, then turned to Bryson. "Good-bye Bryson. I'll call you when I arrive."

He reached into his pocket where he kept his wallet. Slowly, he pulled it out. I thought, he was going to give me my sign before I left. He pulled a business card out and handed it to me. "Here take this. I'll be waiting for your call," he said, as he walked back to his van.

I went into the house for a final check, locked the doors, then drove off with Carlos, bound for Myrtle Beach. We stopped in Florence, South Carolina at the Wal-Mart to buy a few items. Number one on my list was a camera. It seemed like every year, I bought a new, cheap camera for the feast. This year was no exception. I only wanted to spend thirty-five dollars for a camera, nuts, soda and film. Carlos wanted a toy to occupy him for the ride. We made our purchases, ate at the Chick-fil-A across the street, then continued our journey.

Less than two hours later, we reached Myrtle Beach. I spent thirty minutes trying to find the Beach Cove Resort in North Myrtle Beach. Not being familiar with the layout of the city, and not knowing the difference between the south end and the north end of town, I drove around needlessly until I became fully oriented. Myrtle Beach was a beautiful city with many attractions for families. I hoped it lived up to its reputation because Carlos and I planned to stay for two weeks.

After checking in, I called Bryson and left my telephone number on his answering machine. I called to check on Little Carl then Carlos and I canvassed the resort. Outside was a pure white beach; a multi-level sun deck with three large pools; two hot, swirling whirlpools; a kiddy pool and a fountain. Inside, we found another pool, an arcade, saunas, a restaurant and a lounge. Carlos played in the arcade before we went back to our suite to unpack and relax.

Bryson called at 8:30 p.m.. He was glad I arrived safely, but was missing me already and couldn't wait until I came back home. Three times he called my answering machine just to hear my voice. He now understood how I felt when he went home to Aiken, South Carolina, to visit his mom. The shoe always feels different when it's on the other foot.

The next morning, I took Carlos aside. I told him he couldn't do anything before we had our Bible study.

"Ahhh, Mama. We're on vacation! There are too many fun things to do, like swimming, going in the ocean, playing games in the arcade, sight-seeing, watching movies, and..."

"And having Bible study," I added, picking up my Bible from the end table.

"Mama, I'm a kid! I came to have fun, not a Bible study. You can have your Bible study while I watch TV. I promise I won't disturb you."

"No, son. We came here to honor God. The other things are secondary. Turn the TV off. The sooner we begin, the sooner we end." Reluctantly, he turned the TV off. I opened my Bible to Leviticus 23:33-36 and read. *`And the Lord said to Moses, "Say to the people of Israel, on the fifteenth day of this seventh month and for seven days is the feast of booths to the Lord. On the first day shall be a holy convocation; you shall do no laborious work. Seven days you shall present offerings by fire to the Lord; on the eighth day you shall hold a holy convocation and present an offering by fire to the Lord; it is a solemn assembly; you shall do no laborious work."*

"I thought this was the Feast of Tabernacles, not the feast of booths," Carlos mentioned, picking up the remote control.

"Some Bible translations say `booths,' others say `tabernacles.' Whether booths or tabernacles, it's the same feast. Booths are small compartments. The Israelites were instructed to make small temporary housing to celebrate this feast. Today, we have hotels. The point is, God wants us to leave our homes and go to a place where He has chosen, to worship Him for seven days."

"How do you know that? That's not what you read."

"In verses 42 & 43, it says, *`You shall dwell in booths for seven days; all the natives in Israel shall dwell in booths, that your generations may know that I made the people of Israel dwell in booths when I brought them out of the land of Egypt: I am the Lord Your God.'"*

"Mama, God is talking to the children of Israel, not us! This is 1995. God said that to the Israelites before Jesus came. That's the Old Testament. We're living in the New Testament, even I know that. This Bible study is over. I'm watching TV," he said, flipping it on.

"Not so soon. Turn the TV off. I'll tell you when I'm finished."

"I should have stayed at home with Little Carl because you're gonna Bible study me to death! I'm a kid, Mama. I came to have fun, miss some days from school, swim, watch movies, and spend your money."

"You'll get a chance to do all that, plus worship Jesus. You left Him out of your game plan, but He's why we're here. Give me your undivided attention, so I can explain why the Feast of Tabernacles is for us today."

"You have five minutes. My program comes on then."

"Jesus is the God of both the Old and New Testaments. Hebrews 13:8 says, *`Jesus Christ is the same yesterday, and today and forever.'* He kept the feast when he lived on earth. In John 7:2,14, and 37-39, the Bible says, *'Now the 'Jews' Feast of Tabernacles was at hand.... About the middle of the feast Jesus went up into the temple and taught.... On the last day of the feast, the great day, Jesus stood up and proclaimed, 'If any one thirst, let him come to Me and drink. He who believes in Me, as the Scripture has said, Out of his heart shall flow rivers of living waters.' Now this He said about the Spirit, which those who believe in Him were to receive; for as yet the Spirit had not been given, because Jesus was not yet glorified."*

"Mama, the Bible called it the 'Jews' Feast of Tabernacles. Why are we celebrating it? We're not Jews," Carlos complained.

"No, we're not, but Jesus was. At that time in the Scriptures, Jesus had not died, or been glorified, or sent the Holy Spirit to begin His church, which started on Pentecost, another Holy Day. After His death, it was no longer the 'Jews' feast only, but a Christian festival." I explained.

"You haven't mentioned it being a Christian festival in the Bible. This is a Bible study isn't it?"

"I'm glad you asked that question. In Acts, Paul kept the same Holy Days Jesus kept as a Jew. Acts 18:21 says, *"...but he took leave of them saying, 'I must by all means keep this coming feast in Jerusalem....'* He was referring to the Feast of Tabernacles which is sometimes just called the feast. *Acts 20:6 says, '...but we sailed away from Philippi after the days of Unleavened Bread....'* Verse 16 of the same chapter says, *'...he was hastening to be at Jerusalem, if possible, on the day of Pentecost.'* And finally, Acts 27:9 mentions the Day of Atonement, or Yom Kippur, a day of fasting when God commands us to afflict our bodies. It says, *'...because the fast had already gone by,...'*

"Mama, I believe you, whatever you say. Now, can I watch TV? My program is on, and I'm missing it!"

"Jesus doesn't want you to believe what I say, but what His Word says. I have a couple of more Scriptures, then I'll be through."

"Mo-o-o-m, my program will be over by the time you finish! I've missed half of it listening to your Bible study. It's only fair if I don't have to listen to the other half of the Bible study, so I can watch the end of my program," he argued.

"Son, one of the first lessons you learn in this world is life is not fair. Your interruptions are only prolonging this Bible study. 'Silence is golden.'"

"...And a good child is divine," he added, knowing it was one of my common phrases around the house.

"The Feast of Tabernacles represents the millennium, the thousand year reign of Jesus when He returns after Satan is bound. The world will be filled with peace, joy, happiness, health, and prosperity. Revelation 20:2-6 explains. 'He laid hold of the dragon, that serpent of old, who is the Devil and Satan, and

bound him for a thousand years; and cast him into the bottomless pit, and shut him up, and set a seal on him, so that he should deceive the nations no more till the years were finished. But after these things he must be released for a little while. And I saw thrones, and they sat on them, and judgment was committed to them. Then I saw the souls of those who had been beheaded for their witness to Jesus and for the word of God, who had not worshipped the beast or his image, and had not received his mark on their foreheads or on their hands. And they lived and reigned with Christ a thousand years. But the rest of the dead did not live again until the thousand years were finished. This is the first resurrection. Blessed and holy is he who has part in the first resurrection. Over such, the second death has no power, but they shall be priests of God and of Christ, and shall reign with Him a thousand years.'

"I feel like this Bible study will last a thousand years. Aren't you finished yet? Or do you plan to end when the millennium begins? Mama, have mercy on me. I'm only a child."

"I'm almost finished. I have two last Scriptures."

"Thank God! I can't take much more of this Bible study stuff. I'm going to go to the beach, and swim in the pool since I've missed my program. Maybe, we can go to the Waffle House as my reward for being a good listener."

"Jesus wants to give us eternal life for being good and faithful servants. And all you want for a reward is breakfast?" I demanded.

"By the time this Bible study is over and I eat breakfast, I will have eternal life because Jesus would have returned."

"At least you're paying attention. All right, let me read the last two Scriptures. In the future, after the millennium, Jesus will send a plague to all the nations that do not keep the Feast of Tabernacles. Zechariah 14:16-17 says. *'And it shall come to pass that everyone who is left of all the nations which came against Jerusalem shall go up from year to year to worship the King, the Lord of hosts, and keep the Feast of Tabernacles. And it shall be that whichever of the families of the earth do not come up to Jerusalem to worship the King, the Lord of hosts, on them there will be no rain,'"* I said, closing my Bible.

"Amen!" Carlos shouted.

"Do you have any questions?"

"Now, can I eat?"

"Yes, son. Let's get ready. I'll take you to the Waffle House."

We got dressed, ate breakfast and enjoyed the rest of the two weeks with church services, recreation, good food and fun. We truly experienced a time of joy right here on earth.

SEVENTEEN

On the morning of Friday, October 20, Carlos and I left our millennium haven and went home. I had gained ten pounds from eating junk with Carlos. He looked the same, except darker from swimming in the sun. His affinity for water was equal to that of a fish. I often teased him by calling him my "scaleless fish wonder."

When we arrived home the grass was freshly cut with yellow ribbons wrapped around the mailbox and the two front trees. A large white banner hung from the porch that read: Welcome Home Vanessa and Carlos! I Love You.

"Mama, look at that!" Carlos exclaimed, pointing to the banner. "I wonder who did it?"

"It couldn't be anyone but Bryson."

"What about Dad? He loves me, and he still loves you."

"No, you're wrong. It had to be Bryson. Yes, it's true your father loves you, but he stopped loving me a long time ago; that's why I divorced him. He loved his golf, his sisters and brothers, his mother, his single friends, and himself. He loved everything and everybody except me. I was last on his love list. As his wife, I should have been first. Make sure when you get married, you put your wife first. Otherwise, your marriage will end the same way, with a divorce."

"I still say Dad did it. I'm gonna call him and see."

"Help me unload the car before you get on the phone."

"Do you have any film left? This is neat!"

"Yes, you're right. I'll take some pictures with my camera." I reached for the camera, near my purse. I took several shots at different angles. Carlos took a few shots, too. We unloaded the car after the shooting session.

Bryson pulled up as Carlos took the last package in the house. I grinned from ear-to-ear.

"Who did this?" he asked as he approached.

My grin vanished. "I thought you did."

"I checked on the house while you were gone. I came by Wednesday, and this was not up. I didn't have a chance to get by here yesterday. I was tied up all day."

"Mama! Mama!" yelled Carlos, as he ran out the door. "Daddy put up the banner and ribbons! See, I told you so! Daddy still loves you, and he loves me, too!"

When Carlos saw Bryson, he went back inside. He didn't care for Bryson, and neither did Little Carl, or Big Carl for that matter. I'm sure they all felt Bryson was the reason I divorced Carl. They were wrong. The marriage was over when Bryson and I met. But I'm sure I could never convince them of that. I can only pray that one day they understand the truth and accept it.

"Didn't you call the police before you left to notify them you were going out of town, and that you had a trespassing warrant out on Carl, so they would check the house?"

"Yes. I called the police."

"Well, he just snuck one in on us. I'll be damned."

"Mama, telephone, "Carlos announced, sticking his head out the door.

"Who is it?" I asked.

"Your mama."

"Okay, son. Tell her I'm coming. Excuse me, Bryson, while I go talk to Mama. Do you want to come inside?"

"No. I'll stay here until you come back."

"Okay," I said as I went into the house. While I was still on the phone talking to Mama, Bryson came inside with the ribbons and the banner in his hands.

"I don't think you'll be needing these. I'll put them where they damned well belong," he said, as he walked back outside.

I was sure he was going to the trashcan outside. "Mama, Bryson just took down Carl's ribbons and banner," I said over the phone.

"Nessa, you go from the frying pan to the fire. Don't you know how to find a good single man? I worry about you everyday. You being with another woman's husband and all. Sometimes, I'm tempted to put an ad in the paper for you a good, single Christian man with a good job, but I know you'd tell me to mind my own business and stop meddling in yours. But...."

"Mama, I got to go," I said, cutting her off. "Bring Carl home, or I'll pick him up later."

"You haven't seen your son in two weeks, and what's the first thing you do when you get home? You got that married man in your face. Tell him to go home to his wife. He's just blocking you from finding you a single man. And another thing...."

"Bye, Mama. I'm getting off the phone."

"Don't you want to speak to your son?"

I sighed, "Yes, put him on the phone."

"He's not here. He's over to Xavier's house."

"Why did you ask me if I wanted to speak to him if he wasn't there?"

"I just wanted to see what you'd say. I wanted to see how important he is to you."

Mama, you know I love Little Carl. You're talking crazy. I'm getting off this phone right now. Good-bye."

"Nessa, ask Bryson if he can come by here and look at my den. I need him to widen it for me."

"But, Mama, I thought he was no good."

"He's good for repairing things. I saw all the work he did to your house. I like his work. I just don't like him being your man. He's good for something. Now when you find a man that can't do nothing, you really have a mess on your hands."

"Bye, Mama. I'm gone this time."

"Bye, Nessa. And don't forget to ask Bryson."

"Okay. Bye."

Bryson came inside as I hung up the phone. He had a look of victory on his face. I guess he felt he was the man of this house, and neither Carl nor any other man would invade his territory. At least, not if he could prevent it. "Mama wants you to expand her den. I'll give you her number. You can call her later," I said, writing the number down on a piece of paper near the phone.

"You've picked up some weight," he said, looking me over.

"Yes, I noticed it, too. But I didn't think it was that obvious."

"I notice everything about you. The least little change gets my attention."

"You're different from Carl then. When I became uncaged, I went through a million changes. The only thing he noticed was my decreased interest in sex."

"Yeah, that will definitely get a brother's attention. But when a man truly loves a woman the way I love you, he will not only notice everything about her, but he will also do everything in his power to keep her happy."

"There's only one thing that will make me happy with you."

"And I know what that one thing is, but I'm unable to divorce Helen at this time. It's not that easy. I have a plan which will take some time."

"What's your plan?"

"I can't discuss it now. But I have to make sure I can support myself when I leave. Right now, I'm not in that position. Be patient."

"I can be patient, but I must face reality. I'll be forty next year. That means my biological clock is ticking out. Here I am, seeing a sterile, married man who can't support himself. I have two daughters to birth before my clock runs out. Do I stay with you and wait until you're free? Or do I move on to bigger and better fish?"

"Only you can answer those questions," he said, holding me close to his chest.

"I'll stay, Big Daddy," Viva suddenly said, as Bryson kissed me. "I'll wait as long as it takes," she said, when the kiss was over.

"Mama! Mama!" Carlos yelled, coming down the steps. "Carl left a message for you to pick him up when we got home. I talked to him, and he's ready to come home."

"Okay, Carlos. Put your shoes on and we'll go get him."

"I guess this means my visit is over," Bryson said, looking into my eyes.

"I'm afraid so. I haven't seen my son in two weeks, and I really need to spend some time with him."

"That applies to me, too."

"I know it does. Let's get together tomorrow evening. The boys will probably be with their dad. Maybe, we can go dancing."

"Let's go dancing another time. I want to be with you alone. We have two weeks to catch up on."

"Okay. Maybe, I'll fix some appetizers."

"You're all the appetizer I need."

"Come on Mama, I'm ready," announced Carlos, as he came back down the steps.

"Let me use the bathroom first, then I'll be ready."

"You should be ready now. Carl is waiting on us."

"I know, son, but it won't take me but a minute."

"Why don't you tell Superman to leave so you can pick up your son?" Carlos asked, glaring at Bryson.

"That won't be necessary," Bryson said. "I'm leaving. I'll see you tomorrow, baby."

"Baby! Mama, you're a grown woman. Why is he calling you `baby'?" Carlos asked, as I walked up the steps.

"`Baby' is a term of endearment when speaking to someone you care about. It's used like `honey', `dear', and `sweetheart'."

"Daddy never called you any of those names. You were either Vanessa, Van, or doll."

"I know. Maybe if he called me honey, or sweetheart sometimes, we'd still be together. Excuse me, honey. I need to use the bathroom, then we can pick up Carl."

"Honey! I'm Carlos, your son."

"I know. But I love you more than you'll ever realize," I said, closing the bathroom door.

Carlos and I picked up Little Carl, who was more glad to be home where he could freely use the telephone than he was to be with us. He got into a fight at school and was suspended for three days. Although Xavier enforced good study habits, as soon as Carl came back home, he reverted to his old "no study" habit ways. I was really at a loss about what to do with Carl. The more I talked, the worse he got. His "I don't care" attitude made it impossible for me to get through to him. It was hard for me to watch my son do nothing with his life when he had the potential to be exceptional. As his mother, nothing I said or did made a difference. He was on a self-destructive trip going no where.

Our reunion evening together was short-lived when Carl came by to spread his bittersweet joy. He arrived at 7:30 p.m., unannounced. Little Carl, Carlos and I were at the kitchen table, catching Little Carl up on the highlights of the trip when the doorbell rang.

"I'll get it!" shouted Carlos, as he ran to open the door. "It's probably Dad. I know he wants to see me since I'm back home."

"I bet it's Marlon. He called earlier and told me he was coming over," corrected Little Carl.

"No, more than likely it's Bryson. He was probably in the neighborhood," I said.

"I was right!" Carlos shouted again. "It's Dad!"

"Well, I'm glad somebody in here is glad to see me," Carl said, hugging Carlos as he entered the house.

"I'm glad to see you, Dad. I need some money. Let me have twenty dollars. I have some things I need to do."

"I guess you want some money, too," he said, looking at me. "Every time you see me you think I should pull all the money out my pockets and put it in your hands."

"I don't want all your money, only my child support payments."

"What happened to the banner and ribbons I put up?"

"Bryson took them down," I answered, getting up to fix me a glass of soda. "Would you like something to drink?"

"I told Mama you still love her, and you love me, Dad. I knew you put the banner and ribbons up. Mama thought Bryson did it."

"What are y'all talking about?" chimed Little Carl. "I didn't see no banner or no ribbons."

"Dad made a banner that said, 'Welcome Back Vanessa and Carlos. I Love You.' And he tied yellow ribbons on the mailbox and the two trees in the front yard."

"Did you really do that, Dad?" asked Little Carl in disbelief.

"Yes, son, I did. I wanted your mother to come back home to me. I wanted her to know how much I care for her and want her back, but I see I was a fool for thinking such a thing."

"Carl, I told you it was over between us before the divorce. I'm not dating you. I'm not doing anything with you. You had twenty-five years of my life. I wasn't important to you then. Why should I feel like I would be important to you now?" I asked.

"I guess I was hoping you would let bygones be bygones, and we'd pick up the pieces and get back together. But I see I just made a damn fool of myself," he complained.

"Dad, I love you," said Carlos, giving him another hug.

"Me too," added Little Carl, getting up from the table.

I didn't join the "I love you" chorus. My love for Carl was gone forever. All I wanted from Carl was for him to spend time with his sons, pay me child support, and stay out of my life. Right now, I also wanted him out of my house. Obviously, he either read my mind or felt my vibes.

"I came by to pick up Carlos and Carl. Y'all get your things so we can go," he said, lighting up a cigarette.

The boys went upstairs to pack. I sipped on my soda while Carl smoked.

"So, apparently, you're happy with your repairman?" he asked, breaking the silence.

"Yes, I am. I felt broken before the divorce, but now, I feel whole. Divorce agrees with me. Even my blood tests are normal. While we were married, I was anemic. But thanks to Bryson introducing me to vitamins, I have a normal C.B.C.. Even my P.M.S. is gone. I feel good and I'm happy."

"Well, I feel like shit, and I'm not happy. Divorce is a bitch!"

"And our marriage was a beach for you and a bitch for me! Our divorce made me realize God is a just God. Life is fair," I said. By this time, the boys were ready to go.

"See ya, Mama," they both said, as they walked out the door.

"So long, Miss Sea Shell. Don't get too happy 'cause your man might throw you back in the sea," Carl said, closing the door.

Good-bye, Carl," I whispered to myself. "The shoe always feels different when it's on the other foot."

EIGHTEEN

The next night, Bryson came over. We made up for the two week separation and then some. He said he'd been saving himself for me. From the load he had, he was telling the truth. I don't know what he and Helen did in the bedroom, but whatever it was, it couldn't be too much because he was always ready for me. I really loved Bryson, despite his situation. He was my man. He was just married to someone else.

The following Friday, on October 27, Chestnut mailed chapters of "Uncaged" to four publishers. I received two rejection letters and an acceptance letter from Winston-Derek. The fourth publisher never responded. The letter from Winston-Derek read:

DEAR AUTHOR:

SO FAR WE LIKE WHAT WE HAVE READ PERTAINING TO YOUR MANUSCRIPT. IF YOU WISH TO CONTINUE THIS VENTURE, PLEASE SEND IN A COMPLETED MANUSCRIPT.

THANK YOU FOR YOUR INTEREST IN WINSTON-DEREK PUBLISHERS, INC.

LET US HEAR FROM YOU AT YOUR CONVENIENCE.

SINCERELY,
Maggie Staton
THE EDITORIAL DEPARTMENT
WINSTON-DEREK PUBLISHERS, INC.

P.S. PLEASE ENCLOSE A SASE, MANUSCRIPT SIZE.

I was working on chapter eight when I received this letter. Eight chapters down and only Christ knew how many more chapters to go. The letter encouraged me, but I was nowhere close to the end. I kept Winston-Derek's letter in mind as I continued to write "Uncaged."

In November, I received my first child support payment from Carl's employer, Tri-State Dairy, Inc, for $258. My last payment from Carl had been in July for $86. If I relied on Carl instead of Jesus to supply my needs, the boys and I would be outdoors, naked and starving to death. But Jesus helped me. I often recited Psalms 121 when I cried out to Him, especially the first two verses. *"I lift up my eyes to the hills—From whence comes my help? My help comes from the Lord who made heaven and earth. He will not allow your foot to be moved; He who keeps you will not slumber. Behold, He who keeps Israel shall never slumber nor sleep. The Lord is your keeper; The Lord is your shade at your right hand. The sun shall not strike you by day, nor the moon by night. The Lord shall preserve you from all evil; He shall preserve your soul. The Lord shall preserve your going out and your coming in from this time forth, and forevermore."* Knowing that whatever happened, Jesus would supply all my needs, always gave me peace. The peace of Christ continued in my life no matter what else happened.

Everything was going well until Bryson called me the Monday before Thanksgiving and told me he had just been fired from Grady. He said he and another officer were sitting in the break room and got into a verbal confrontation. The other officer called him a bitch. Bryson then called the officer a bitch. The witnesses got scared and reported them to their superiors because they thought Bryson was going to start shooting. They were both fired for using profanity on the job. A forty-three year old man loses a job for using profanity. He reminded me of Carl when he lost his $37,000 a year job at Lockheed for fighting over a twenty-five cents cup of coffee. I asked myself, Lord where did I go wrong? How do I end up with such low character men?

As I pondered the question, Carl called to ask me if the boys could spend the week of Thanksgiving with him. It had been awhile since they had an opportunity to spend a whole week with their dad. I gladly granted him his request.

While they were gone, I worked on "Uncaged." The joy I had all week long vanished when the boys returned home Sunday evening. I should have known a week with Carl could only spell disaster. When I saw the diamond stud earrings in their ears, I became irate. "What have you done to your ear!" I asked Carlos as he entered the house.

"We all got our ears pierced, including Dad."

I looked at Carl's pearl earring protruding from his left earlobe when he unloaded some of the boys' things onto the floor by the door. He looked foolish. "What's up with the earrings?" I asked Carl.

"It was my idea. I thought it would be cool to get an earring. I got my ear pierced first, then Carl wanted his done, then Carlos decided to try it, too."

"The last thing either one of you needed was another hole in your heads. Carl, you're supposed to be an example for your sons. You're supposed to be a positive guide not a negative influence. They have enough to deal with from their peers. They don't need you to lead them astray. Don't you realize you have boys, not girls?"

"You're just a nag. We have our own minds. We can do what we want to with our bodies, whether you like it or not."

"Mama, I've been wanting an earring, but I knew you wouldn't let me have one. It's really cool! I love it!" Little Carl added.

"Fine," I said, throwing up my hands. "There's nothing I can do about it anyway, now. I just thought I'd never see the day when my sons and ex-husband would wear earrings."

"We're cool, Mama. We're the three Lewis men," Carlos said, putting on his shades.

Carl walked out the door as Carlos finished his short spiel. He was the nut and my sons were nut-ees. I sensed the earrings were their way of having a common bond, a pact, that made them one.

In my opinion, boys should look like boys, not girls. I never thought my sons would ever get their ears pierced because of how I felt. Big Carl knew my feelings on the subject. I believe he did it to hurt me, and he did.

By the time I went for my annual PAP smear, a few days later, I had accepted that my sons had an extra hole in their heads. So be it. During my examination, I asked Dr. Barclay to remove my I.U.D. since it expired in January and I didn't need it anymore. Although Bryson was sterile, I hoped, in the back of my mind, he would get me pregnant. Now, with the I.U.D. removed, maybe a miracle would happen. Maybe, he would be the father of my two daughters.

Only God knew how much I longed to have my daughters. I couldn't wait to hold them, nurture them, love them, and watch them grow. Sometimes, when I saw a little girl, I thought of my daughters. A strange feeling engulfed me. Will they ever get here? Even when I saw grown women, I'd think, one day my daughters will be grown. So many times I felt like Sarah. I'm too old, and it's taking too long for these promised seeds to arrive.

The boys thought I was nuts for wanting more children at my age. My mom told me I needed my head examined, instead of my butt when I told her I was going to get a PAP smear. Nobody really understood how I felt, but that was okay. God knew how I felt. He knew I was robbed of having my daughters earlier in my prime childbearing years because the marriage with Carl was unstable and unbearable. Luckily, Bryson was in my life to erase all those miserable years with Carl.

November 29 was Bryson's 44 birthday. I invited him over and prepared a special birthday meal. As he came to the door, I was taking the cornbread out the oven. Everything else was ready. He let himself inside. I was standing at the stove when he entered the kitchen. His eyes lit up when he saw the roast beef, turnips, fried corn, cornbread and candied yams. "My, my, my, it sure smells good in here," he said, taking a deep whiff.

"Happy birthday! This dinner is your birthday present," I said, fixing his plate.

"I hope dessert is included," he said, giving me a wicked smile.

"Yes-sir-ree, I made candied yams."

He walked over to me and placed his arms around my waist. "Candied yams are fine, but that's not what I had in mind."

"Look, Bryson, the boys are here. Candied yams will be your only dessert. Unless you want ice cream?"

"The boys haven't stopped us before."

"Your plate is ready. What do you want to drink?" I asked, ignoring his last remark.

"Do you have cranberry juice?"

"Yes. I'll pour you a glass."

"That's fine. I'll go wash my hands while you do."

"Okay. I'll fix the boys' plates, too." I fixed the rest of the plates. The boys came and got theirs, then went back to their rooms. They never ate with us. They preferred eating in their rooms anyway, and Bryson being over was a good excuse.

"I'm starved. Everything looks delicious!" Bryson said as he placed his plate in front of him.

"I hope it is. I added a few special touches," I said, sitting in my seat, ready to eat. We bowed our heads and Bryson said grace.

"Dear Lord, thank you for this wonderful meal that has been prepared. I pray that it will provide health and nourishment to us all. Bless the cook. And thank you, Lord, for allowing me to see another year. Amen."

"How does it feel being forty-four?" I asked, reaching for my fork.

"The same as twenty-four and thirty-four. Once I stopped being a teenager, the rest of my birthdays feel the same."

"I had my I.U.D. taken out yesterday," I said, scooping up my turnips.

"What's that supposed to mean?" he said, eating his roast beef.

"I can get pregnant."

"By who? I'm sterile. I haven't been able to make a baby for nearly twelve years."

"I know. But miracles do occur," I said, biting my cornbread.

"I hope for both our sakes, Jesus passes over us this time."

We ate the rest of our meal, mostly in silence. I was digesting his last comments, while he probably was digesting mine. We ended the evening with a glass of wine. I toasted to his health, long life and happiness. He toasted that we always be together because I was the source of his happiness.

How long our relationship would last, only God knew. I knew, if a miracle didn't happen soon, he would have to go. I loved Bryson, but I couldn't let him stop me from having my daughters.

My sons wanted to spend Christmas break with their dad, but they spent it with me because Carl had found a new love and didn't have time for the boys. I took some time off work to spend quality time with them. They each wanted company to spend the night. We went bowling, rented movies, ate out, went skating, shopping and had fun. The boys were easy to please as long as they had enough food and money.

I spent January 1, alone. The boys spent the night with friends. Bryson called me the next day to tell me what a great time he had with Helen and his two brothers who came into town with their wives. He said he started to call me to go with them because Helen was acting funny. But at the last minute she got dressed and went.

Bryson always tells me how much I mean to him and how little he cares for Helen. But every time he goes somewhere, she's with him instead of me. It began to bother me that I never met his family. He's never offered to take me to South Carolina to meet his mom. I guess my place was at home where he can come and go as he please. This way he could put on a facade, to look like the faithful husband. That's okay, Bryson. All the dirt comes out in the wash. One day the truth will be known.

On January 10, 1996, my obsolete wedding anniversary, Carl came by the house. The boys were in school. When I opened the door, he stared at me. I knew what was on his mind. This day used to have meaning, but now it was just another day. I didn't say anything to him. His eyes said everything. Finally, he told me to open the burglar door. As I opened the door, he put his arms around me, held me momentarily then walked away. I watched him as he got into his car and drove away. I locked both doors, then went back upstairs to my bed. Farewell, Carl Lewis. This day used to be special, but it's not anymore, I thought as I fell back to sleep.

My aching breasts made it difficult to sleep. I knew I didn't have P.M.S. because the vitamins eliminated all my symptoms months ago. I noticed my stomach was swollen also. Coming fully awake at the thought of being pregnant, I got out of bed to look at my yearly planner where I record the first day of my cycle. My eyes widen as I discovered the last date was December 3. My cycle was like clockwork. It sometimes came early, but it never came late unless I was pregnant. Oh, my God, I thought, not knowing what to do. The phone rang while I sat on the edge of the bed in a daze.

"Hello," I said in a low scratchy voice.

"Van, what's wrong with you? Are you sick?" Bryson asked concerned.

"I think I'm pregnant."

"That's impossible. You know I can't have any children."

"I know, but I'm a week late. I'm never late unless I'm pregnant."

"Why don't you take a pregnancy test to be sure."

"I will, tonight at work."

"It's probably your nerves or something. You've been stressed lately. I've noticed how uptight you've been."

"I haven't been uptight!" I said snapping at him.

"Whoa, maybe you are pregnant. I never heard you act bitchy. You remind me of my ex."

"Suppose I am pregnant? What will you do?"

"First, I would go to the doctor and get checked out. I know it could be possible although it is highly unlikely. A miracle could happen."

"Suppose you don't check out?"

"Don't worry about me. Take the test first, then we'll go from there."

"Suppose I am pregnant, and you do check out? Then what?" I asked, quizzically.

"Then you will become Mrs. Vanessa Collier."

"How can you say that when you already have a wife?"

"If you're carrying my child then I want to help raise it."

"But if you can get me pregnant, then you can also get Helen pregnant. You could have two women carrying your seed."

"That's true. However, Helen has irregular cycles. She has a period twice a year. The chance of her getting pregnant is almost impossible."

"Bryson, if I'm pregnant, I want this baby. That way, I know I'll gain you, too."

"You already have me."

"Right! You're over there with Helen, and I'm over here, alone."

"Look, Van. Take the test, then we'll discuss our options."

"There are no options except having this baby."

"I wasn't talking about getting rid of the baby. I was talking about us."

"Oh. I'll call you as soon as I find out."

"Everything will be all right. I have to go. I'll be waiting for your call."

"Okay. Bye."

"Bye, love."

After I hung up the phone, I crawled back into bed. Visions of being Mrs. Bryson Collier filled my head.

NINETEEN

Carlos woke me up just as I marched down the aisle with my father. The sparkle in Bryson's eyes let me know he was waiting eagerly for me to reach him. He gave me his million dollar smile, which grew larger the closer I got to him. His arms were folded in front of him as he bounced on his feet. My father and I were at arm's length to Bryson when Carlos kissed my cheek and Bryson disappeared.

"Mama, Mama, wake up!" Carlos demanded, leaning over me.

I slowly opened my eyes. I couldn't believe I was at home in my bed. The dream seemed so real. "Hi, son," I said, fully waking up.

"Mama, look what I got today at school!" he said excitedly, as he went through his book bag. He pulled out five test papers with one hundreds on them.

I sat up, took the papers and reviewed each one. Three were in math, his favorite subject; one was in social studies where he correctly identified all fifty states and their capitals; the last paper was an English essay, 'What He Would Do To Make The World A Better Place.' "These are excellent papers, Carlos! Keep up the good work!"

"Mama, you owe me $5," he said with his hand opened.

"You're right. Give me my purse."(For any test score of 95 or above, I gave the boys $1.) He handed me my purse, and I gave him a crisp five dollar bill.

"Thanks, Mama," he said, leaving the room. "You can go back to sleep."

"No, I'm up now. I'll start dinner."

"What are we having?" he asked from his room.

"What do you want?"

"Tacos!"

"Tacos, it is. I'll start dinner after I get dressed."

"Okay, Mama. I'll do my homework. Call me when the tacos are ready."

I got up, washed up, dressed, then made tacos. Little Carl came home as I was ready to fix the plates. He had a wide smile on his face that spelled trouble.

"How is the best mother in the world?" he asked, coming over to kiss me on my cheek.

"I'm fine, but what else is on your mind?"

"Nothing. I just want to hug and kiss my sweet mother. Is that a crime?"

"No. But, maybe what you've done is. Out with it, son! I can take it," I said, walking to the table to sit down.

"I need you to sign my progress report," he said, handing me the report.

I unfolded it. His grades were three D's, two C's and a B. "Carl, you're a smart kid. There is no reason for you to make grades like these. You're an A-B student. Why are you making D's and C's?"

"I'll work hard and pull those D's up before the quarter ends. Mama, I know you made all A's and two B's in high school, but I take after Daddy who graduated with a low C average. My name is Carl, Jr."

"That's no excuse. You can do better than your dad. You can make A's and B's."

"Mama, don't get so uptight! I'll bring those grades up, I promise."

"Carl, there's more to it than making good grades. When you can do better and don't, then you're not living up to your potential. Low grades will make it hard, if not impossible, for you to get into college. Without a college education, you won't be able to get a decent job. Low grades equal low wages, which means you'll have to work two or three jobs to afford your basic necessities."

"Mama, I said I'll pull up my grades. I don't need a lecture."

"See, that's your problem! You don't want to listen to me or your teachers. You need to take school seriously. It's your key to a bright future."

"Okay, Mama, I hear you. Are you listening to me? I said I'll pull up my grades."

"I hear you son, loud and clear. Make sure you do. Are you ready to eat?"

"What are we having?"

"Tacos."

"Sure. Fix me three. I'm going to my room first, then I'll be ready to eat."

I made the tacos. We ate and talked about the day's activities. Afterwards, Little Carl said he wanted to live with his dad. I told him, he had to earn the right to live with his dad by doing well in school first. He thought I was crazy and didn't understand what grades had to do with the decision. Because he was his dad's son, that's all that mattered. My feelings were, if he truly wanted to live with his dad, then he would be motivated to do well in school since his grades determined if he went.

I asked Carlos if he wanted to live with his dad, too. He shrugged. He hadn't thought about it, he finally said. His life was just fine the way it was. I'm glad I asked. I always want to know what's going on in his head. Divorce is hard on kids, and anything I can do to make it easier, I will.

For the rest of the evening, I thought about being pregnant. From the looks of my swollen breasts and abdomen, I knew I was. A glowing sensation came over me at the thought of being pregnant. My daughter was on her way. Soon, I'd get a chance to hold her.

The first thing I did when I got to work was perform a urine pregnancy test. It can detect the HCG of a ten-day-old fetus. If I was pregnant, my fetus would be twenty-one days old. I put three drops of urine in the intake well, then waited five minutes to read the results. A plus sign meant positive, and a minus sign meant negative. After five minutes, a minus sign appeared. My heart sank as I read the results.

Bryson called at 12:30 a.m.. I told him the results. He was just as disappointed as I was. We both hoped the next time would be different. He told me again I probably was stressed out. He was coming by today to give me a full body massage. Maybe once I relaxed, my cycle would start. I accepted his offer. I guess, he was right. I must be stressed.

Jenny and I were busy that night. We went non-stop. If I was stressed, it was due to the job not home. While I was accessioning specimens, I felt my period start. I immediately went to the ladies room. A wave of disappointment enveloped me as I saw the blood. Was I really stressed out? Or was I hoping for a different outcome? The mind can play tricks with the body. I think my mind and body wanted to be pregnant. Therefore, they signaled a false delay.

When I returned to the lab, I called Bryson and left a message that I had started. I also canceled the massage because my flow would be too heavy. He called to see how I felt. I told him I was okay, but he heard the disappointment in my voice. He said he was hoping I was pregnant because he knew how much it meant to me.

For the remainder of the shift to get my mind off not being pregnant and not becoming Mrs. Collier, I occupied myself by thinking of "Uncaged." I remembered Chestnut would be in town for the January 20 meeting. I was working on chapter fifteen, but wanted to give him chapter sixteen as well. For some reason, I originally thought "Uncaged" would end with sixteen chapters. But when I reached chapter sixteen, I realized there was more to write. I decided I would no longer count chapters. My main focus was getting the story down; every detail; every prayer; every prophecy; every thought.

Chestnut took chapters 14-16. He said he wouldn't start editing until I completed the entire manuscript. With each chapter I gave Chestnut, I felt a sense of accomplishment. It didn't matter if he read it or not. I felt good knowing the more chapters I completed, the closer I was to the end.

While checking my messages after the I.B.W.A. meeting, one message stood out. It was from Herman Lowe, a member and good friend of my church. He said he missed me today at services and hoped I was doing well. I called him after I heard all my messages.

The telephone rang three times before he answered.

"Hello, Herman, this is Vanessa. I just heard your message."

"Oh, Miss Vanessa," he said with a slight accent. He always called me Miss Vanessa. "How are you doing? I didn't see you at church today."

"I'm fine. I wasn't at church today because I went to a writer's meeting. You know I'm writing a book."

"Oh, yes. I remember you mentioning it before. I thought you were kidding. I didn't know you were a writer."

"This is my first serious attempt. I was commissioned by God to write my book."

"Well if God told you to write it, then you have to be obedient."

"That's my feelings exactly."

"I want you to know, I've been praying for you to reconcile with your husband."

"Why?"

"I know you loved your husband and probably divorced over a misunderstanding."

"No, you're wrong. The marriage was over. We'll never get back together."

"Well, how are your creatures handling the divorce?"

"They're taking it well. Little Carl's grades are low, but that's because he's putting forth no effort. He's not taking school seriously these days."

"What a shame. What are you going to do about his grades?"

"I pray for my sons, daily. Besides beating his butt and taking away all of his privileges, I don't know what else to do."

"I will pray for him, too."

"Thanks. Prayer changes things."

"Miss Vanessa, you know we've been friends for a long time. You knew my ex-wife and was a guest in our home. I always felt comfortable around you, which is odd because I'm generally shy."

"Yes, we've always enjoyed each other's company. You're a walking library with your numerous spiritual books. I've read many of your books. They've helped me through a lot of spiritual battles."

"Shirley was very fond of you. She talked about you all the time."

"We were close. We walked together, took the kids to the park, and I came over your house just to chat."

"Shirley and I have been divorced for two years. She lives in Florida with the creatures. We both have moved on with our lives."

"That's good. That's the way it should be. Life goes on."

"Maybe, we could talk sometimes, over dinner perhaps."

"That sounds good. We always have something to say to each other when we're together. I must warn you, I don't plan to get serious about anyone until after I write my book. Now is my transition period, where I'm working all the kinks out."

"That's an excellent plan. But if you don't mind, I would like to call and talk sometimes. My dinner invitation still stands. Maybe one evening after church? I'll take your creatures, too."

"Okay, I'll take you up on it. Just let me know when."

"Okay. Good-bye, Miss Vanessa. I know you are a busy lady. I won't take up any more of your time."

"Good-bye, Herman. And you don't have to call me Miss. Just call me Vanessa. I'll see you in church next week."

Thoughts filled my head as I hung up the phone. Herman was a very handsome man, medium dark complexion, with thick straight black hair. He had an excellent job with a good salary. He would be perfect for me because we communicated well, always had fun together, and respected each other. We also had the same beliefs. Everything said yes except one thing. I was a friend of his ex-wife.

"I have another reason," Viva rudely interjected. "He's not Bryson. No one can take the place of Big Daddy."

"Who asked you, Miss Thang? You don't determine who I see."

"Oh, yes I do. As long as I'm around, Big Daddy is in and Mr. Encyclopedia is out!"

"You're the one that's out! I'm going to get you out of my life if it's the last thing I do."

"Don't hold your breath, girlfriend. I'm in your blood. And another thing, Miss Vanessa. Do you really think you can get pregnant as long as I'm around? I think not!"

TWENTY

For some reason, I couldn't get Shirley off my mind. She kept leaving Herman while they were married, going to her mother's in Arizona. Without notice, she'd packed the three kids up and leave. When Herman came to church without his family for an extended time, I knew Shirley was gone. I'm sure the other church members knew, too.

Shirley was an attractive, level-headed woman. She was friendly and always a pleasure to be with. Our conversations ranged from discussing the sermons, to the latest things going on with the kids, to the frustrations we both experienced with our mates. Although she was a housewife, she seemed more frustrated and burdened than me. Her biggest complaint was not having enough money to buy personal items, such as nail polish. Her second complaint was how indifferent or inhospitable Herman was to relatives and friends when they came over. His not speaking to them when he entered the house really pissed her off.

Shirley never mentioned why Herman and her teenage son, Shane, didn't get along. I heard through Herman how he went to the ministers for counseling after they fought. I tried not to get into their business or ask any questions, but if they wanted to talk, I listened and said my piece.

The next week at church, Herman asked me out to dinner. Since the boys were with me, he treated all of us. Herman treated my sons as if they were his children. He was totally different from Bryson who never took them anywhere or spent any money on them. I loved Bryson, but I wasn't going to let a good man like Herman slip through my fingers.

The boys liked Herman because he was friendly, easy going and generous with his money. They hoped we would get together; that way, they would have everything they wanted. They had visions of having expensive clothes, shoes, and gadgets; something they'd never had before.

Herman started calling almost daily. We talked for hours at a time and never ran out of things to say. Herman was a methodical person who asked a series of questions. Many times, I'd forget what I said in past conversations, but Herman would quickly remind me of my previous reply, as if he had written it down. The question and answer sessions unnerved me sometimes, but I knew it was Herman's way of learning me from the inside out. He felt as he hadn't known

Shirley as well as he should have. Obviously, he didn't want to make the same mistake twice.

By March, my relationship with Herman looked promising. We continued to eat out after church occasionally. He respected my main priority of writing "Uncaged." Therefore, he tried not to take up too much of my time. Talking to him made me realize how shallow my relationship was with Bryson. I felt like Mr. John Newton, who wrote "Amazing Grace." "I once was lost, but now I'm found; was blind, but now I see." With my eyes fully opened, I saw Bryson had stopped loving me. He only wanted sex. His time with me started dwindling as he became preoccupied with work. I also believed he was seeing someone else. He told on himself after a sex session when he quickly jumped up and washed himself off. He had informed me early in the relationship that he immediately washed up to prevent getting any diseases. Since he had been with many women, his method seemed to work. There was a time when he didn't jump up, but now he had started back.

By June, I knew Bryson and I were through. Now, his work took up all of his time. He was working on an unoccupied house that needed major repairs. The owner was eager to move in. I know he used the house as an excuse for his other fling. I never told him how I felt. However, I did tell him about Herman, my church friend.

Herman called me in late June to ask for my assistance in helping him buy new living room and bedroom furniture. Shirley had cleaned the house out when she left the last time. He wanted his life full again: first with new furniture, then with a new wife.

Herman only bought what I liked although our tastes were different. I selected a beige sectional sofa, beige and white, marble glass coffee and end table. For his bedroom suite, we chose a queen-sized cherry, high gloss Victorian style with nightstand, chest of drawers, and a dresser. Herman said he was buying the bedroom suite now, but didn't plan to sleep on it until he had his new wife. He paid for all the furniture with a check.

Two weeks later, Herman asked me to help him find a car. His car had been totaled in an accident last November. Until now, he had been unable to drive due to neck injuries. We went to a Toyota dealership on Highway 78 where he saw a tan Camry he liked. I haggled the salesman down to the price Herman wanted to pay. After a brief rebuttal, he made his purchase with a check, then we left.

As I drove home, I couldn't help but think of Herman. I was glad to help him get his life back together. Maybe, one day I'd be able to fully enjoy the purchases he recently made.

Bryson was at the house when I arrived. From the expression on his face, he'd been there for a while. He opened the door as I reached the steps.

"How long have you been here?" I asked, crossing the threshold.

"Too long. Where've you been?"

"I helped Herman find a car. I told you last week, he asked me to go with him," I said, sitting on the sofa.

He stood directly in front of me. "Can't you see what he's up to?"

"No. What?"

"First, he wants you to choose his new furniture. Second, he wants you to help choose his car. Next, he'll ask you to marry him, so the two of you can enjoy his new purchases. You weren't born yesterday! You know what's going on," he said, walking away.

"I think you're jealous," I said, kicking off my shoes. "It's okay if I sit here in this house and rot while you work all the time. But when someone takes an interest in me, you get all uptight. If I didn't know any better, I'd think you thought I was getting married."

"You know he likes you. I'm a man. I know how another man thinks."

"Speaking of think. I've been thinking that this relationship isn't working. You don't have time for me anymore. Next week when the Olympics begin, you'll have even less time for me when you start working twelve hour shifts, seven days a week, for a month."

"Are you trying to get rid of me to make room for Herman?" he asked contemptuously, turning to face me at the steps.

"That's not such a bad idea. Herman is a lonely man with plenty of time and money on his hands. Two things which you never have."

"I told you from the beginning, I stay busy. You know my financial situation. My ex gets over half my take home pay from MARTA. I have to work my ass off to pay my bills."

"I'm tired of being neglected. I need someone who will take me out and spend time with me. You treat me like a rag."

"That's what you said about Carl. Don't compare me with him."

"If the shoe fits, wear it."

"When the Olympics are over, I promise I'll spend more time with you. We'll go dancing. You're right, we haven't been out in a long time."

"I want more than you have to offer. Even after the Olympics, you can't give me what I want."

"I know what you want to hear, but I can't say it!" he said, raising his voice.

I felt tears well up in my eyes. I quickly ran passed Bryson up the steps so he wouldn't see me cry. Minutes later, he came into my bedroom where I was crying. He sat down beside me, facing my back.

"Vanessa, I'm sorry," he said, placing his hand on my back. "Normally, I walk away when a woman cry. But with you, it's different. I love you, I really do. Please, understand that I'm a busy man. The one thing that I don't have is free time. I'm beginning to realize that time is more important than money. I didn't realize how much I've been neglecting you."

I stopped crying. Lying perfectly still, I stared at the wall. Finally, I spoke. "I have nothing to hope for with you Bryson. You just said so yourself. All I have to look forward to are more lonely days. I can't take much more."

"Look, baby. I'll make it up to you. Don't give up on me now," he pleaded, turning me over to face him.

"Bryson, I'm like you. The one thing I don't have is time. I have two babies to birth before my clock ticks out. Next month, I'll be forty. While I'm waiting on you, I'll miss out on what I want in life."

"I thought you wanted me."

"I do. But today, you told me I'll never have you." He didn't say anything. He slowly stood up and left. Only God knew how much Bryson hurt me that evening. I took his words as a final wake up call.

Herman called minutes after Bryson left.

"Hello," I said, thinking it was Bryson calling on his cell phone.

"Hello, Miss Vanessa I hope I am not disturbing you?"

"Oh no, Herman. I was just lying on my bed."

"I called to thank you for helping me today. I still can't believe how you got the price so low. I never would have gotten such a great deal without you!"

"God was with us today. He made the deal possible. I prayed while you conducted business."

"To show my appreciation, I would like to take you to dinner Friday, alone."

"You don't have to take me to dinner to thank me. It was my pleasure."

"I know you've been busy writing your book. And I have tried not to interfere, but being with you these past few weeks makes me anxious for us to spend more time together. I really enjoy your company."

"I enjoy being with you, also. We do have a lot of fun together, just doing simple things. I'd be glad to go out with you Friday. What time?"

"Six o'clock. I don't like to eat too late. It's not good for the digestion."

"Six will be fine."

"Oh, Miss Vanessa, I need you to help me pick out some curtains for my living room to go with my new furniture."

"Okay. Just let me know when you want to buy them. I'm busy, but I'll make time for you."

"Thank you. I've taken up enough of your time today, already. I will let you go because I know you're busy."

"Okay, Herman. I'll see you Friday at six."

Thoughts filled my head after I hung up the phone. I could never tell Herman about Bryson. How do you tell a Christian man who is interested in you, that you have been sleeping with a married man? He would think I was as wicked as the woman who was caught in adultery in the Bible. And he would be right. I definitely couldn't tell him about Viva, either. Then he really would think I was an abomination. Somehow, I would have to keep both of them a secret.

Bryson wasn't thrilled when I told him I had a date with Herman. I broke the news to him during our conversation on Wednesday. He wasn't fond of the idea of another man moving into his territory. Especially a man who had more time, more money, more education, better looks, and more pizzazz!

Promptly, at six o'clock on Friday, Herman rang my bell. As I opened the door, I saw his navy blue suit, white shirt and a gold, black, blue and white patterned tie. His thick black hair was combed to the side with a few strands touching his gold, wire-rimmed glasses. He smiled as I unlocked the door.

"Wow! You look wonderful!" he exclaimed, admiring me in my knee-length white dress that buttoned down the back with a V-neck collar and a wide gold belt. I had on white and gold pumps to match.

"So do you," I replied, admiring him, too. "Would you like to come in?"

"No. I'm ready if you are."

I locked the door then we walked to his car. He opened my door and watched me gracefully settle inside. We smiled at each other as he closed my door. He quickly walked to his side and opened his door. The radio was on a soft jazz station as he cranked the car.

"Where are we going," I asked, adjusting my seat.

"There's a nice Italian restaurant close to my office. I always enjoy the food. The service is excellent. I thought it would be the perfect place to take you, today."

"It sounds great! I can't wait to get there."

"If we have time, I want to show you my office. I need to pick up a couple of papers."

"Sure. I'd love to see where you work."

"Let's go!" he said, backing out of the driveway.

We talked the entire thirty-five minutes it took to arrive at "A Taste Of Italy," where it was nestled in a complex with other restaurants and shops. Patrons entered and left as we reached the entrance. The host seated us at a table near the window. Waiters and waitresses were busy serving tables. Pictures lined the wall of different scenic views of Italy.

"Is this table to your satisfaction?" the host asked with a slight Italian accent.

"Is this location acceptable?" Herman asked me, before replying to the host.

"Yes."

"Yes, this table will be fine," Herman said, nodding his head.

Herman pulled my chair from the table, and I sat down. He gently pushed me to the table and sat in the adjacent chair. Simultaneously, we reached for the menus the host left. Scanning the selections, the only items I recognized were spaghetti, pizza, ravioli, veal parmesan, and lasagna.

"What do you usually order?" I asked, hoping he'd say something that sounded better than lasagna.

"A spinach pasta dish covered with ricotta cheese, antipasto salad, eggplant parmigiana, or the vegetarian lasagna. All are excellent!"

"Are you a vegetarian?"

"No, but I believe in eating plenty of vegetables. I seldom eat meat."

"That explains why you're thin."

"I've never been big, even when I ate more meat. What would you like to order?" he asked, looking into my eyes.

"I'll try the lasagna with a salad."

The waiter came to take our orders while I spoke. Herman gave our selections, including wine. He must have ordered his spinach pasta dish because whatever he said didn't sound familiar. Within minutes, the waiter came back with the wine. He poured a small amount into Herman's glass after he opened it in front of us. I watched as Herman rolled the wine over his tongue.

"Is the wine satisfactory, sir?" the waiter asked, holding the bottle in his hand.

"Yes. It's perfect!"

The waiter then filled our glasses with wine. I couldn't wait to taste it. I had never been served wine like that before. Carl and Bryson never ordered wine when we ate out. We usually had a bottle waiting for us when we returned home.

"What do you think?" Herman asked as I sipped my wine.

"It's delicious!" I exclaimed, sipping more. I could tell it was expensive. I already had a buzz going. Those Italians know what to do with grapes, I thought as I emptied my glass.

Would you care for more?" Herman asked, reaching for the bottle.

"Sure. Why not?"

He filled his glass also. He lifted it up as if to propose a toast. "To Miss Vanessa, a wonderful woman I hope to know better."

I then lifted up my glass. "To Herman, a man of character, charm, poise and the wisdom of God. May your days be filled with joy, peace and happiness."

The waiter brought our entrees as we finished our toasts. A small, freshly baked loaf of whole wheat bread was placed on the table with our meal. My lasagna was covered with cheese; so was Herman's spinach pasta dish. Herman bowed his head to say grace.

"Dear Father, our God in Heaven, Creator of the universe. Thank you for blessing us with this meal. I pray that You remove any impurities from it that may be detrimental to our health. I pray that You provide for those who are

hungry and do not have anything to eat. Please, let them not go hungry. Bless this evening. And let everything be said and done to Your glory. Again, I give thanks. Amen."

"Amen."

The candle light glowing on the table gave it a very romantic setting. Herman and I continued to talk as we ate the delicious cuisine.

"Miss Vanessa, one thing bothers me about you," Herman said, wiping his mouth with his linen napkin.

"What is it?" I asked, putting butter on my bread.

"I can't seem to get close to you. I think you have a fear of intimacy. I feel as if something is between us."

"Herman, I don't have a fear of intimacy. I've told you many times, I think of you as friend. The fact that I was close to Shirley has a lot to do with it. But I haven't told you this—the next man in my life must give me a sign. If you give me my sign, it will overrule my feelings about Shirley. So the thing that is between us is my sign."

Herman looked at me as if I had lost my mind. "What do you mean by a sign?"

"Before my divorce, I prayed to God concerning a certain action I wanted the next man in my life to take to identify himself as being THE ONE for me. I made a mistake with Carl. I don't want to make another mistake."

"What do you want? Some man to come to your door with a Santa Claus on his back?"

"No, Herman," I said, laughing.

"You want him to come and ring your bell?"

"No," I said, laughing harder. "God has to reveal it to you. Pray about it. Maybe, God will show you what it is."

"You're some lady, Miss Vanessa. I don't know about your sign. I think it's crazy!"

"You can think what you want. I must have my sign before I remarry. I have to make sure I have the right man."

He lifted up his glass of wine. "Here's to your sign. May God reveal it soon."

"I'll toast to that," I said, lifting up my glass.

TWENTY-ONE

Thirty minutes later, Herman and I finished eating. He asked if I wanted dessert, but I was too full and too high. He also passed. He's not one to eat sweets. The waiter came with the check while we were talking, eating the last of our food. My eyes instantly focused on the tab: $76.46 Wow! I thought, the food was good, but I didn't realize it was that expensive! The wine must have been flown, special delivery, straight from the vineyards of Italy. Herman, however, didn't blink an eye. He reached into his wallet, and laid five twenty dollar bills on the table.

"Keep the change," he instructed the waiter, as he picked up the money. "Are you ready to leave, Miss Vanessa?" he asked turning toward me, smiling.

"Sure. I want you to know, I had a great time! We must do this again."

"Tonight, you said your birthday is coming up next month. If you don't mind, I'd like to take you out then. Tomorrow, I pick up Herman at the airport. He will spend four weeks with me. I plan to take him to Disney World Sunday. While he's here, he will take up all of my time. He'll leave Wednesday, August 14."

"I'll be happy for you to take me out on my birthday. Is there anything I can do for you and Herman while he's here?"

"I do have a special favor to ask of you before he leaves. I want you to go shopping with me to buy back-to-school clothes for Herman and his sister. I told their mother I would buy them clothes."

"That sounds like fun. I've never shopped for a little girl before. The stores have so many pretty things for them to wear."

"Fine. Since that's settled, are you still up to going to my office?"

"Yes. I'd love to see where you work."

Herman pulled my chair back and we made our way to the door. Within a few minutes, we pulled up to a small office complex, a couple of blocks away. He parked in front of the last red brick building. The buildings were well maintained. Herman's building was number 367. "Flannigan & Associates Financial Services" was written on the window, in italicized blue letters.

"Well, this is where I work, Miss Vanessa. Let's go inside. We'll only be here a couple of minutes," he said, opening his door. He then came to my side to open mine.

Unlocking the office door, we entered a reception area with a small black desk and black leather chairs for clients to sit. Herman took me down a corridor to the left. We passed several closed doors before reaching his office at the end of the hallway. His office had a large brown desk with a computer on one side. Two black leather chairs faced his desk. A picture of the Flannigan team was on the wall, their motto posted underneath: Let our trained experts work for you. Your money is in safe hands with us. Flannigan & Associates is a name you can trust.

"What exactly do you do?" I asked, after reading the motto.

"I invest my client's money, give sound financial advise for them to build wealth, and provide their insurance needs."

"You have a nice office. It's hard to picture you sitting behind your desk talking to clients. You seem so shy sometimes."

"That's true when I'm not working." He searched through the papers on his desk. Retrieving three papers from the stack, he said, "I'm ready to go now. I found what I came for."

"Okay," I said, admiring a large picture of him behind his desk. "That's a nice picture of you."

"Thank you. I took that picture three years ago. I didn't want to take it, but Mr. Flannigan insisted. He said a picture puts the clients more at ease. They feel closer to you."

"Mr. Flannigan is a smart man. I agree with his philosophy."

"You are something else. May we leave now. Or do you want to look at my picture longer?"

"No. I'm ready. Let's go!"

We walked out of his office, down the corridor, and out of the front door. He drove me home, talking all the way. Herman spoke of a new foreclosure mortgage business venture he was in. He paid $500 for the start up materials and another $200 for video tapes. He was considering buying seminar videos for an additional $375 to boost his earning potential. He knew a guy who had been in the same business for six months who wanted Herman to become his partner. They both felt, together, they could do better than alone. Herman also knew someone who had money to give him whenever he found a foreclosed home. His excitement grew the more he discussed the business. I didn't have the heart to tell Herman I thought he was being taken for a money merry-go-round. In time, he would find out for himself he was a sucker being licked.

When we arrived home, the evening was still young. We both stared at the door as he parked the car.

"Would you like to come inside?" I asked, picking up my purse from the floor.

"No. Maybe some other time. I have many things to do before I pick Herman up tomorrow."

"Okay. I'll give you a rain check." He opened my car door then walked me up the steps, never touching me. With my keys in hand, I unlocked the door.

"Goodnight, Miss Vanessa," he said, as I opened the door.

"Goodnight, Herman," I said, turning around with the door opened. "Thank you again, for a wonderful evening!"

"My pleasure. I look forward to next month."

"So do I." He walked down the steps, then suddenly turned around.

"Miss Vanessa, is your sign when you kiss a man he passes out?"

"No," I replied, laughing. "Is that why you didn't try to kiss me?"

"No, but I did want to know before I did."

"Goodnight, Herman," I said, before I closed the door.

I heard the car start then leave the driveway. Herman is such a good man, Lord, I thought, as I walked to my bedroom. Will he give me my sign? I know, I can't go by sight or lean to my own understanding. I must rely on You to identify the next man in my life. Please, give me patience and wisdom while I wait.

The phone rang while I was taking off my clothes. On the second ring, I picked it up. "Hello."

"Why are you breathing hard? What are you doing?" Bryson demanded.

"What do you think I'm doing?"

"Screwing Herman."

"Do you? Do you think I screw every man who takes me out? I believe you're jealous of Herman, and you should be! We had a wonderful evening together. And get this, our meal cost $76.46."

"You know I can't compete with him!"

"We both know that. That's why you're acting this way."

"What all did you do?"

"Why should I give you an itinerary of my date?"

"Because I asked!"

"We talked, ate dinner, and drank wine."

"And?"

"And that's it. Nothing else happened, Sherlock."

"He didn't kiss you goodnight?"

"No, but I think he wanted to."

"If he tried to kiss you, would you let him?"

"I have to wait and see. I can't answer that question right now."

"Don't let him kiss you. You belong to me."

"Helen belongs to you. She's your wife. I don't have a husband, therefore, I only belong to Jesus, the head of my life."

"There you go again. I told you I need more time to get out of my situation."

"I'm giving you all the time in the world. I'm just not sitting in this house, holding my hands, while you get out of your situation. Life goes on. The world doesn't stop turning for no one."

"All right, Van. You talk all that crap! I know Herman and no other man can take my place. You love me, admit it!"

"Yes, Bryson, I love you. But sometimes you have to leave someone you love when the relationship is not working."

"I know, I haven't been spending much time with you lately. I've been working on that house too long. I finished today because I wouldn't have time while the Olympics were here. Next Saturday, I'll pick you up and take you to the Olympic Park. I'll still be working, but we should be able to spend some time together."

"Okay. That sounds good. I'm taking Carlos to see the women's gymnastics on Thursday."

"What about Carl?"

"He said he didn't want to go to anything."

"I won't have time to go to any of the events. Not working twelve hour shifts, seven days a week." "That's too bad. Sounds like another case of all work and no play."

"Speaking of work. I have to go. I need to answer my radio."

"Okay, bye."

Bryson was a trip. He knew his good thing was ending. I wonder what else he had up his sleeves to keep this relationship going. Whatever it was, I may not be around long enough to find out.

The weekend passed quickly. Before I knew it, it was time to go back to work. I hadn't seen or heard from Herman or Bryson since Friday. Not having company gave me plenty of time to work on "Uncaged."

The work shift started out quiet, which was typical for a Sunday night. I was the accessioning/Hitachi person, therefore, I was at the front window. By 1:00 a.m., I noticed an unfamiliar security guard kept passing by the window; he didn't stop to talk. At first, I didn't think too much about it. The lab corridor leads to the Emergency Room, the snack bar, and outside where people go to smoke. Consequently, it's usually busy with people. Once, I caught him looking at me. When I came out of the ladies room later in the shift, this same officer approached me.

"Excuse me," he said, as I locked the bathroom door. "May I speak with you for a few minutes?"

"Do you mind talking while I walk back to the lab? It was busy when I left. I just stepped out to go to the bathroom," I said, walking fast.

"Will it be possible for us to talk when you take a break?" he asked walking next to me, keeping up with my fast pace.

"I don't take breaks. When the work slows down, I sit in the office."

"My name is Raymond Miller. How can I talk to you if you don't take breaks?"

"You can come by the window and talk," I said, standing in front of the lab window.

"I'd feel like I was on stage. What's your name?"

"Vanessa Lewis. It was nice meeting you, Raymond, but I have to go back inside." I said, punching the keypad code. He walked off as I opened the door. From the expression on his face, I knew I would see him again.

Raymond was a short, slender man. I guessed his height to be about five-six. He wore large, brown glasses that covered half his face and his complexion was a shade darker than mine. He looked younger than me, but I couldn't guess his age. I definitely was not interested in him. I had my hands full with Bryson and Herman. The last thing I needed was another man to deal with.

Since I didn't see Raymond anymore that night, I assumed he gave up on me. I hoped my lack of interest scared him away. Besides, he was not my cup of tea, I liked my men tall, dark, and old. He was short, brown and young—the wrong combinations. I kept shaking my head, every time I thought of Raymond.

The next night, I saw Raymond again when I was leaving the ladies room, it was the only time I left the lab. I knew he was watching me when I saw him approach me again.

"Excuse me, Miss Lewis, may I talk to you for a few minutes?"

I thought about saying no, but I wanted to hear what he had to say. Maybe if we talked, he would also realize I was not for him. "Sure. I have a few minutes. What do you have to say?" I asked, moving from the bathroom door to the adjacent wall.

"Can you take a break, now? I would like to talk in private."

"No. I don't have time for a break, but I do have a few minutes to talk."

"I would like to get to know you. I've been watching you from the back hallway. Every time I see you working, something goes through me, like you are the one for me."

"Oh, really?"

"Yes. "I know it seems odd. I came from the day shift to act as lieutenant for this shift. I've been on the night shift since March. This feeling came over me in June. At first, I tried to dismiss the whole idea, but each time I see you, the feelings come back. This is all strange to me because I haven't been in a relationship for over five years, since I divorced my children's mother."

"You mean to tell me, you haven't been with a woman in over five years?"

"No."

"Why not?"

"I've been divorced twice. My last divorce turned me off with women until I saw you."

"Are you serious?"

"Yes. I am."

"What's so special about me?"

"I don't know. That's why I want to get to know you to find out."

"Right now, I'm busy writing a book about my life. I don't want to start a relationship until I finish. I'm on chapter twenty-nine. I don't have too much more to go to finish the book. I call this my transition period. Maybe, after I complete the book, we can talk."

"What time do you get off?"

"7:30."

"Would you mind if I walk you to your car?"

"No, that would be nice."

"Okay, I'll be waiting for you outside the lab at seven-thirty."

"Okay," I said, not knowing what else to say. "I've got to get back to work before Jenny thinks I've deserted her."

"I'll see you at 7:30," he said, walking away smiling.

As I walked back to the lab, I asked myself, what have I gotten myself into? I must practice saying the word `no' when it comes to men. No, you can't walk me to my car. No, I'm not interested in getting to know you. No, I have someone else in my life. No, you're wrong for me. But then that was not me saying no; it was Viva. Maybe, he was right for me, Vanessa.

TWENTY-TWO

At 7:27 a.m., I saw Raymond standing outside the lab waiting for me. Seeing him waiting, I clocked out. Jenny and the others on the day shift acted as if they didn't notice my visitor.

"Have you been waiting long?" I asked, as I came out of the door.

"Two or three minutes. Are you ready to go?"

"Yes. What time do you leave?"

"My shift is over at seven, but I usually don't leave until eight or eight-thirty. It takes me that long to complete all my paper work."

We walked out of the Pratt Street entrance near the pharmacy. While walking, I thought, how nice it was to have someone walk me to my car. I felt special. I also remembered how Bryson only walked me to my car once in the nine months he worked at Grady.

"What are some of your interests?" Raymond asked, as we approached the parking deck.

"I like dancing, writing, reading, and going to plays. What are yours?"

"I'm interested in building wealth, which includes investments, obtaining foreclosed properties, and eventually giving seminars."

"I have a friend who is doing the same thing. He works with a financial planning firm. Do you plan to work with a firm?"

"No, I plan to work for myself. My goal is to become financially independent. I'm well on my way to reaching my goal."

"Have you bought your start-up materials to obtain foreclosed properties?"

"Buy what start-up materials? Everything I need to know is in the public library for free! I don't believe in spending money needlessly. I'd rather invest it and let it earn interest."

"You sound like a man who has his act together," I said, approaching my blue Subaru. "Here's my car."

"May I walk you to your car again tomorrow?"

Viva wanted to say, Get lost half-pint! Go check on your investments. But I said, "I would love for you too. I enjoy your company." I unlocked my door. He quickly reached to open it for me. "Thank you," I said, getting inside the car, holding the door open.

"My pleasure. I must run. I have some unfinished business to tend to before I leave. I hope you have a nice day. I look forward to seeing you again tonight."

"Okay. Same to you," I said, as I closed my door and cranked the car. He walked off while the car warmed up.

What a coincidence, I thought, both Herman and Raymond are in investments. Herman appears to be successful while I'm not sure about Raymond. He just seems like an ordinary guy, trying to make it. Sometimes, those are the ones who'll fool you. And then again, sometimes those are the ones who really don't have anything. Only time will tell which way the coin will fall.

Raymond continued to walk me to my car every morning. Each night he tried to persuade me to take a break with him, but I came up with excuses. I couldn't believe his persistence. Hearing no, night after night, and not giving up. I admired his determination, if nothing else.

I told Bryson about Raymond when he called me to confirm our plans for Saturday. "You're talking to that pip-squeak! He's all wrong for you. You can do better than him," Bryson responded.

"He seems like a nice guy. I really haven't given him a chance to talk to me yet. I've been stalling. Although, he does walk me to my car every morning."

"He's a loser! Don't waste your time with that chump. I didn't call you to talk about him. Tomorrow is our night. I'll pick you up at eight o'clock."

"Okay, I'll be ready."

"I'll see you tomorrow, love. Bye."

"Bye, Bryson."

The thought of spending an evening with Bryson excited me. We hadn't been out in a long time. Maybe, tomorrow would be a turning point for us. Our relationship had been shaky up to this point. Spending quality time together would help mend our wounded affair. With both Herman and Raymond knocking at my door, tomorrow may be the decisive factor whether we make it or not. Why should I sit around this house and rot when I have two men who would be glad to take me out? Watch out, Bryson. Either play ball, or go to the dugout.

The telephone rang as I ran my bath water before bed. "Hello," I said, as I picked up the phone running from the bathroom.

"Miss Vanessa, did I call you at a bad time?" Herman asked, hearing my heavy breathing.

"No, I was just running my bath water. Hold on a minute, let me turn it off." I laid the phone down and went back into the bathroom. A minute later, I returned. "I'm back, Herman. Sorry to keep you waiting."

"I called to see how you're doing. I bought you and your creatures gifts from Disney World."

"That was very thoughtful of you. How was your trip?"

"Herman and I had a grand time. It's hard keeping up with a 5 year old when you're forty-one."

"I bet it is. What all did you do?"

"We did everything. We rode all the rides, played all the games, saw all the sights for his age group. I bought a camcorder for the trip. Herman spilled his drink on it; now, it's not working. I took a lot of wonderful shots that will never be seen. I was planning on sending the video home to his mother and sister."

"Can't you get it fixed?"

"No. The soda ruined it."

"What a shame! It seems like lately, you're just a money tree that's being shaken too much."

"I don't mind the money. It's the lost memories that I regret."

"You're one-of-a-kind. I would be upset with losing my money."

"Money is relative; memories are relevant. How many times will I take Herman to Disney World at the age of 5?"

"Probably, once."

"Exactly! Now those images are gone forever."

"I see your point. I'm sorry about your camcorder."

"That's life! Herman will be with me tomorrow at church. If you and your creatures don't have any plans, I would like to take you out to dinner."

"My boys aren't here. They're spending the summer with their dad. But, I would love to have dinner with you and Herman."

"Good. I will give you your gifts tomorrow after dinner."

"That'll be fine."

"I won't keep you any longer. Go take your bath! I'll see you tomorrow."

"All right Herman, good-bye."

"Good-bye."

At the sound of the click, I hung up the phone. I went to the bathroom to add more water and bubble bath in the tub. I sat in the tub while it filled up. My mind shifted from Herman, to Bryson, to Raymond before I was completely relaxed, enjoying the soothing suds.

I prayed silently as I bathed. *Lord, I don't know what's going on, right now, but You do. Please direct my steps. Don't let me make a mistake. Why do I have three men interested in me? All I want is one.*

I slept soundly that night, trying not to think of any man. Instead, I thought of "Uncaged." I was working on chapter twenty-nine, the chapter that revealed my sign. I wondered if it was forthcoming, if it would be the decisive thing to select the one man in my life. Surely, it was coming! Hopefully soon. Tomorrow would be a perfect day to get my sign, I thought, as I went to sleep.

121

I woke up to the sound of birds chirping at my window. Sunlight peeped through the blinds. A perfect day to get my sign. I prayed and studied my Bible first thing. Then I ate and lounged with a cup of coffee before going to church.

Looking at my cranberry carpet, I guessed, my days of being cheerful and optimistic had arrived. I felt all those things. God knew I would have days like these. That I wouldn't have to suffer all my life. I thanked Him for the joy, peace and happiness I was experiencing. And prayed that they would never end.

At 1:30 p.m., I started getting ready for church. I had chosen my navy-blue sailor dress, white stockings and blue pumps. I put my hair up in a french twist with bangs that looked smashing. "This is a day that the Lord has made. Let me rejoice and be glad in it," I recited Psalm 118:24 to myself as I drove to church.

Herman met me at the door; little Herman was with him. It felt good having my own personal greeters. Herman led me to our seats on the third row from the rear. This was the first time Herman and I sat together. Usually, I sat on the front row, and he sat near the rear. Little Herman sat between us.

While Mr. Joseph McNair, our pastor, read the announcements, little Herman said he had to go to the bathroom. I volunteered to take him. We came back right before the special music began, a solo by Mrs. Carolyn Calhoun, a long time member. She sang, "If I Can Help Somebody, Then My Living Won't Be In Vain." Mr. McNair returned to give the sermon as she finished.

"Good afternoon, brethren!" he said, with a jovial expression. "The special music is a perfect introduction to my sermon. Thank you, Mrs. Calhoun for the special music," Opening his Bible and putting a glass of water underneath the podium, he placed some objects underneath where the water was. Fingering through his ash-blonde hair, he began his sermon.

"The title of my sermon today is, 'Whatever We Do For Jesus Christ Is Not In Vain.' Please, turn with me to Ecclesiastes 1:1. I'm sure all of you are familiar with this Scripture. It says, *'The words of the Preacher, the son of David, king of Jerusalem. Vanities of vanities, says the Preacher, vanities of vanities! All is vanity. What does a man gain by all the toil at which he toils under the sun? A generation goes and a generation comes, but the earth remains forever.'* King Solomon was the wisest man who ever lived. To him everything we do on this earth while we live is vanity. Do you agree brethren? Most people might say, yes. But if you are a Christian, your answer should be no. There does exist vain works of man. But at the same time, we as Christians should have profitable works of Jesus Christ. We need to know the difference between works of vanity and works of Jesus Christ that come with a reward.

Now read Ecclesiastes 2, beginning with verse 4. *'I made great works; I built houses and planted vineyards for myself; I made myself gardens and parks, and planted in them all kinds of fruit trees. I made myself pools from which to water the forest of growing trees. I bought male and female slaves, and had slaves who were born in my house; I had also great possessions of herds and flocks, more than any who had been before me in Jerusalem. I also gathered for myself silver and gold and the treasures of kings and provinces; I acquired singers, both men and women, and many concubines, man's delight. So I became great and surpassed all who were before me in Jerusalem; also my wisdom remained with me. And whatever my eyes desired I did not keep from them; I kept my heart from no pleasure, for my heart found pleasure in my toil. Then I considered all that my hands had done and the toil I had spent doing it, and behold, all was vanity and a striving after wind, and there was nothing to be gained under the sun.'*

Here was a man who had everything his heart desired, yet he understood it meant nothing. It was all vanity. Life without Jesus Christ produces a life filled with vanity. Jesus knew the futility of this life. That's why he said in John 10:10, *'The thief comes only to steal and kill and destroy; I came that they may have eternal life, and have it abundantly.'*

Jesus Christ came to give us eternal life. That is our reward for accepting Him as our personal Savior; believing He died and rose again for our sins; and living His Way of life. When we yield our bodies as living sacrifices for Jesus, by allowing Him to live in us, then we can begin to experience a life that has meaning. Then what we do for ourselves and others are not done in vain, but it is done in service to Christ.

Turn in your Bibles to Matthew 25:31. It says, *'When the Son of man comes in his glory, and all the angels with Him, then He will sit on His glorious throne. Before Him will be gathered all nations, and He will separate them one from another as a shepherd separates the sheep from the goats, and He will place the sheep at His right hand, but the goats at His left. Then the King will say to those at His right hand, "Come, O blessed of my Father, inherit the kingdom prepared for you from the foundation of the world; for I was hungry and you gave me food, I was thirsty and you gave me drink, I was a stranger and you welcomed me, I was naked and you clothed me, I was sick and you visited me, I was in prison and you came to me." Then the righteous will answer Him, "Lord, when did we see you hungry and feed you, or thirsty and gave you drink? And when did we see you a stranger and welcome you, or naked and clothe you? And when did we see you sick or in prison and visited you?" And the King will answer them, "Truly, I say to you, as you did it to one of the least of these my brethren, you did it to me."*

"So brethren, you can live your life in vain, striving after the things of this world. Or you can submit your life to Jesus Christ, live according to His Way and serve your fellowman. Then you will be rewarded when He returns."

Mr. McNair reached under the podium and pulled out a large balloon and began blowing it up. "This is a life of vanity," he said, pausing between breaths.

The balloon filled to its capacity, then he held it up for us to see. "This is a life full of the things of this world. When we live a life of possessing more and more material things, until we can't acquire anymore," he blew into the balloon again, causing it to burst, "then our lives will be like this balloon, vanity, a bunch of wasted hot air. But when we live our lives for Jesus Christ," he said, reaching under the podium again, pulling out a world bank, "then the works that you do in this life will be remembered by Jesus Christ and He will reward you when He returns," he said, dropping several coins in the bank. "The choice is yours brethren, a life of obtaining or a life of serving others." He lifted up the bank, then said, "As for me and my house, we will serve the Lord!" He then walked off.

Mr. Charles Calhoun took his place to conduct the last hymn, "Who Is On The Lord's Side?" by Frances Havergal. At the end of the song, Herman gave the closing prayer.

"Dear Great Eternal God, Father of our Savior, Jesus Christ. We thank You for Your presence here, today. Thank You for sending Your Son, Jesus here to teach us Your Ways. Help us to come out of this world and live Your Way of life. Guide us into all truths. Bless all Your people worldwide. Heal those who are sick. Clothe those who are naked. Provide all the needs of Your people. Protect us as we travel home. Keep Your angels encamped around us throughout the week in order for us to return again next week to hear Your Word expounded. Amen."

After the prayer, we mingled with the other church members before going to Shoney's to eat. While we ate, little Herman talked about his Disney trip. Seeing Mickey Mouse, the castle, the shows, the rides and the parades excited him. His enthusiasm grew the more he spoke. Finally, Herman had to calm him down by telling him to do more eating and less talking because he was getting food everywhere.

Herman and I exchanged few words. Most of our time was spent listening to little Herman. At the end of the meal, Herman gave me my bag of gifts. They were two Mickey Mouse T-shirts for the boys and a dress with Minnie Mouse on it. I thanked him for his thoughtfulness and left.

When I got home, I had just enough time to bathe and get ready for Bryson to pick me up at 8 o'clock. Browsing through my closet, I pulled out an olive green, sleeveless pantsuit with gold stripes and flat gold shoes. I flipped my hair on both sides. By seven forty-five I was ready.

At nine o'clock, Bryson called to tell me he couldn't make it. His supervisor was present and he couldn't leave. I hung up the phone then went upstairs to take off my clothes. As I looked at myself in the mirror, Viva came forth. "Big Daddy, You have messed up now! YOU HAVE PISSED ME OFF!"

Viva's disposition turned to red hot fury. "Who does he think he is, canceling our date?" she said, in front of the mirror. "How dare he stand me up! This is the last straw. I'm not taking anymore of his shit! Vanessa, you can have Mr. Encyclopedia and Mr. Super Nerd. May the best man win your wimpy ass!"

"I'm just as disappointed as you about tonight," I replied. I'm sorry Bryson stood us up. But I'm glad you're finally letting me live my life as I see fit. Herman is a wonderful man. Raymond, I don't know enough about to judge. So far, he seems okay. With you out of the picture, they can really get to know me."

"Go for it, girlfriend. I'll stay in my place. You won't hear a peep out of me. Unless of course, Big Daddy redeems himself. Then girlfriend, you'll have to step back, because I will take over forever! You can kiss both of your charming chumps good-bye," she said, blowing a kiss in the mirror.

"You evil witch! I'll be glad when I can kiss you good-bye."

"Don't hold your breath, girlfriend. I may be mad, but I'm not demented."

"I may be wimpy, but I'm not pliant! Your days are numbered, Miss Thang! I just don't know when."

"Goodnight, Miss Goody Two Shoes. I won't wrangle with you all night. I have better things to do, like figure out how to even the score. Four is a party. Three is a crowd. Two is a delight. One is a lonesome number. What will it be Vanessa, dear? You and me and the two investment boys. Or you and the two boys? Or you and a boy? Or me? Sweet dreams, girlfriend. I hope yours will be as sweet as mine."

I looked at myself in the mirror and shook my head. "Lord, how did I ever get myself in this mess?"

TWENTY-THREE

I spent the remainder of the weekend reading, writing, and listening to the radio. Viva kept quiet; Bryson and Herman kept their distance. My work consumed all my energies. I knew the sooner I completed "Uncaged", the sooner I could go on with my life. Needless to say, I was ready for my transition period to end.

Carlos and I went to the Women's Gymnastics Olympic Competition at the Georgia Dome, Thursday, July 25. On the way, Carlos told me he had a dream, before I bought the tickets, that he would attend one of the competitions. He loved women's gymnastics. He not only watched them on TV, but he checked out many library books on gymnastics in general. We found our seats in time to watch the warm-up activities. Dominic Mocearu was Carlos's favorite. He cheered her on each time she performed. The U.S. team performed well, but made too many errors to win the gold. They were still our favorites in spite of their loss. After the competition, we bought T-shirts and other items from vendors then we walked through the crowded Centennial Olympic Park. Briefly, watching a performer on stage, we decided to call it a day. Neither Carlos nor I cared for crowds. We'd rather be home in the comfort of air conditioning, watching more events on TV.

Bryson called later in the evening to apologize for Saturday. I told him I needed to speak to him in person. He said his schedule was too hectic for him to come by before the Olympics were over. Then he asked me if I would go dancing with him to make up for Saturday. And since he would be on vacation the following week, it would be his way of celebrating my birthday. I accepted his invitation because I loved dancing with Bryson.

That night at work, I saw Raymond as I returned to the lab from the ladies room.

"Excuse me, Vanessa. Do you have a few minutes to talk?" he asked, as he approached me.

"Sure," I said, turning around.

"I haven't seen you for a few days."

"I've been here. Last night I took off to go to the Olympics with my youngest son."

"How was it?"

"Great! Do you plan to take your kids?"

"My children are in Augusta with their grandparents. They always spend the summer with them."

"Do you have pictures of your kids?" I asked, curious to see them.

He pulled out his wallet. "I have a picture of my two daughters, but not of my son."

"How old are your children?"

"Here's a picture of my oldest daughter from my first marriage. Her name is Brandi, but we call her M & M's or M's." Brandi was a dark-skinned girl with two long, thick plaits and a grin from ear to ear.

"How old is she?" I asked, smiling.

"She's thirteen now. She's eleven in this picture." He then turned to another picture. "Here's my youngest daughter, Francine. She's six. She took this picture last year."

Francine looked like a living doll. Her complexion was close to mine. She even resembled me. She had pink ribbons in her hair that matched a pink scarf draped around her neck. I fell in love with Francine on sight. "She's cute! I can see she's daddy's girl."

"Yes, she is. She's very attached to me."

"I have pictures of my two sons in my purse in the lab. Maybe one day I'll show them to you."

"Okay."

"I really must get back to the lab. I can't stay gone too long."

"Will you take a break later?"

"No."

"May I walk you to your car?"

"Sure."

"I'll see you at 7:30 then."

"Okay," I said, as I walked back to the lab.

When I went back into the lab, I couldn't get Francine off my mind. She was so cute! Somehow, from her photograph, she had stolen my heart. I thought about my daughters to come. I wondered when they were coming, and if somehow they would look like Francine.

Raymond tried to persuade me to take a break with him every night. And every night, I said no. Finally, on the night of July 31, he gave me his pager number and told me to page him when I could take a break. Feeling his desperation, I took the number. It was close to 2 a.m.. At 5:45, I paged him only because I knew he was expecting it. Seconds later, the phone rang.

"Emergency Clinic Lab, Lewis," I answered.

"This is Raymond Miller, returning your page."

"Raymond, I can't take a break now. I just wanted to talk. Since you gave me your pager number, I knew you expected me to call you."

"Actually, I'd given up on you calling me. I thought you weren't interested."

"I'm interested. I was busy up until now."

"Vanessa, I've been trying to talk to you for a week and a half! We've talked briefly while I walked you to your car. But I have things to say that will take more time."

"Go ahead. I'm listening."

"I'd like for us to be more than friends. There's something about you that makes me want to know you more. Let me tell you something about me."

"Okay. I'm still listening."

"I will never lie to you. I'll always tell you the truth. I will never tear you down. I'll only build you up. I will provide for you. You won't have to work. I prefer my woman to stay at home, taking care of the family. With my investments and other income, I'll make more than enough to support us comfortably."

"That sounds good. Now, I have something to tell you about me. First off, the next man in my life must give me a sign. Before I divorced last year, I prayed for a sign to identify my next husband. Without the sign, we can only be friends. Also, I will have two more children, daughters, to be exact. On August 18, I'll turn forty. Therefore, I don't have time to waste on a man who's not serious about a relationship."

"I am serious. I have been from the beginning. I thought you wanted to play games," he said, sarcastically.

"No, I don't have time for games. I just don't want to waste my time on the wrong man," I explained.

"There are two things I will require of you to make our relationship work."

"What are they?"

"Honesty and fidelity."

"Those are my two strengths," I answered, eagerly.

"Good. By the way, I love children. I want six."

"Well, you have the wrong woman. I will only have two more. But, if you count my two sons, that will be a total of seven. That's one more than what you wanted. It's also God's number for completion."

"We'll talk about children later."

"I told you how old I am. How old are you?"

"My birthday is June 29. If you don't kick me to the curb by then, I'll tell you."

"Your age really doesn't matter. You can tell me now."

"No, I'll wait."

"Raymond, I have to go. My work is piling up."

"I'll see you at seven-thirty."

"Okay, bye."

As I hung up the phone, Jenny put more urine samples and C.B.C.s on my station. I processed them, then completed three blood gases at the same time. I had several pregnancy and cardiac marker tests coming off the Axsym to answer. The work was nonstop until seven o'clock. Jenny and I took a real break then because the day shift was present to complete the work. Before I knew it, Raymond was waiting for me outside the lab. I clocked out and joined him. We talked on the way to the car. The more he said, the more I wanted to hear. I realized, as I got to the car, talking to Raymond had completely healed my mind. I felt truly whole again. He had a way with me different from Bryson or Herman. It was satisfying, and invigorating.

It was as if Raymond finished the job Bryson started. I felt a healing with Bryson, but it was incomplete because my mind wasn't healed. Bryson only mended my broken body, while Raymond healed my wounded mind. I knew with the healing of my mind, my transition period was officially over. Being healed in both body and mind made it possible for me to move on into the next phase of my life. Surely, my sign was forthcoming.

I was off the next night, but I thought of Raymond all day. Several times I picked up the phone to page him, but resisted the urge. I wanted to hear more of his words. The more I fought the temptation to call him, the more I wanted to talk. At 1:05 a.m., I paged him. The telephone rang two minutes later.

"Hello, Raymond" I said, knowing it was him.

"This is Raymond Miller. Someone paged me from this number."

"Raymond, this is Vanessa. Are you busy?"

"Oh, Vanessa, what a pleasure to hear from you!"

"I have a confession to make. I've been thinking about you all day. I've resisted paging you until now; I couldn't fight the impulse any longer. I had to call."

"I'm glad you did. It makes me feel good to know you were thinking of me. I think of you all the time."

"I can't remember all you said last night, but I wanted to hear more. I feel like you've healed my mind."

"I told you I'd never lie to your or tear you down and I meant it. Everything I do for you, or with you, will be to build up. I have many things I want to do with my life, and I haven't really begun yet."

"What are some things you hope to do?"

"I plan to buy a house in November. I'd like to coach a Little League football team. I visit the library regularly to get the latest information on investments and obtaining foreclosed properties. I listen to motivational speakers to learn how to give financial seminars."

"When do you plan to get started?"

"Spring of next year. Right now, I'm collecting information."

"Where would I fit into your plans?" I asked, desiring to share his plans.

"I haven't thought about that yet, since I've been alone for over five years. I've spent all my energy on my family and reading information on starting up my business. Are you saying you'd like to be a part of my life?"

"I don't know. Would you like to be a part of mine?"

"Yes, if that's agreeable with you. At least, I'd like to get to know you."

"I feel the same."

"Good. May I keep your number?"

"Yes."

"I have a call I need to answer over the radio. May I call you tomorrow?"

"Yes. You can call me anytime."

"Okay, good-bye Vanessa."

"Good-bye, Raymond. I'm glad I paged you."

"So am I. Good night."

"Good night." I felt good all over. I was glad I gave into my temptation to page Raymond. He was all man; I just had to get used the way he was packaged.

It's been said, you can't judge a book by its cover. You also can't judge a person by height, weight, age or looks which determine how a person is packaged. The real person is underneath the physical appearance where the heart and mind are located. They produce character, the real fingerprint of a person.

Raymond and I continued to talk every day. He told me why his two marriages failed; why he didn't finish at Georgia Tech after completing three years; how he fought for custody of Raymond Jr. and Francine; and how at one time, he had all of his children at home to rear. He mentioned his two years of unemployment after being laid off by Sears. One thing he said, that really caught my attention, was he'd never ask me for sex. A man not wanting sex? A man who's not been with a woman in over five years must be one in a million. That was my phrase for Raymond, my one-in-a-million man.

When I told Mama about Raymond, she gave me some unsolicited advice.

"Nessa, I'd try that man out before I married him. Ain't no such thing as marrying a pig-in-a-poke these days. Ya got to know what ya getting before ya get it in ya bed every night. He might've been the problem with his other wives. They were probably frustrated. Honey, ya better try him out before ya say 'I do.' Ya don't want to be frustrated, too. If a man leaves a woman frustrated he can be one in ten million, won't nobody want him. Don't ya get stuck with him."

I generally don't ask Mama for personal advice, but she volunteers it anyway. I disregard ninety-nine percent of what she says, but the other one percent has merit. She would never be an Ann Landers or Dear Abby. What happened to, "Don't have sex before marriage?"

Bryson called minutes after I hung up with Mama. He was on his way to pick me up. He wanted to make sure I hadn't canceled our date. I told him I'd be ready when he arrived.

While I dressed, I decided to wait until we returned home to tell him what I had to say. Why get him in an attitude before we had fun. I knew, after I said my piece, this would be our last date.

Bryson arrived twenty minutes later, dressed in a dark green suit with a black shirt and no tie. His cologne tantalized my nose as I let him inside.

"You look and smell nice," I said as he entered, stopping at the door.

"Thanks, so do you."

"You don't usually compliment me when you first arrive. You usually wait until hours or days later."

"I haven't seen you in weeks. I guess what I'm trying to say is, it's good to see you again."

"You're a busy man, remember? You don't have time for me anymore," I said, gathering my things.

"The Olympics are over although I'm still not finished with the house. The owner found more work she wanted me to complete before she moves in."

"I'm ready. I don't want to hear about your work."

"You said you have something to tell me. Let's talk first then, go. You act like something's bothering you."

"I'll tell you when we come back. Let's go!"

He locked the doors, then led the way to his van. Being polite, he opened my door. My peach dress barely covered my upper thighs as I settled in my seat. I crossed my legs to tease him on the way to the club. When we arrived, signs were posted advertising a male review night.

"Do you still want to go inside, or would you rather go someplace else?" he asked, as he parked the van close to the entrance where the sign was visible.

"Let's go in! I've never seen a male review. I'll get two treats for the price of one."

"Okay. This is your night, whatever you say," he said, opening his door.

I waited until he came to my side to open mine. I made sure he got a peek of what he wasn't going to get. Our eyes met as he closed the door. We both smiled, but for different reasons. His hand clasped mine as we walked to the front door. At the window, Bryson paid the twenty dollars admission, and we entered through a black, glass door.

Inside, people were jamming. Bryson ordered drinks before we joined in. While drinking our drinks, we couldn't wait to dance to the throbbing beat of the music. Laughing and dancing on five songs, we started sweating and acting silly on the floor. He did the robot while I jitterbugged.

On the sixth song, the disc jockey asked everyone to clear the floor for the male review. Bryson ordered another round of drinks. We drank, watched and laughed at the almost naked men on stage. The funniest part was seeing the reactions of the sex-starved women who stuffed money in the men's crotches. One bride-to-be practically had her tongue in one man's crotch. She licked him up and down when he stopped at her seat.

Bryson and I left before the show was over. I'd seen enough of naked men parading around, exciting pathetic women. Bryson said we could finish where they left off when we got home. I didn't have the heart to tell him, "I don't think so." I just smiled and let him think whatever he wanted. He asked if I wanted to get something to eat while we were out. I told him, no I wasn't hungry. I wanted to hurry home and tell him what I had to say.

By the time we arrived home, Bryson sensed something was wrong. "Come on, out with it!" he demanded, as we entered the house.

"Have a seat first," I said. He sat on the sofa while I sat on the loveseat. His eyes were transfixed on mine as I opened my mouth to speak. "We've been together for a year and a half. In that time, you haven't given me my sign. I know now that you never will." He started to interrupt, but I raised my hand. "Let me finish before you speak, please. Next week, I'll be forty. I don't have anymore time to waste. I'm ready for my sign, so I can move on with my life. When I met you, I was broken, sick, not quite myself. To continue our relationship after discovering you were married proves I was ill. Recently, I realized I'm no longer sick, but whole again in body and mind. You're a repairer, and God sent you to repair me. However, in the process of repairing me, you were repaired, too. Your heart of stone was turned into a heart of flesh. You've been through a lot in past relationships. I thank you for all that you've done for me. You were a part of my life when I needed someone, but God has shown me that all you can offer me is milk or sex. When I was sick, milk was all I needed. I wasn't ready to have a real relationship because I was not healed. But I'm healed now. I'm whole again. I need more than milk.

Another thing, I no longer want to be your side dish that you sample now and then. I'm ready to be the main course. I have two men who have prepared a banquet for me. One is of rich foods, the other is a simple spread. Milk is not enough anymore. I want to taste what they have prepared for me. I'm starving on your milk diet."

Tears ran down his face. He didn't attempt to wipe or conceal them. He moved close to me and held my hand. "I love you Vanessa. I know you've been unhappy with our relationship because I haven't spent enough time with you lately. Starting tonight, I planned to change all that. Tonight is a new beginning for us. I want to give you everything you want and deserve. Give me another chance to show you how much you mean to me," he said kissing the back of my hand.

I pulled my hand back. "No, Bryson. Your time is up. I've given you too much time already. It's time for us to go our separate ways."

"Okay, If you want me out of your life, I'll leave," he said, looking into my eyes.

"Bryson, I want more than you can offer me. I want a filled package. I can't settle for an empty box anymore."

He stood up. "I won't be needing these," he said, taking my house keys, which he never returned, off his key ring.

I held out my hand for my keys. "Thanks for understanding. I want you to know, you'll always have a special place in my heart."

He walked to the door, then slowly turned around. "I have one request before I leave."

"What is it?"

"Can I have one last dance?"

"Sure. I guess that's the least I can do. Wait right here while I get us some music." I went to my bedroom and turned on the radio. When I came down the steps, he held out his arms. As I reached him, another song played. It was, "If This World Was Mine" by Luther Vandross. We danced, holding each other close. His heart pounded wildly next to mine. Tears fell from his face to my hair. He held me as if he never wanted to let go. We danced slowly to the song, not saying a word. Our hearts throbbed rhythmically, saying what our mouths wanted to say.

When the song ended, he kissed my forehead. "Thank you," he said, releasing me.

I opened the door to let him out. "Thank you for all you've done."

"Can we kiss then say good-bye?" he asked, standing at the opened door.

"Yes."

He pulled me to his chest, lifted my chin and tenderly kissed my lips. "If you're really mine, I must let you go, to see if you'll come back to me again," he said, as his lips parted from mine. "Good-bye, my love," he said, as he walked out the door.

I locked the doors as he left.

"Good-bye, Big Daddy," Viva said while the key was still turning.

TWENTY-FOUR

When Bryson left, I read my Bible then prayed.

Dear Heavenly Father, forgive my trespasses. Please, wipe my slate clean with the blood of Your Son, Jesus Christ. I feel like the Israelites, who wondered in the wilderness for forty years after You freed them from Egyptian slavery. I feel as if the first thirty-nine years of my life have been a time of trial and testing. Now, I'm ready to enter the Promised Land You have prepared for me. Let my past and the wilderness be far removed from me. In a few days, I will be forty, a number of deliverance. Please deliver me from Viva so that I may serve You with my whole being. Let her not have dominion over me. Help me to live a holy and righteous life from this day forward. I'm reminded of Isaac who took his wife, Rebekah, when she was forty. I too pray that You will bless me with my next husband at forty. I thank You and ask these things in the name of Your Son, Jesus Christ. Amen.

That night, as I slept, I decided to start a relationship with Raymond. Raymond and I took a break together Sunday night at work. I had some things to tell him in person. Once we were settled in a cafeteria booth, I gave my spiel.

"Raymond, I've been thinking a lot about us lately. I really would like to see how far we can go. But there are somethings about me you need to know first. I've made a lot of mistakes in my thirty-nine years of existence, most of which occurred in the past few years."

"Your past is your past," Raymond interrupted. "I'm only interested in your present."

"I have to explain some of my past in order for you to understand me now."

"Go ahead."

"I've been dating a married man since my divorce a year ago. He worked here, in security. His name is Bryson Collier."

"I know him."

"I broke up with him this weekend because I want to live right before God."

"Right is right, and wrong is wrong. It was right for you to end the relationship," he said, reaching for my hand.

"You don't have a problem with me being with a married man?"

"Not if the relationship is over. That's your past. It's behind you now."

"I'm glad you understand," I said, taking a deep breath. "There is one more thing I have to tell you."

"I'm listening."

"There are two of me," I blurted out.

"What?"

"I have another personality. Her name is Viva. She is worldly and comes out at anytime. If you're with me and I act differently, that's Viva."

"Whom am I talking to now?"

"Vanessa."

"Who dominates?"

"Me most of the time."

"Do you think I should be concerned about Viva?"

"Not really. But I wanted you to know she exists in case she comes out."

"Thanks for informing me about Bryson and Viva. I don't have a problem with either one," he said, looking at his watch. "Is there anything else you want to tell me before we leave? Our time is up," he said, getting up.

"So, you're not going to kick me to the curb?" I asked, sliding from the booth.

"No."

I smiled. "So we are an item now?"

"Yes. Unless you object?"

"No. You truly are one in a million."

He laughed as we walked out of the cafeteria and back to work.

I paged Raymond later in the shift to talk again. For some reason, I felt a constant desire to listen to him. His words were music to my ears; music that didn't need a dance beat to enjoy.

Bryson called before I clocked out. He wanted to talk with me at home and would be waiting in the driveway. I told him I had nothing more to say. He said he did, and it was my turn to listen to what he had to say.

Promptly at 7:28, Raymond stood outside the lab to walk me to my car. I surprised him by being ready when he arrived.

"You must be glad to see me?" he asked, smiling as he saw me waiting.

"Yes. I couldn't wait until you came."

"Let me carry your bag."

I gave him my bag of stuff. "You're spoiling me, you know."

"I'm just being a gentleman,"

"I know. I'm not use to being in the presence of a gentleman. I usually do everything myself."

"Do you have plans for your birthday?"

135

"Yes, a church friend of mine will take me out. He asked me last month before I met you."

"I wouldn't be able to take you out anyway. I don't have a day off until the thirtieth. Would you like for me to take you out then?"

"Yes, I'd love that. Do you always work so much?"

"I try to work as much as possible while my children are away. When you don't have someone in your life, what else is there to do besides work?"

"I've never experienced that before, but you do have a point. I can cook dinner for you next Friday, before you go to work, if that's okay?"

"That would be nice."

By now, we stood in front of my car. "I enjoy your company Raymond."

"Thank you. The same here."

"What do you like to eat?" I asked, opening my car door.

"Food is food. I eat anything."

"You make planning easy."

"I'm glad," he said, opening my door. "I wish I could say the same. I have no idea where to take you since I don't go out."

"I'm easy to please. Whatever you decide will be fine with me. I don't go out much, either."

"Be careful," he instructed, closing my door.

"I will. Call me when you get up," I commanded.

"Okay, I will. I can't stay any longer, I gotta run. I have several more things to do before I leave."

I drove off when he disappeared down the parking deck steps. On the way home, I thought of Raymond then Bryson. I wondered what Bryson was up to? *Whatever it was, Lord, make me ready. Give me the spiritual armor to fight his fiery darts.*

Bryson's van was at the mailbox. He stepped out as soon as I pulled in the driveway. I took a deep breath, then opened the door. He walked passed me to the bottom of the steps.

"We can talk right here," I said, standing by my car.

"No, I want to talk inside."

"Why?"

"Are you scared of me or something? Or, are you afraid you might do something you want to do?" he said, pissed.

"Bryson, I'm tired! I've been up all night. Say what you have to say so I can get some sleep!"

"I'm not moving until you open the door. The longer you stall, the longer it'll take you to get to bed."

I walked to the door. I was too tired to fight or play games. I knew the sooner he talked, the sooner I could go to bed. "I hope what you have to say is brief. I'm really tired," I said, unlocking the door. He went inside and sat on the sofa. I sat on the loveseat, close to the opened door.

"I've thought about what you said the other evening and I've decided I'm not going to let you go. If you want to see other men, you still have to see me. I'm not out of the picture."

"You don't have a choice. You are out of the picture. I have moved on."

"You can't throw away what we have built in this past year in a half. You still love me, no matter what you say. I know I haven't spent much time with you lately. But I've made up my mind to give you more time. Last Friday was going to be a new beginning for us. I'd planned to take you out more and do all the things you've said I wasn't doing."

"You're too late. Our relationship is over! You need to get that through your thick head. I already told you, I'm ready for my sign. You've never given it to me, and you never will!"

"Damn your sign! My feelings are more important than a stupid sign. I love you, Van! Doesn't that mean anything to you? Isn't my love worth more than a sign?"

"No. Anybody can say `I love you,' but only the right person can give me my sign."

"Baby, give me another chance! We can make it work. I promise I'll spend more time with you, take you out more, and anything else you want me to do," he said, leaving the sofa, coming to the loveseat.

"No, Bryson! I'm already talking to someone else."

"Raymond Miller! You'd rather have him over me? I told you he's all wrong for you. I'm the man for you!"

"You're married. He's single," I retorted.

"Oh, so that's it! It's my status. I am my status! You know my status has nothing to do with us! You feel like I'm the wrong man. Isn't that it, Van?"

"Yes. Right is right. And wrong is wrong. It's wrong for me to be with you."

"Well, I have something to tell you, baby," he said, walking to the door. "I'm not out of your life! It'll take more than Raymond Miller to take my place. Tell your boyfriend, you have a man. Remember, baby. It's not over until the fat lady sings," he said, as he walked out the door.

I stood up and locked the doors, making sure he did not return. Exhausted from both work and the confrontation with Bryson, I went to bed. I didn't sleep, however, because I tossed and turned thinking of my predicament. How could I be with Raymond while Bryson was still in the picture? How could I get Bryson out of my life so I could be with Raymond? Where did Herman fit in? I had questions with no answers. The more I thought, the more questions I had. When will this merry-go-round end?

While I slept, I dreamed up a solution. It wouldn't be right for me to see Raymond as long as Bryson wouldn't leave me alone. I didn't want Raymond to get hurt. Therefore, I decided until I got Bryson completely out of the picture, I wouldn't see Raymond. I knew Bryson. He'd cause confusion, something I didn't want Raymond to deal with. The more I thought about it, the more it seemed like the right thing to do.

I decided, that night at work when Raymond and I took our break, I would tell him my decision. Raymond wanted to go outside to talk. We walked along Pratt Street, in front of the pharmacy. A warm breeze blew as we walked.

"Let's stop here," Raymond said, reaching the midpoint of the sidewalk.

"Isn't this a beautiful night," I said, looking into the sky.

"It's beautiful because you're here with me."

My gaze went from the sky to Raymond. "Raymond, I have something to tell you."

"What is it? You look troubled," he responded, staring at me intently.

"What I have to say isn't pleasant. It's not really what I want to do, but under the circumstances, I don't have a choice. I'm battling a demon, a Goliath, in my life. Although I broke up with Bryson, he won't let me go. I don't want you caught in the middle of my war. Until I can get this resolved, I think it would be best if we didn't see each other."

"I understand. I've been through this before. If you want me out of your life, I'll leave you alone."

"I think that would be best. I'll call you when this is over."

"Let me take you back inside," he said, turning back toward the entrance to Grady.

We slowly walked back to the lab. His grim expression captured my mood. I felt bad having to end our relationship before it really started. But under the circumstances, I hoped he really understood, like he said. I knew Bryson would make our lives miserable. Raymond was too good to be tangled up in Bryson's web.

"Vanessa, explain one thing to me?" Raymond asked as we reached the lab.

"What?"

"If the relationship is over between you and Bryson, why is there a problem?"

"It's over as far as I'm concerned. I just have to convince Bryson. He's not going to hand me over to you on a silver platter. I know him. He has to be conquered by the power of God just like David defeated Goliath."

"Suppose you can't defeat him?"

"Then God will have to send me a David to slay him."

"I'll be waiting."

"Thanks Raymond. I hope it won't take too long," I said, punching the keypad numbers to enter the lab.

"Me too," he said as he walked off as I went inside. He did not offer to be my David.

TWENTY-FIVE

For the rest of the night, I had a sinking feeling. Breaking up with Raymond was not easy because I had grown attached to him in the short period of time. A thought came to me as I sat at the computer verifying my chemistry results. I would look up Raymond's name and find out his age. Going into the patient information function, I typed in Raymond Miller. Eight names appeared. Two had employee codes, but only one had a birth date of June 29. When I looked at the year, my jaw dropped. 1963! Raymond was thirty-three years old, seven years my junior. He's just a baby, I thought.

I worked the remainder of the shift thinking about Raymond and his age. Not that it mattered, but I couldn't believe he was so young. I also couldn't believe how much I wanted us to be together again. Bryson called that evening from the MARTA office. "What are you doing?" he asked when I answered the phone.

"Washing dishes."

"I'm not busy here. I was thinking about coming over."

"Why?" I asked not sure I wanted to see him.

"I want to see you, that's why. Will what's his name object?"

"Raymond and I are no longer seeing each other thanks to you!"

"You're finally coming to your senses. You should thank me for getting you out of that disaster."

"Being with Raymond is not a disaster. A man who hasn't been with a woman in over five years will treat her like gold. You treat me like a rag."

"Don't you believe that bull-shit! He's lying. I saw him talking to a woman before he met you. Wake up, baby! He's running a game on you."

"I believe him. He's a good man, and I was a fool for letting him go."

"That's the only smart thing you've done with him."

"Bryson, let me tell you something. Sunday, I asked God to forgive me of all my sins, to help me live a righteous life. I can't live a righteous life being involved with you! Starting now, it's forever over between us! Raymond is out of my life and so are you. I need time to myself, without any man."

"I'm coming over!" he screamed, slamming down the phone.

I quietly hung up the phone. What on earth did he plan to do? He's acting like a mad man, refusing to accept the fact that our relationship is over. Lord, please slay my Goliath. He's too much for me to conquer.

Fifteen minutes later, Bryson rang my doorbell. I let him in.

"I just walked off my job to come over here!" he shouted as I let him inside. "What's gotten into you? Don't you know how much I love you?" he asked, shaking me.

"Right is right and wrong is wrong. Right has nothing to do with love."

"You keep saying that. Why all of a sudden does my status matter?"

"Because right is right and wrong is wrong." I kept repeating Raymond's words.

"What's with all this right and wrong stuff. Van, we've broken up before. Why does this time feel different? You make me feel like I'm the wrong man for you," he said, trying to kiss me.

"You are! Right is right and wrong is wrong," I said, moving my head, avoiding his advance.

"Oh, you don't want to have anything to do with me anymore? Is that it?"

"Yes, that's it"

"I'll see about that," he said, picking me up. "I love you, Van, and I'm not letting you go," he kept repeating as he carried me down the steps to the den acting like a crazy mad man.

"Put me down!" I screamed as he continued to move toward the sofa.

"No! You're mine! I want you now, and I'm going to have you!" he snarled, ripping off my clothes.

"No! Stop, Bryson!" I shouted, trying desperately to keep my clothes on. Bryson forced me down on the sofa, shoving my pants down. I couldn't stop him.

"Baby, is it good to you?" he asked between breaths, humping over me.

I didn't answer, hoping he would hurry up and finish. I separated my mind from my body to endure it. Viva was enjoying it while I was waiting for it to be over. Letting out his typical Tarzan yell as he climaxed, Bryson went limp. I kept still until he got up. Then I watched him carefully as I pulled up my clothes.

"That was good," he said, getting dressed.

"Good! My God, Bryson. That was rape!" I screamed at him.

"Don't give me that rape shit! You wanted it. Sometimes, I think you go into a closet and come out a different person."

I knew he was referring to Viva, whom I never told him about. "I said no, Bryson. N-O, no. You had no right to take me like that!"

"No, I knew that's what you wanted, and I was right," he said, standing over me with a half grin on his face.

"Bryson, I am a different person. I'm going to say this for the last time. Right is right and wrong is wrong! It's wrong for us to be together. Get out of my life Bryson!" I demanded, getting up.

"All right. If that's what you want, I'll do it."

"Yes, that's what I want." I said, going toward the door. I let him out the door.

Turning around, holding the door open, he said, "I want you to remember one thing: I will always love you. You mean more to me than sex." He closed the door behind him.

I quickly locked the doors, watching him enter his van. This time it was for real. My Goliath had been slain by the words of Raymond. Indeed, Raymond was my little David.

I prayed when Bryson left for God to forgive my trespass against Him. I told God today would be the last time I disobeyed Him. I wanted to serve Him with my whole being with no hypocrisy. I asked Him to wash me again with the blood of Jesus to make me clean, whole and righteous.

I spent the remainder of the evening reading my Bible and praising God before going to sleep for work. I thanked Him over and over again for His victory in my life. Now, that my Goliath was defeated, what was I suppose to do next? I pondered the question, and only came up with, `nothing' as the answer.

After Bryson's encounter, I needed a period with no man in my life. I told myself after Herman takes me out for my birthday, I'll be through with men for a while. I'll take this time to renew my relationship with God.

Herman called Friday evening to confirm our date. Since his plans included both Saturday and Sunday, he would be over at six p.m. Saturday to pick me up. After he called, I thought, maybe by getting Bryson and Raymond out of the way was God's plan for showing me Herman was the man for me. He'd been trying for seven months to get close to me. In all those months, Herman never could get Bryson out of the picture. But one month with Raymond did the trick. God knew, Bryson had to go. He sent Raymond, my little David, to conquer Herman's foe.

Early Saturday morning, my doorbell rang. To my surprise, a delivery man was at the door with a beautiful bouquet.

"Are you Vanessa Lewis?" he asked as I opened the door.

"Yes."

"These are for you," he said, handing me the bouquet.

"Who are they from?"

"Read the card," he said, walking back to his van.

I smelled the cluster of gold chrysanthemums, near the top. The bouquet was filled with white, purple, gold and pink flowers. Closing the door, I reached for the tag. It read, "To: Vanessa Lewis. Happy 40th Birthday." I turned the tag over to see who it was from, but there was no name listed. I then took the flowers to the phone and dialed the florist's number on the card.

"Season All Flower Shop," a woman answered.

"Hello, my name is Vanessa Lewis. I just received flowers from your florist, and I want to know who sent them. No name was on the tag."

"Hold on, please, while I check." A minute passed. "Miss Lewis, your flowers were paid for in cash yesterday. We don't have a name of who sent them. I'm sorry I couldn't be of more help."

"Thank you," I said, hanging up the phone. "I wonder who sent these?" I asked aloud, finding a place for them on the glass end table between the sofa and loveseat. Admiring them, the thought occurred to me that Bryson sent them. He paid for them yesterday before he went to Florida on vacation with Helen and their family. It was his way of observing my birthday in his absence. It was also his way of staying together. I smiled at his craftiness. No one had ever sent me flowers before.

Herman arrived promptly at six p.m. in a navy blue suit, white shirt and tie. His hair was combed to the side. He looked very handsome.

"Are you ready, Miss Vanessa?" he asked as I opened the door.

"Yes. Let me grab my purse from upstairs." I ran up the stairs, then back down with my purse. "Where are we going?" I asked as I went to the door.

"Dante's Down The Hatch by Lenox Square Mall. Have you ever been there?"

"No. What kind of food do they serve?"

"Fondue."

"What's fondue?"

"Strips of meat cooked in hot oil, then dipped in a sauce."

"That sounds good! I've never had fondue before."

"It's delicious! I think you will like it."

"Let's get this show on the road," I said, closing the doors. The clouds began to blacken as we reached the car. "Herman, I need to get my umbrella before we leave. It's sure to rain soon."

"Don't worry," he replied opening my door, "I have a large umbrella in the trunk. If it rains, it will give us an excellent opportunity to get close. Hey, that's not such a bad idea. I think I'll pray for rain."

"It doesn't have to rain for you to get close to me. All it takes is a little nerve."

"Well, I'll pray for rain and nerves," he said, closing my door. He then went to the trunk of the car. "This is for you," he said, handing me a hanger with plastic covering a garment as he entered the car. "Happy birthday!"

"What is it?"

"Take the plastic off and see."

Slowly, I pulled the plastic from the hanger. Underneath was an aqua blue dress that buttoned down the front with a white collar. "It's beautiful! Thank you, very much." I looked at the tag in the back. It was a size ten, my exact size. "How did you know my size?"

"There was a woman in the store your size. I asked her what size she wore. She said ten."

"Where are we going tomorrow?"

"To the Fox to see "Annie.""

"This dress will be perfect for tomorrow. I'll wear it then," I said, putting the plastic back on.

"Hear let me hang it up in the back," Herman volunteered, taking it from my hand. He hung it up, then we drove off.

Raindrops splashed against the windshield by the time we reached the I-20 West ramp. Strong gusts of wind accompanied the rain and lightning streaked through the sky.

"Do you think we should turn back? I asked, looking at the black clouds, seeing the lightning, and hearing the thunder.

"No. I prayed for rain. God just threw in the lightning and thunder as a bonus. I see it's working. You need me to comfort you," he said, reaching for my hand.

I held his hand the rest of the way to the restaurant. He was right. I felt both comforted and close to Herman as a result. God works in mysterious ways. This was one of them.

We reached the restaurant thirty minutes later. Herman dropped me off at the door before he parked the car. The rain was coming down harder than ever. Herman was soaking wet when he came inside. We held hands as the waitress took us to our reserved booth in the back. I ordered the chicken fondue with honey mustard, teriyaki and horseradish sauces. Herman ordered the steak fondue with the same sauces. We both ordered strawberry daiquiris.

The waiter came first with two pots of hot oil that had gas flames underneath. Next he brought our drinks, then our food. Salad and a small loaf of warm wheat bread and butter came with our meal. Herman and I enjoyed our drinks, ate and talked. My head felt woozy from drinking the daiquiri. The more it spun, the more I laughed at Herman. He looked awkward cooking his meat in the oil. Herman was all thumbs when it came to cooking. This time was no exception.

A white male singer sang popular white songs. We wanted to dance, but the beat was not right. I couldn't even tap my foot in sync to the beat. Herman rocked back-and-forth a little. Obviously, the white patrons present didn't have the same problem we had. They frequently got up to dance.

"Would you like to go dancing?" Herman asked when we finished eating.

"Yes. I would love it!"

He paid the $78 tab and left a $15 tip. We walked out talking, laughing and holding hands. The rain had stopped. We walked cuddled up to the car. Herman opened my door releasing his arm around my waist. I eased in my seat, smiling at him the whole time. He smiled back as he closed my door. He put the umbrella in the trunk before entering on his side.

"What club are we going to?" I asked as he started the car.

"There's a new club on South Hariston I want us to try. It's really nice. I'm sure you will like it," he said, reaching for my hand again.

I held his hand. "I see God answered both requests."

"Yes, He did."

"What else is on your agenda?" I asked, anxiously.

"You'll have to wait and see."

The night is young, I thought, as we drove to the club. How will this night end?

TWENTY-SIX

We reached Club Hariston's by 8:10 p.m.. A valet took the car when we drove into the parking area. Herman handed him the keys while another valet opened my door. Lionel Richie's song, "Three Times a Lady" played as we entered the club. Herman paid the admission, gripped my hand, and led me to the crowded dance floor. The people present appeared to be thirty-five and up, mostly mid-forties and early fifties. Finding a small area near the glass wall in the back, we danced. Herman tenderly held me close to him as our bodies swayed back-and-forth to the music. I closed my eyes, pretending I was in heaven because the way he held me made me felt as if I was.

When the song ended, he looked into my eyes and smiled. His eyes were filled with joy. He really cares for me, I thought, as I felt his love radiate. All I could think of was how I had put him off all this time. He was a good man who deserved the best. Tonight was his night. If he played his cards right, it never had to end.

Several fast jams played back-to-back. Herman was an excellent dancer. The longer the songs played, the harder and faster he moved. He swung his arms from side-to-side, shaking his head to the beat. We both laughed while we danced. Perspiration poured from us by the sixth song. We wiped the moisture from our heads onto our clothes and kept dancing.

"Would you like to take a break and have a drink to cool off?" Herman asked as the song ended.

"Yes, that would be nice."

"There's a vacant table next to the dance floor," he said, pointing to the right where twelve tables and booths were arrayed.

We left the dance floor holding hands. Herman led the way. He held my chair, then sat down in his chair across from me.

"What would you like to drink?" he asked, signaling a waiter to come to our table.

"A Long Island Iced Tea."

"How may I help you, sir?" The tall, slender waiter asked, leaning toward Herman.

"I would like one Long Island Iced Tea and one Scotch on the rocks."

"Would you care for anything to eat with your drinks?" the waiter asked, writing our drink order.

"No," we replied.

"That will be all," Herman instructed the waiter.

"Yes, sir," he said, walking off.

"This is a very nice place," I said, canvassing the club. "I really like the atmosphere." A large bar with more tables and booths were to our left. Outside steps led to a balcony where live jazz played according to a sign posted on the door. Behind me was the dance floor, another bar and more tables and booths. People were eating, drinking and having a good time without being rowdy. Men wearing expensive suits were standing near the small dance floor checking out the ladies.

"I heard it was a good club to come to. I see the service is excellent, too." Herman said as our waiter came back with our drinks.

"Long Island Iced Tea for Madame. And a Scotch on the rocks for you, sir," he said, placing our drinks before us, respectively. "That will be ten dollars, sir."

Herman pulled out his wallet and gave the waiter fifteen dollars. "Thank you."

"Thank you, sir," the waiter said, nodding his head before leaving.

"This Long Island Iced Tea is superb!" I exclaimed, tasting my drink. "How's your drink?"

"They use quality Scotch," he replied, sipping his drink.

"Where are you going for the feast this year?" I asked, trying to start small talk.

"Do you remember reading in the church's newspaper about the single's feast at Lake Tahoe?"

"Yes. Do you plan to go there?"

"Yes, and I want you to go, too."

"I have plans to go to Myrtle Beach."

"Would you go to Lake Tahoe if I paid your way?"

"How much does it cost?"

"One thousand thirty-six dollars, not including airfare."

"That's too much money! Why don't you come to Myrtle Beach? You can hang out with Carlos and me."

"The money is no problem if you want to go. I think it would be great for both of us," he said, sipping on his drink.

I sipped on mine as well. "Herman, thanks for the offer, but I'm going to Myrtle Beach. I have my hotel reservations, and travel plans set to go. Maybe, next year I can plan to go, if I'm still single."

"You can take your creature. He won't be a problem."

I laughed at Herman who always called children creatures. "Carlos is not the reason I'm turning down your offer."

"What is?"

"I'm independent. If I can't afford to pay my own way, then I won't go."

"You're some kind of lady," he said, smiling and finishing his drink.

"I hope you still think so after I finish this drink," I said, sipping the last of it. "It really has a kick."

"Are you up to dancing again?"

"Sure. I hope I can keep my balance after drinking that drink though."

"Don't worry. If you fall, I'll pick you up. We'll pretend it's a new dance step. Come on, let's go boogie down," he said, standing up reaching for my hand.

"Okay. You're sure, you'll catch me?"

"Trust me," he said, taking my hand, leading me to the dance floor.

Herman found a spot in the center of the floor where we danced our hearts out. The Long Island Iced Tea had a good buzz going, but it didn't hinder me from dancing. The DJ got down with one oldie after the next. Popular music is all right at times, but nothing beats the music of the seventies and eighties to me.

Herman and I swayed to the music. His steps mimicked mine. Our only problem was avoiding big butts carried away by the music. One time, Herman fell on the floor when a "Bertha Butt" hit him at an angle. I tried not to laugh, but I couldn't prevent it, especially when Herman started laughing, too.

"Are you all right?" I asked between laughs.

"I'm fine. I'll feel better in a more serene setting. That lady has some butt," he said, wiping himself off. "It's almost a lethal weapon."

"Let's go to the balcony and listen to the live jazz."

"That's a good idea before I get hurt on this dance floor."

We squirmed through the dancers to get to the steps leading to the balcony across the room. The steps led us to a man in his sixties, wearing a black tuxedo, playing jazz on a keyboard. His fingers glided across the keys while he sang, mesmerizing the crowd. "Would you like to sit here?" I asked Herman, standing next to an empty table a few feet away from the performer.

"Sure. Let me help you with your chair," he said, assisting me. "Would you like another drink?" he asked after he finished.

"No, but I see some water in the corner. I would love a glass of water."

"I'll go get you a glass before I sit down."

"Thank you." A waitress came to our table when he returned.

"Would you care for anything to eat or drink?" she asked, standing over Herman.

"Do you want something to eat?" Herman asked me, handing me my glass of water.

"No."

"I would like a Scotch on the rocks." The waitress took his order then went to another table. She returned a few minutes later.

"Here's your drink, sir. Will there be anything else?"

"No, thank you," Herman said, handing her eight dollars. She took the money, then went to the next table with her tray of drinks.

"I'm glad we came up here," I said, rocking to the music. "It's good to get away from the crowd."

"Yes, this is a pleasant change. At least, up here, I don't have to worry about being butted."

We both laughed. Herman drank while we listened to the music. He leaned back and smiled as the old man played another song.

"Are you enjoying yourself?" Herman asked, smiling at me.

"Yes, I am. Thank you for a wonderful evening!"

"My pleasure. You know, there is more in store tomorrow?"

"Yes. And I know it will be just as entertaining as tonight."

"Do you think you will remarry?" Herman asked, finishing his drink.

"Yes. I plan to marry the man who gives me my sign. I will have two daughters by him."

"Don't you think you're too old to have more children? It's dangerous for a woman your age."

"With God, all things are possible. I won't be single long. Hopefully, I'll get married and have my daughters soon. Don't you remember Abraham and Sarah who were one hundred and ninety years old when Isaac was born? If God can bless Sarah's womb at ninety, surely, He can bless mine at forty."

"You're some lady, Miss Vanessa. You know what you want out of life."

"Do you want more children?"

"I haven't thought about having more children. If I remarry and my wife wants more children, then I'll have more children," he said, turning his head to the performer. "I like his style. He's really good."

I listened to the music as well. We spent the next forty-five minutes on the balcony, talking and enjoying the entertainment. By that time, we decided it was time to retire. We didn't want to be tired tomorrow.

"Did you like the flowers?" Herman asked as we pulled from the parking lot.

"Yes, they were lovely. But I didn't know who sent them."

"I stopped by the florist yesterday on my way home. I wanted to surprise you."

"Well, you succeeded. No one has ever sent me flowers before," I said, turning looking back at the road, wrapped up in thought. Here I am giving Bryson credit for what Herman did. So that meant, Bryson didn't do anything for my birthday. He probably didn't even think about me. On the other hand,

Herman has gone over and beyond to make my birthday special. I'm glad Bryson's out of my life. He's only blocking me from having a fulfilling relationship.

The rest of the way home I continued to think how special Herman was in comparison to Bryson. This was the best birthday I had ever experienced. And I owed it all to Herman, a kind, thoughtful and caring friend. Herman interrupted my train of thought as he broke the silence.

"I talked to my son Herman last night. He mentioned our shopping trip. He said he now has two mommies."

"He called me 'mommie'?"

"Yes. He thinks of you as a mommie. I told him not to get ahead of me. You're not his mommie, yet," he said, looking at me, taking his eyes off the road.

"That's the highest compliment a child can give a woman is to call her mommie."

"I think so too. You've stolen both our hearts," he said, pulling into my driveway.

Herman opened my door and retrieved my dress from the back after he parked. We walked to the door holding hands "Would you like to come inside?" I asked, unlocking the door.

"Yes. I would."

When we got inside, I took the dress and laid it on the sofa. Herman remained standing three feet from the opened door. "Would you like to sit down?" I asked, standing in front of him.

"No, I won't stay long."

While I looked into his eyes, Viva spoke to me. "Girlfriend, you need to find out how he kisses! See if he can make the fireworks start. See if he can make us feel like Big Daddy did before he went crazy." Before I could stop her, Viva kissed Herman with everything in us. He held me, kissing me passionately. His hand glided passed my breast, kissing me intensely.

"Wow!" Herman exclaimed when the kiss was over. "That was some kiss. Are the creatures home?"

"No. They're with their dad."

"Do you want to go upstairs, or go to my house for some wine?"

I pretended I didn't hear the first question which completely turned me off. Who does he think I am? Does he think he can wine and dine me then take me to bed? I know, I haven't been abstaining, but I'm not an easy lay either. "It's late," I said, answering the second question. "I'm ready to call it a night. We have a big day planned tomorrow."

"Okay," he said and headed for the opened door. "I'll be here at one o'clock tomorrow."

"Goodnight, Herman. I'll see you then. Drive safely," I said, closing the door. He left and I went upstairs.

"Girlfriend, that kiss wasn't shit!" Viva responded as I walked up the steps. "Can't nobody kiss us like Big Daddy. You're out of your mind if you let him go. So what if he lost his temper! Herman could never get a fire started with us."

"Shut up, bitch! Herman's a good man. Bryson is married, and I don't have any business kissing him anyway!"

As I finished my last words, the phone rang. I knew, it wasn't Herman because he was heading home. Maybe it was Raymond; he couldn't stand us not talking any longer. I felt the same way. I wanted to talk to him badly, but I wanted him to call me. I enjoyed my evening with Herman, but when it was over in the back of mind, I thought of Raymond. I missed him.

"Hello," I said, running to pick up the phone on the first ring.

"Why are you breathing hard? What are you doing?" Bryson asked irately.

"Why are you questioning me? Aren't you vacationing with your wife in Florida?"

"Is Herman there?"

"That's none of your business!"

"I'm in Florida and my woman is going out with another man. That makes it my business!" Bryson yelled.

"You're with your woman in Florida."

"What happened tonight, Van? Don't lie to me. I ain't no fool. Tell me what happened!"

"None of your business. We're through Bryson!" I yelled back.

"Don't get smart with me! What happened?"

"I kissed him."

"Is that all? I want you to know I cried all the way to South Carolina to pick up my mother, and all the way to Florida. Helen kept asking me what was wrong? Van, I love you! I can't stand being without you. Can we talk Monday when I get back?"

A million thoughts went through my mind. I wanted to say no, because I didn't trust Bryson anymore. But Viva said, "Yes, we can talk Monday."

He sighed in relief. "Good. You don't know how much this means to me. I must go now. I'm on my cell phone in the van. I love you. Good-bye."

"Good-bye, Bryson," I said, hanging up the phone.

"Viva! Why did you say yes?" I screamed, removing my hand from the receiver.

"Calm down, girlfriend. Viva knows what's best for us. You won't be sorry. Besides, your little David is no longer around to slay your Goliath. Or do you expect Prince Charming to rescue you this time?"

I threw myself on my bed and cried out. "Jesus! Please deliver me from my sinful flesh. Remove both Viva and Bryson from my life. You said in 1 John 5:14&15, *`Now this is the confidence that we have in You, that if we ask anything according to Your Will, You hear us. And if we know that You hear us, whatever we ask, we know that we have the petitions that we have asked of You.'* I need Your help Jesus. I need Your help!"

TWENTY-SEVEN

Herman arrived early to pick me up. He was all smiles when I opened the door, dressed in an aqua-blue and white leisure suit. I was determined not to let his suggestion last night spoil my mood today, even though it was in the back of my mind. Wearing the dress he bought me for my birthday, I waited to see his reaction.

"Wow! You look great!" he said as I opened the door.

"Thank you. It's a perfect fit," I said, turning in a circle and modeling for him.

"I'll say! Are you ready?"

"Yes," I said, closing the door.

"I have a card in the car," Herman said, walking down the steps.

When I held the card as I sat in my seat, I thought of my sign. Maybe, Herman put fifty dollars in it! If he did, then he was my man. The timing was ideal with both Bryson and Raymond out of my life. Was this God's plan? I thought as I opened the card. I closed my eyes and took a deep breath. To my disappointment, the card was empty.

"This is a very nice card. Thank you, again, for making this birthday special," I said, trying not to sound disappointed.

He smiled as he started the car. "You're a special lady. I wanted to buy you a necklace, but I didn't know your taste."

"You have excellent taste. I'm sure whatever you selected would have been fine."

"I hope you enjoy "Annie"," he said, pulling out of the driveway. It's one of my favorite plays." We drove to the Fox Theater downtown, parked the car, bought popcorn and sodas and found our seats. During the performance, Herman placed his arm around me. He told me how glad he was to have me with him and hoped I liked the play. I told him, I felt as if I was watching "Annie" for the first time since I had forgotten most of it. For some reason, after the play ended, I wanted to go see my parents.

I had talked about my parents numerous times to Herman before. They lived between downtown and my house. We took the Maynard Terrance exit off I-20 East to reach them. Since they didn't know we were coming, our arrival was a surprise. I had talked to Mama about Herman, and now she would get a chance to meet him.

Mama came to the door as we pulled into the driveway and watched us get out of the car. When she saw me, she came outside. Herman and I slowly approached her.

"Nessa, I didn't know who was riding in that nice car," she said, giving me a hug.

"Mama, this is Herman. You remember me telling you about him?" I asked, hugging her back.

"Hi, Herman," she said, holding out her hand. "It's nice to meet you. Y'all c'mon inside. Y'all really look good together. Let me get your dad. He's inside watching the game."

"It's a pleasure to meet you, Mrs. Grant," Herman finally said when Mama stopped talking. "I've heard good things about you."

"You young folks don't have time to talk about me! I'm sure you have more important things to talk about."

"Herman and I talk about everything, including you and Dad."

"C'mon inside," Mama said, leading the way to the steps. Her short legs outpaced us as we followed her inside. "I can't wait for your dad to see you and Herman. Y'all make a nice-looking couple. Xavier!" Mama shouted as we entered the house, "Nessa's here with her friend Herman!" Then she turned to us. "He's in the den. Y'all go on inside. He's not going to budge from that game until it's over." Mama led the way to the den. Dad was sitting on the purple and green flowered loveseat near the door. The top of his head was bald with gray hair surrounding the bald area. He looked like a harmless, aging man who wouldn't hurt a fly. He reminded me of Big Mama, my great-grandmother, who raised him.

"Dad, this is Herman Lowe, a good friend of mine," I said as we entered the den.

"It's a pleasure to meet you, sir," Herman said, shaking Dad's hand.

"Same here," Dad said, looking back at the game.

"Nessa, why don't you and Herman sit on the sofa. Can I get you anything to drink?" Mama asked, standing behind us.

"No, thank you," we replied.

"What about something to eat?"

"No, thank you," we both replied again.

"We plan to eat after we leave," Herman explained.

"Mama, Herman bought me this dress for my birthday."

"Oh, that's real nice. It looks good on you, too."

"He had flowers sent to the house, and he took me out to eat and dancing yesterday. Today, he took me to see "Annie" at the Fox, and we're going out to eat again. Plus, he bought me a card."

"My, my, my, he really spent a lot of money on you! Y'all must be serious?"

"Vanessa says she only thinks of me as a friend, Mrs. Grant. I'm trying to persuade her to change her mind and think of me in a more serious manner," Herman replied as he sat on the sofa.

"Nessa, can be down-right bullheaded at times. But she needs to wake up and smell the coffee while it's still percolating. Don't you agree Xavier?"

"Uh? Betty, you know, I'm watching the game. I ain't listening to your conversation."

"Herman, what do you do?" Mama asked.

"I work with an investment firm to help build financial wealth for my clients."

"That sounds like a good job," Dad replied, glancing away from the TV. "Vanessa, you do need to wake up before it's too late. Once the feeling is gone, you may never find it again."

Herman, Mama and I laughed at Dad's sudden interest in Herman. I guess a well-off, prospective son-in-law was enough to get Dad's attention momentarily.

"So, how much do you make a year, Herman?" Dad asked, inquisitively.

"Over fifty thousand dollars, plus income from my investments, sir."

Dad flipped the TV off and walked over to his small liquor table next to the TV. "Can I fix you a drink, Herman?" he asked, fixing himself one.

"No, thank you, sir."

"Vanessa, let me get this straight," Dad said, tasting his whiskey and cola on ice. "This man has taken you out twice this weekend, bought you a dress, makes good money, sent you flowers and you think of him as a friend?"

"Yes."

"Why?" Dad asked.

"Because I was a friend to his ex-wife."

Dad almost choked on my words. "Are you divorced, Herman?"

"Yes, sir. For three years."

"Vanessa, either this drink is getting to my head where I can't think clearly, or you're a damn fool for not trying to hold on to a man like Herman!" Dad shouted.

"Daddy, Herman is a very nice man. I made a mistake once when I married Carl, twenty-one years ago. I don't want to make another mistake. If Herman gives me my sign, then I'll know he's the right man for me."

"Herman obviously cares for you. He gives you his money and time. What more do you need for a sign? A talking ven-tril-o-quist," Dad muttered, "to say, here I am?"

"No, Dad, that's not my sign."

"I agree with you, Mr. Grant. I think her sign idea is crazy."

"I don't care what anybody thinks, my sign is important to me. I have to be absolutely sure I have the right man."

Dad fixed himself another drink. "Here's to your sign," he said, lifting up his glass. "I hope Herman is the right man."

"Thanks, Mr. Grant. I need all the help I can get."

"Nessa, your sign is the most foolish thing I've ever heard of! Herman seems like a good man. Forget your sign. A bird in the hand is better than a thousand flying around," Mama added.

"It's easier to find a good bird than it is to find the right man," I said, looking at my watch. "Mom, Dad, it's time for us to go. Come on, Herman," I said, standing up.

"Okay, we'll leave if you're ready to go," Herman said, standing up too.

"It was nice meeting you," Mama said, walking us to the door.

"Come back, Herman," Dad said as we were leaving. "You're welcome anytime."

"Thank you, sir. It would be my pleasure," Herman said, walking out the door.

We went to the Sizzler's to eat after leaving Mom and Dad. While we ate, he told me of his plans to get a Ph.D. in theology via a home study course. He also planned to buy a bigger house soon, to accommodate the new wife he hoped to marry within the next two years. By then, his real estate business would be up and running, bringing in more money than he'd know what to do with. I wished him well in his studies and business. I told him I would keep him in my prayers.

On the way home, I thought of how wonderful it would be to Mrs. Lowe. I knew Herman would shower me with countless gifts. My closet would be filled with expensive clothes. We'd eat out, go dancing, and have fun. Life would be a bowl of pitted cherries—sweet, through and through. But then I thought about Shirley. She must have thought the same thing. Her dream of living a life of luxury was shattered by actually living near poverty. I didn't want to fall into the same trap she did. Remembering conversations with Shirley made all of Herman's money and future plans seem like pipe dreams.

"What happened between you and Shirley?" I asked as we neared my subdivision.

"Shirley made life difficult for me. I had to claim bankruptcy once when I had to pay a $20,000 hospital bill."

"Don't you sell insurance? Why didn't you have any coverage?"

"Her hospital bill was over one hundred thousand dollars. My insurance paid eighty percent. I was responsible for paying the balance. The hospital wanted their money within ninety days or would start collection procedures. Since I didn't have the money, I filed bankruptcy."

"Oh. What else happened?"

"Every month she had three to five hundred dollars in phone bills from calling her mother four or five times a day, every day, in Arizona. I was the only one working which made paying all the other bills economically challenging. Several times I went to the ministers to see if they could talk some sense into her."

"Did counseling help?"

"No. It only made her angry. Once she hit me so hard in my chest, I had to go to the doctor. She also constantly spent money we didn't have buying the creatures clothes they didn't need."

"Why was she so unhappy? Why did she keep leaving you?"

"I never could get her to tell me why. I asked her those very same questions. I was good to Shirley. I don't know why she was unhappy."

Shirley hadn't told me about the phone bills or the bankruptcy. No wonder she didn't have but one color of nail polish. From what Herman just revealed, she was lucky to have a roof over her head. Here I was thinking he was a villain, when in actuality he was a saint. His marriage was a horrendous trial that I'm sure he was glad to get out of.

Herman pulled into my driveway, but kept the motor running. He opened his door, then came to my side and walked me to the door without attempting to kiss me goodnight.

"Good evening, Miss Vanessa," he said as I opened my door.

"Good evening, Herman. And thanks again for giving me a wonderful birthday. I'll take you out on your birthday in October."

"That won't be necessary."

"I know. It's not something I have to do. But it's something I want to do. Don't make any other plans. October 21 is our day."

I thought about what you said last night. I think I will go to Myrtle Beach for the feast. We can go in my car. Your creature can come, too," he offered.

"That sounds great. I'm glad you changed your mind about Lake Tahoe."

"I'm glad you're glad."

I closed the door as he walked down the steps. His car pulled out of the driveway as I kicked off my shoes. Immediately, I went to my phone to see if Raymond had called. For some reason, I kept thinking of him while I was with Herman. The stutter tone on my phone signaled someone had called. I dialed my voice mail to retrieve the messages. The first caller hung up without leaving a message. The second caller was Bryson. He loved me. He wasn't having fun on his vacation because he kept thinking of me. He'd call me back later.

I went upstairs and undressed. As I took off my clothes, the excitement of the weekend weaned. In my mind, I kept thinking of negative things that had transpired in the past two days. Herman didn't believe I should get pregnant again at my age. To me, he showed a lack of faith. His loose spending was a potential problem. It was okay while we dated, but if we were married, I would object to how, he currently managed his money. His drinking was excessive which might be a problem later. I also kept thinking about Shirley's comments concerning Herman's inhospitable side. If Shirley could hit him and send him to the doctor, then Herman was too fragile. I needed a real man, not one I could walk over or beat up. On the other hand, I didn't want a man who would walk over or beat me up either. My absence of feelings for Herman bothered me causing my high from the weekend to hit rock bottom. Herman, you're a wonderful man but...are you the right man for me? I thought as I lay down on the bed. Before I closed my eyes, I prayed.

Dear Lord,
I have three men who are interested in me. Please identify the one You have chosen. Right now, I'm confused, and I know You're not the author of confusion. I ask this in Jesus name. Amen.

As I slept, God answered my prayer. First, He took me down a dark, deserted street where abandoned cars were parked. At the end of the street was a large yellow and black sign that read, "DEAD END". He said, "This is Bryson." Next, He took me to a race track with one car running around the track. Red flags kept going up in the air as whistles blew. "This is Herman." Last, I saw a traffic light with the green light on. "This is Raymond," He said as the green light came on.

TWENTY-EIGHT

I dreamed about God's revelation. Raymond was my man, my green light. God sent me a light to clear up the confusion in my life. It all made sense now. Raymond was young. I was forty, wanting more children. At my age, my main concern was living long enough to rear them. With Raymond being younger, his chances of outliving me were better. If my next husband was older than me, his chances would drastically decrease. I kept thinking of how Samuel chose David to be king of Israel. God didn't choose the oldest, or the biggest, but the youngest of Jesse's sons. I also remembered I Samuel 16:7, *"But the Lord said to Samuel. `Do not look at the appearance or at his physical stature, because I have refused him (Eliab, Jesse's oldest son). For the Lord does not see as man sees; for man looks at the outward appearance, but the Lord looks at the heart.'"*

My alarm clock jerked me from my sleep. My next task was reuniting with Raymond. I hoped he still wanted me. Tonight at work, I'd see.

Thoughts ran through my mind of what to say to Raymond. I prayed as I dressed that God would intercede. I knew prayer always worked. My confidence soared as time passed.

At 3:30 a.m. when the worked slowed down, I called Raymond and asked if he could take a break because I wanted to talk. He said he needed to wrap a few things up, but would be able to meet me in ten minutes.

I waited outside the lab by the elevators, our meeting place. Raymond ambled down the hallway, near the snack bar.

"How are you?" he asked as he approached me with a blank expression on his face.

"Fine. I'm glad you could take a break," I said as the elevator doors opened. We both stepped on, and Raymond pressed number two. "I kept hoping you'd call me this weekend," I said as the elevator closed.

"I didn't have a reason to call you. I was giving you all the time you needed to deal with your Goliath."

"My Goliath is dead. That's what I want to discuss," I said as the elevator doors opened. We exited and walked to the cafeteria. Our favorite booth was empty so we automatically walked to it and sat down. Raymond sat across from me with his hands clasped on top of the table, waiting for me to begin. "I want you to know I've been thinking about you every day since we broke up. Even after Herman took me out, I thought of you."

"Yeah, right."

"No, it's true. When I came home, I hoped you'd called. I wanted to talk to you, and tell you I've missed you this past week."

"Vanessa, cut the bull out and get to the point."

"The point is, I want us to get back together. You're the man for me. God revealed it to me in a dream before I came to work tonight."

"Sure He did," Raymond muttered.

"Let me finish. I prayed concerning you, Herman, and Bryson. He showed me Bryson was a dead end; Herman was red flags; and you were a green light."

"How did God show you that?"

"In my dream, believe me. I'm telling you the truth. Will you take me back?"

"My feelings for you haven't changed. I'd love for us to be together. Are you sure Bryson and Herman are out of the picture?"

"Yes. You are my green light and my little David."

He smiled. "There you go again. What am I going to do with you?"

"Love me for starters. I'm sure you'll come up with something else."

"So does this mean I'm still coming over for dinner Friday?" he asked, unfolding his hands and grabbing mine.

"Yes. And it also means our date for the thirtieth is still on. This time we will last."

"How can you be so sure?"

"Trust me. I know what I'm talking about."

"By the way, happy birthday."

"Thank you. You are my birthday present. You are hand picked by God and sent special delivery."

He laughed. "Sometimes I think you're crazy."

"You might be right, but I know what I'm talking about. Forty truly is a number for being delivered. I'm a witness to that."

"What are you talking about?"

"Never mind. If I try to explain it, you might send me up to the psyche ward."

"Sometimes, I think that's where you belong."

"I'm not crazy. I'm just different. Last week, I looked your name up in the computer, Raymond Eugene Miller. I also know your age now. I admit. I was surprised when I found out."

He laughed. "Does my age bother you?"

"No, I've gotten over the shock. As a matter of fact, everything makes sense now. Your age is a plus not a minus. By the way, how tall are you, five-six?"

"No, five-eight. Your little David just grew two inches. I need to get back," he said, looking at his watch. We laughed as we slid from the booth. "I'll walk you to your car at seven-thirty," Raymond announced as we stood up.

Raymond called me when he returned to his office. He told me how good he felt about getting back together. It seemed as if a heavy weight had been taken off his shoulders. I told him I was glad, too. We looked forward to Friday when we could be alone outside of Grady Hospital's campus.

Raymond returned at 7:26. It felt like old times seeing him waiting on me. He carried my bag as we talked on the way to the car.

"This feels right," I proclaimed as we reached my car.

"It sure does. I missed our walks more than I realized."

"I missed you more than you'll ever know."

He smiled showing most of his teeth. "I'll call you later today," he said as we reached my car.

"Okay," I said, unlocking my door, getting inside. Raymond walked off as I started my car.

I smiled all the way home. I was happy Raymond and I were back together. This time I hoped it would never end. He was my green light. Surely, that meant he was my man forever. The phone rang as soon as I got home. I ran to answer it hoping it was Raymond. "Hello," I answered, excitedly.

"Oh, I'm glad you're eager to hear from me," Bryson responded.

"I thought you were Raymond. We got back together last night."

"What do you see in him? He's not your type."

"Yes, he is. He's exactly what I need."

"I'm what you need. I can't believe you're running around with different men while I'm gone."

"Believe it! I'm having the time of my life. As a matter of fact, Raymond's coming over for dinner, Friday. And we're going out next Friday."

"Can't you hold off until I get back and we talk?"

"Is that what you really want me to do?"

"Yes. Tell me something. How can you love me and be with him?"

I couldn't answer that question. But I did have a question of my own. "How can you love me and be with Helen?"

"I told you Helen got me out of a jam. I owe her. Love has nothing to do with it. I love you."

"Bryson, I'm tired. I'll talk to you next Monday."

"Are you still going to keep your dates with Raymond?"

Suddenly, I felt remorseful. Was I doing the right thing? Am I moving too fast? Should I wait until Bryson returns? "Let me think about it," I replied.

"Van, please wait until I come home before you do anything. Remember I love you."

"Good-bye Bryson. I love you, too." I laid the phone down and went to bed.

Bryson and Raymond entered my dreams while I slept. God's revelations kept churning in my head. Bryson was a dead end. Raymond was a green light. Why should I be involved with Bryson when God has already revealed to me where he stands? I need to put Bryson behind me and go forward with Raymond. Monday, when I talk to Bryson, I will end the relationship. Although I keep telling him it's over, he refuses to let me go. I can't ignore God's revelation. Bryson's a dead end—with no opportunity for marriage. He's already tied up in his third marriage. Even if he leaves Helen and we get together, what would be my reward? A cheating husband who does not honor his vows. With Bryson, I lose no matter what happens. God is right. I'll just be another abandoned car or wife on Bryson's dead end street of life.

The boys came back home that evening because school started in a few days. They were full of energy and in good spirits. The summer apart did us good. Now it was time to settle down to our normal routine. Tomorrow, I'd take them back-to-school shopping. Today, we caught up on the summer's activities.

They laughed when I told them I had dumped Bryson. They laughed even harder when I told them about Raymond and his age. Little Carl told me, as long as I was happy, it didn't matter who I was with. Carlos wanted to meet Raymond first, and of course, he wanted to know what kind of car he drove. I told him, I didn't know. I never saw Raymond's car. Besides, I can't judge a man by the car he drives, but by the content of his heart and mind, his character. I stressed to Carlos what's inside of a man is more relevant than what he owns. Carlos understood, but he had his own criteria for judging.

On Friday, Carl picked the boys up before Raymond arrived. They were disappointed because they wanted to see him and what he drove. I reassured them they would have another opportunity to meet Raymond. He would be around for a long time.

Raymond arrived thirty minutes later. He drove up in an old, beat up Mercury Marquis. It had to be at least twenty years old. I watched him as he got out of his car, wearing his blue uniform, smiling as he came to the door. "Did you have a hard time finding me?" I asked as I opened the door.

"No. You gave excellent directions. I didn't have any problems."

"Dinner is ready, if you're ready to eat?"

"Sure. Let me wash my hands first. Where's your bathroom?"

"Up the steps. The first door on the right. I'll fix our plates while you wash your hands." I went to the kitchen and dished out baked cornish hens, wild rice, broccoli, tossed salad, rolls and tea. For dessert, we had carrot cake.

I was still fixing the plates when Raymond came into the kitchen. In a previous conversation, he had told me he had a healthy appetite, so I piled food on his plate.

"Can I help you do anything?" he asked, standing behind me.

"You can grab the mats from the top of the refrigerator and put them on the table."

He did as I instructed. I sat the plates on the mats. He poured the tea while I put the salad in bowls. I placed the rolls, butter, napkins and salad dressings on the table before I sat down. Raymond pulled my chair back and pushed it forward as I sat down. He blessed the food, then we ate.

When he cleaned his plate, I asked if he wanted more. He had had enough. I finished my food, then cut the carrot cake. We moved to the living room after eating the cake. I sat on the sofa; he sat on the loveseat. We talked and laughed for two hours. When it was time for Raymond to leave, he raised up one finger and said, "I'm not going to kiss you tonight."

"Why not?" I asked, as if he had read my mind.

"I'm not ready," he said, standing up walking to the door.

"You're not ready," I laughed. "When will you be ready?"

"I don't know."

"Okay, we won't kiss until you're ready." I never met a man before who wasn't ready to kiss. There's a first time for everything. And this was definitely a first. We said our good-byes and he left.

While I was cleaning up the kitchen, reminiscing over the evening, the phone rang. "Hello?"

"Miss Vanessa, how are you doing?" Herman asked.

"Fine."

"I was wondering if you had any plans for after church, tomorrow?"

Raymond and I had planned to go to my church tomorrow. I hadn't talked to Herman since God revealed he was red flags. "Herman, I'm seeing someone else. I prayed to God Sunday evening after you left concerning you and this other person. I was confused, but God showed me where each of you stood with me. I can't refute God's answer. You are red flags and he is a green light."

"I didn't know you were seeing someone else."

"Actually, I wasn't. We started talking in July then we broke up. My friend is coming to church with me tomorrow."

"I had things planned for you and your creatures," he said, indignantly. "But now I have to cancel them."

"Thanks for thinking of me and my sons. They really like you."

"Good-bye, Miss Vanessa. There is no further need to converse."

"Okay, Herman. Good-bye." I yanked the phone from my ears as he slammed it down on his end. God was right about Herman. God knew this side of Herman that was carefully concealed from me. I didn't know he had a temper, but God knew. I thanked God, I didn't have to rely on my own limited understanding.

TWENTY-NINE

Saturday afternoon, Raymond arrived wearing a gray suit, white shirt and a pink, gray, and lavender tie. He carried a bouquet of flowers that matched his clothes. He ran up the steps as I watched from the opened door.

"These are for you," he said, handing me the flowers.

"Thank you," I said, sniffing the whole bouquet. I replaced Herman's flowers for Raymond's. I was elated receiving two bouquets of flowers, one week apart, by two different men. This time, however, I hoped to keep the man. "You look very handsome in your suit. This is the first time I haven't seen you in your uniform."

Raymond smiled to the point of blushing. "Thank you. I like your dress. It's very becoming."

I had on a red dress that stopped above my knees. It had a wide V-neck collar that laid on my shoulders. The red belt made my waist small and my hips and bust stand out. "Let me take a picture of us holding the flowers," I said, getting my camera from my purse. "I'll take you first by the table." I took Raymond's picture in the kitchen. "Here take mine by the door," I instructed, handing Raymond the camera. He handed me the flowers. "Just press the green button on top. I'm ready when you are." Raymond took my picture then I placed the flowers back on the end table.

When we arrived at church, Herman was sitting near the back. Raymond and I sat in the front. Eyes rolled our way as we sat down. My congregation had never seen me with anyone but Carl, during his infrequent trips to church. Most of my congregation knew I was divorced. I think the ones who didn't stared the hardest. I smiled, opened my hymnal and sang to the Lord. Raymond joined in, singing most of the lyrics. We both sang out of tune, but that didn't stop us from worshipping God with our voices.

After the service, a few members came up to meet Raymond. They welcomed him to our church. We talked briefly with other members before we left. It was a good service. The fact that Raymond was with me made it special.

For dinner, we ate at Red Lobster. I ordered grilled salmon. Raymond ordered shrimp. We talked while we waited for our food.

"Have you told your kids about me yet?" I asked, squeezing the lemon in my tea.

"Not yet. I feel it's too soon. You must remember, they have never seen me with a woman. They were one and three years old when I divorced their mother. I don't want to act too hastily. I want to be sure about us first," he said, picking up his tea to drink.

"You're my green light. What else do you need?"

"More time to make sure it doesn't turn yellow or red."

"My sons know about you. Maybe, they'll get a chance to meet you Friday. Have you decided where we're going?"

"'Ray's on the River.'"

"That's a nice place. Great atmosphere. You can watch the Chattahoochee River while you eat."

"Speaking of eating, when is our waiter coming with our food?" he asked with a chagrined expression.

"He'll be here soon. The restaurant is crowded. Besides, the longer we wait, the more time we'll have together. I'm sure, as soon as we leave, you'll have to go home and get some sleep."

"That's right. I'm feeling tired already."

"Cheer up! Here's our waiter."

"Good, I'm starved!"

The waiter placed our food on the table. Raymond said the blessing, then we ate. "What did you think of my church?" I asked as we finished eating.

"It was okay. You know, I'm an old Baptist from Dublin, Georgia. Our services are different. I'm used to fire and brimstone sermons. In my church, the men sit on one side and the ladies sit on the other. We also sing our hymns without music. I'm used to that 'old time religion,' some people might say."

"Well, that 'old time religion' has made an upright man out of you. I'd love to visit your church."

"You'll get your chance. My church meets every second Sunday. If you're finished, we'll leave," he stated, looking at his watch. "I really must get some sleep."

Raymond signaled for the waiter to bring our check. During the drive home, Raymond talked more about Dublin. He planned to live there once he got his business up and going. Atlanta was only his temporary home until he could make enough money to live comfortably in the country. He asked me if I wouldn't mind living in Dublin, in a big house with lots of land and a lake on the property. I told him it sounded wonderful, but I would have to see Dublin first.

When we reached my house, Raymond walked me to my door but didn't come inside. We said our good-byes then he drove off. I spent the remainder of the evening writing "Uncaged." I thought about Raymond as I wrote. In my mind, I also tried to picture Dublin. I imagined a small country town with plenty of chickens and cows. As far as the eye could see were acres of corn growing in fields. There probably was only one store, one gas station, and one traffic light in the whole town. Surely, I was wrong. But what if I was right. I guess it wouldn't matter since I would be living in my big house on lots of land with the lake. I'd pretend I was someplace else, anyplace besides Dublin.

The remainder of the weekend passed quickly. The next thing I knew it was time to go back to work. I told Raymond about the meeting with Bryson, Monday morning. He didn't like it, but he understood. I assured him, it would be the last time I'd be with Bryson. I was only meeting him because Bryson requested it. The relationship with Bryson was over no matter what he had to say or what Viva thought.

Monday morning when I drove home, Bryson was parked at my mailbox. As I parked, he got out of his van. He looked forlorn. My eyes studied him as he approached me.

"I guess you know you ruined my vacation," he said, standing directly in front of me.

"You're giving me too much credit. I didn't ruin your vacation. You did. You didn't have to think about me while you were with your lovely wife, mother, and children," I responded, sarcastically. "I'm sure y'all had a barrel of fun."

"Let's go inside," he suggested.

"We can talk right here."

"What? Are you afraid you won't be able to control yourself or something?"

"No. I can control myself. But the question is, will you control yourself?" I demanded.

"Yes, I just want to talk."

We went inside. Bryson sat on the sofa. I sat on the loveseat and left the door open. He started talking as soon as his butt hit the cushion.

"While I was away, I had time to think about many things," he said, spreading his arms across the back of the sofa. "I didn't realize how much I love you until we broke up. It seems like all my life you're what I've been searching for. It scared me at first. I didn't know what to do. I realize now, I kept too much back from you. When we were together I made a lot of mistakes. My biggest ones were not telling you how much you mean to me and not spending enough time with you. My errors cost me the most precious thing on this earth—you," he said, leaning forward reaching for my hand. I folded my arms, preventing him from grabbing my hand. I didn't say anything because I wanted him to finish.

"Every since my sister died," he continued, putting his hand in his lap. "I stopped feeling for anyone, until you came in my life." He paused and looked me dead in my eyes. "I'll do whatever you want me to do, just don't leave me, Van! Don't walk out on me now," he pleaded.

I exhaled before I spoke. "Bryson, it's too late for us. What we had is over. I've moved on. You don't realize how much guilt I carry being with you. I feel guilty knowing I'm with another woman's husband. I'll feel guilty if you and Helen divorce because of me. No matter what happens, I'll feel guilty. The breakup is the best for both of us. You know I'm right, even if you won't admit it."

"Sometimes what is right is the wrong thing to do. It's right for us to be together," he said, moving to the loveseat.

I stood up. "Stay over there! Don't try to get something started!"

"What we have, started a long time ago," he said, trying to kiss me.

"Stop it, Bryson!" I yelled, going toward the door.

He pulled me back, making me fall on the loveseat. "You know you want me. You don't want our relationship to end," he said with his lips almost touching mine.

With everything in me, I pushed him off me. "Stop it, Bryson! Get out of my house!"

"Okay, okay, if that's what you really want. I'll leave," he said, walking to the door. "But remember one thing. You haven't seen the last of me yet. When you get tired of your young plaything, then you'll come running back into my arms. And I'll take you back because I'll always love you, and you'll always love me."

"I'm not coming back. It's over Bryson. Why can't you accept it!"

"It's never going to be over," he threatened, walking out the door.

I locked the door when he left. He drove off speeding from the cul-de-sac. I hoped that was the last time I'd see him, but my intuition told me differently.

That night at work, I told Raymond about the meeting. He had been concerned that we met at my house. He felt we should have met on neutral territory. I assured him we only talked, that Bryson was able to get everything off his chest. The meeting signaled the last of Bryson, even if he didn't want the relationship to end.

For the remainder of the week I was excited, anticipating my date with Raymond. When Friday finally arrived, I was overflowing with joy and could hardly wait for six o'clock to come. Raymond arrived wearing a dark lavender suit. His face beamed as he came to the door. Little Carl and Carlos came downstairs as I let Raymond inside. Little Carl laughed when he saw how short Raymond was. Little Carl at six-one towered over both of us. Carlos went to the door to inspect Raymond's car.

"Ha! This is your new man? He looks like a nerd, Mama. Come here, Carl, and see his car," Carlos said, laughing.

Carl went to the door and started laughing, too. "I thought, Daddy drove pluckers. Yours beats his."

"Mama, why don't you like men who have cheese in their pockets? Where do you find these broke men?" Carlos asked, laughing going up the steps.

"Raymond these are my two rude sons, Carl and Carlos."

"Hi guys," Raymond replied still bearing a smile.

"Hi guys," they both repeated, laughing. "He looks and sounds like Steve Urkle."

"Hey Raymond," Little Carl said, shaking Raymond's hand. "I don't know much about you, but you seem to make my mama happy. You're all right with me."

"No cheese. No shake," Carlos added.

"Thanks, Carl. Maybe, one day, I'll let you take my car for a spin to test it out, to see how it purrs like a kitten when you're behind the wheel."

"No thanks. I don't want to drive your car. I'd rather walk. What model is it?"

"An 81," Raymond answered, proudly. "Well, it was nice meeting you, Carl, even if I am a nerd who drives a plucker."

"Truth is truth," Little Carl said, going up the steps.

"Raymond, I hope my sons didn't hurt your feelings. I can't control what comes out of their mouths. They sometimes act like Bebe's kids. They take too much after their dad."

"They didn't hurt my feelings. Like Carl said, truth is truth. They spoke the truth. I don't have a problem with them telling the truth. Are you ready?"

"Let me tell them good-bye." I went upstairs and kissed them. I also told them how rude they were. I would deal with them later about it. When I went back downstairs, Raymond and I left.

"Would you prefer going in your car?" Raymond asked as I locked the door.

"No. I'm not ashamed to ride in your car. Besides, I can sit close to you since you don't have bucket seats."

"You do have a point," he said as we walked to his car. "I want to go to South Dekalb Mall first if you don't mind?"

"Why?"

"Because I want to buy you something special."

"What is it?" I asked, excited.

"It's a surprise. You have to wait and see." We reached South Dekalb Mall five minutes later. We went to every jewelry store in the mall. "What are you looking for?" I asked, not being able to take the suspense any longer.

"A chain with a key on it. It will signify that I have the key to your heart. I can't find it today, so I'll have to go somewhere else, another time. It's getting late. We need to head over to 'Ray's On The River.'"

No one had ever bought me a key necklace before, I thought, going back to the car. No one had ever wanted to have the key to my heart. Although we didn't get the necklace today, I hoped Raymond would be able to purchase it another day. He was different. I liked the difference more and more.

As we drove up to 'Ray's On The River's' valet parking, the attendant's eyes lit up. I'm sure he wasn't accustomed to parking cars as beat up as Raymond's. Raymond opened my door from the inside because the handle was jammed and only he knew how to jiggle it open. Once I was outside the car, he gave the attendant his keys, then we went inside.

We went to the waiting area where the hostess informed us we had a thirty minute wait. She directed us to the lounge in an adjacent area. We sat at a table across from the bar. I ordered pineapple juice. Raymond ordered water. At first we talked with our hands on the table. Then Raymond grabbed my hands and held on to them as if his life depended on them. I enjoyed his touch. I squeezed his hands as he held mine, not ever wanting to let go.

Forty minutes later, the hostess called Raymond's name. A tall thin host took us to our table at a window facing the river. We stared outside the window as the river's calm waters moved slowly. We looked at the river and talked while we waited on our dinners. The candles glowing on the tables gave the room a romantic atmosphere.

At the end of the meal, Raymond suggested we walk along the river. It seemed to beckon us to come. We noticed other couples strolling by the river, holding hands, talking, in their own world.

Raymond and I exited through the same side door we'd watch other couples use while we ate. A stone walkway led to the river. Four benches lined the river, spaced a few feet apart. We walked along the pathway until we reached the third bench.

"Would you like to sit down?" Raymond asked as we approached the bench.

"Sure," I said mesmerized by the water. The moonlight glistened on its surface. Crickets chirped near our feet. Occasionally, something stirred the water while we watched. Raymond put his arms around me, holding me tight. The clean, crisp air penetrated our nostrils, giving a euphoric sensation.

"The water has a way with me, sitting here with you. Looking at the river makes me feel like I'm in heaven. I never want this moment to end," Raymond said, holding me tighter.

"Me either," I chimed, feeling totally lost in his embrace; in his presence; in his love. What can top this? I asked myself as we continued to sit by the river. He doesn't need a piece of jewelry to possess my heart. He had it already, the moment he put his arms around me.

THIRTY

The next day, after church, Raymond and I went to Service Merchandise to buy the key necklace. The chain and key were gold with a small diamond heart in the center of the key. I wanted to wear it then, but he insisted on waiting for the 'right moment'. Now is the right moment, I thought. You already possess my heart. Are you waiting to control my mind as well?

After we left Service Merchandise, we made plans to bring his kids over to my house, the next Sunday. I told him we could bake cookies.

When we reached my house, I asked Raymond how long I had to wait for the 'right moment'? He said he didn't know, but to be patient, because he would know when.

I wondered if the 'right moment' included him kissing me. If it did, I was in for a double treat. My anticipation rose as he left. I began to imagine how his kiss would be. Would it be like anything I'd already experienced, or would it be different? I could hardly wait to find out.

Thursday and Friday nights were Raymond's nights off. He came over Thursday evening. I came up with the idea to go to Stone Mountain Park to see the laser show while we talked on the sofa. He agreed that was a good idea. When we arrived at the park, we were told after Labor Day, the show was only shown on the weekends. Not letting the bad news spoil our evening, we decided to park the car and walk along the scenic routes in the park. We parked near a big white building with benches and a cozy walkway nestled behind it. Raymond and I decided we'd rather talk first, walk later. We settled down on the bench closest to the building. Once seated, Raymond put his arms around me. I rested my head on his shoulders, admiring the scenery.

"This was a good idea you had," Raymond said, turning his gaze toward me.

"I know. It's good there wasn't a laser show. I like this better."

"Every time I'm with you, I feel good inside. There's something magical about you. I don't know what it is."

I looked into his eyes, begging for him to kiss me. "I feel as if we were meant to be together. Maybe, what you feel is God's blessing, His assurance that we were meant to be."

He let go of me. I sat up. "What's wrong?" I asked, shaken from my dream-like state.

Raymond ate his chicken first, smiling as he ate.

"This food is delicious!" Raymond Jr. responded, eating his macaroni and cheese. "You're a good cook!"

"Thank you. My recipes have been kid-tested. Kids won't eat just anything. It has to look and taste right, or they won't eat it. My kids made me perfect my cooking. You're just reaping the benefits of many trials and errors."

"I'm glad I wasn't around then," announced Raymond Jr. "This food is good! Can I have some more macaroni and cheese, please"

"Eat the rest of your food first. Then you can have more," I said, biting my chicken.

"Okay," he said, picking up his broccoli with his fingers.

"Francine, would you like something else?"

"No. I'm not greedy like Raymond."

"I'm not greedy."

"You are too."

"Stop it, Francine and Raymond!" Raymond interrupted. "Or you'll be sorry."

They settled back down and finished eating their food. After dinner we baked cookies.

It was the first time Raymond and Francine baked cookies. They thought the cookies were wonderful and should be sold to their friends although Raymond and I had a different opinion. We felt they were too greasy and too crumbly. The kids didn't seem to notice. They thought the cookies were delicious! Raymond and I decided not to say anything. Since they thought they were wonderful and delicious, nothing else mattered.

Raymond and the kids left at six o'clock, taking some cookies home to share with their friends and grandmother, Carrie, at home. Raymond Jr. and Francine stole my heart even more. I could tell, they were receptive to me as well. I felt an instant bonding that only God could have placed between us.

My sons came home shortly after Raymond left. They had had a good time with Carl. Little Carl asked me again if he could live with his dad. Again, I told him, no, because his dad was unstable. He needed to learn how to support himself, first, before he took on the additional responsibility of supporting his kids. I stressed also the importance of making good grades. If Carl made good grades—A's and B's—then I would let him live with his father, starting next summer. His long face told me he didn't like my decision, but there was nothing he could do about it.

As I looked into my son's sad eyes, I thought about the harshness of divorce. It destroys the family sense of balance and structure. The unity is gone. The children, wanting to live with both parents, now must be content with only living with one. I could see the pain on my son's face, a hurt I tried to avoid.

Sometimes in this life, we must live through painful situations. I wished I could bear his pain, but I couldn't. He must bear it alone with Jesus Christ.

Carlos, as far as I could tell, was having no adverse reaction to the divorce. His grades, countenance and temperament were the same. He never asked if he could live with his father. Therefore, I assumed he was okay and I hoped my assumption was correct.

Being a single mother was harder than I imagined. While I thought Carl was doing nothing in our home for us, I was wrong. His presence here, if nothing else, made a difference in the cohesiveness of the family. Before the divorce, I never paid any attention to the "cohesiveness" because it somehow always existed. It wasn't until after the divorce, when it was gone, did I miss it, and I'm sure the boys did, too.

Friday, Raymond and I went to the Starlight Drive-In on Moreland Avenue to see "A Time To Kill." We stopped and bought fish from Fish Supreme on the way. Raymond always had a way of making me feel special. While we waited for our fish, he held me close to him, as if to say, "she's mine." I liked his possessiveness. Carl always treated me as if I was community property—I was free to be with whomever I pleased although I was his wife.

We watched the movie, eating our fish and fries. By the time, we finished eating our food, the white men in the movie were indiscriminately killing black men for the alleged rape of a white slut. My pulse rose with each new scene. I enjoyed the movie, but I was glad when it was over.

Raymond started talking as we exited the movie, stalled in the outgoing traffic. "I just want you to know I have attended several home buyer's seminars in the past few months. I plan to buy a house in November."

"That sounds good. What kind of house do you plan to buy?"

"I haven't decided. I was hoping you would look at homes with me. I want to buy what you like since we would probably live in the house together."

"When do you plan to look?"

"Soon," he said smiling, making his way through the cars.

My heart raced wildly as he spoke of buying a home and including me as if I would be part of his family. I touched my heart to slow it down, but touched the key necklace instead. As my finger stroked the small diamond, I wondered if the necklace was a fulfillment of my sign since it cost at least fifty dollars. I pressed it close to my heart. It stopped racing. I looked at Raymond and gave him a big smile, thinking I've got my man. The only other thing I needed now was a ring. If he was planning on buying a house by November, I would get it soon.

THIRTY-ONE

Since the fall Holy Days were coming up, I needed to prepare myself spiritually for them. The Feast of Trumpets, or Rosh Hashanah, was the next day. It signified the return of Jesus Christ, the next occurrence in God's plan of salvation for humanity. The first three steps of His seven step plan have been fulfilled with Passover, signifying Jesus' death; the Days of Unleavened Bread, signifying Jesus' resurrection; and Pentecost, the pouring out of the Holy Spirit upon man. The last four steps are fulfilled in the fall Holy Days. The Feast of Trumpets represents Jesus' return. The Day of Atonement, or Yom Kippur, represents when humanity will be at one with God. It is a time when Satan will be bound for one thousand years to usher in the millennium reign of Jesus on earth, called the Feast of Tabernacles. The last and final step occurs on the eighth day following the seven day festival of the Feast of Tabernacles. It is called the Last Great Day. It's mentioned in John 7:37, *"On the last day, that great day of the feast, Jesus stood up and cried out, saying, `If anyone thirsts, let him come to Me and drink.'* The Last Great Day represents when all mankind will be granted salvation, even those who were not part of the first fruits of the first resurrection, or the incorrigible wicked of the third resurrection who will be burned in the lake of fire.

I read my Bible for several hours, then meditated on God's Word. God's plan of salvation always made me respect His love for mankind. If only we could reciprocate what He does for us, the world would be a better place.

The boys and I attended the Feast of Trumpets service together on Saturday afternoon. Afterwards, we ate dinner with Herman at the Gwinnett Place Mall food court, near the Gwinnett Arts Center, where services were held. We all chose Chinese food.

We found a table at the end of the food court. The boys sat across from each other. Herman sat across from me.

"How is school?" Herman asked, putting a napkin on his lap.

"Fine," they both answered.

"Did you enjoy service today?"

"No. There are no pretty girls in the church," Carl answered, drinking his soda.

"Church is boring. I come because Mama makes me," replied Carlos, picking up his honey chicken.

"Put that chicken down!" I demanded. "We haven't said grace."

"I'll say grace," Herman volunteered. "I'm sure they're hungry."

We bowed our heads while Herman blessed the food. As soon as Herman said "Amen", the boys devoured their food. They acted as if they hadn't eaten in days.

"What did you think about the sermon?" I asked Herman, eating my pepper steak.

"The sermon was most fitting. It captured the true meaning of the day, the return of Jesus Christ. Mr. McNair really painted a vivid picture of all the events that will take place when Christ returns."

"I agree with you. It was an excellent sermon. I can't wait until the feast to hear more of God's word expounded."

"Speaking of the feast, I don't think I'll be able to go with you on the twenty-seventh."

"Why? Is it because of my male friend?"

"No, of course not. I'm not concerned about him. But Carlton Smith is very sick. He was diagnosed with cancer last month. He's like a father to me. I wouldn't feel right leaving, with him being so sick. I plan to stay here and help his wife, who is like a mother to me. They need me. They took care of me after my accident. This is my way of repaying them," Herman said, picking up his fork to eat his rice.

"I'm sorry to hear about Mr. Smith. I didn't know he was sick. I'll keep him in my prayers. Carlos and I'll miss you. We were both looking forward to you coming with us. You would have been a welcome change."

"Maybe next year, if you're not married," he said, drinking his tea.

"The way things are going, I will be," I said, eating my egg roll.

"Well, it's probably best I'm not going with you. I don't want your fiancé to get the wrong idea."

"I'm not engaged. Raymond knows we're just friends. I told him about the feast and your birthday."

"Ah, you've got to be kidding," he said, laughing. "You don't have to do anything for my birthday."

"I know I don't have to, but I want to. You made my birthday special. I want to do the same for yours."

"Okay, Miss Vanessa. If you insist."

"I do, and you can't back out of it. I hope Mr. Smith will be doing fine by then."

"I do, too. He's a tough old man. It will take more than cancer to take him out of here. He'll probably be around when Christ returns."

"If not, he'll at least be in the first resurrection. Either way he wins."

"I wished I had his odds with you. Being a red flag gives me only one choice—a loser."

"Only one thing can change your odds," I said, smiling.

"What?"

"My sign. If you give me my sign, then you will be a winner."

"Has your green light given you your sign?"

"I'm not sure. Sometimes I think so, even though it's not exactly what I prayed for. I would have never thought to pray for what he gave me."

"Mama, can I have some money?" asked Carl, interrupting the conversation. "I want to buy a CD in the music store.

"Me, too," added Carlos. "I have something I want to buy."

"Okay," I said, reaching for my purse. "Be back in twenty minutes." I gave them money, and Herman and I continued to talk until they came back, thirty minutes later.

We left the mall going our separate ways. On the way home, I thought of Herman. Only my sign could change our course. Only my sign could cancel out Herman's red flags. Would he give me my sign? Only time would tell. I didn't know, but God did. I would have to wait and see.

Although Herman was nice, charming, intelligent and spiritual, he was not the man for me. He didn't ring my bell. Sometimes, I wished I felt differently, but I couldn't lie to myself. God knew the kind of man I needed. That's why he sent Raymond into my life. Raymond not only rang my bell, he caused an explosion to go off inside of me every time we kissed. The way he treated me made me feel special. It was a refreshing change not being treated as a sex object. I thought about Raymond all the way home.

We heard the phone ringing as we opened the door. Carl ran to answer it.

"Mama, it's for you!" he yelled, extending the phone to me.

"Thanks, son," I said, reaching for the phone. "Hello?"

"It's good to hear your voice. I've dialed your number many times and hung up. Today, I had to talk to you. I couldn't take it any longer," Bryson explained.

"Bryson, I told you our relationship is over! You have no business calling me."

"I know, but I can't help myself. Van, I still love you. I've been trying to forget you, but I can't. I love you too much. And I know you love me, too."

"Bryson, I'm involved with Raymond now. I'm not coming back to you."

"Let me come over to see your face one more time. I promise I won't do anything to you. I just want to see you again."

"No. I won't see you anymore. The last time we talked, was the last time for us to be together. It's over Bryson. You might as well accept the truth." I hung up.

Bryson called back.

"It's not over yet because you still love me. As long as we both have feelings for each other, it will never be over. And I will never give up! If I give up, then I'll never have you again. But, if I keep trying, then one day, you'll be mine. You belong to me, Van. I should have never let you go."

"You didn't let me go. I left you. You're a dead end. You'll never leave Helen, so I don't have any choice but to move on."

"That's not true. I do plan to leave Helen. I'm just not in a position to leave right now."

"Good-bye, Bryson."

"Van, I'm not giving up, no matter what. You're coming back to me because you're mine."

I hung up the phone. What would it take for Bryson to leave me alone? How long will he pursue me before he realizes he's fighting a lost cause? I pondered these questions for the remainder of the evening, hoping for an answer. Since no answer came, I decided not to waste any more time thinking of Bryson. All my energy would be focused on Raymond.

The relationship with Raymond continued to escalate. His gentle, caring nature ignited a spark in me that I didn't know I possessed. He not only healed my mind, he made me feel like the woman I always wanted to be. Somehow, Raymond had a way of bringing out the best in me. And, I think, I brought out the best in him.

I knew it would be hard going to the Feast of Tabernacles without Raymond. I hated leaving him behind. But, Carlos and I went anyway, from September 26 to October 7.

When I returned, Raymond and I picked up where we left off. We missed each other which was evident in the built-up passion we both displayed. I hoped I never had to leave him behind again. He assured me that I wouldn't because he wanted us to get married when he found a house.

The house he wanted had to have four bedrooms, two bathrooms, with a finished basement and big yard. The basement would be for Little Carl and office space. Carlos, Raymond Jr., and Francine would have their bedrooms in the main living area. Preferably, the house would be in a quiet neighborhood with lots of land between each house.

I wanted what he wanted with a formal living room, dining room and den. We both preferred a ranch style house with a two-car garage. He said his price range was $100,000 or less. We both felt we could easily find what we wanted within his range.

The two weeks following the feast, we looked at houses. We drove in different neighborhoods to get a feel for the market in various locations. After driving around, we saw a few houses we liked from the outside. From the sign in the yard, we wrote the agent number down for future reference. Along with house hunting came the time to take Herman out for his birthday. Raymond understood my wanting to repay Herman for how he treated me on my birthday. I explained to Raymond that Herman and I were only friends, that he had nothing to worry about. He said he had only one stipulation—we do not slow dance. He did not want Herman or any other man close to me. I told him, I would abide by his stipulation. I would not slow dance with Herman. I also told him, I would call him at work when I got home.

Raymond and I went to church and ate at Red Lobster on the day I planned to take Herman out. By the time I got home from Red Lobster, it was almost time for Herman to pick me up. Since I didn't have time to change, I kept on what I wore to church.

Ten minutes after Raymond left, Herman arrived. I was glad to see he had on his same church clothes, too. I didn't buy Herman a gift. My gift to him was to pay for our night out.

Herman came to the door smiling. His handsome face radiated warmth like the sun. I could tell he was glad to get another opportunity to be with me.

"I'm ready," I said as he rang the bell. "Remember, this is your night. I'm paying for everything."

"Miss Vanessa, you must be kidding," he said, laughing. "I can't let you do that. What kind of man do you think I am?"

"It's okay, Herman. It's my gift to you."

"Come on, lady. Let's go boogie down."

We both laughed as we went to the car. Twenty minutes later, we drove up to Club Hariston's. Herman tipped the valet before I got out of the car. When we checked in our coats, he tipped again. I spotted an empty table at the end of an aisle to the right. As we sat down a waiter immediately came for our order. Herman ordered the chicken finger dinner. I ordered the New York cheese cake and coffee.

"Is that all you're eating?" Herman asked after I ordered.

"Yes. I ate at Red Lobster with Raymond earlier. I can't eat another meal."

"Why didn't you tell me you didn't want to eat? I never would have ordered food."

"Eating dinner is part of the evening. I'll help you eat your food if it'll make you feel better."

"Yes, it will."

"Whatever makes you happy. This is your day. By the way, happy birthday."

"Thanks, Miss Vanessa. Indeed, it is."

Our food came while we talked. Herman's plate was loaded with chicken fingers and stir-fried vegetables. He ate most of the vegetables, and I ate most of the chicken fingers. They were delicious dipped in the honey-mustard sauce. Herman paid for the meal and left the tip. I insisted on paying, but he wouldn't have it any other way. Once the waiter disappeared with the paid check, we left the table and headed for the dance floor.

I found myself thinking of Raymond while I danced with Herman. Sometimes I felt guilty that Herman could not hold my attention. This was his day, I told myself, he deserved my undivided attention. Herman didn't seem to notice, my lack of focus, he was having too much fun. I tried to pretend I was having as much fun as he was although I wished he was Raymond.

By the tenth song, we stopped for drinks which Herman paid for. A slow song played while we enjoyed our drinks. I was glad we weren't on the dance floor. How could I tell Herman I couldn't slow dance with him? Lucky for me, I was spared a dilemma.

A couple of songs later, we returned to the dance floor. My luck soon ran out, however, when a slow song played. As I motioned to leave the floor, Herman grabbed me and held me close to him. His arms wrapped around me, holding me to his chest. I didn't have the courage to tell Herman I couldn't slow dance with him. Not knowing what else to do, I laid my head on his chest and closed my eyes, wishing the song would end soon. As it ended, another slow song played. Herman maintained his hold. His eyes met mine as I lifted my head. Joy filled his eyes. I closed my eyes and pretended he was Raymond, hoping he would understand another man was in love with his woman.

THIRTY-TWO

It was after two o'clock in the morning when Herman brought me home. I paged Raymond at work when I got inside. The phone rang two minutes later. I took a long deep breath, then answered the phone.

"Hello, Raymond," I said, picking up the receiver.

"Are you just getting home?" he asked pissed off.

"Yes. I wasn't watching the clock. Besides, I didn't know I had to be home at a certain time."

"I expected you home by twelve at the latest. I'm here at work while my woman is out partying with another man. I kept looking at my watch, thinking you would be home soon."

"I didn't know I had a curfew. I am a grown woman, not a child. I can stay out as late as I want to!" I said, indignantly.

"When you're with me, yes. But not when you're with someone else."

"Well, you don't have to worry about that happening again. Herman's birthday is over. I won't be going out with him anymore."

"Did you slow dance?"

"Yes, several times."

"I told you not to slow dance! I don't won't no other man near you! You deliberately went against my instructions!"

"No, I didn't! When a slow song came on, I attempted to walk off the floor, but Herman held on to me, preventing me from leaving."

"If he tried to have sex with you, I guess you couldn't stop him from doing that either!"

"Sex and dancing are two different things! He didn't try to have sex with me."

"If he did, would you have let him, like you let him slow dance with you?"

"Of course not!"

"I'm not so sure. I'm getting off this phone before I blow a fuse. I already feel my blood pressure rising. We'll talk about this later. Good-bye."

"Good-bye," I said as the phone clicked in my ear.

I stared at the phone for ten minutes before I went to bed. I was determined not to let Raymond spoil a perfectly good evening. I said my prayers, then dozed off to sleep.

The next day, Raymond came over wearing tight jeans and a white T-shirt. He was still pissed off. Few words passed between us because of his ill temper. I was still determined not to let his mood change my good disposition. He brought up the slow dance thing again, but decided to let the matter rest after I did not add more fuel to the fire. Assuming the fire was out, I suggested we visit my parents. I had already told Mama about Raymond. She and Dad wanted to meet him. Today might be their last chance if he didn't get over last night.

We drove to my parents house, ten minutes away. Driving his car, going the speed limit, took an extra five minutes. Raymond was a stickler for driving at or under the speed limit. Sometimes he drove me nuts when we went places because I consistently drove over the speed limit. I knew this was not the time to tell him to speed up since I was already in the doghouse.

Mama answered the door. She had on a loose-fitting house dress that was unusual for her. She usually either wore tight fitting pants or a dress with a belt to show off her good figure. Even at sixty-one, my mama could turn some heads with her youthful physique.

"C'mon in," she greeted us with her southern charm. Noticing Raymond's clunker in the driveway as she opened the door, she politely asked, "Is that your car, Raymond?"

"Yes, ma'am," he answered, crossing the threshold.

"How old is it?"

"It's a 1981 model."

"That's the same age as Carl Jr.. Isn't it Nessa?"

"Yes, Mama. It's fifteen years old."

"My, my, my. That's an old ass car. How does it run?"

"Sometimes the transmission slips. Other than that, it drives like a new car."

"That's good. C'mon inside. Your father's in the den watching TV."

The three of us walked to the den with Mama leading the way. Her dress swayed back and forth as she walked. Raymond and I held hands going into the den. Mama sat on the loveseat beside Dad, near the door. Raymond and I sat on the sofa next to the seat facing the door.

Dad was in his typical position, watching TV. Turning a beer to his lips, he greeted us with a wave. "Honey, this is Vanessa's new friend I was telling you about. The one with the two children."

"Dad, this is Raymond, the next man of my life."

"Hi, Raymond. Nice to meet you," Dad said, extending his beerless hand for Raymond to shake.

"My pleasure, sir."

"Would you like a beer?"

"No, thank you. I don't drink alcohol."

"You don't have to be bashful. Vanessa can go get you a beer out of the fridge," Dad said, turning his can up again.

"Leave him alone, Xavier. Raymond don't drink, smoke, cuss or gamble."

"He don't?" Dad asked with a chuckle. "If you don't do all those things, ain't nothing left for a man to do except have sex."

"He don't do that either. He ain't been with a woman in five years," Mama added.

"Sho' nuff? I'll be damned," Dad said, finishing his beer.

"Obviously, Vanessa has told you everything about me," Raymond said with slightly clenched teeth, squeezing my hand.

"Stop, Raymond, you're hurting me!" I exclaimed, pulling away my hand.

"I see you can get upset. I was beginning to think you were queer or something," Dad added, turning his hand back-and-forth to the side. "I can use another beer. Vanessa, do you want one or do I have to drink alone?"

"No, thanks. I don't care for one either."

"Betty, go get me another beer."

"I just want you to know Raymond is not himself today. Last night, I went dancing with Herman," I said, looking at Raymond smiling.

"Don't be smiling at me! You know you were wrong. I told you I didn't want no man touching you!"

"Has Raymond given you your sign?" Mama asked, standing up to get Dad's beer.

"No. Not yet. At least, not the way I prayed for."

"Good," Mama said without thinking. "I mean, goodness. Let me hurry up and get that beer. Nessa, come give me a hand. I'm sure you and Raymond want something to drink."

"No, thank you," we both said together.

"I won't have no for an answer. Y'all got to taste my ice tea."

I stood up, getting Mama's drift. I figured she had more than ice tea on her mind. We walked out, leaving Dad and Raymond watching TV.

Mama went into the kitchen, opened the refrigerator and pulled out a gallon jug of tea. Reaching for three glasses, she filled them with ice, then poured the tea.

"Nessa," she said handing me two glasses. "I'm not trying to get in your business, but I don't think Raymond is right for you. He tried to hurt you in the den! You don't need a man like him. What happened to Herman? He treated you right. He had class. Raymond ain't got nothing but them children."

"Mama, Raymond's a good man. He's just upset today. On the outside, Herman seems to have more than Raymond. But what Herman has doesn't seem real to me. Raymond, on the other hand, appears to have nothing, but I see him having more than Herman."

"Trust me, Nessa. Raymond ain't got shit! I can see that with my natural eyes. I don't know what eyes you're using."

"Betty! C'mon with that beer!" Dad yelled from the den.

"We'll talk later," Mama said, opening the refrigerator to get a beer. "Raymond is probably boring your daddy to death. You need to get back with Herman and leave Raymond alone."

"Mama, Raymond is a one in a million man. It's hard to find a man like him these days."

"If he's one in a million, I'll take the dime a dozen men like your daddy. At least, I know what I got. I ain't too sure about Raymond. He ain't got nothing and pretending he got everything. Men like your daddy ain't got nothing and ain't ashamed to admit it."

"Mama, Raymond is good to me and good for me."

"Don't let him fool you. He just want what's between your legs like any man. And he wants you to be a mother to his children. Open your eyes, Nessa, and wake up before it's too late," Mama said as we reached the den door. "Here's your beer," she said to Daddy.

I sat next to Raymond, giving him his tea while drinking mine. Mama lit a cigarette, inhaling deeply. Smoke filled the room when she exhaled. She pulled on the cigarette continuously until it disappeared.

"Mama, I thought you quit smoking two weeks ago?"

"I did, but my nerves are damn near shot. I need something to help me relax," she answered, reaching for another cigarette.

"Well, we have to leave," announced Raymond, standing up.

"Why?" I asked, surprised by his announcement.

"I can't tolerate cigarette smoke. Come on, let's go!"

"Okay, let me finish my tea first. I have a little bit left."

He gulped his down also. "It was nice meeting you, Mr. and Mrs. Grant."

"Come back again," Mama added, finishing her second cigarette.

"This might be the first and last time you see Raymond if he doesn't get over what happened last night."

"Good. I mean, good evening. Y'all drive safely." Mama said, trying not to put her foot further into her mouth.

"If I don't see you again, I understand. A man gotta do what he gotta do," Daddy said, shaking Raymond's hand.

"You're right, Mr. Grant. And I'll do what needs to be done."

"Raymond, you're just talking nonsense. You're not going to do anything," I said, pulling him toward the door.

We went back to my house after we left my parents. Silence filled the ride home. Raymond seemed more pissed now than before. I tried to think of something to say to remedy the situation, but was at a complete loss for words.

Why was he making such a big deal out of slow dancing? I could understand him being upset if I had had sex with Herman. All I wanted to do was take Herman out for a good time and look what happened. Raymond is acting like a spoiled kid who didn't get his way. "Your parents don't care for me," he finally said, breaking the silence.

"Well, you weren't Mr. Congeniality. What did you expect?"

"No. It had nothing to do with how I acted. They don't think I'm the right man for you, especially your mom."

"Mama is Mama. She speaks her mind whether you like it or not."

"Maybe, she's right."

I looked at him in disbelief. He went from not talking, to talking crazy. His last words made me silent the rest of the way home. Minutes later, he pulled the car into the driveway, parked and turned towards me instead of getting out. I knew something was up. I held my breath waiting for his next move or word.

"I'm not going inside. I've been thinking, this relationship will not work. You deliberately went against my wishes. I don't know if I can trust you. I've been through this before, and I can't go through this again. I'm sorry, Vanessa, but our relationship is over."

Swallowing a big lump in my throat, I managed to say, "I'm sorry I hurt you. I didn't do it intentionally."

He looked at me with a stone face. I studied his eyes which were cold as ice. I turned to open the door that I could never open. Raymond reached across me and wiggled something that caused it to open. I grabbed my purse, then got out. He didn't move. I walked up the steps alone, and opened my door without turning back. I heard Raymond drive off as I locked the door. Will he ever be in my life again? I asked myself, slouching on the loveseat.

"Not if I can help it, girlfriend," Viva responded. "Correct me if I'm wrong. The deal was, I would rule if you lost both Encyclopedia Man and Library Man. Well, from what just happened, you have no man. That means, I rule this show now. Get up! You ain't got time to sulk. Go get Big Daddy on the phone!"

THIRTY-THREE

Viva was above herself. She had made those stipulations in the past, not me. I told her under no circumstances would I ever allow her to rule me, and I was not calling Bryson. She said, under no circumstances would she be subordinate again. Her goal now was to get Bryson back, no matter how I felt about Raymond. The battle was on. May the best woman win!

That night when I left for work, Bryson's van was parked by the mailbox. As I walked to my car, I kept watching for him to get out. By the time I reached the door of my car to unlock it, he appeared from the dark side of the house at the beginning of the driveway.

"Ah!" I screamed as he came to the light. "You scared me! What are you doing here?"

He walked toward me from the front of the car. "I had to see you. I knew this way, you couldn't say no."

"I don't have time to talk. I have to go to work."

"I know. It will only take a few minutes to say what's on my mind," he said, standing in front of me.

"Go ahead. You have two minutes," I said, looking at my watch.

"Van, the bottom line is, I can't live without you. I've tried not calling or coming by, but you're all I think of, day and night. I want to hold and kiss you again," he said, leaning forward to kiss me.

Viva said to me, "This is the moment I've been waiting for. Welcome back, Big Daddy!" She ruthlessly took control.

His arms gripped my waist as his lips touched mine. We kissed softly at first, then passionately, holding each other close. Tears streamed down Bryson's face when the kiss was over. Holding me even closer, his tears began to wet my hair.

"I thought I'd never be able to hold or kiss you again. I knew you still loved me. Tonight, proved I was right."

"Bryson, I must go," I said releasing Viva's hold.

"I know," he said. "Thanks for not rejecting me. I love you. And I know you love me, too."

I drove off, leaving him in the driveway. He watched me leave before he walked back to his van. I noticed the kids' bedroom lights were on when I left. I hoped they didn't see Bryson kiss me.

Bryson's kiss lingered with me on the way to work. It felt good being in his embrace. Although I thought I was over him, his kiss told me I wasn't. Then I thought, was I still in love with Bryson, or was it Viva's love I felt? Since I wasn't sure, I counted it as Viva's. Her flame for Bryson wouldn't go out no matter how I felt or who I was involved with. Surely, there's something I can do to extinguish the flame, I thought as I drove to work.

By three o'clock, I had forgotten about Bryson because I wanted to see Raymond. We usually took our breaks then. I missed him and wished he would come to his senses soon. I kept expecting Raymond to pass by. He never did. Clocking out at seven-thirty with no sign of Raymond, I knew the relationship was over for good.

Walking to the parking lot, I kept looking for Raymond, hoping I was wrong, and he had changed his mind. My hope turned to despair causing me to be listless as I drove home. Get over him, I kept telling myself. There are more fish in the sea. My right hand touched the key necklace underneath my shirt, pressing it to my heart. But this fish held the key to my heart. I couldn't let him get away.

Feeling despondent, I went to sleep without eating breakfast. Food was no substitute for Raymond. I wanted him and nothing else. Only he could fill the void I felt. Only he could turn the key to set my heart free.

I slept until Carlos came barging into my room when he came home from school.

"Mama! Was that Bryson outside with you last night?" he shouted, sprawling on my bed next to me.

"Yes," I answered sleepily, throwing the covers over my head.

He pulled the covers back to expose my face. "Did you kiss him?"

"Yes."

"How can you kiss two men? That's nasty! If my old girlfriend tried to kiss me, I'd tell her to get out my face. No way I'd be kissing on her and my new girl, too."

"You're right, Carlos," I said, sitting up. "I didn't mean to kiss Bryson. It just happened."

"A kiss doesn't just happen, Mama. You could have pushed him away or said no. I was watching you last night. You let him kiss you, and you kissed him back. I wish my old girlfriend would come up to me. I'd take her down with some karate kicks," he said, acting like Bruce Lee.

What wisdom comes out of the mouth of babes. Carlos was right. I felt like a complete fool. I had to make sure it never happened again. No matter how I, or Viva, felt. "Carlos, do you have a request for dinner?" I asked getting up, trying to change the subject.

"Do we have some of those little chicken wings?"

"Yes."

"Then I want hot wings. Make 'em extra hot."

"Extra hot, hot wings coming up," Carlos karate-kicked his way out of my room into his room. I hoped he'd forget about last night, like I was trying to do.

Bryson called after dinner. I told him Raymond and I had broken up. He took the breakup as an invitation to start over for us. I quickly dismissed the notion. Regardless, of what happened with Raymond, Bryson and I were never getting back together. I would use this time to be alone and complete "Uncaged."

Viva wanted Bryson back. Every time she tried to say something contrary to how I felt, I overruled her. I could tell she was upset with me when the conversation ended because I heard her cussing me out. I told her to get a grip. I was the captain of this ship. If she didn't like it, she could jump overboard. She told me where to jump more explicitly.

By Tuesday night, I was going crazy. I wanted to hear from Raymond badly. Several times I found myself picking up the lab phone to call, but put the receiver back down. I reminded myself it was his idea to breakup. Therefore, he had to make the first move to get us back together. I must move on, I kept telling myself. He's gone forever. It's probably for the best. God knows for sure.

I went home Wednesday morning with the weight of the world on my shoulders. Raymond where are you? Why are you doing this? I kept asking myself.

Wednesday evening, Bryson came by unexpectedly. I was at the kitchen table working on "Uncaged" when the door bell rang. Carlos answered the door.

"Mama, Bryson's at the door."

"Let him in," I said finishing a sentence.

"I thought you dumped him."

"We're not seeing each other. But let him in since he's at the door."

Carlos let Bryson inside, then went back upstairs. Bryson walked into the kitchen and sat directly in front of me in his favorite seat at the table.

"Would you like to sit in the living room?" I asked, looking up from my word processor.

"No. I'm fine right here," he said, staring intently into my eyes.

"What brings you over?" I asked, putting the cover on my keyboard.

"You."

"Don't think for a minute that we're getting back together because Raymond and I have broken up."

"That's what you say. I know differently."

"How are Helen and the kids?"

"Don't try to change the subject. I'm talking about us. Leave Helen out of it."

"I can't. She's a part of you. The two of you are one since you're husband and wife."

"I know my status. You don't have to remind me of it, okay."

"The way you're talking, I thought maybe you'd forgotten."

"Van, what happened Sunday night lets me know I'm not fighting a losing battle. You still love me, regardless of what you say," he said, walking towards me.

He pulled me out of the chair. I stood up, facing him. "Don't think what happened Sunday will happen tonight," I warned him. "You caught me off guard. I'm myself tonight," I said, walking to the loveseat. I felt Viva ready to take advantage of another opportunity to get something started with Bryson. Keeping her subordinate with Scriptures, I continued talking to Bryson, who was walking toward me. I knew trying to keep both of them under control was a mighty task. Without saying a word, he pulled me from the loveseat, into his arms. I fought both him and Viva, until she came forth.

"Mmmmmmmm, you smell magnificent. What is that you're wearing?" she asked with her head on his chest.

"Ladies' Choice. I bought it yesterday, just for you," he replied, sensing the mood change and taking advantage of it by kissing my lips. I felt his penis harden while his hands glided across my back. Viva held him closer as if to say she wanted everything he had to give.

"Damn! You feel good. I've been waiting for this moment for a long time. I thought I'd never be in your arms again," she cooed, running my fingers through the hairs on his chest.

"You just don't know how much I've missed you. Being near you excites me. I want you, baby, and I know you want me, too. Let's go downstairs before we both explode," Bryson muttered kissing my neck. My nipples responded to his touch. I felt wet between the legs. My body yearned for his although my mind would not give into him. At that point, I took over before Viva had me doing something I would regret.

"You must leave now," I said, pushing him away.

"No," he said, grabbing me again.

"Let go of me, Bryson! It's time for you to go!" I said, pulling away, walking to the door.

Carlos and Carl came to the steps. "What's going on?" Carl asked.

"Nothing, sons. Bryson was just leaving." Bryson walked to the door, shaking his erection down. The boys went back into their rooms when I closed the door. I heard the wheels of Bryson's van spin from the driveway. I hoped he got the message—ain't no freebies at this house. Sorry, Big Daddy, the thrill is gone!

Shaken by Bryson's visit, I sat on the sofa, reliving the event and thinking about what could have happened if I had not gained control. Viva was dangerous. If she ever, truly took over, I'd be in trouble. There must be a way to get rid of her and Bryson. They both spelled trouble. God would have to show me how because I was at a complete loss on how to get rid of them.

At work that night when I was talking to Tia, my new co-worker, I wanted to discuss my dilemma, but I didn't have the nerve to tell her I was involved with a married man. Tia was young, twenty-six, and more liberal minded than Jenny, who was prudish and much older. The three of us talked frequently about many things. Tia was a sister who kept me abreast of what was going on. Although she was fine and foxy, she concealed her shape and looks by wearing granny glasses, putting her long hair in a pony tail, and wearing baggy clothes. She said she only wanted to look good for her husband. If I had what she had, I would look good for everybody.

Tia often spoke of a girlfriend who was involved with a married man. Her disgust for her friend let me know not to bring the subject up concerning me. Jenny knew what was going on, but minded her own business and never said a word. By the time Tia started working with us in September, Bryson and I had officially broken up. And since he no longer worked at Grady, the only person she saw come to the window was Raymond.

"I haven't seen Raymond stop by lately," Tia queried, adjusting her glasses while reading the newspaper.

"He kicked me to the curb Sunday."

"Why?" she asked, peeking over the paper.

"Because I slow danced with another man the night before."

"Oh, he's a jealous jackass. He couldn't take the heat so he got out the kitchen."

"I guess you can say that. He told me before I went dancing, not to slow dance."

"He has his nerve! I wish a man would try to tell me what to do," she said, putting the paper down. "I'd put him in his place so fast he wouldn't know what to think. Don't no man tell me what to do, not even my husband!"

"I'm more passive than you. I try to please my man.

"I do, too. But there are limits and he better not cross over my boundaries, or he can jump back in the sea with the other fish who are trying to get me."

The telephone rang as she finished speaking. Tia answered. "Emergency Clinic Lab, Tia speaking. How may I help you? Hold on, please," she said putting the phone on hold. "It's for you. Your fish is on the line."

"Who?"

"How many fish do you have?"

"None."

"Well, pick up the phone and see."

"I'll take it at Becky's desk." I picked up the phone, curious who it was. "Hello," I answered nervously.

"Vanessa, this is Raymond. You did say we can be friends?"

"Yes, I did."

"I was wondering if we could take a break together, to talk."

"When?"

"Now, if you're not busy. I'm down the ramp at Mr. Cox's station."

"I'll be right out," I said, hanging up the phone. "Tia, Jenny, I'm going on break!" I shouted as I headed for the door.

"Sounds like your hook is in the water," Tia commented as I was leaving.

"Yeah. And if I pull him back out this time, he won't ever want to jump back in," I said, pushing the exit button.

THIRTY-FOUR

Feeling my hair to make sure every strand was in place, I boldly walked down the ramp to where Raymond was waiting. He looked better than I remembered, standing with a smile on his face. Mr. Cox, the Pratt Street door security guard, was standing beside him directing a patron to the Emergency Clinic. Raymond stood perfectly still, watching me come to him.

"Hello, Mr. Cox," I said, passing by him to get to Raymond.

"Hello, Miss Lewis. How are you doing tonight?" he asked, sitting in his chair at his post.

"Wonderful! And you?"

"I'm blessed. I thank God it's not too bad. I worked in the yard all day and I'm tired," he answered, looking weary.

"Hopefully, you'll get some rest when you go home this morning."

"I hope so, if my wife don't have a list of things for me to do around the house."

"Well, Mr. Cox, we'll see you later," Raymond said, signaling me to go with him outside.

"All right," he said, standing back up, stopping a man who just came from outside.

Raymond and I walked outside, but decided it was too cold. We then walked up the ramp to the elevators to go to the cafeteria. Walking in silence, I didn't know what to expect from this meeting. It felt good being with Raymond again, even if it might be for a brief time. We sat in our usual spot. I looked into Raymond's eyes, waiting for him to speak. He looked into mine, cleared his throat, then continued.

Folding his arms on the table facing me, he said, "Vanessa, I've been through a lot of changes these past three days. I felt like Jonah in the belly of the whale. God has been dealing with me concerning you. He knows you're everything I've been looking for. You're the type of woman I need. When I tried to run from you, He pulled me back and threw me in the whale's belly. What I'm trying to say is, I want us to be together again. Will you take me back?"

A smile covered my face. I couldn't believe my ears. Raymond wanted me back! And I wanted him as much as he wanted me. "Of course, I'll take you back! You have no idea what I've been through these past few days. So God put you in the whale's belly?" I asked, laughing. "It serves you right for kicking me to the curb. I wonder what He'll do the next time you try to leave me?"

"I don't even want to think about it. I promise you, there won't be a next time. I'm here to stay. I've learned my lesson the hard way."

"When God deals with you, you've been dealt with," I said, laughing again.

"It's not funny. You don't know what I've been through," he said, looking green.

"And you don't know what I've been through either, so we're even. That's behind us now. Let's move forward," I said, pulling the key necklace from inside my shirt to let it rest on the outside where it could be seen by the whole world.

A huge smile broke out on Raymond's face when he saw the necklace. "I thought you would have taken it off."

"How could I when you still have the key to my heart?"

He reached for my hand across the table and placed it inside his. "I've been such a fool. Will you please forgive me?" he asked, caressing my hand.

"Yes, I will. I'm just glad we're back together."

"So am I," he said, releasing my hand. "We better get back to work," Raymond said, looking at his watch.

"Raymond, I have one question to ask you," I said, sliding from the booth.

"What is it?"

"How did it feel being in the whale's belly?"

He grinned waiting for me to stand next to him, "Not good. Come on. Let's get back to work."

Tia was still in the office reading the paper when I entered the lab. I went into the office to get some water as well as update her on the meeting. Beaming with joy, I pulled the paper from her face.

"You don't have to say a word," Tia said, looking at me. "It's written all over your face. You're back together."

"Yes. I'm so happy I could burst!" I exclaimed, spinning around.

"Don't get too excited yet. Men are jerks from Mars. He might do something else."

"I don't think so," I said, getting a cup of water. "He learned his lesson. He said he felt like Jonah, trapped in a whale's belly."

"That's the damnedest thing I ever heard of. Either he's lost his mind, or you've lost yours."

"That's okay, Tia. I know there are some things you can't understand. We're back together. That's all that matters."

"I'm glad, because your face was so long these past few days Jenny and I thought we might step on it."

We both laughed. I finished my water, and she went back to reading her paper.

The relationship blossomed between Raymond and I in the days to follow. The breakup made us realize how much we really cared for each other. Neither one of us could stand living without the other one. After the reconciliation, we saw each other regularly. Most of the times, our kids were with us. Although they clashed, especially Francine and Carlos, we were not going to let them determine the course of our relationship. We figured, eventually, they would except each other and get along. Carlos had the most acid disposition because he didn't want to share his mother with any other kids.

I met Raymond's mother, Mrs. Carrie Simmons. She was a plain, country woman with a friendly disposition most of the time. However, she could be moody like Raymond. They were two of a kind. But for the most part, we got along fine. When she was in a good mood, she talked my head off. I said more to her on our first visit than I said to my ex-mother-in-law in twenty-five years.

I started washing and pressing Francine's hair, every third week. Normally, the only time she got her hair fixed was when her grandparents, in Augusta, picked her up for a visit. Since the grandfather had open heart surgery in July, their visits had diminished from every other weekend to whenever they could make the trip. Unfortunately, Francine's hair suffered because Mrs. Simmons was unable to fix her hair due to her handicapped leg, and Raymond didn't take it upon himself to take her to a beautician. Therefore, I became Francine's beautician.

I was beginning to love Francine and Raymond Jr. I filled a mother's void in their lives. And they filled my heart with joy. Whereas, my sons took me for granted and favored their father. Francine and Raymond Jr. thought I was the greatest mother on earth. I found myself wanting to spend more and more time with them. And they wanted to spend more and more time with me. It was strange, but they felt more like my family than my own sons. The way they made me feel was a refreshing change.

By the time I finished "Uncaged" on November 12, Raymond and I were very close. We had started heavy petting that made me want more. Everything about him drove me crazy. In my heart, I wanted to do right, but my flesh was getting weak. I didn't know how long, I could control myself. I wanted to say forever. But my body said, not long.

Finally, on December 28, on a Saturday evening, when we were all alone and passion was flowing thick, we went all the way. Raymond had a problem keeping an erection since he hadn't had sex in over five years. His problem was something new to me. Neither Carl nor Bryson were impotent. Nor had they been without sex in over five years either. I told myself I would not hold his abstinence against him. Besides, he was living his life according to God's way.

Who was I to count his obedience against him? I loved Raymond despite his problem because he satisfied me outside the bedroom. I remembered how Carl satisfied me in the bed but frustrated me in all other areas of our relationship. Being satisfied outside the bedroom was more important to me at this stage of my life.

Speaking of Carl, my sons came home to announce Carl had gotten married. He and Yvette went to the courthouse, Monday morning. I remembered a prayer I prayed before Carl and I divorced. I knew, Carl had cheated on me at least once. I felt strongly, however, that there had been other times. I prayed to God that each time Carl was unfaithful to me, it took him the same number of years or relationships before he found the right person. Carl himself told me when he met Yvette, last December, she was the eighth person he had been involved with since our divorce in March. With his own mouth, he answered my prayer.

Raymond and I continued our lovemaking sessions. I knew I had found the man to father my daughters. Although I wasn't married, I was ready to get pregnant because of my age.

I kept track of when I ovulated. In January, Raymond and I had sex during that time. I waited patiently to see if I would miss my period. I didn't. I was crushed when I started at work. I broke the sad news to Raymond when we went on break. I waited until we were seated at our booth before I told him.

"What's wrong with you?" Raymond asked, sensing something was wrong.

"My period started tonight. I was hoping this would be the month our daughter would be conceived."

He reached for my hand and held it tight. "Don't worry. We'll try again next month. We'll keep trying until you get pregnant."

"This is the time. It will happen soon."

"Yes, it will. Cheer up. Next month will be different."

"There's something I have to tell you, that I've never told anybody else."

"What is it?" he asked concerned.

"The day of my divorce, I saw an image of a baby wrapped in a blanket as I was driving to the courthouse. I said to the image, 'I'm coming. I'm coming, baby girl. Mama's coming,' before it disappeared. Then as I was driving from the courthouse after my divorce was final, I saw another image. This time it was a very pregnant image of me. Suddenly a big book came in front of the image of me. A voice said, 'Your book will be published first before you deliver.' The image then disappeared. I finished writing my book "Uncaged" in November. Lawrence Chestnut is editing it now. I should hear from him any day now to send it off to the publishers. Do you understand what I'm saying, Raymond? Since my book has been written, now is the time for the image to be fulfilled."

"I understand. And It will. Our daughter will be coming soon," he said reaching into his shirt pocket, pulling out a key. "Here, take this," he said giving me the key. "This is my apartment key. I've been meaning to give it to you for awhile. Feel free to come by any time."

"Thank you," I said, reaching into my pants pocket for my keys. "These are the keys to my life," I said removing my car key and a set of house keys from my key ring and handing them to him. "I have an extra set in my purse. Since you are the man in my life, you will be the possessor of the keys to my life. Your car stopped running last month. We can share my car until you get yours fixed."

"Thank you," he said, taking the keys. "I won't put any more money into my car. The transmission is gone. I'll have to buy a new vehicle. Thanks for giving me my own key to your car. It makes it much easier than passing one key back-and-forth."

"There's one more thing I need to tell you."

"What is it?"

"After I saw the last image, the same voice said, `There will be a question about my name. It will be changed before the book goes to print.' Vanessa Lewis will not be on the book. My name will be changed first as if in a marriage."

"I like the sound of Vanessa Miller, both on and off the book," he said, examining my marriage finger.

"I do, too. One thing for sure, Lewis will not be on the book. Miller would be a perfect substitute."

"Mrs. Miller, it's time for us to leave," Raymond said, standing up, helping me out of the booth.

"I'm not Mrs. Miller yet."

"You will be, soon. You have my word on it," he said, as we walked.

THIRTY-FIVE

When I got back to the lab, Viva had her say. She was cool while Raymond and I talked. Most times, she left me alone because I was quick to put her in her place. I guess, since she couldn't add her two cents earlier, she let it rip in the lab.

"Hold up, girlfriend," she started as I put on my lab coat. "What do you think you're doing, wanting to have a baby by brother-man? He can't fuck? Have you lost your mind? Your man has to satisfy me, even if he doesn't have to satisfy you. I'm telling you, right now, my ass is not being satisfied. I'm frustrated, girlfriend, and I can't take no more. Tell him to check out 'Love Making 101' from the library. My nerves are on edge and I need relief!"

"Viva," I said, talking to her in my mind. "You might as well get a grip. I love Raymond. He's a good man. He's the type of man I want. I'm sorry if he doesn't rock your world. He makes mine come alive."

"That's fine and dandy for you, girlfriend, but I need more than sweet words, nice gestures, and pleasantries! I need some 'Dr. Feel Good' loving like Aretha sings about. The kind that makes your toes curl up. I need a man who can throw down in the bed. Raymond makes me want to throw up. I need the kind of man Aretha had in her bed. Whoever he was, she got rich singing about his good-loving ass."

"You're overruled, Viva! I want Raymond to be the father of my daughters. He's a good man and a great father."

"Do you really think you're going to have a snotty-nose, pissin', shittin', waking me up at all hours of the morning, baby, as long as I'm around?"

"I'm having my daughters soon, whether you like it or not."

"I don't think so, girlfriend. You'll never have your daughters with me in your life. I will prevent it like before, remember?" Viva taunted.

"Yes, I remember what you said when you first came out. This is a new day, Miss Thang. I know I'm having my daughters because I saw the image of a baby and an image of me pregnant. Flesh is not greater than God."

"That's true, but flesh can conquer you," she said then subsided.

I went into the office where Tia and Jenny were to get a cup of water. The lab was unusually slow. Jenny was drinking a cup of coffee while reading a book. Tia was knitting a blue blanket for her sister, who was having a baby in May.

"When you finish your sister's blanket, you can start on mine," I announced, getting a cup.

"Are you pregnant?" Tia asked, looking over her glasses.

"Not yet, but I will be soon. I'll have a girl. I want a pink blanket."

"I only knit pink or blue blankets after I know the ultrasound results."

"You can start on mine before I get an ultrasound. I know I will have a girl," I said, turning to the water cooler.

"I don't go by wishful thinking. I go by concrete evidence like an ultrasound."

"Vanessa's going by what she wrote in her book," added Jenny, who read each chapter as I completed them. "She thinks she's going to have two daughters."

"No, it's not what I think. It's what I know. I will have two daughters. They are coming just as sure as I'm standing here."

"Okay, Vanessa. Whatever you say. Just let me know after your ultrasound. Then I'll start your blanket."

I drank my water, then went to the window to accession specimens I heard clocked in while we talked. While I worked, I thought of Raymond, Viva, and Tia. Would I have my daughters? Was I going crazy? Why didn't I get pregnant this month since I had sex when I ovulated? Was Viva right? Or was Madame Lee right, the seer who prophesied back in 1980 that I would have four children, two boys and two girls? She also said I would leave Carl, and I did in '95. Everything she said came to pass except my two daughters. But didn't the images I saw in '95 confirm her prophesy? I then thought about the six initials Madame Lee gave me of the men who would be important in my life. They were B.C., L.C., Z.A., H.L., D.J., and R.M.. B.C. was Bryson Collier; L.C., Lawrence Chestnut; Z.A., Zakee Abdul-Rauf; H.L., Herman Lowe; and R.M., Raymond Miller. Who was D.J.? Why wasn't Mike Taylor included in the list? Madame Lee knew he would not be significant enough to list. Knowing Mike led me to pray for the sign to identify the next man in my life. Madame Lee knew he would not be the bearer of the sign, only the initiator of it.

Knowing I must get ready for my daughters, I called my family doctor, Dr. Duane Barclay before I went to sleep. He delivered Carlos in '86. He was my OB, GYN and pediatrician all roll up in one. Naturally, I wanted him to deliver my new arrival when the time came, so I requested a PAP smear with a complete physical.

Raymond called me that evening, saying he made an appointment with a urologist to diagnose and eliminate his problem. He was tired of being frustrated by his inability to maintain an erection. He remembered the days before his abstinence when he performed at will. His high sex drive drove his first two wives nuts. When he wanted sex, he had to have it, regardless if they wanted it or not.

He also knew I must be frustrated as well. He loved me enough to please me in every way. He wanted me to experience him at his best. I told him I loved him for him. Sex was just the icing of a relationship—it made it sweeter.

Raymond had a way of making me feel wonderful without an orgasm. I loved how he put his arms around me and held me close. We'd sit for hours wrapped in each other's arms. My head, often times, laid against his chest, hearing his heart beat, feeling his lungs expand. Those were the times when I wished time stood still, when nothing else mattered but us.

Raymond and I were on top of the world. We spent as much time as possible with each other. He'd come over some mornings after work. We'd have breakfast together, then go to my room to make love before falling asleep. We'd set the alarm to make sure we were dressed by the time Carlos came home from school. I'd take Raymond home after we ate dinner.

Taking Raymond home gave me an another opportunity to spend time with Francine and Raymond Jr., who were always glad to see me. Sometimes, I'd wait in the car while Raymond picked them up from the after-school program. Each time they saw me, they'd break out running to the car. They too had a way of making me feel special. I felt blessed being a part of their lives.

Just when everything was going well with Raymond, Bryson called during a terrible thunderstorm. I started not to answer the phone because a bolt of lightening had flashed nearby. The heavy rain mixed with thunder was not compatible with talking on the phone. Letting the phone ring three times, I picked it up, thinking it might be Raymond.

"Hello," I shouted over the thunder and rain. When the phone popped, I started to hang up.

"Hello, Van. Don't hang up," Bryson coaxed.

"It's storming outside. I need to get off the phone."

"I'm at Exchange Park on my cell phone."

"Bryson, have you lost your mind? You could be killed in this storm."

"Would it matter to you if I was killed?"

I thought about what he said before I answered. For some reason, his question really hit home. "Yes. It would matter." The storm subsided as I answered, and so did my wall of defense. Sensing the tone in my voice, Bryson used it to his advantage.

"Van, I want to see you. I'll do anything for another chance to look at you again."

"No, Bryson. You can't come over. I shouldn't even be talking to you over the phone."

"I won't stay but a minute. I just want to see your face one more time."

"No," I said less sternly. "You can't come."

"Baby, I love you. You don't know how hard it is to be away from you. I try not to call or come by, but I long to be with you so bad! Baby, please let me come this last time," he pleaded in such a way my heart melted.

Viva grabbed control. "Okay. But only for a minute."

"I'm on my way," he said hanging up the phone.

Exchange Park was around the corner from my house. It was also the first place we had met outside of Grady Hospital. By the time I got off the phone, the storm had been reduced to moderate rain. Bryson weathered both storms—the one outside and the one with Raymond. As he drove to my house, I wondered what would make this man give up. So far, nothing I'd said or did made a difference.

Within minutes, Bryson rang my bell. He hovered close to the door, dodging the steady rain. I noticed his beige shirt and brown pants were soaking wet. His face lit up when I opened the door.

"Have you lost your mind, being out in this weather?" I scolded as I let him inside.

"If I have to lose my mind to gain you, then it's worth it."

My heart melted again. Bryson knew how to make my walls come tumbling down. As a result, Viva came forth.

"Come here," he said softly, pulling me to him. "I don't want to hurt you. I want to love you."

Before I knew it, I was in his arms, laying my head on his chest, engulfed in his embrace. For a long time, neither one of us said a word. He held me tight, and I held him back.

"Van, we have no business being apart," he said, breaking the long silence. "We were meant to be together."

Everything I ever felt for Bryson resurfaced. "Bryson, I can't deny my feelings for you. They're strong and real. These past few months, I've been trying to deny them, to pretend they did not exist. Today, has proven, I've been lying to myself. I don't know what to do."

"There's only one thing to do—start over. We can make it, baby. We can."

I thought about Raymond and having his child. "Bryson, it's too late for us. We can't start over. I plan to have Raymond's child," I said, releasing myself from his embrace.

"Screw, Raymond! What about us?"

"There is no us! What we had is gone. It can't be resurrected."

"If Jesus can raise Lazarus from the dead, he can restore our relationship. I'm not giving up until you're mine again," he said, reaching for me as I walked to the door. "One thing you can't take from me is my faith and the belief in the Almighty God, Who can turn this situation around."

"There are two ways you can get me back," I said, opening the door. "If you give me my sign. Or if you get me down. If you ever get me down, it's over between Raymond and me."

He smiled. "Sometimes, when I think of us making love, I see myself saying your sign," he said as he stood up.

"I'll give you a hint. It's not something you just say, but something you do and say."

"Okay, love, we'll play it your way," he said, walking to the door.

"Bryson, if we're meant to be together, then nothing and no one can keep us apart. I have to be absolutely sure about the next man in my life. So far, you haven't proven to me that you're the one."

"Van, we both know, I am the one and only man for you. The next time you see me, I'll prove it," he said, walking out the door. I stared at the door five minutes after he left. I didn't like the sound of his last remark. I knew he would be something to reckon with later. Would God reveal my sign to Bryson? Or would Bryson get me down? Either way, I'd be his again.

While thinking of Bryson, I felt a sharp sensation from my left ovary. I went to the calendar in the kitchen to note my last cycle date with today's date. The date confirmed I was indeed ovulating. Raymond and I planned to go to Dublin Saturday and stay for church Sunday. Maybe, this will be the month our daughter will be conceived, I thought as I looked at the calendar.

Raymond's urologist appointment had been this past Monday. Dr. Wesley Smith ruled out high blood pressure, which Raymond had, and diabetes. Raymond's problem was poor penile circulation and low testosterone levels. He was given medication to correct both. I hoped by Saturday the medication would make a difference in his performance. Although I understood Raymond's condition, I was ready to have an orgasm.

Saturday, turned out to be different from our other lovemaking sessions. Raymond was erect enough to satisfy me. He said he could tell the difference, but he still wasn't his old self. He wanted me to have multiple orgasms so he could drive me crazy in bed. He knew how he was capable of performing, and it hurt him that he wasn't able to live up to his expectations. I told him, one day, we'll be able to do everything he desired. But we had to take it one day at a time. Today was an improvement. Hopefully, each day would show signs of progress.

My appointment with Dr. Barclay was the Monday after we returned from Dublin. I told Dr. Barclay my plans of getting pregnant. He performed a pelvic exam, PAP smear, and physical and read my urinalysis, chemistry and C.B.C. reports. After reviewing all the data, he said I was a picture of health and shouldn't have any problem with a pregnancy.

Since my last cycle date was January 22, I waited patiently for February 22 to arrive. I hoped this month my cycle would not come. On Friday morning of the twenty-first while I was at work, I felt a flutter in my abdomen as if I was pregnant. I went to the ladies room to collect a urine sample to perform a pregnancy test. To my surprise it was positive. I looked at the faint plus sign for several minutes before discarding the test. I was so excited, I told Jenny and Tia before calling Raymond. He picked up on the second ring.

"Security Services, Lieutenant Miller speaking."

"Lieutenant Miller, congratulations! You're going to be a father."

"Are you sure?" he asked.

"Yes. I did a urine pregnancy test and it was positive."

"Well, that's good news. How do you feel?"

"Like the most blessed woman on earth!"

"And I feel like the most blessed man."

"Good. I'm not going to keep you. I know you're busy. I just had to call and tell you the good news!"

"I'm glad you called. I love you."

"I love you, too," I said, hanging up the phone, rubbing my abdomen, comforting our child.

THIRTY-SIX

Raymond was beaming when he walked me to my car at seven-thirty. Both of us were so happy we couldn't contain our joy. He kept asking me, how I felt? I kept telling him, fine. By the time, we reached my car, he had asked me at least ten times. The tenth time he asked, I said, "Look, Raymond. If you ask me one more time how I feel, I'm going to scream! I'm fine, fine, FINE! But I won't be if you keep asking me the same thing."

We both laughed. "Don't get testy," he said, grabbing my hand. "I'm concerned about your well-being. You are carrying my child."

"I'm not being testy. You just got on my last good nerve and wore it out. If you continue at the rate you're going, I'll have lost my mind before the baby is born. Do you understand?"

"Yes, let me help you in the car," he said, opening my car door. I got inside with the door still opened. Raymond leaned forward and kissed my lips. "I love you," he said, smiling at me. "Drive home safely. I don't want anything to happen to either of you."

"Thanks for being concerned," I said, closing the door. "Don't change. It feels good to have somebody who cares."

"I'll call you when I wake up. I've got to get back," he said as he walked off.

I started the car, let it warm up, then drove home feeling good knowing I had a part of Raymond inside me. I couldn't wait until our daughter was born. I'd been waiting for her arrival since 1980. I remembered how upset I was with Madame Lee, in 1980, when she told me I would have four children, at the age of twenty-four. Back then, I didn't want that many children. However, at forty, I was thrilled with the concept of having three, possibly four children.

When I got home, I called Dr. Barclays' office to set up my first appointment. However, I was informed by the receptionist he no longer did OB, GYN. I hung up the phone dazed. If he didn't do OB, GYN, why didn't he tell me earlier?

Luckily, open enrollment for insurance had been changed from November to March. In my sixteen years at Grady, this was the first time open enrollment was in March. And it was for a special purpose because the hospital planned on having a second mandatory open enrollment in November also. God knew I needed to change insurance providers since I had to find another doctor to deliver my baby.

All weekend long, I thought about my daughter. I rubbed my swollen abdomen in an attempt to caress her. Raymond and I spoke about her, over the phone, as if she was already here. I couldn't wait to take a serum pregnancy test Monday to see my HCG titer. The urine test could detect 25 mIU/ml. A titer greater than or equal to 25 is considered positive on both urine and serum tests.

Sunday night at work, I had my blood drawn for my serum pregnancy test. The titer registered thirty-five. I was somewhat disturbed that it wasn't higher. Then I dismissed the results as being contributed to very early pregnancy. My suspicions turned to horror when I started bleeding at work Monday night. At the first sight of blood, I called Raymond to tell him of the blood and demanded he pray for our child. Despite our fervent prayers, the blood continued to flow. Within an hour of the first sight of blood, I had to put on a sanitary pad. By the time I left work, I was bleeding profusely. All hopes of having this baby were gone. Loosing the baby made me realize I needed to get "Uncaged" ready for publication. I remembered the pregnant image of me with the big book coming in front of the image, and God saying, "Your book will be published first before you deliver." I knew the image and saying were certain. I also knew, getting a book published could take over a year. With that in mind, I went through my manuscript again to rewrite and proofread. I called Chestnut to see where he was with editing "Uncaged." He said he hadn't started. I knew I couldn't wait on him. Therefore, I had to get it ready myself.

God always gives me what I need when I need it. He sent me Howard Livingston, a computer wiz, whom I was helping write his first novel, The Bid. Howard called me up on November 12, the day I finished "Uncaged". He typed my entire manuscript into his computer since I didn't have a computer, nor was I computer literate. I had typed "Uncaged" on a cheap word processor with no disk capacity.

It took until March 12 to complete the revisions. On that day, I mailed eleven query letters to publishers. Of my queries, two said I needed a literary agent, one sent a nice rejection letter, and one was interested in receiving more information. The interested publisher requested that I submit a brief summary, a table of contents, an annotated chapter by chapter outline, three sample chapters, marketing information, an author biography, and a self-addressed, stamped envelope. I prepared everything the publisher requested and mailed it.

Also in March, I had a doctor's appointment with my new insurance provider, Kaiser Permanente. I chose Kaiser because the premiums were cheaper and the out-of-pocket expenses would be less in the event of a pregnancy. The doctor checked me over to make sure everything was well with me, and it was. He said he couldn't find anything wrong with me to prevent a normal pregnancy.

I immediately thought of Viva after his examination. She had to be the culprit. I knew then I had to get rid of her before I could have my daughters.

That was easier said than done because both Viva and Bryson were active in my life. The closer Raymond and I became, the more they interfered. Bryson called daily. He had to know everything that was going on with Raymond and me. I ended up telling him about Raymond's impotency. Raymond was improving, but he still wasn't up to par.

Viva and I were both happy. She had Bryson and I had Raymond. All was well until Bryson wanted Raymond out of the picture. I believed Raymond sensed Bryson's presence because we were having problems.

Raymond looked disturbed when we went on break one morning. The stern expression on his face coupled with his silence let me know something was wrong. I didn't say anything. I waited to let Raymond speak first as we sat in our usual spots. Raymond clasped his hands, then looked into my eyes before he spoke. "Something has happened to us in the past few months. I feel as if there is someone else in your life. We're not as close as we used to be."

"Raymond, there's no one else but you in my life. I know it's hard for you to trust me or any other woman because of your past experiences, but I have been faithful to you."

"Something is missing. My instincts tell me you're fooling around. I been through this before, Vanessa. I know all the signs."

"You're wrong this time. What can I do to convince you otherwise?"

"Vanessa, my mama didn't raise no fool. Something's wrong, and I can't stay in this relationship the way it is."

"Okay, Raymond. If you want to end the relationship, return my keys. Those keys are the keys to my life. They represent everything of value I own," I said, looking into his eyes.

His countenance soften as I stared him down. "Oh, I see you're trying to play hard ball. Now, it's up to me."

"Yes, it is. You have the key to my heart," I said, pulling the chain to emphasize my point. "What more do you want? The ball's in your court. What are you going to do?"

"I have to think about it. I'm not sure what I want to do at this point," he said, sliding out the booth. I knew that was the cue to leave. We walked out of the cafeteria silently, each in our world.

When Raymond didn't show up to walk me to my car that morning, I knew we were no longer together. My heart felt heavy as I walked alone. It seemed as if it took forever to reach the parking deck. I kept looking around, hoping Raymond would join me at any moment. To my despair, he never appeared. I've lost him again, I thought. This time for good.

The next evening when Bryson dropped by, I had not heard from Raymond. I knew it was over between us, and I was deeply hurt. I told Bryson about the breakup. He took it as an invitation to get back together.

Bryson came inside and immediately tried to kiss me, but I shunned him. He reached for my breast and had it almost out of my blouse before I backed away. "Vanessa, I want you. I got to have you now!" he said, coming toward me.

"No, Bryson! Settle down. Nothing's going to happen!"

He grabbed and pulled me to the sofa, pinning me down with one hand and pulling out his penis with the other. "I've waited long enough! You're mine, and I'm going to get you back," he said, pulling my pants down. "You can have all this, baby. I know you want it."

"No, Bryson. Stop! My cycle is on. I can't do anything," I exclaimed, reaching for my pants. I was glad my cycle was on, then I had an excuse to prevent him from doing something I didn't want him to do. Bryson was quick and strong. The combination was too much at times to keep under control.

He picked me up from the sofa and pulled me up the steps with his penis exposed. I squirmed, trying to free myself from his grip, but he held me too tightly. I thought he was headed for the bedroom but he went in the hall bathroom instead. He held me with one hand and masturbated over the toilet with the other hand.

"Why are you doing that?" I asked, watching from his side.

"This is what I do now since we broke up. I'm not ashamed to admit it. I wanted you here because you turn me on," he said, pulling his penis back and forth.

"What about Helen? She's your wife. What's she doing?"

He made noises as if he was reaching his climax. Semen spilled from his penis into the toilet. At that point, he let me go. With his free hand he wiped his penis with tissue then put it back in his pants. Turning to me, he said, "Ahhh! That felt good." He smiled with a look of relief. "Helen and I are like two ships passing in the wind. We hardly see each other. She works seven nights a week. When she's home, she's asleep. She has no interest in sex. This is what I do to relieve myself."

We went back downstairs and sat on the sofa. He was calmer now than before.

"Baby, I want you back," he said. "Sometimes, I get frustrated with our situation. No matter what I do I don't know how to get you back. I sit at home and think of things to say and do to get you back into my life. I've never loved a woman the way I love you," he said, resting his head on the back of the sofa.

Bryson had a way of touching my heart. "Look, Bryson. Raymond and I are no longer together. Give me a week to think about it. But, I want you to leave now for me to clear my head."

"Okay. You have one week," he said, getting up smiling. "I'll be back next Sunday."

Feeling relieved and in control again, I was thankful for the turn of events. I was sincere. I would think about getting back with Bryson in the upcoming week. Letting him out the door, I said, "If I make a decision before the week is up, I'll call you."

He walked out the door happy. I was happy too until I closed the door. Immediately, the guilt I once felt being involved with a married man hit me like a ton of bricks. I knew then, I could never get back with Bryson, but I would wait until the week was over to tell him my decision.

Carlos came home an hour after Bryson left. It was only the two of us now. Every since mid-March Little Carl started living with his dad. I had two choices at the time Little Carl left—juvenile detention or his father. I didn't care which. All I knew was he had to leave my house.

Before Little Carl left, he stayed out too late. One of my house rules was to be in by ten p.m.. He was coming in after I left for work at eleven. I wouldn't tolerate my son being in the streets all hours of the night. He either lived by my rules or he had to go. Since I had to work, I couldn't stay at home to monitor when he came home.

Carl wanted Carlos, too. I told him not until the school term ended because I didn't want Carlos to start a new school in the middle of a term. The arrangement worked well since both Carl and Carlos wanted to live with their dad. I wanted them to be happy even if it meant giving them up.

I knew something had to be done when I slapped Little Carl twice for being disobedient. I thought of my father, the way he slapped me when I was growing up. I didn't want my son to go through what I experienced. He had to leave before one of us got hurt.

It was during this time, I also threatened him with a baseball bat. I was determined to knock some sense in him since he didn't want to listen to me. I realized then how much divorce had broken our family. Satan is very shrewd. His primary goal is to kill, steal and destroy. He works by dividing and conquering. He divides families so he can conquer them one at a time.

Carlos and I talked before I laid down to take my nap for work. He had a great weekend at his dad's. He spoke highly of Yvette. It seemed as though she made up his family now instead of me. Kids need a sense of family. It's something that God imbues in them. I was blessed that Yvette was good to my sons, and they had a substitute for me. My absence in their lives was another price I had to pay for my divorce. I prayed they would always know how much I loved them, regardless of how much time we spent together.

That night at work, at two forty-five a.m., Raymond called, wanting us to take a break in fifteen minutes. He had time to think about our relationship and wanted to discuss his decision. I told him three o'clock was fine. I'd be waiting by the elevators.

When three o'clock came we met at the elevators and rode up to the second floor cafeteria. We walked to our booth and sat down. I didn't say a word. I waited to hear what he had to say. I held my breath, expecting the worst.

"I've been thinking about our relationship all weekend. I came to a decision this evening. I've decided, I do want our relationship to continue. This summer, while my children are in Augusta, we will look for a house and get married soon."

I breathed slowly. I couldn't believe my ears. "I'm glad you came to your senses. This also means our Disney World trip is still on in August?"

"Yes. Hopefully, we will have found a house by then and can get married after the trip."

"What about our baby? Should we wait until we move and get married?"

"No, we don't have to wait unless you want to. Anytime will be good for our child to come."

A smile of joy spread across my face. Just when I thought the relationship was over, it was only beginning. God had a way of turning lemons into lemonade. And how sweet it was to drink!

THIRTY-SEVEN

Growing impatient with the publisher, who was interested in "Uncaged", I mailed out more query letters. This time, I included literary agents. Two agents had either moved or were out of business because my letters were returned unopened with a postal sticker addressed unable to forward. Two agents weren't interested, and I never heard from the other agents or publishers. It was now June and I was beginning to become discouraged.

The only thing that helped me through these times was the prophecy from God when he told me before I wrote a word of "Uncaged". "This book will be written, and it will be published." God's word is truth, and I knew "Uncaged" would be published. I just didn't know who would publish it or when. My task was to find a publisher. I sent more letters out.

June was a good month. Raymond Jr. and Francine went to Augusta after the last day of school. Raymond and I looked at several houses. One house I particularly liked was located in Stockbridge. The two story house had three spacious bedrooms upstairs with a bonus room that could be used for another bedroom or den. A combination bath/utility room was also upstairs. Downstairs had the master bedroom, large living room, dining room, an oversized kitchen with a large screened porch that led to a large fenced yard. I thought it was the perfect house for us. The neighborhood had a pool and a park within two blocks. The houses were well kept with manicured lawns. Even the price was within Raymond's range. At the end of our tour, Raymond told the real estate agent he we would call him later if we decided on buying the house after looking at more properties. Raymond had the notion that he had to look at one hundred houses before he bought one. I'm different. When I see one house I love, I'm ready to buy.

By the time we looked at three more houses in a two week span, I knew Raymond was not serious about purchasing a home. Therefore, I lost interest, too. I stopped glancing in the Homefinders section of the Sunday paper and stopped picking up the free Home Buyer's book in the grocery store. So much for living in a dream house with Raymond. I'll be content with living in my small house in Decatur, I thought as the days passed by.

Raymond's thirty-fourth birthday was Sunday, June 29. For his birthday, I took him to Steak and Ale. It and Red Lobster were our two favorite places to eat. Raymond loved their steaks and salad bar. Once seated, at a table in a room with four other people, we gave our order. As the waitress left, Raymond led the way to the salad bar. When we returned to our seats, we were both eager to eat our salads. Raymond immediately said the grace.

"Happy birthday! I see we made this day even with you kicking me to the curb several times," I said, picking up a fork full of salad.

He laughed, drinking his tea. "I guess it has been a stormy eleven months. Hopefully, it will be smooth sailing from here on out."

"I hope so because I'm pregnant again."

He put his glass down and smiled. "How far along are you?"

"One week. I didn't tell you earlier because I wanted the news to be your birthday gift."

"Thank you for such a special gift," he said, putting his fork in his salad. "That's the best gift—besides you—I can get."

I blushed, feeling both happy and embarrassed. "I hope you always feel that way."

"I will. And another thing," he said, chewing his food.

"I'll never leave you for a younger woman."

I looked at him in total amazement. I had never thought of him leaving me for any woman, especially not a younger one. I always felt he was committed to me. His last statement proved me right. "I'm glad to hear that," I said, eating more salad.

"When is the baby due?"

"February 28." (Jenny taught me how to calculate my due date by subtracting three months from my last cycle date and add seven days.)

"Have you made an appointment to see the doctor?"

"Yes, Wednesday, July 16, at one-thirty."

"I'm going with you. I'll make sure I mark that date in my planner. I received the check for the down payment on our house yesterday, in the mail. I guess, we need to look at more properties this week."

"Yes, I guess so. It would be good to buy a house before the baby comes."

"Hopefully, before the summer is over, we can move."

"That would be perfect!" I said as the waitress came with the main course. We finished our salads and ate the whole wheat loaf bread with our meal. After dinner, we went to my place for a romantic evening alone. At the conclusion of the evening, Raymond told me he enjoyed his birthday, and I enjoyed him.

The next week, we looked at houses but didn't find anything suitable. I asked Raymond to inquire about the house I liked. He did, only to find out it had been sold. All of the other homes we looked at didn't grab me like it did. I found myself losing interest and could tell Raymond felt the same way.

After our last house hunting adventure, I changed my focus to getting "Uncaged" published. The last batch of rejection letters had returned by July 11. Only Winston-Derek, the self-publishing company in Nashville, Tennessee, whom I sent the first three chapters to in October of '95, sent me a positive response. Their letter requested the completed manuscript. I mailed it off the next day.

Marvin Miller, an I.B.W.A. member, told me about Lisa Brown, his teacher at Clayton State College and University in Morrow, Georgia. He said she wanted to publish his manuscript when it was completed because she felt it was very good. His manuscript would be the first book her company, Advance Publishing and Literary Services was considering publishing. Marvin told me of a writer's meeting Lisa was having with her students at a coffee shop in Fayetteville, on Saturday, July 12. I went with my manuscript in hand. Lisa and I talked briefly after the program, where her students went to the microphone and recited or read their works. We exchanged numbers, then set up a meeting for Monday, July 14, at the IHOP on Highway 85 and Highway 139.

Lisa pulled up in her silver Mercedes Benz as I waited inside. The sun made her cocoa complexion glisten as her tall, sleek body eased from the car. I watched her shoulder length braids bounce when she opened the back door and reached for her briefcase. Locking her door, she waved when she saw me in the window.

"Have you been waiting long?" she asked as she entered the restaurant.

"Fifteen minutes," I responded, looking at my watch.

"Sorry, I'm late. I had a few last minute things to do."

"That's okay. You're here now," I said, walking toward her.

"Welcome to IHOP," greeted a friendly hostess. "How many are in your party?"

"Two," replied Lisa.

"Smoking or nonsmoking?"

"Nonsmoking," we both responded.

The hostess walked us to a table in the second row, handed us each a menu, then walked off. We studied the menus and placed our order when the waitress returned.

"What can I do for you?" Lisa asked when the waitress left with our order.

I put my manuscript on the table. "I need you to publish my manuscript."

"Do you want me to edit and evaluate it?"

"No, I need you to publish it. I'm pregnant. My baby is due February 28. I need my manuscript published before my baby comes."

"Let me read it first."

"Sure," I said, handing her the manuscript. "Marvin said you planned to publish his manuscript first. That's why I contacted you. I know his is not completed. If you're in a position to publish his, maybe you can publish mine."

"Marvin is an excellent writer. I really like his work. Let me get back with you after I read your manuscript. I will let you know then what I can do."

"Okay," I said, glad she considered reading my manuscript. "How long would it take to publish?"

"Three months."

"Good," I said, relieved the book could be published before the baby came.

The waitress came back with our food. We talked for two hours while we ate. Lisa and I hit it off instantly. I hoped she would consider publishing "Uncaged" because I thought we could work well together. If she turned me down, my only other option was Winston-Derek. Either one would be able to get "Uncaged" published long before my due date.

Raymond and I arrived for the doctor's appointment on Wednesday ten minutes early. We were told the first visit was an orientation class. The participants were given a large maternity notebook and instructions on what to do and expect during the pregnancy. We had to schedule another appointment for our first visit with the doctor or midwife. I scheduled mine for the following Wednesday, July 23 at 9 a.m..

Raymond went with me to the next appointment. We were excited for me to be examined by the doctor. Shortly after we arrived, I was called from the waiting area to be weighed in, have my blood pressure checked and a urine sample taken. From there, I was taken to an examining room where I waited until a midwife appeared. She asked me questions and gave me a food diary to complete for the next visit. When I told her about my miscarriage in February, she grew alarmed. She requested I take an ultrasound to see how the baby was doing. I went to get Raymond from the waiting area before I went into the ultrasound room because I wanted him to see our baby. I took my clothes off from the waist down as instructed. Raymond and I watched the screen as the midwife moved an instrument in my vagina. She kept moving it around until finally she took it out and asked us to excuse her. A few minutes later, she came back with an Asian-looking male doctor. He took the same instrument and probed some more.

He turned to Raymond and me and said, "I'm sorry, but you do not have a viable pregnancy. You have had a miscarriage."

The smiles disappeared from our faces. I looked at him in disbelief. "How can I have had a miscarriage when I have not had any signs of bleeding or experienced any pain?"

"You no longer have a fetus in your uterus. You have miscarried," he said showing us the empty uterus on the screen. "I'm sorry," he said as he left the room.

Pam, the midwife, said, "I want you to have a pregnancy test performed, today. Come back on Friday to have another test drawn. If you are pregnant, the HCG levels will double in forty-eight hours. If indeed you have miscarried, I suggest you get genetic testing done before you try again. Get dressed. I will put your lab request into the computer. Go across the hall to have your blood drawn. I will call you next week with the results. Do you have any questions?"

"He's wrong, Pam. I haven't lost this baby. I haven't had any signs of a miscarriage."

"Sometimes it takes a while. The two pregnancy tests will verify your status."

"Okay," I said, getting up from the table. Pam left the room. I was glad Raymond was with me. I wouldn't want to hear such bad news alone. I thought the doctor was a quack. I had not miscarried. I didn't care what he said.

Pam called me Monday, July 28, with the results of both pregnancy tests. The HCG level on the 23rd was 12,000 mIU/ml. The one on the 25th was 11,891 mIU/ml. She instructed me to get another sample drawn on Monday, August 4, then once a week until the titer was less than ten. Pam confirmed the doctor was right although I didn't want to believe him. I wanted to cry but didn't. I knew, in my heart, Viva had struck again. How could she destroy my baby? Why was she so mean?

On Sunday, August 3, at four a.m. while I was at work, my back started hurting. I was in labor. The fetal tissue passed forty-five minutes later. When the tissue passed, the pain stopped and my cycle started. I went to the ladies room to clean myself and recover the tissue sample for Pam.

The HCG level the next day was 4,434 mIU/ml. I told Pam, I wouldn't be able to take a test the following week because I was going out of town. I gave her the tissue sample to examine before I left. Friday, was our day to leave for Orlando, Florida. I was glad to get away. I needed to get over the hurt of losing another baby. Will I ever have my daughters? I thought as I packed Carlos's and my luggage for the trip.

I received a letter from Winston-Derek the same week. They wanted to co-publish my book, meaning I would have to share the cost of the first printing of the book. All subsequent printings would be their responsibility. They would send me the exact figures if I was interested.

Lisa also called. She liked the manuscript and wanted to publish it. We set a date to go over a contract. I told her I wanted to hear from Winston-Derek before I signed. She agreed.

The morning of August 7, my last night to work before we left for Disney, my old security guard friend, Isaiah Avery, stopped at the window.

"Viva!" he shouted at the window. (To a few of my Grady friends, I called myself Viva.)

I walked to the window from the back of the lab. "Long time, no see," I said, sitting in the chair at the accessioning station.

"Congratulations!"

"About what?"

"You and Ray-mon-o are getting married."

"Raymond hasn't asked me to marry him."

"Captain Lindsay announced tonight during roll call Lieutenant Miller was getting married. He is dating you, isn't he?"

"Yes, but he hasn't asked me anything."

"Oh, excuse me," he said, looking embarrassed.

"Why would Raymond tell the captain before asking me?"

"Because he knows you will say yes. Won't you?"

"I'm not saying."

Isaiah's attention suddenly shifted to someone in the hallway. "Have you seen Helen Collier yet?" he asked, looking back at me.

"No. All I know is she's tall and dark. That could be a lot of women."

"Well she just got on the elevator."

"How does she look?"

"You look better than her. But I'm not one to talk about another man's wife."

"Oh, I forgot you are Reverend Avery. I need to give you more respect," I said, bowing my head.

"Reverend or no Reverend, I better go. I don't want Ray-mon-o to see me talking to you. He might get the wrong idea."

"Bye, Isaiah. I hope you have a good night."

During the night, other officers congratulated me, too. I told them the same thing I told Isaiah, Raymond had not asked me anything. They usually smiled and kept walking.

Around 2 a.m. when I went to the ladies room, I saw Bryson in the hallway by the elevators. I stopped to talk.

He smiled when he saw me turn the corner from the D hallway. "You look good," he said, admiring me.

"Thank you. What are you doing here?"

"I came to see some old friends. I come down periodically to visit."

"This is my first time seeing you here since you were fired."

"I hear Raymond has bought you a ring," Bryson said, leaning against the wall by the elevator.

"When did you hear that?" I asked with a puzzled expression.

"That's what he's telling the guys in the department. I thought you knew."

"No. This is my first time hearing about it."

"I guess he plans to pop the question soon."

"You would think so."

"Has he given you your sign?"

"No."

"He could be waiting until he gives you your sign, or hoping you'll damn forget about it," Bryson said, laughing.

I started laughing, too. Bryson had a way of making me laugh. All of a sudden a thin, dark-skinned woman wearing shorts came down the hallway.

"I can hear you all the way down the hall," she scolded Bryson like she was his mother.

Bryson stopped talking to me and went with her down the D hallway. He turned around and silently said, Helen. I could tell Helen kept him in check when she was around. He acted liked a puppy dog on a leash. I went back to the lab feeling sorry for Bryson and glad Raymond was going to ask me to marry him soon.

THIRTY-EIGHT

I anticipated Raymond asking me to marry him while we were on vacation. I envisioned a romantic setting when he popped the question. Of course, I'd act surprised as if I had no idea he was even considering asking me. Looking at my ring finger, I imagined a large diamond engagement ring on it. I wondered what else he had up his sleeve. If it had not been for Isaiah and Bryson, he would have taken me completely by surprise.

Carlos and I loaded up our things in the car. When we finished, there was hardly any room left. I wanted to make more room, but I couldn't think of one thing I could leave behind. Carlos was the same way. I hoped Raymond traveled light or we would be in trouble.

When we arrived at the apartment, Raymond's things covered a forth of his living room floor. Since this was their first trip, I guess they decided to bring everything. It took Raymond an hour to load up the car. I couldn't believe he managed to get everything inside the car and still had room for five passengers, but he did.

During the eight hour drive, Carlos, Francine, and Raymond Jr. kept something going. Carlos didn't want Francine, who was sitting next to him, to touch him. Francine complained she didn't have enough room for her legs because Carlos's boombox was taking up too much space. Raymond Jr. whined because it was taking too long, and Francine was messing with his toys. Raymond kept driving because if he stopped to discipline them, one or all three of them would not have made it. We were determined not to let our kids spoil the trip, even if it meant grinning and bearing it for eight long hours.

At one point, I almost lost my cool, but Raymond calmed me down in time before I hurt somebody. Carlos and Francine were the worst because they couldn't stand to be next to each other. I kept thinking, what would happen if I had to put up with this every day? I would either go insane or wished I was.

When we arrived at the three bedroom condo, Raymond unloaded the car while I got the kids settled in. Francine wanted the bedroom across from the master bedroom. Carlos wanted to sleep in the living room on the sofa bed. Raymond Jr.'s bedroom by default was next to the kitchen. Since each child had their own space, I hoped it would cut down on the confusion for the week.

Raymond and Raymond Jr. went to the grocery store and KFC after he unloaded the car. I unpacked all the clothes, putting them into drawers and closets. Francine played with her dolls in her room. Carlos watched TV. The remainder of the evening was peaceful despite a few minor eruptions.

After dinner, Raymond and I settled into our bedroom. We took our showers and were ready for bed when a bright idea came to my head. I put on my house coat and went to the kitchen to get some grapes. When I returned, I walked over to Raymond's side of the bed, carrying the washed grapes in a bowl. He propped his head on his pillow when he saw the grapes.

"You know the story of Adam and Eve?" I asked placing the bowl on the end table then sitting by his hip on the bed.

"Yes," he answered, looking at me puzzled.

"They lived in the garden of Eden surrounded by fruit trees of every kind. Eve was the only woman for Adam, and Adam was the only man for Eve. I'm sure they fed each other fruit from the trees. What I'm trying to say is, you're my Adam, and I'm your Eve. There is no other man or woman for us to choose from. To symbolize our oneness, I'm going to feed you grapes," I said, placing a grape in his mouth. "I want you to know, I've never done this to any man but you. It's my sign to you that you are the man in my life," I said, feeding him more grapes. I then gave him the bowl and he fed me. We fed each other until the last grape was gone. I placed the empty bowl on the end table, then got into bed next to Raymond. We kissed and fell asleep in each other's arms.

The next day, Raymond bought five four-day passes to Disney World. We went to Magic Kingdom the first day; Epcot the second day: MGM Studios the third day; and back to Magic Kingdom the fourth. We were planning on going to Universal Studios the fifth day, but our nerves were too frayed. Raymond and I couldn't take another day of Carlos and Francine constantly being in each other's throats. They both competed for me. If Francine held my right hand, Carlos wanted to hold it, too. If Carlos stood on my left side, Francine wiggled her way in between us. Whatever one did concerning me, the other one had to do it, too.

The last two days, we spent shopping, sight-seeing and at the condo pool. By Thursday night, we were all exhausted. I demanded that Francine go to bed early because she was getting on everyone's nerves. She had lost too much sleep during the week and was very cranky. At the conclusion of the trip, I knew I would never, ever do this again. The next time, Raymond and I would go alone.

Before we left Friday morning, we cleaned the condo, spotless. I also washed and dried the last load of dirty clothes.

Raymond loaded up the car. Amazingly, he was able to get everything inside including the new things we had bought. We checked out by 10:30 a.m., thirty minutes before the deadline. Naturally, the kids didn't want to leave, but it was time to go.

On the way home, I experienced a letdown. I was disappointed Raymond hadn't proposed. I knew then, if he hadn't ask me in Florida, he never would. I made up my mind then, to distance myself from him. I would concentrate on getting "Uncaged" published and start writing my second book, "The Bearer of the Sign". Although I had not received my sign yet, I would start writing anyway because I knew, eventually, I would get it.

I thought about the last miscarriage. God said, "Your book will be published first, before you deliver." Now I understood that I could deliver any time after the book was published. At first, since I saw the pregnant image and book together, I thought, both events had to occur simultaneously. This last miscarriage, coupled with the fact that I had two publishers interested in my work, gave me the new understanding.

Also, I thought about the sixth initials, D.J., whom I had not met. Now I understood I would meet him, the last man in my life. Then I would get married. After him, there would be no other man for me to be involved with because he would give me my sign. The pieces of my life were coming together as I drove up I-75.

I went home with a new zeal. I was determined to get my life straight. Since Carlos would be living with his dad, I would have plenty of time to work on my next book. For the first time in my life, I would be by myself. I would use this time for me.

My first order of business was to get my body back right. I had an appointment with Great Shapes, an inch loss program, for my birthday. It was my gift to myself. I wanted to get rid of the pregnant look in exchange for my Viva is alive and well look!

At Great Shapes, I lost twelve inches my first visit and signed up for ten more. Those lost inches made a big difference in how my clothes fitted. By the third visit, I was wearing my old clothes. I felt good about my appearance again. I liked looking a certain way. I could tell Viva was being restored.

The next day, August 19, I took another pregnancy test. The result was 23 mIU/ml. I didn't go back anymore. I knew the next time it would be less than ten.

After taking the last pregnancy test, I made up my mind, I wouldn't get pregnant again without being married. I told Raymond of my decision. He hurt my feelings by not asking me to marry him after miscarrying two of his babies. My eyes were open now. I realized he liked to tease me about marriage, buying a house, starting a business and buying a car. He said many things he didn't mean. I was tired of hearing lies and dreams. I would make my own dream come true by getting my book published.

I met with Lisa on August 21, as scheduled. She had a preliminary contract drawn up. I looked it over, then told her what changes I wanted before I signed.

She consented with my changes. I felt good working with Lisa because she listened to what I said. If we disagreed on something, we worked it out until we were both satisfied. I took the contract home but told her I wouldn't sign until I heard from Winston-Derek.

I called Winston-Derek when I got home. The person over the phone said they had moved. It would be another month before they could mail me a contract. I hung up the phone then called Lisa to tell her, "Let's get started in two weeks." We decided on Friday, September 5. That would give me enough time to carefully read over the contract and get my money for the first three installments. I was ready to get this show on the road. I didn't have time for Winston-Derek to get their act together.

Friday, August 22, I started writing "The Bearer of the Sign". Although I had not received my sign, I knew God would answer my prayer. I wrote by faith and not by sight. If I relied on sight, my sign would never come.

On September 5, I signed the contract with Lisa. She said she would have to edit the manuscript first which was covered with the first payment. She needed another payment when she took it to the printer. The third payment would be due when it came back from the printer in November. The printer would give us galleys to proofread before he bound the book. The whole process would be completed by December 1. I would need the last payment then for marketing. Raymond came over the same evening. I gave him a small photo album of the Disney World pictures I had taken with my camera. After looking through the pictures, he said he wasn't satisfied with the quality of the pictures. I told him, I had a cheap camera. He said he would buy me a better camera. I smiled and thanked him. We spent the rest of the evening reminiscencing about the trip. We laughed at the funny things the kids said and did. We agreed we'd never go on another trip with all three kids again. Their compulsive behavior ruined the trip.

Saturday evening, we went to Wal-Mart on Wesley Chapel Road. They had several good cameras to choose from. Raymond wanted to spend about $80. He saw a Canon Sure Shot and Olympus Stylus models he liked. While we were in the store browsing, the thought came to me, if Raymond buys me the camera, I would count it as my sign since it cost at least fifty dollars. The truth was, I was ready to receive my sign. Today, with the purchase of the camera, I would get it. As I finished my thought, a brown, heavy-set, elderly sales clerk came over to assist us.

"May I help you?" she asked, standing behind the counter.

"I would like to see this Canon Sure Shot camera," Raymond replied, pointing at the camera.

She bent down to unlock the camera cabinet. Searching for a few minutes, she straightened up and said, "We're out of that model."

"What about this Olympus Stylus model?" Raymond asked, pointing again.

"Let me see," she said, bending down. "There's not much down here. We're sold out of everything except the most expensive models. I'm sorry," she said, standing up and adjusting her glasses. "We're out of that model, too."

"We'll go someplace else another day," Raymond said as we walked off.

I couldn't believe what just happened. Here I was, about to get my sign and they were sold out! Lord, will I ever get my sign? I asked myself as we walked out of the store holding hands.

The following week, we went to another Wal-Mart that was also sold out of cameras in Raymond's price range. Kmart wanted $10 more for the same camera. We decided to wait until later. I took what happened as an omen from God that Raymond would never give me my sign.

On Thursday morning, September 18, when Jenny and I were walking to the parking deck, we saw Raymond, in the hallway at the snack bar, opening one of the double doors that were closed.

"Hi, Raymond," I said as Jenny and I saw him open the door.

"Wait a minute. I have something to give you," he said finishing his task, then reaching into his back pocket to retrieve his wallet. Thumbing inside, he pulled out several bills and gave them to me.

"What's this for?" I asked, taking the money.

"It's for you, to buy the camera."

"Thank you," I said holding four twenties, smiling. He walked off and so did we. "Jenny, do you see what's in my hand?" I asked, waving the money in her face.

"Yeah, money."

"This is my sign. Remember, I wrote the next man in my life would give me fifty dollars or more voluntarily. When he gives the money to me, I'll ask, 'What is this for?' His reply will be, 'This is for you, because I am your man.' And indeed he will be from that day on. Jenny you just witnessed Raymond giving me my sign. Don't you agree?"

"Yeah, I guess so. I knew a long time ago, he was right for you."

"Yes, I remember, you telling me that. Well Jenny, he'll be mine forever!"

"That's good. Can you give me a sign to show me how to get my 33 year old son out the house?"

We both laughed as we went through the double glass doors.

THIRTY-NINE

I went to my car excited Raymond had given me my sign. He teased me throughout our relationship that he would never give me any sign. He said the only sign I would get from him was a banner over my front door that read, "Stupid Fool! This Is Your Sign," I called him when I reached the Ingles parking lot on Wesley Chapel Road. I dialed his office number from my car phone.

"Security Services, Lieutenant Miller speaking."

"Raymond, do you know what you did this morning?"

"What?"

"You gave me my sign."

"Nooo I didn't. I told you I wasn't going to give you your sign."

"When you gave me the $80, you gave me my sign. My sign was for a man to give me $50 or more, voluntarily."

"Anybody could have done that."

"That's true. But only you did. Also, when I took the money, I asked you, what was it for? You said, 'It's for you.' The second part of my sign was to say, 'It is for you because I am your man.' And indeed he will be from that day on. See, you even said the right words, for the most part. Congratulation's Raymond, you're the bearer of the sign! That means, we'll be together the rest of our lives!"

"You're talking nonsense."

"No, I'm telling you the truth. You are the bearer of the sign."

"I guess that means, we'll get married soon."

"I don't know how soon we'll get married. But it does mean, you'll be my next husband."

"We'll continue this conversation later. I have to run. I need to go up to the 12th floor. I was on my way out when you called."

"Okay, the bearer of the sign," I said, laughing as I hung up the phone.

I felt good knowing Raymond had given me my sign. I didn't know if we would be married in time to fulfill another prophecy—"There will be a question about your name. It will be changed before the work goes to print." There was no question about it, Vanessa Lewis would not be on "Uncaged." No way was I going to be known to the world by my divorced name, Lewis.

221

Deeva Denez

On the way home from the grocery store, I started thinking of my life with Raymond, Raymond Jr. and Francine. I wasn't sure I was up to the added responsibilities, especially, when my present life was carefree. The more I thought about giving up my freedom, the more disturbed I became. Do I really want to get married again and start a new family? Do I want to be a stepmother? After several minutes of pondering the questions, I answered, yes. Viva, however, answered, hell no!

"Girlfriend, you need to listen to me this time. We don't need to raise nobody else's chulins. We're FREE! We don't have to worry about nobody but ourselves. You're crazy to give all this up to be tied back down with a family. This is the time to please us—to think about what we want in life."

"Viva, you don't understand me. All I know is family life. This single life is not for me. I love coming home to a husband and children. Both have been taken from me through divorce. Marrying Raymond will restore what has been taken from my life. I am a mother and a wife without a husband and children."

"And I am your counterpart who hasn't had a chance to fully enjoy being single. I don't want to be tied down. I want to remain uncaged and unleashed!"

"Your days are numbered. I'm marrying Raymond whether you like it or not."

"Uh, not if I can prevent it. And believe me, girlfriend, I'm going to do everything in my power to come between you and Raymond," she said, going back in.

The days that followed were a power struggle with Viva. She filled my head with negative thoughts and kept telling me how good it felt to be alone, thinking only of myself. Some days, I struggled with myself, trying not to give in.

On Friday, October 5, I met with Lisa to give her the second installment. My manuscript was ready for the printer. Raymond had not proposed. Therefore, I knew, Vanessa Miller was not going to be used as the author. I thought of the perfect name which I discussed with Lisa. The name was Deeva Denez. I changed Viva to Veeva to make her seem like a real person. Then I used a D instead of a V for her name. The name Denez came to me one night at work. Actually, Viva wrote "Uncaged" correcting the wrongs done to me to make them right. Going back over my past was too painful for me to write. Lisa liked the name. I didn't explain why I wanted to use it.

The next day, Raymond saw a good deal on a '91 Nissan Maxima in the paper. We went Sunday morning to inquire about the ad. Raymond thought it was an exceptional value because the car was well kept with low mileage. He left the owner a personal check and told him he'd be back the next day with a certified check to purchase the vehicle.

Monday, we returned with the certified check. The owner said he was offered cash for the car after we left, but he was a man of his word. He told the

222

cash buyer to call back later today to see if Raymond returned to buy the car. Raymond left with the car, a proud owner of a good automobile.

I felt strange not sharing my car. When we had one car, we did everything together, including grocery shopping. Now, with two cars, we did things independently. The first time I went grocery shopping without Raymond, I felt abandoned. My only consolation was knowing one day we would shop again as husband and wife.

Raymond talked of marriage often. He even suggested we live in my house for starters until we could find a bigger place. I knew when he suggested we all live in my house, he had no intentions of buying a house. I also knew I was right a year ago that he wasn't interested in buying a home.

I didn't respond to his suggestion. I hoped, in time, he would change his mind when he saw I wasn't going along with his plan. Neither one of us ever mentioned it again.

During this time, Bryson dropped by, as he customarily did, when he got the notion. I told him three weeks before he had to break his habit of coming over whenever he pleased because Raymond had his own transportation. I shook my head when I saw his van pull up. I watched him as he got out of the van and came to the steps. The only reason I let him inside, I knew Raymond was taking his evening nap.

"What are you doing here?" I asked opening the door.

"I came to see you," he said smiling, coming inside.

"I told you three weeks ago to stop coming over. Raymond may come by unexpectantly."

"I don't give a damn about Raymond," he said making himself comfortable on the sofa.

"Well, I do. He's my man and can come over anytime without bumping into you."

"You're breaking my heart," he said sarcastically.

"Come, sit down next to me," he said, patting the sofa.

"I'll sit on the loveseat. What's on your mind? Why did you come over?"

"I told you earlier. To see you. Damn it! Stop playing games, Van. You know why I'm here."

"Bryson, I'm not playing games. You are. You know Raymond and I will get married soon."

"Has he propose?"

"No."

"Has he bought the house he plans to put you in?"

"No."

"Has he started his multi-billion dollar business he's been filling your head with?"

"No."

"And you think, I'm playing games. Wake up Van! Raymond is full of lies! Maybe, now, you'll believe me. I never tried to swell your head with false accusations. I've been truthful to you from the very beginning."

"Yeah right. You lied about you and Helen. You didn't tell me you were married. And you keep lying now, saying you're going to leave Helen. You lie about getting a divorce. And Raymond lie about getting married. I'm tired of both of you telling me lies. I need to find me someone who is sincere."

"Bull shit! You'll never find someone to love you like I do. I am sincere when I say I love you."

"Admit, you'll never leave Helen. You just want to string me along—to be your side kick. God told me over a year ago, you're a dead end and He was right."

"I should have never let you get up," he said, coming toward me. "That was my first mistake. When I get you down this time, I won't ever let you get up again," he said, grabbing me, pulling me to the floor. "I let you get away the last time. You're not getting away again!"

"No Bryson! Stop! Get off me!" I screamed, fighting him off as he pinned me underneath him.

"I am going to take you right now! Because you're mine. You belong to me!"

I struggled with him to no avail. He was determined to get his prize. Pulling my dress up and his pants down, Bryson was an inch from reaching his goal. "No, Bryson. No," I pleaded, calmly looking into his eyes.

Without saying a word, he got up, pulling up his pants. I got up, pulling my dress down, watching his every move. He sat on the sofa with his eyes closed. I sat on the loveseat watching him. After several minutes passed, he spoke.

"I know you're wondering why I stopped."

"Because I asked you to."

"No. When I saw the look on your face, I knew I could win the battle but lose the war. If I lose the war, I'll lose you forever. I couldn't risk doing that. I love you too much," he said, wiping sweat from his forehead. "Sometimes, I wish I could shake you to make you realize how much I love you. All you see is my status. I wish you knew how I feel on the inside."

I watched silently, taking it all in. "Bryson, I hate to sound like a broken record, but what we had is over. I need more than what you can give me. All you have to offer me is sex."

"I love you more than for sex! We haven't had sex in over a year. If that's all I wanted from you, I wouldn't be here now. Don't you see," he said, getting up walking toward me, "I don't want sex! I want you! You told me yourself, the only way I could get you back was either give you your sign or get you down. I haven't been able to give you your sign. That means, my only chance of getting you back is to get you down," he said, pinning me to the wall.

"You couldn't give me my sign because you're the wrong person for me," I said in his face. "Raymond gave me my sign because he's the right man for me. God told me last August you were a dead end and Raymond was a green light. The fact you're still married, a year later with no signs of leaving your wife, tells me God was right which I never questioned. Coupled with the fact, Raymond gave me my sign, proves again God was right."

"All I know is, I love you and want you in my life. I don't care if it's right or wrong. I'll leave now," he said walking to the door. "But I want you to always remember, I love you."

I didn't respond but silently let him out the door. His presence unnerved me and I wanted him to leave. Lisa called thirty minutes after Bryson left. She said the printer was having problems and "Uncaged" wouldn't be ready until the second week in December. The galleys should be ready the week of Thanksgiving.

On the Friday before Thanksgiving, Raymond came over with marriage on his mind. We were sitting on the loveseat, cuddled up, with my head on his chest and his arms wrapped around me, when he told me what he expected from his wife.

"You have accused me of teasing you concerning marriage, many times. I can sense your frustration. You have told me that I say a lot of things but never do anything. I want you to know, that although you can't see anything, I am doing something."

"Like what?"

"I can't say now. You'll find out later. There is something I want you to know now, though."

"What is it?"

"What I expect from you as my wife. And I do plan to marry you, when the time is right."

"When will that be?"

"I'm working on some things now that will facilitate the process. I don't know when."

"Oh. What are your expectations?"

"I will be responsible for everything on the outside and you will be responsible for everything on the inside."

"There are more things on the inside than on the outside to be responsible for," I interjected, sitting up.

"The inside is yours. You'll have a lot of free time because I don't want you to work, but to stay at home and take care of our family. I'll work and provide for the family. That way, you'll have plenty of time to do everything on the inside."

"So in other words, you want me to be like your mama? I've seen her work herself to the bone while you and the kids do absolutely nothing to help her. I can't be like Mrs. Simmons."

"I'm not asking you to be like my mother. I'm used to living a certain way and that's what I expect from my wife."

"You don't want a wife, you want a maid."

"Let me continue, please."

"Go ahead."

"I'll also expect you to have sex whenever I want it."

"Raymond, this is my body. You can't have sex with me if I don't want you to. We both have to consent to have sex."

"As my wife, your body belongs to me. I will take it if you won't give it to me. I remember with my ex, she laid there while I took it. It made her so mad, but I didn't care."

"I see why y'all divorced. I'm telling you now, you ain't taking nothing from me."

"You won't be able to stop me."

"You're crazy, Raymond. You're talking like a male chauvinist fool! I can't be your wife under these circumstances."

"Sure you can. It's not as bad as it sounds. You'll be able to adjust easily to my demands."

"I don't think so. I'll feel caged up again with no hope of ever being freed."

"You said yourself since I gave you your sign, I will be your next husband. You're stuck with me now," he said laughing.

I didn't laugh because what he said was not funny. However, he was right. Since he was the bearer of the sign, he would be my next husband whether I liked it or not. I have to be careful what I pray for, I thought, as he continued to tell me his expectations.

FORTY

Raymond's expectations greatly disturbed me. So much so, I couldn't see myself being his wife. I felt as if I would be in bondage. I wouldn't be happy; something I cherished at this point in my life. My next husband had to add to my happiness, not take from it. Unless Raymond changed his expectations, I wouldn't be his wife. I didn't care if he was the bearer of the sign.

All day Saturday, I felt gloomy. No matter what I did, I couldn't shake it. Finally, that night, I realized what my problem was. I had strayed so far from God, through my many trespasses against Him, I had come to the end of myself. I needed God in my life, one hundred percent. No longer would I serve him half-heartily. But I would give my whole body as a sacrifice to Him and Jesus Christ. I reached for my Bible and read Romans 12:1-2, *"I beseech you therefore, brethren, by the mercies of God, that you present your bodies as a living sacrifice, holy, and acceptable to God, which is your reasonable service. And do not conform to this world, but be transformed by the renewing of your mind, that you may prove what is that good and acceptable and perfect will of God."*

As I read the Scriptures, my left hand touched my heart and the key necklace. I put the Bible down and walked to my mirror in my room. The diamond on the key sparkled as I stood in the mirror. My hands reached for the clasp to unfasten it. I took the necklace off and dropped to my knees by my bed and prayed.

Dear Heavenly Father and Jesus Christ, my Lord,

My heart belongs to You and You alone. A man no longer has the key to my heart. No one can love me like Jesus, who gave His life for me. Please forgive me for allowing someone else to take Your place in my life. From this day forward, I will serve You with my whole heart. I present my body to You as a living sacrifice. I know You do not desire my money, but my broken will to do Your Will. You can take my brokenness, caused by sin, and make me whole. Forgive me of all my sins, which are many. Cleanse me with the blood of Jesus to make me whiter than snow.

Father, I know, I am not a physical virgin but make me a spiritual virgin for the next man in my life. I repent of all sexual immorality, which is sinning against my body. I desire to be pure in mind, body and spirit all the days of my life. I pray this in the name of your Son, Jesus Christ. Amen.

After praying, I realized, I had the wrong focus. My focus was on becoming the bride of a man instead of being the Bride of Jesus at His second coming. I had to re-direct my life to live by every Word of God. My will had to be in line with God's Will in my life.

Thinking of virgins and being the Bride of Jesus, I turned my Bible to Matthew 25:1-13, *"Then the kingdom of heaven shall be likened to ten virgins who took their lamps and went out to meet the bridegroom. Now five of them were wise, and five were foolish. Those who were foolish took their lamps and took no oil with them, but the wise took oil in their vessels with their lamps. But while the bridegroom delayed, they all slumbered and slept. And at midnight a cry was heard: Behold, the bridegroom is coming; go out and meet him! Then all those virgins arose and trimmed their lamps. And the foolish said to the wise, `Give us some of your oil, for our lamps are going out.' But the wise answered, saying, `No, lest there should not be enough for us and you; but go rather to those who sell, and buy for yourselves. And while they went to buy, the bridegroom came, and those who were ready went in with him to the wedding; and the door was shut. Afterward the other virgins came also, saying, `Lord, Lord, open to us!' But he answered and said, `Assuredly, I say unto you, I do not know you.' Watch therefore, for you know neither the day nor the hour in which the Son of Man is coming."*

I asked God for a full measure of His Holy Spirit so I would be wise and not be left out of the marriage with Jesus Christ at his coming. My prayer and Bible study assured me I was back on the right track. The fruit of God's Holy Spirit would be evident as I lived my life according to God's Will and Way.

Sunday, Carlos wanted to go to the arcades at South Dekalb Mall. He played the games for an hour before I told him, I wanted to go to B. Dalton Bookstore to look at the New Releases section. He didn't object because he had spent all his money on the games.

In B. Dalton's, I visualized my book, "Uncaged" on the New Releases's shelf. By faith, I received it as already done. I knew, one day, my book would be on their shelf.

Carlos wanted to browse in the music store, next door, to listen to CD's while I performed my act of faith. I waited on a bench, near the store, when I finished. As I was sitting on the bench, a man walked passed me then came back. He had on a gray work uniform with Tech America written on the pocket. His features were those of a pure Black man with jet black skin, wide medium nose, small oval eyes and thick lips. He looked to be about five-ten, in his mid thirties with an average build and slightly round waistline. Short black hair crowned his face.

"Don't I know you? he asked, turning around. "You look familiar."

"I've never seen you before. "I'm asked that question all the time. I must have a twin somewhere," I replied, closing my green coat I bought with the eighty dollars Raymond gave me for the camera.

"I travel all the time. I could have sworn I've seen you before."

"Where have you been?"

"I'm from California. I've been in Atlanta for three years. I've traveled to Germany, Jamaica, Trinidad, Africa, Italy, South America, Japan, Puerto Rico, Hawaii, and other parts of the United States," he said, sitting next to me.

"How can you remember seeing someone when you've been to all those places?"

"I could never forget a face as pretty as yours. By the way, my name is Douglas Jefferson."

"I'm Vanessa Lewis. It's nice to meet you," I said blushing.

"You won't believe what happened to me the other day. I received my phone bill last week which had a credit charge on it. So I called Bell South up and asked them what the credit was for? They said because my bill was over paid. I explained to them that I paid what was due and not a cent more. Well, to make a long story short, they wouldn't reverse the $25 credit charges. God is good," he said, smiling, squinting his small eyes.

"Yes, He is."

"Things like that happen to me all the time. Every since I've been paying tithes and staying in the Word, Jesus has been blessing me."

"That makes two of us."

"I was at the card shop buying a card for my son, Melchizedek. I send him a card every week since he lives with his mother in Alabama," he said, showing me the card inside a white bag.

"That's very thoughtful of you."

"I like sending cards to tell him how much I love him and miss him," he said, placing the bag between us. "Why are you here?"

"I wrote a book called, "Uncaged". It will be out next month. I was visualizing it inside B. Dalton's. I call it an act of faith. God wants us to live by faith, not by sight."

"He sure does. It's good to meet another Christian. Do you come here often?"

"No. I'm here with my youngest son. He asked me to bring him to the arcades. He's in the music store now, listening to CD's."

"I work with computers. I can help you with your book."

"I want to put it on the Internet. Can you help me do that?"

"Sure. I can do anything with computers. I build computers."

"I've never met anyone who builds computers."

He reached into his back pocket and pulled out his wallet. "Here is my business card. Call me when you want me to put your book on the Internet. Is there anything else you need me to do?"

"No. I will call you when my book comes out," I said, putting the card in my coat pocket. By this time, I saw Carlos coming from the music store. "It was nice meeting you, Douglas," I said, standing up. "It's time for me to go." Carlos stood beside me as I finished speaking. "This is my son, Carlos. Carlos, this is Mr. Jefferson," I said as Carlos stood by my side.

"Hi, Carlos."

"Hey."

"What is your book about?" Douglas asked, picking up his bag walking with us.

"My life. Everything there is to know about me is written in my book."

"I have to make sure I get a copy."

"I have your number. I'll call you when it comes out," I said, stopping at a passageway. My car was parked in the back, down the hallway.

"Can I have your number?" he asked, quickly.

I thought about it for a minute. Should I give him my number? I don't like giving out my number. I saw something in his eyes that told me it was okay. "555-9663." He wrote the number down on the white bag. Carlos and I walked down the hallway. Douglas went in the opposite direction.

When I got home I checked my messages. Douglas had called twice. He probably thought I gave him the wrong number and was trying it out. I called his pager number to let him know I got his messages. He called me right back. We talked for thirty minutes.

He called again later that evening. We mostly talked about God. Douglas had fascinating stories concerning things God had done for him in his life. One story was, God had told him to only take two dollars to work with him, one day. He had more money, but that is the amount God wanted in his pocket. Consequently, he had to rely on God to supply money for gas and lunch. During the day, he called the college he was attending to inquire about a book. The person answering the phone told him, he had a fifty dollar reimbursement check. Douglas picked up the check later and thanked God for supplying his needs.

Tuesday, when Douglas called, I told him I was seeing someone. He had called everyday, several times a day, since I gave him my number Sunday. He said he understood and only wanted to be Christian friends. I told him I didn't want other men calling my house. He agreed not to call anymore and told me to page him if I wanted to talk because he worked two jobs and was rarely at home.

Tuesday night, Raymond came over. We were both off because we had to work Thanksgiving. I knew he was expecting to make love or accommodate each other as Raymond put it. Since I had repented of all sexual immorality, Saturday, I did not want to have sex.

Raymond arrived at six-thirty. By eight o'clock, we were in the bed. I felt so guilty during the love making session, I didn't enjoy a minute of it. He couldn't tell the difference because he thoroughly enjoyed himself. I told myself, later, that I would never let it happen again. My heart and body belonged to Jesus. Somehow, I would have to let Raymond know.

Wednesday, Lisa called to say the galleys were ready. I opted not to proofread them because I trusted what was submitted. She assured me they would be exactly what we had corrected at our last meeting. We both wanted the book to be published without delay.

For Thanksgiving, Raymond, Carlos and I went to my brother's house. Everyone was eating when we arrived at 4:30 p.m.. It was the first time Raymond met my whole family. Sheila's, Xavier's wife, family was present also. I introduced Raymond to everyone before we ate.

After Raymond ate, Xavier invited him into the loft area of the house to be with the other men. They watched TV, talked and drank alcohol, all except Raymond, who didn't drink and barely said a word. He was the opposite of Carl who kept everybody laughing and drank liberally.

I socialized with the women. We talked about our men, kids, jobs and new recipes. Sheila had the younger kids make gingerbread houses in the garage. They were out of our way having fun which made the occasion very pleasurable.

By seven o'clock, Raymond and I left because we needed to take a nap before we went to work. We left Carlos behind since he wasn't ready to leave. My sister, Beverly, volunteered to keep him overnight.

Raymond and I went home and got in the bed. When we cuddled up to each other, something came over me. I would not be disobedient this time. I had to tell Raymond everything on my mind.

His arms wrapped around me. We had already kissed goodnight. My back was against his chest. By the movements of his hands, I could tell he was ready to get something started. It was at that point, Viva said her piece.

"Raymond, I don't want to be tied down with more children. I won't be happy being your servant either! I won't be responsible for everything in the house because it'll be too much for me to do. I don't know what kind of woman you think I am, but my body is my body. You can't have sex with me if I don't want you to. And besides that, you haven't satisfied me in weeks! You don't care if I come or not. That tells me you don't love me the right way."

I then spoke, "I need someone who is interested in my well-being. Someone, who will add to my happiness and not subtract from it. It took me too long to reach this point in my life, where I am happy! I treasure my happiness more than anything on earth. And I will not let you or anyone else take any of it from me.

Furthermore, I'm not having sex anymore without being married first. I'm doing everything God's way from this day forward."

Raymond didn't say a word after I spoke. He continued to hold me as we fell asleep. We got up when the alarm sounded, got dressed and went to work. When Raymond didn't call me during the shift, I knew he was upset. I didn't call him either. I was giving him time to think about what I said. I hoped we could talk about it later after it had time to sink in.

I started a fast Friday, beseeching God to remove everything that came between us. I prayed for Him to remove Viva from my life. During this fast, I wanted my flesh to be crucified forever! And to let His Will be done with my relationship with Raymond.

I left a message on Bryson's phone for him not to ever call or come by my house again. If he called, I'd hang up on him. If he came by, I wouldn't let him inside. I had had enough of playing with God. It was time to become a real Christian again!

I programmed all my automatic channels in my car to AM gospel stations. One station, 860, had ministers speaking throughout the day. The other stations played a mixture of gospel music and sermons. All I wanted to hear while I drove was either the Word or praises to God. I located my gospel tapes to make sure they were in the car.

I turned the radio inside the house to the AM stations as well. I had to renew my mind and not conform to this world. I couldn't risk giving place to Satan any longer. I wanted to get rid of everything in my life that did not glorify God. I placed prayer and Bible study at the top of my daily to do list.

Bryson called Friday evening. I immediately hung up the phone when I heard his voice. When he didn't call back, I knew the fast was working. I felt like a yoke had been removed from me.

The whole weekend passed without a word from Raymond. I knew then our relationship was over. I tried not to think about how hurt I was. I kept my mind on God. I prayed for strength to see me through. Jesus lifted my spirits by having Douglas call me Sunday afternoon who shared more Christian stories that made me praise God more.

At the end of the conversation, Douglas asked me to eat dinner with him. He had just gotten out of church and wanted us to eat together and talk. I said okay. Later, it dawned on me as I hung up the phone, his initials were D.J..

FORTY-ONE

Douglas asked me to meet him at the Amoco station, in twenty minutes, across from South Dekalb Mall. Not wanting to wear the jeans I had on, I chose a beige pants suit with a green, brown and rose flowered top. Pulling it from the closet, I slipped it on. My hair was up, but I took it down. I looked in the mirror and was pleased with the final results. I wanted to look good for D.J..

I drove to Amoco feeling uneasy about the meeting. I had second doubts, thinking, I shouldn't be doing this because I was still Raymond's woman. We had not officially broken up. We were just going through another episode of noncommunication.

I parked on the side away from the pumps, looking into every car that came up. Twenty minutes after our appointed time, Douglas had not arrived. I took it as a sign I was not suppose to meet him. Therefore, I went back home.

As I walked in the house, the phone rang. I answered on the third ring. "Hello."

"Vanessa, I'm at the Amoco station," Douglas stated.

"I left a few minutes ago. I didn't think you were coming."

"Come on back. I'll be waiting. I got tied up in traffic on I-285. A truck overturned."

I hesitated a minute before responding. "Okay."

"Good. We'll go to a barbecue restaurant on Chandler Rd."

"I'm on my way." We said good-bye and hung up.

I got back in my car and met Douglas at Amoco. I drove up to my same spot on the side. Douglas was parked by the telephones on the left, driving an old, red Pinto. I recognized his eyes through the windshield. Waving at me, he drove his car next to mine.

"Follow me," he shouted from the driver's side with the passenger window rolled down.

I followed him out of the Amoco, onto Chandler Rd, to Hodges Barbecue Restaurant. We parked adjacent to each other in front of the building.

He smiled as we walked into the restaurant together. I liked Hodges food. Barbecue was my favorite food to eat. I ordered the barbecue chicken dinner with macaroni and cheese, and lima beans. Douglas ordered the beef tips with collards and potato salad. We both had tea with our meals.

We sat at a table in the back of the restaurant by the window. Six other people were eating at three different tables. Douglas pulled my chair out, pushed me up, then went to his seat in front of me. He said grace as we bowed our heads.

"How was church?" I asked, putting a napkin in my lap after the grace.

"God is good. I go to World Changes with Pastor Creflo O'Dollar. He preached to the single men on how to find the right Christian woman. He reminded us from the Scriptures, it's not good for man to be alone."

"I read an article about your church a few months ago. That's the church Evander Holyfield goes to. And the members gave your pastor a Rolls Royce."

"The media loves to emphasize the Rolls Royce. They don't understand Pastor O'Dollar and his ministry. He teaches the Word. He gets members to live by the Word by understanding it in its simplest form. The media never has anything positive to say concerning my church."

"Why do you have a work uniform on?"

"I have to go to my part-time job this evening. I wore it to church. We go as we are. I never wear suites and ties to church."

"Do you ever have a day off?" I asked eating my lima beans.

"No. I work seven days a week."

"Why do you work so much when it's only you?"

"Work keeps me occupied since my son is gone, and I don't have anyone in my life."

I noticed he wasn't eating his food. I ate a piece of my cornbread and sipped on my tea. He sat with his hands in his lap, looking at me. My cycle was on and I needed to change. "Excuse me. I need to go to the ladies room. I'll be right back," I said, grabbing my purse from the floor, pushing my chair back. When I returned five minutes later, he had eaten all his food. I thought it was odd, but I didn't say anything. I kept thinking, either he was too bashful to eat in front of me or he ate like a pig. I didn't know which.

"The Holy Spirit told me to ask you out today. He said you would say yes."

"He did? What else did He tell you?"

"That you like me, and if I called you to come back to the Amoco station, you would come."

I laughed, picking up my chicken to eat. "You have a way with me. I should say no when I say yes."

"The Holy Spirit told me to ask for your number the first day we met. He said, `Douglas get that number, or you will never see her again.' When you gave me your number, I felt good, knowing the Holy Spirit was right."

"I don't give out my number to strangers. But your eyes told me it was okay."

"God is good," he said smiling, squinting his small eyes.

I looked at Douglas, wishing he was Raymond sitting across from me. I ate my food while Douglas talked, telling me more about instructions from the Holy Spirit and stories of his life. We left one hour later when I used my last pad.

I went home having mixed feelings about our date. Douglas was a very nice, spiritual man. I couldn't get into him, however, because I still loved Raymond. I wanted us to work things out. I didn't want to start over in a new relationship.

That night at work, Raymond called me to talk. We took a break at three o'clock. I didn't know what to expect. I hoped for the best when we sat down at our booth. Raymond's face looked troubled. I knew that was a sign of bad news.

He put his elbows on the table, holding his hands together to cover his mouth. Looking into my eyes, he stared for a minute before speaking. Putting his hands on the table he said, "I've been rehashing our relationship for the past year and three months. It seems as if, we've been going on a roller coaster ride with all our ups and downs. I can't take anymore. Thursday, when you told me how you felt, I realized I don't know you as well as I thought I did. I think it would be best if we go our separate ways."

"If that's what you want, then I don't have a choice. But I do want you to know, part of our problem is Viva. I'm working on getting rid of her. We'll never make it as long as she's around."

He looked at me. He was all too familiar with Viva. He knew she made me do things out of character. Whenever she came out in his presence, he'd tell me, "Put Viva back in the box!" Sometimes, I told him, "Viva wanted to come out and play." And she did.

"I will give it more thought. I'll let you know later in the week. You said Thursday, you're not happy with me. I will end the relationship if that will make you happy."

"I said, I am already happy. I treasure my happiness more than anything on this earth. It took me too long to reach this point in my life. I will not let you or anyone else subtract from my happiness. You can add to it but not take from it. I wouldn't be happy living up to your expectations."

He took a deep breath. "I need time to think things through. I'll let you know later."

"Okay."

We slid from the booth and went back to work. I didn't know what his decision would be, but I hoped we could still make it work. I prayed to let God's Will be done, regardless of the outcome.

Douglas called Monday morning before I went to sleep. I told him, I was going through something with my friend and didn't want to talk to anyone else until the situation was resolved. I would call him when I was ready to talk.

My heart felt heavy when I fell asleep. I loved Raymond more than I realized. The thought of losing him was more than I could bear. I cried myself to sleep.

Viva said, "Dry your eyes, girlfriend. I told you, I was going to get rid of Raymond. He could never make me happy. His ass had to go!"

"You have to go, Viva," I said, wiping my tears. "I'll never be happy with you in my life. I'm working on getting rid of you. I don't know how long it will take."

"Girlfriend, I ain't going no damn where! I know you been getting into the Word, lately. Listening to the Word all damn day. Praying, fasting and meditating. But, I'm telling you now, I'm here to stay. Like it or not!"

"Let me sleep, Viva. I will continue in the Word of God all the days of my life. One day, you'll be gone if I keep doing what I'm doing."

"Sweet dreams. I'll be here when you wake up."

I finished my sleep in peace, thinking of Raymond and me getting back together.

Raymond called me at 3:30 a.m. Thursday morning. He said he had made his decision and wanted to return my keys. He was on his way down to the lab. Choking back the lump in my throat, I told him to come on. I'll have his house and car keys ready.

Five minutes later, Raymond appeared at the window. I was sitting in the chair facing him.

"Here are your keys," he said, handing them to me through the opening.

I had his keys in my opened hand. He took his keys, leaving mine.

"Thank you," he said, putting his keys on his key ring as he walked away.

My heart ached looking at the keys in my hand. They meant our relationship was over, and I was free to move on.

For the remainder of the shift, I fought back tears as I worked. Tia and Jenny left me alone. They sensed I was going through something when I didn't join in their conversations. I had told Tia earlier, Raymond and I were on the verge of breaking up. She saw tears in my eyes when Raymond left, but didn't say anything because the expression on my face said it all.

Tears flooded my eyes as I drove home as if a dam had erupted. No longer could I hold them back, crying all the way home. Raymond didn't have to do this, I kept telling myself. All we had to do was talk and work out our differences. "Lord help me get through this," I pleaded. "Help me see the rainbow on the other side."

"Girlfriend, dry your damn eyes. You ain't lost nothing but trouble, heartache and misery. Out of all the men in Atlanta, you end up with twerps, slurps and quirks! There are some FINE brothers in this city! I'm getting embarrassed with your men. You've gone from Steve Urkle to Kuta Kinte. And another thing, girlfriend. You probably know the only man in the U.S. who still drives a fucking Pinto!"

"Viva, leave me alone. I'm not up to your harassment. Can't you see I'm heartbroken?"

"Cheer up, girlfriend. Losing Raymond was the best thing to happen to you."

"Shut up, Viva! In the name of Jesus Christ, get out of my life!"

"I'm outta here, girlfriend!"

I pulled into the driveway as Viva made her exit. I was glad to be home. All I could think of was getting in my bed and falling asleep. The phone rang before I went to bed. I answered it quickly, thinking it was Raymond, changing his mind.

"Hello," I said, trying not to sound as if I had been crying.

"Hello, Vanessa. Are you all right?" Douglas asked.

"No. I'm very upset. I broke up with my friend this morning."

"The Holy Spirit told me to call you. I told Him you didn't want me to call you anymore. He said, `Call anyway.'"

I smiled. I hadn't heard from Douglas in three days. Today, the Holy Spirit was right. I was glad to hear his voice. I also believed this was God's way of getting me through this.

"Vanessa, are you there?"

"Yes, I'm here. I was thinking how good it is to hear from you this morning. The timing is perfect."

I leave for Germany, Saturday. I would like to see you before I go."

"Douglas, I'm not up to starting a new relationship. I need time to get over my friend. I'm very hurt by our breakup."

"I understand. It would mean a lot to me if I can see you for a few minutes before I leave, I'll be gone for three weeks."

Three weeks, I repeated to myself. That would give me time to get my head straight. "Why are you going to Germany?"

"I'm in the reserves. Once a year, I have to leave for three weeks. Every month, I have to leave for a weekend."

"Will you be fighting?"

"No. I'll be in training and relieving solders working on the base."

"When did you want to see me?"

"I was hoping, tomorrow night. I have to leave early Saturday morning to drive to Alabama. From there, I'll go to Germany."

"Let me think about it. Call me tomorrow. I'll tell you then."

"All right."

I hung up the phone and went to sleep. I slept like a baby. I was at peace although I was still hurting. I knew God was working something out. I had to wait to find out.

FORTY-TWO

Lisa called Friday morning to tell me there was another delay with the printers because the picture on the cover was not clear on the first run. Consequently, "Uncaged" would not be ready until after December 19. In addition, my coming out party, scheduled for the 13th, had to be canceled.

Douglas called shortly after Lisa hung up. He wanted to know my decision. I told him he could come by for a few minutes and gave him directions to my house. He was delighted and looked forward to this evening. At 9:30 p.m., Douglas called to say he was on his way. Since he lived in Marietta, I knew it would be awhile before he arrived. I waited nervously tiding up the house.

Douglas arrived forty-five minutes later dressed in green and brown army fatigues with black boots. In his hand was a bouquet of plastic purple and yellow flowers and a white envelope. I opened the door to let him inside.

"I can't stay," he said, handing me the flowers and envelope. "I wanted to see you before I left and give you these things to remember me by while I was gone. I will call you when I get to Germany. Can I get a hug before I leave?" he asked, standing at the door shivering.

I put the flowers and envelope on the floor then hugged him quickly. "Drive safely. Thank you for the card and flowers," I said as he turned and walked away. I watched as he drove off. After locking the doors, I picked up the flowers and card. Since the colors of the flowers didn't match anything in the living room, I decided to put them in my bedroom. Finding a place on Carl's old dresser, I laid them down before plopping on my bed to read the card.

On the outside of the card was the face of a black couple looking into each other's eyes. I opened the inside and read, 'There are few things in this life that have meaning. The friendship we share is more precious to me than all the riches of this world. When we met, my life changed for the better. Your friendship is a valued treasure, I hope I will always possess. Thinking of you, Douglas.'

I placed the card next to the flowers. Staring at them both, I thought of Douglas. He was a very thoughtful person. I prayed for his safe return as I looked at his gifts. I prayed God would mend my broken heart and make it new again to receive the next man in my life. If that man was Douglas, please reveal it to me before he returned.

I removed my Bible from the dresser and read it before I went to sleep. I thought of Douglas as I read. The three weeks he's gone, I'll get a lot of writing done. I didn't know what I was going to do when he came back. It has been said, "Absence makes the heart grow fonder." I'll have to see if it applies to us.

Douglas called me early Saturday morning. I couldn't believe how glad I was to hear from him. I sensed, I missed him already. He said he would be flying out within the next few hours. He had to hear my voice before he boarded the plane. I told him how much I enjoyed his card and flowers. Every time I looked at them, they reminded me of him. "God is good," he said before hanging up.

Before I went to church, I spent the morning writing, "The Bearer of the Sign". I had written twelve chapters. My goal was to complete it in one year.

Sunday, I found myself wanting to hear from Douglas again and was very disappointed when he didn't call. I read his card several times, hoping he would feel me missing him. I couldn't believe how much I thought about him. Didn't I just break up with Raymond? Why am I thinking of Douglas? I've only known him for two weeks. This is crazy, I kept telling myself. It's something about Douglas that turns me on. I don't know what it is, but I have to find out when he returns in three weeks.

To my delight, Douglas called Monday evening. He said he would be back in town, Friday evening and would complete the rest of his time at Dobbins Air Force Base in Marietta. Unfortunately, he wouldn't be able to call me again before Friday. But he wanted to see me Friday night when he got back in town. I told him, okay.

Friday evening was my regular novel writing meeting with I.B.W.A.. Douglas called shortly after I got home from the meeting to say he was on his way. He said he had gifts for me and hoped I liked them. I told him I was easy to please.

At 11:55 p.m., he rang my bell. I hugged him without being asked.

"How about a kiss, baby?" he asked after I hugged him.

"Okay," I replied, wanting to kiss him, too. His lips touched mine, sending a warm sensation throughout my body. We embraced briefly before pulling apart.

"These are for you," he said, showing me the contents in his hand.

"Thank you," I said, opening the bag. Inside was a yellow, brown and beige necklace and earring set. It looked like costume Indian jewelry. It was too bulky and colorful for my taste in jewelry. He also gave me a large gold pendant with a red rose that said, Jesus. I loved the pendant and immediately put it on my green coat.

"Do you like your gifts?" he asked, hoping I did. "I didn't know what you like. I didn't know what to get."

"They're fine. I especially like the pendant. The earring set is for pierced ears. I wear clip-ons."

"I'll take them back and exchange them for the kind you wear. You have to forgive me for buying the wrong kind. Did you miss me?" he asked pulling me close to him.

"What do you think?" I asked smiling, enjoying his touch. "Have a seat. Make yourself comfortable," I said, pulling away.

"Do you have any coffee?"

"Yes."

"I sure would love a cup.

"I'll make you some coffee. I'll have hot chocolate," I said, going into the kitchen. He followed me and sat at the table. I sat in the chair facing him after I put the water on to boil. "How was Germany?"

"Cold. I was in classes all day. I thought about you in the evenings. Is the coffee ready? I'm cold. I need something to warm me up."

"It will be ready in a few minutes. I just turned it on."

"Let me read your eyes while the water gets hot," he said, reaching for my hands.

"What do you mean, read my eyes?"

"I can look into your eyes and tell everything about you. The Holy Spirit will reveal things to me."

"Okay. What do I do?"

"Look into my eyes without blinking."

It took a few seconds for me to look at him without blinking and smiling. But I managed to do so when he gazed into my eyes. He looked for a few seconds then spoke.

"I see you had a troubled childhood. You weren't happy. I see a lot of sadness in your eyes. You and your father didn't get along. Something happened between the two of you to cause you to leave home. I can't see what happened. Your eyes are getting blurry."

"Everything you said is true. I explain my life in my book, "Uncaged"."

"Baby, I don't have to read your book. I can read your eyes and tell everything about you."

I felt close to Douglas after he read me. I felt as if he knew me from the inside out. Nothing about me could be hidden from him. My life was an opened book to him without the book. "The water is ready now. I'll make your coffee," I said, getting up. I made our beverages then sat back down. As I sipped on my hot chocolate, the thought came to me to tell him of my two future daughters. "How do you feel about having more children?"

"I'm forty-two. I raised my son by myself because his mother rejected him at birth. He's now 15. I'm at a point in my life where I want to do as I please without the responsibility of raising more children."

"Well, I will have two daughters."

"How old are you?"

"Forty-one."

"Do you know how old you'll be in twenty years?"

"Yes. Despite my age, I will have my daughters. My only problem is finding the right man."

He drank half of his coffee as I spoke. "Before I married my ex-wife, I took her to meet my family. My grandmother was blind at the time. She held Sylvia's hand and told me she wasn't the right woman for me. She also told me, I would raise our child by myself."

"Why didn't you listen to your grandmother?"

"I thought she didn't know what she was talking about until it happened. Now, I wished I had listened to her a thousand times."

"I wished I could have met your grandmother."

"Me, too."

We talked two more hours before he left. He told me more about his grandmother, and I told him more about me. At the end of his visit, we kissed again as we said our good-byes.

Douglas had reserve duty every morning, but his evenings were free to spend with me. Wednesday evening we went to the midweek service at his church. Friday evening we went to Bible study. I enjoyed each service. Douglas bought sermon tapes and books after each service. The next day, he gave me a copy of the sermon. We talked about the Word all the time. Our lives evolved around the Word and each other.

Douglas told me from the beginning, he wasn't going to touch me. I told him I had repented of committing fornication because I wanted to be a spiritual virgin for my next husband. He told me, he saw me repenting many times on my knees, crying out to God. I told him, that was true, but I meant it this time.

On Friday, December 19, when we came home from Bible study, we sat at the table, drank coffee and talked.

"God showed me a baby girl last night, and you gave her to me. The night before, I saw someone giving me a baby girl, but I didn't see the face. Last night, I saw it was you."

"But you don't want anymore children."

"I didn't before I saw you giving her to me. She had my color. Her name will be Righteous."

I smiled at his new revelation. I felt as if this was my cue to tell him more about me. "There's something I want you to know. I had two miscarriages, this year, by my friend who I broke up with."

"The Holy Spirit is telling me, you'll have Righteous. You can work full-time until you conceive, then you must not work at all or work part-time."

"What else is The Holy Spirit saying?"

"To ask you to marry me."

I looked at Douglas stunned. "It's too soon for me to say yes. We need to get to know each other more."

"I don't mean right away. But, sometime next year," he added.

"I want to be divorced three years before I re-marry. I don't want to get married before March."

"We can get married in May. I have a plane reservation for Trinidad on Sunday, May 10. I can change the ticket for two, to go to Jamaica. It can be our honeymoon."

"I want marriage counseling first. I didn't have it for my first marriage, but I want it for my second one."

"World Changes have marriage counseling. I will get the information and pass it on to you."

"How long do you think the counseling will take?" I asked, finishing my coffee. "Probably, two to three months."

"That's good because I don't want to rush into anything."

"Me either. I learned my lesson from my first marriage," Douglas stated, finishing his coffee, too.

"That makes two of us. It's getting late. Shouldn't you be leaving? Don't you have to get up early in the morning?"

"Yes, but I don't want to leave. Let me stay here with you tonight. I'm not going to touch you."

"I'm not worried about you touching me. I told you, I've repented of committing fornication."

"I'll get up early in the morning to go to the base."

"Okay. I'll get some covers from the hall closet and make a mat on the living room floor." I ran up the steps to get the covers. Douglas was at the base of the steps, watching.

"I won't be able to come by tomorrow," he said as I loaded my arms with comforters.

"Why?"

"I'm going to Alabama to give Mel his Christmas present."

"What are you giving him?"

"One hundred dollars. That's what I always give him."

"You can make the mat while I get the pillows and alarm clock. Here catch!" I said, throwing him the covers. He caught the covers and started making the mat. "I have to work tomorrow night anyway. So it's good you're going out of town," I said going into my bedroom. Looking at my empty bed, I thought of Raymond and the many times we had shared it. I didn't feel right letting Douglas sleep in my bed although we weren't going to have sex. I felt like my bed was Raymond's bed.

I went back downstairs where Douglas had the mat ready. He was sitting on the sofa waiting for me to come down. We kissed before we laid our heads on the pillow. He said a prayer as he put his arms around me to fall asleep. I had my back to his chest as I pulled the covers over us. We both said goodnight then cuddled up to sleep.

As I lay beside Douglas, God told me to give him my full attention; to put nothing before him except Jesus. I took it as God's blessing to go full speed ahead with Douglas. I was convinced, Douglas was my man, sent by God.

Early in the morning, I heard someone ring the doorbell. They rang again and again. It woke me up, but Douglas was fast asleep. I didn't move. I never answer my door all hours of the night. I stayed on the floor trying to think who it could be. Was it the kids? Why would they ring the bell when they had a key? Was it someone in trouble and they wanted to use the phone? Was it one of Carl's friends, who hadn't heard we were divorced? I couldn't figure it out, but I wasn't curious enough to peek out the window. Whoever it was, it was the wrong time of the night to come to my house and get inside.

When the alarm sounded at 6:30, I asked Douglas if he heard anyone at the door in the early hours of the morning. He said no. I dismissed it from my mind and made us breakfast. I fixed Douglas his coffee first. He drank it while he dressed. We ate breakfast then kissed good-bye.

I realized when Douglas left, he made me happy. He showered me with love the whole time we were together. For once in my life, I felt truly loved with no strings attached. If he ever asked me to marry him again. I would say yes. Didn't God give him a heavenly sign that he will be my next husband by showing him our daughter, Righteous? Surely, a heavenly sign overrules an earthly sign of unrighteous mammon.

FORTY-THREE

For some reason after Douglas left, I thought about the loose pictures I had of Raymond, Francine, Raymond Jr. and me. They included pictures when we went to church in Dublin, snaps around the house and snaps with his mother. I had bought a small photo album months ago but never put the pictures inside. I decided this was a good time to fill the album and give it to Raymond tonight. It was my way of saying, it's over, brother. This was what you gave up. Eat your heart out!

That night at work, I looked for Raymond but never saw him in the hallway. Isaiah stopped by the window as I picked up the phone to call Raymond.

"Miss Viva! What's happening?"

"You are, Isaiah. Have you seen Raymond? I have a package to give him."

"He started his vacation, tonight. He was scheduled to work but called in."

"I'm jealous. When we were together, he never took time off," I said placing the phone back on the receiver.

"Well, he won't be back until January 6."

"Thanks, Isaiah. I'll hold on to my package until then."

"Glad to be of assistance. Is there anything else you want to know?"

"Yeah. What is a good man like you doing walking the halls of Grady?"

"I've been asking myself that same question for years."

We both laughed before he walked away, and I left the window to finish my work in the back.

Sunday evening, Douglas came over with Jamaican jerk chicken which we both loved. We ate our dinner of jerk chicken drummetts, fried plantain, rice, and tossed salad before he wanted to read my eyes. I cleared the table first then scooted my chair close to his.

He stared into my eyes. I looked into his without blinking. A few minutes later he said, "You're nervous about getting married again. The Holy Spirit is telling me to tell you, `You have nothing to fear. You will re-marry and it will be right.'"

Douglas hit the nail on the head. What he said was true. Although I knew I would re-marry because of my daughters to come, it made me nervous. I never verbalized it to myself, but I felt it within. I had gone through so much with Carl, I didn't know if I could do it again.

"I'm nervous, too," he added. "I haven't been married in fifteen years," he said, reaching for my hand.

"Didn't you meet someone in all that time that you wanted to marry?" I asked, squeezing his hand.

"I was too busy raising Mel to think of re-marrying. I wanted to give him all my time."

"What is it about me that you want to marry me in such a short period of time?"

"You're different from any woman I've ever met. You're the kind of woman I've always wanted in my life."

"I'm flattered".

"I mean it. I've never felt the way I feel about you before with any other woman. I have something for you," he said, going to the sofa where he had his things.

"What is it?"

He reached inside a plastic bag and pulled out some small white books. Coming back to the table with a handful of books, he gave them to me. "These are for you to give to people who need Jesus in their lives."

I took the books, reading the cover. It read, "Daily Bread." "I've never had one of these."

"Keep one for yourself and pass out the rest. I pass them out all the time. Whenever I see someone with pain on their face, I walk up to them and say, here, take a "Daily Bread". It can give you the answer you need. They usually take it and thank me for it. I used to go house to house ministering to people for the church. I told God I would do His Will. My life was His to do as He pleased."

"Have you always served the Lord?"

"No. I had my mind on the flesh before I started attending World Changes in September. I was living with a woman until I kept hearing Pastor O'Dollar preach against fornication. I knew I had to repent and get my life right. To me, you're my reward for being obedient."

"I've never been a reward before. I guess, you're my reward for repenting of my sins and becoming a spiritual virgin. If you think about it, we're both spiritual virgins, who want to live our lives for the glory of Jesus Christ, our Lord."

"Yes, that's where I am in my walk with the Lord. We'll raise Righteous in a loving Christian home. We'll take her with us when we travel out of the United States to do missionary work. I want to go back to South America to witness for Jesus."

"That sounds fine to me. I've never been to South America," I said, releasing my hand from his to rub my shoulder.

"Do you need a massage?"

"Yes, I stay tensed up. I usually get Carlos to give me a massage when he comes over."

"I'll massage your shoulders and back. I went to Life College to be a chiropractor for three years. I'll even give you an adjustment if you need it," he said, coming over to me.

Douglas gave me the greatest massage I've ever had in my life. He also adjusted my neck. When he finished, I felt wonderful! Everything he did made me feel good. Douglas was the best thing that ever happened to me.

Sunday night, at work, I passed out "Daily Breads". I was surprised at how receptive people were to receive them. For once in my life, I felt like a true Christian soldier doing the work of Jesus. No longer was my life revolved around me but helping other people.

Monday, December 22, Lisa called and told me "Uncaged" was ready and to come to her house to get some books. I went. She showed me "Uncaged" as she opened her door. The cover was orange and yellow with Gina, a model, coming out of a cage. The title was written in bold black letters. Finally, what God told me in April of '94 had happened. He said, "This book will be written and it will be published."

I gave Douglas an autographed copy of "Uncaged" when he came over that evening. He skimmed a few pages, commenting on the profanity. I told him as a writer, I had to write people as they were, not as I wanted them to be. Unfortunately, almost everyone I knew cursed. According to my mother, Big Mama, my great-grandmother was a curser although I never heard her use profanity.

Douglas gave me another card and more flowers. It was rare for him to come over empty handed. I appreciated him and his gifts. He treated me like I'd never been treated before. When we sat at the table to drink coffee, he told me more about his grandmother. "My grandmother first died when she was 47," he said as he drank his coffee. "But she lived to be 104 years old."

"How can she die at 47 and live to be 104?" I asked bewildered.

"People were gathered at her funeral and the minister was giving the eulogy when she rose up from the casket. She sat up and looked around and said, 'What's going on?' Half the people ran out of the church."

"That sounds like a normal response. What happened? Was she really dead?"

"Yes, according to the medical reports. My grandmother said a lot of people in town wouldn't have anything to do with her for a long time. They thought she was a ghost that had come back from the dead."

"What really happened?"

"Come to find out, the doctors had made a mistake. She wasn't dead."

"What about the mortuary employees? Didn't they embalm her?" I asked, drinking my coffee in suspense.

"As far as I know, they did. It's one of those supernatural acts of Jesus that can't be explained except by the power and Will of the Almighty God."

"You always have something fascinating to say about your grandmother."

"Did I tell you about her making a cake with no flour?"

"No."

"My grandmother was very poor, but she was rich in faith. She was also close to God. Sometimes she'd go into the kitchen to make a cake with no flour. She'd get her sifter and use it as if it contained flour. Praying while she turned the empty sifter, flour appeared from no where going into the shifter and from the sifter into the mixing bowl. The first time I saw it, I ran and told my mother. I was ten years old at the time. My mother said she had seen it many times. It was nothing new."

"That's amazing. It illustrates the power of God and what faith can do. It reminds me of James 2:5, `...Has God not chosen the poor of this world to be rich in faith and heirs of the kingdom which He promised to those who love Him?'"

"Prayer and faith are the two most powerful tools a Christian can use to breakdown strongholds in our lives."

"I agree. Would you like more coffee?"

"Yes, baby. I would," he said, handing me his empty cup.

I made Douglas more coffee and we continued to talk until I had to get ready for work. He talked about his plans for becoming certified by May so he could make $100,000 or more income. He had turned down several offers recently, to make more money, because he wanted to be certified first. His aspirations were to have his computer business again. Last time he made $15,000 a week before it folded. Douglas said his downfall was a woman he became involved with who got his mind off the business. His employees kept telling him, she was wrong for him. They begged him to leave her alone. But he didn't listen and lost the business, two years ago. He said he learned his lesson. He had the right woman this time. He only wanted the best for me and Righteous.

Douglas wanted to buy us a big house and a 4X4 Jeep. He saw a six bedroom house in Swanee he liked. One day, he'd take me to look at it. He also had $15,000 cash and could get a V.A. loan when we were ready to buy a house. I told him that sounded great, but we couldn't plan anything before the counseling sessions. We weren't engaged yet. He then asked me to marry him again. I said, yes.

Since we couldn't be officially engaged until after counseling, we set a tentative date for Saturday, May 9. We felt as if that would give us enough time to plan a small wedding and not feel as if we were rushing to get married.

When Douglas left, I felt more in love than ever. He was a good man; heaven sent. I felt blessed being his woman. I knew we would have a happy life together.

Wednesday evening, Douglas and I went to the mid-week service at World Changes. A special skit was performed which we enjoyed. Later, Pastor O'Dollar delivered a dynamic sermon. He emphasized the purpose of Christmas. He said, "Jesus was born to deliver us from our sins. Jesus is our gift."

Thursday, Christmas Day, Douglas called his mother in California to wish her a merry Christmas and tell her the news of him getting married. I talked with her for a few minutes also. We couldn't wait to meet each other. Next, I called my parents. Mama wanted us to drop by before we went to a Christmas dinner at one of Douglas's co-worker's house. I told her we'd be over within the next half-hour.

Douglas prayed for Jesus' protection and blessing upon the day before we left. We had just enough time to visit my parents for thirty minutes before the dinner started at 4 o'clock.

On the way to my parents, I felt nervous. The last time I took Raymond to meet them, it wasn't a pleasant visit. I hoped this time would be different with Douglas.

Carl's van was parked in the driveway when we arrived. Douglas and I parked close to Little Carl's Toyota, I bought him in September. When Mama opened the door, she welcomed us inside and took us to the den where Carl, Yvette, Dad, Little Carl, Carlos and Teneshia (Little Carl's girlfriend) were sitting.

As we entered the den, Carl and Yvette immediately got up from the loveseat. They left a minute later. Although Carl was married, I could tell it bothered him to see me with another man. Little Carl was snuggled up to Teneshia. Carlos was sitting next to them watching TV. Mama sat in the chair next to the door, close to Dad.

"Merry Christmas!" Douglas said, breaking the silence and tension as we settled in Carl and Yvette's vacant seats.

"Merry Christmas," everyone replied at once.

"Ah, Carl just brought Carlos over to see us," Mama explained, nervously.

"Mama, you don't have to explain anything to me. This is your house. You can have him over whenever you please," I said trying to ease her guilt stricken mind.

"Can I get you something to drink?" Dad asked Douglas.

"No thank you. I don't drink."

"You, too," Dad said without thinking.

"Everyone, this is Douglas Jefferson," I said, jumping in trying to save Daddy's face.

"It's nice to meet you, Douglas," Mama replied. "What do you do for a living?"

"I build and service computers. I plan to have my own computer company again soon."

My parents looked at each other, nodding their heads.

"How much money you make?" Carlos blurted out.

"Carlos! That's none of your business," I shouted.

"Yes it is. He's your man isn't he?"

"Yes."

"Well, I need to know these things. I need to know if I can buy Air Jordans or Reeboks."

"Carlos, you can excuse yourself. Go watch TV in Mama's room. You're getting into grown folks business," I commanded.

Carlos left the room.

"We're leaving, too," Little Carl announced. We're going over to Teneshia's aunt house to eat. It was nice meeting you," Little Carl said, shaking Douglas's hand before he left.

"Same here," Douglas responded.

"Bye son and Teneshia. Who's keeping Carlos?" I asked, realizing both Carl and Little Carl were leaving him behind.

"Beverly's coming by later. He'll spend the night with her," Mama responded.

It dawned on me since I'd met Douglas how little time I'd spent with Carlos. Now Carlos seemed like an oddity. Everyone was paired off except him. I vowed to myself to spend more time with him next week before he went back to school.

After Carlos left, Douglas had my parents spellbound talking about Jesus. They clung to every word, shaking their heads in agreement to everything he said.

"Douglas, it's time to go," I announced, looking at my watch thirty minutes later. We don't want to be late for the dinner."

"Mr. and Mrs. Grant, I want you to know I want to marry your daughter," Douglas said, grabbing my hand. "I love her and want her to be my wife."

"Nessa, you didn't tell me it was this serious," Mama said, looking into my eyes.

"I've only known Douglas for a short time. Everything is happening so fast. I can't believe it myself. But, yes. It is this serious. We want premarital counseling first before we make it official."

"It's a done deal as far as I'm concerned. The Holy Spirit has already told me Vanessa will be my wife."

"Thank God for The Holy Spirit! She's better off with you than...," Mama paused catching herself, "than with anyone else I've met."

"On that note, we're leaving," I said, standing up holding Douglas's hand to pull him up, too. "Come on Douglas. I don't want to be late for the dinner."

"Come back again," Dad said, nursing his drink.

"Thank you for the invitation."

"He'll be back. You'll see a lot of him," I said, smiling.

"Good," Mama replied, walking us to the door. "Nessa, I'm glad to see you're finally coming to your senses. Douglas is a good man. See if you can hold on to him."

"Bye, Mama," I said walking out the door.

"Merry Christmas, everybody!" Douglas shouted as we left.

And indeed it was. I felt both blessed and merry; two things, I hoped to experience for the rest of my life.

FORTY-FOUR

The dinner at Keith's house made us closer. Douglas introduced me as his fiancee. Each time I heard him say it, it made my love for him grow. By the time we got to my place, we could hardly control ourselves. As we sat on my sofa, our kisses became very passionate. We had to stop several times to compose ourselves. Once he had me pinned down on the sofa. I could tell he wanted more. Something came over him, however, and he got up. I sat up, looking at him walk around.

"I guess I got carried away," he said as he sat back down next to me. "If it wasn't for The Holy Spirit keeping me under control, we would have had sex eight or nine times by now."

I continued to look at him. I had no idea he had been wrestling with himself to stay off me. I thought he had everything under control. "Although he got carried away, I had no desire to have sex. I'm for real about being a spiritual virgin. I will not have sex before marriage."

"We might have to move our wedding date up. I don't think I can wait until May."

"I understand how you feel. May is a long time away. We have to wait at least until March 13. I don't want to get married before then."

"I want to put a ring on your finger now," he said, holding my hand, examining my ring finger.

"Did you ever get the counseling information?"

"Not yet. I won't be able to while I'm in reserves. Saturday is my last day. I will get the information, first thing next week."

"It's time for me to get ready for work," I said, looking at my watch.

"You know, I don't want to leave. It's getting harder and harder for me to depart from you," he said, pulling me close to him.

"One day, you won't have to worry about leaving. My home will be your home."

"I'll be glad when that day comes. I love you, baby," he said, drawing me into his arms, kissing me passionately.

We kissed good-bye for ten minutes. I hurried upstairs when he left because I had thirty minutes to get dressed. Neither one of us wanted to depart. Our only consolation was we'd see each other again tomorrow at Bible study.

On the way to Bible study, Douglas said his car kept losing speed, but somehow he made it to church. Not sure how reliable his car was, he wanted me to follow him to my house. I tailgated him to the Flat Shoals Road exit off I-285. At the exit, he went left and I went right. I didn't panic when we separated since we were only minutes away from my house and his car was running fine. I figured he had a stop to make before he reached the house.

When I reached my cul-de-sac, Bryson's van was parked at the entrance and he followed me to my driveway. I waited for him to get out of his van as I stood by my car door. Whatever he wanted, I wished he'd make it quick because I knew Douglas would be coming soon. Looking GQ wearing a black leather jacket, black pants, fitting brown buttonless shirt and a brown cloth hat, Bryson stood over me. Observing him closely, I realized, I was completely over him. My heart didn't skip a beat nor did my pulse change. The attraction I felt for him was gone. I took it as a confirmation, Viva was gone as well.

"I had to see you," he said, searching my eyes. "I know you want me to leave you alone, and I have tried to stay away, but tonight, I had to see your face."

"Bryson, what we had is over. You have a family. You can't give me what I desire—a family of my own. Our relationship worked for awhile. We had good times together. We even healed our brokenness. We were two broken, incomplete, people trying to find happiness. And we did in each other. But now, what you have to offer me is not enough. I need more than crumbs from your table; scraps from your time schedule. I need more than what's leftover when Helen, your jobs, and other responsibilities are done."

"Damn it, Van! I don't have anything to give you but the little bit that's left when everything else I do in my life is done. I work like I work because I have to. You know that. And as far as Helen is concerned, we're just two people trying to make the best of a bad situation. I don't love her. And by her actions, she doesn't love me either. Van, how many times do I have to tell you, it is you I love. I LOVE YOU," he emphasized. "Stop playing games with me. I know you're blaming me for the breakup with you and Raymond."

"Don't you think you had a part in it? You are partly responsible. He never had me to himself. You were always in the picture."

"I couldn't stand the thought of you being with anyone else but me. You don't know how much you hurt me when you got pregnant. The pain went all through me. I was hurt because he could give you what I couldn't. And I know how much having another baby means to you. But I want you to know, I wanted you then, pregnant and all. And I want you now. I want you in my life, Van, anyway I can have you. And don't think for a minute, if you get married, I'll be out of your life. Because I won't. You're mine, Van; even if I have to share you with another man."

A car came up as Bryson finished. I looked to see if it was Douglas. The car looked like his, but it kept going. I watched it drive out of sight then turned back to Bryson.

"Van, tell me to my face, you don't want me in your life anymore and I promise you, I will leave you alone. I don't ever want you to accuse me of being the reason for problems in your other relationships," he said, looking into my eyes, waiting for me to respond.

"Bryson, I want you out of my life. I want to be free to live with the man who God gives me to be my next husband. We both know that man is not you because you are committed to Helen regardless of what you say."

"Remember this one thing, Van. And don't you ever forget it. I will always love you. You will always have a place in my heart."

"Good-bye, Bryson. I'm tired and I'm going into the house."

"Good-bye, my love," he said as he turned to go to his van.

I walked to the steps, not looking behind. I heard the van pull off as I closed the door. He's gone for good, I told myself. I was finally free to live my life without him or Viva around to quench my happiness. I was ready, now, for the next man in my life.

I waited an hour for Douglas, but he never came by. I started to page him but decided to go to bed instead. I wasn't sure if that was his car I saw that turned around. I prayed for his safe return home before I want to sleep.

I didn't see Douglas again until the following Wednesday. He said he decided to go home instead of coming over because he experienced car problems again. Saturday morning, he called his mechanic to see if his Toyota was ready. It would be ready Monday. He couldn't come over, however, because reserve was over, and he was working two jobs again.

The Celica barely got Douglas home Monday. He became frustrated with both cars but wouldn't buy the 4X4 Jeep he wanted because The Holy Spirit had not told him to buy it yet.

Wednesday evening while sitting at the table talking, drinking coffee, Douglas wanted to read my eyes again. I positioned my chair in front of his and looked into his eyes without blinking.

"I see a green 1995 van," he said after gazing for a few seconds.

"That van belongs to Bryson Collier, an ex-male friend of mine. He came by Friday when we separated after Bible study."

"Do you have feelings for him?" Douglas asked still looking into my eyes.

"No. Our relationship is over."

"The Holy Spirit is telling me, you missed out on many blessings for being disobedient."

"Really? I feel very blessed. I can't imagine what I could have missed."

"It was a lot. Now, you'll never find out."

"I guess not. Would you like to go to church with me Saturday since you're not in reserves?"

"I'll go to your church. But you do know, when we get married, we'll go to World Changes. That will be our church since I will be the head of the house."

"I respect you being the head of the house. I also know how important it is to worship together as a family. While I enjoy services at World Changes, I love my church. I wouldn't totally want to give up going to my church. I've been attending it for fourteen years."

"You can go once a month," he said, drinking his coffee. "We have to go where the Word is preached."

I thought about what he said. Was I willing to give up my church for him? Would that be idolatry? I have to give this marriage thing more consideration. Right now, I'm not so sure I want to get married after all. "My church preaches the Word," I finally said.

"I'll be the judge of that Saturday when I go. How is your back?"

"I feel tensed ."

"Let me give you a massage," he said, getting up from the table.

While massaging my back, Douglas discovered my pelvis was out of alignment. Pressing down on my hips, he corrected the problem. I felt like new when he finished. It never failed. Whenever I was with Douglas, I felt wonderful!

Friday, after Bible study, Douglas wanted to stay again. This time, we slept on top of my bed with our clothes on. Neither one of us wanted to sleep on the hard floor anymore. This time, I could handle Douglas sleeping on top of the bed but not under the covers.

During the night, Douglas kissed me every hour on the hour and told me he loved me. I kissed him back and told him the same. When I got up the next morning, I was more fatigued than before I went to bed. Douglas loved me more than anything in this world. And I loved him, too.

Douglas wore his uniform clothes to my church, Saturday. He stuck out like a sore thumb with his uniform, old dirty brown coat and run over bucks because my church was traditional. He looked like something I dragged off the street and invited to services.

After church, Douglas wanted to go to his place to get some money to take us out to eat. He told me I was curious about where he lived anyway. And he was right. Douglas had a way of reading me even when he wasn't looking into my eyes. I felt as if I had no secrets with him.

"What did you think about services?" I asked when we got into the car.

"Your church has too much singing and not enough Word," he responded, icily. "Thanks for inviting me, but I won't be coming back."

"How much of "Uncaged" have you read?" I asked, changing the subject.

"I'm on the second chapter. I've been too busy to read it. Don't worry. I plan to read every word."

While he drove, I thought about his comments concerning my church. It disturbed me to say the least. Everything else about Douglas, I could live with. But his strong, negative opinion about my church, I didn't know if I could accept. I also thought about my sons. With his plans to travel all over the world, he would take me away from them.

We reached his apartments, forty minutes later. The large gray complex was well maintained with white winding steps and three levels in each section. Douglas lived on the bottom level at the end.

"That's my truck," Douglas said, parking beside an old rusty white pickup.

"Why don't you drive it?"

"It needs a transmission, sticker and insurance."

"Oh."

"I have a roommate. He might be home. The apartment owner rents out rooms in the apartments. We each have our own bedrooms and share the rest of the living space. I sleep on the sofa in the living room because my room is so small. Come on. Let's go inside," he said, opening his door. I trailed behind.

Taking his keys from his pocket, Douglas opened the apartment door. A brown and tan herculon sofa took up half the space in the tiny living room. A table and component system took up the remainder of the room. Douglas walked down a narrow hallway to his room and unlocked the door. Inside were a bookcase, lamp, large plastic bottle bank and twin bed with no covers. There was just enough space to take three steps to the bed and bookcase.

"You see why I don't sleep in here. It's too small. I need to get more money to eat with," he said, reaching under his mattress, pulling out an envelope. I stood next to him. The envelope contained twenties, fifties, hundreds, and travelers checks in the same denominations. My estimation of the amount the envelope contained was between $2,000-$3,000. He took out two twenties then put the envelope back under the mattress. Locking the door back, we left the apartment to go to the Jamaican restaurant not far away.

As Douglas drove to the restaurant, I thought about my sign. Seeing all that money in the envelope made me think about it again. I wondered, as he handled the money, if he would pull out fifty or more dollars and give it to me. I was disappointed when he didn't. Since he didn't give me any money then, I felt as if he never would.

FORTY-FIVE

Sunday, Douglas went to church without me because I worked the night before. He called me after church to tell me his car caught on fire in the parking lot, and he needed me to pick him up. I got dressed and went to his rescue.

By the time I reached Douglas, a tow truck had arrived. I waited inside my car until he and the attendant finished talking beside his car. After the conversation, Douglas removed some valuables from his car to put into mine. We watched as his Pinto was towed away. He was glad his Toyota would be ready soon.

Douglas asked me to take him to Marietta where his Toyota was being repaired. He felt by some chance it might be ready. We drove to a small mechanic shop where his car was parked outside. Douglas started the car with no problem. We took off with both cars. First, to get something to eat, then to go to my place.

His car drove satisfactorily to my house although a red light kept coming on. Douglas said he would take it back tomorrow to inquire about the red light. With his Pinto down, he needed his Toyota running.

Once we got home, I tried to make him forget his car problems by fixing him a cup of coffee. He drank two cups before we went to the sofa to talk.

"I want you to know, I know how to satisfy a black woman," he said, putting his arms around me.

"Why are you telling me this? I've never questioned you whether you could or couldn't."

"I don't want you to think just because I haven't tried to have sex with you, that I don't know how to satisfy you."

"I'm satisfied right now, just being in your arms. It doesn't take much to satisfy me."

"I'm part Jamaican. We Jamaican men know what it takes to please a woman."

I instantly thought about How Stella Got Her Grove Back. Her young lover was one hundred percent Jamaican. Someone in the book referred to Jamaican men as having fire hoses between their legs. I didn't need a firehose to satisfy me. A normal size penis would do. Of course, I thought of Raymond and his performance problem. Douglas sounded too good to be true.

"First, I would start at your breast," he continued. "I would caress and suck each one. Then I would work my way down to between your legs and give you a thrill you've never experienced before. When I feel like you're ready for me to enter you, I will. I won't stop until you came again and again and again."

"I have something to look forward to, don't I?"

"You certainly do. I will do everything in my power to make you happy. I want the best life for you and Righteous."

"There's no doubt in my mind that you will make me very happy. I'm happy now. I can't imagine being happier than what I am already."

"Good," he said, turning me to kiss him. We kissed for a long time. His hands glided up and down my back as we kissed.

I kept thinking of his Jamaican heritage, anticipating my treat. "It's time for you to leave," I announced, looking at my watch at the conclusion of our kissing session. "I have to go to work."

"You know I hate leaving you. Tomorrow, I will give you the counseling number. I left it in the Pinto."

"I'll call tomorrow as soon as you give it to me.

"Kiss me good-bye before I leave," he said, kissing me again. He left ten minutes later.

Monday evening, Douglas called to ask me to take him to get a rental car. It turned out, the Toyota was not ready. The red light indicated another problem. He checked with the people who had his Pinto. It was driveable but still needed more work on it to make it reliable. The cost to get it fixed was more than Douglas wanted to pay. Therefore, he decided to wait until Thursday to get the Toyota back.

We went to a rental place by the airport. When we got back, Douglas asked if he could leave his Pinto in my driveway. That was okay with me since it wouldn't be in my way.

Late Tuesday evening, Douglas called to give me the marriage counseling number. I told him since it was so late, I'd call first thing Wednesday morning. I'd page him after I talked to them.

Tuesday was also January 6, the night Raymond returned to work. I made sure I carried the photo album to work with me to give to him. I saw Raymond on my way to the snack bar at midnight. He was talking to another officer.

"Vanessa, I want to talk to you," he said, interrupting his conversation with the officer.

"Okay," I said, walking toward him, waiting for him to end his conversation. He immediately came over to me, leaving the officer who walked off.

"I would like to sit down and talk to you later. How does three o'clock sound?"

"That sounds okay. I have something to give you. I'll wait until then."

"I have to run. I'll see you at three," he said, leaving.

He walked off and I went to the snack bar. My mind was on Douglas. I had no idea what Raymond wanted to discuss. Whatever it was, I didn't even care. I was very happy with Douglas. I should thank Raymond for breaking up with me so I could experience this much joy.

When three o'clock came, I told Tia where I was going before I left. She told me Raymond would try to get back together. I told her she was crazy. I hadn't heard a word from him in five weeks. The relationship was over. Besides, I was very happy with Douglas.

I went to the elevators to wait for Raymond who came a minute later. We got on the next elevator and went to the second floor. I had the album in my hand but decided to wait until we were seated to give it to him. We sat down in our booth. Raymond looked at me with a hurt expression on his face. I had never seen him like that.

"Vanessa," he started, taking a deep breath. "I have been an emotional wreck these past few weeks. I came by your house the Friday night before my vacation and a red car was parked in your driveway. I knocked on the door several times, but you didn't come to the door. I thought about the times we were in bed and you didn't answer the door at night."

"So, that was you at my door. I couldn't figure out who it was. It never occurred to me, it would be you. Especially, on a night you worked. It's not like you to leave the job."

"I was sitting at my desk when something told me you were with another man. I've been through this before, Vanessa. I know all the signs. I got up and left. I had to find out. When I pulled up and saw the car, I knew I was right. I was deeply hurt," he said with his voice cracking. "It's a good thing you didn't come to the door. I don't know what I would have done."

"My friend wanted to stay over. We were on the living room floor sleeping. I heard you knocking. But at that hour of the night, I didn't care who it was. I wasn't going to the door."

"All I could think of was you were in the bed with another man. I completely lost it! I went back to work, talking loud. Somehow, I finished the shift but signed up to take Saturday night off because I was too upset."

My heart went to my feet as he talked. I never knew how much Raymond loved me until now. It hurt me to know I hurt him although he started it by breaking up first when he returned my keys.

"I want to know one thing," he continued, talking with his voice cracking, fighting back tears, "have you moved on with this other man?" He paused for my response.

My mind said yes, but my heart and mouth said, "No."

"Does this mean we can get back together?"

My mind said no, but my heart and mouth said, "Yes."

"Good," he said, exhaling a deep breath. "Vanessa, there's one thing I don't understand. How can you be with someone else so soon? I love you so much. I would have given my life for you."

I felt two inches tall. "I wasn't looking for someone else. He just came into my life. When I didn't hear from you, I thought you were gone forever."

"I wanted you to be happy. From what you said before we broke up, I didn't make you happy."

"Under the conditions you wanted me as your wife, I wouldn't be happy. That's the point I was trying to make. We could have talked about it and worked things out. We didn't have to break up. You returned my keys to hurt me," he smiled because I was right, "but you ended up hurting yourself."

"You're right. I'm sorry for hurting you. Will you forgive me?" he asked, reaching for my hand.

"Yes, I forgive you. I have something for you," I said, handing him the album. He turned each page slowly.

"I don't understand how we came to this point from looking at these pictures. We were happy together. These pictures prove it."

That's why I wanted you to have them. To show you what you kicked to the curb."

He smiled again. "Well, that's behind us now. We're back again. Aren't we?"

"Yes, we are. Does this mean, you'll call me this evening?"

"Yes, I'll be calling you everyday," he said, sliding from the booth.

We went back to work. I was bewildered to say the least. I had gotten back with Raymond although that was not what I really wanted to do. Something happened in that meeting that I didn't understand—the power of the heart over the mind. In my mind, I had move on. But Raymond ruled my heart. He still had the emotional key to my heart even though I had gotten rid of the physical necklace.

I guess the expression on my face, clued Tia that something was wrong when I came back. She came behind me as I walked to my station.

"What happened?" she asked, standing next to me.

"You know how I told you about Douglas and how happy he made me."

"Yeah."

"And how he asked me to marry him."

"Yeah."

"And how I said yes."

"Yeah."

"And how he was going to be the father of our daughter, Righteous."

"Yeah."

"And how he made me feel good by giving me massages."

"Yeah."

"Well, forget all that. I just got back with Raymond."

"What on earth happened to make you dump Douglas for Raymond?"

"I don't know. When we were talking, my mind was thinking one thing but something totally different came out of my mouth. It was the strangest thing. I still don't believe it. But I don't know what to do."

"See both of them until you make up your mind. I did before I married Derrick. I was seeing Lanel five years before I met Derrick. They knew about the other one. Then I realized I was in love with Derrick. Lanel was messing around anyway. So I let him go and married Derrick."

"I can't do that. I get confused if I see more than one man at a time. Since I told Raymond we were back together, I have to tell Douglas it's over. I was suppose to call for counseling today, too."

"Sounds like you're up shit creek without a paddle. If I were you, I'd give it more time and see both of them until you make up your mind."

"Thanks Tia for the advice. But I don't have any other choice but to break up with Douglas."

"All righty then. You do what's best," she said, walking to the front.

I was a basket case for the rest of the shift. My biggest concern was breaking the news to Douglas. How would I tell him it's over between us because I'm back with Raymond? How did Raymond come back into my life? What happened in the cafeteria? What's going to happen now?

On the way to the parking deck, Raymond told me he wanted to come over Thursday morning after work. I told him, fine, that sounded like a good idea.

As I walked in my house, the phone rang. I picked it up and said, "Hello."

"Vanessa, have you called the marriage counselor yet?" Douglas asked, excitedly.

"No. I just walked in the door. I won't be calling today after all."

"Why? Have you changed your mind?"

"Yes. I got back with Raymond tonight."

Silence filled the other end of the phone. "I thought it was over between you and him."

"I did, too. I don't know what happened. I can't explain it. All I know is I agreed to get back together. Believe me Douglas, that's not what I want to do."

"What do you want to do?"

"Stay with you."

"Why did you get back with him?"

"I don't know. I still don't understand."

"I need you to go with me to take the rental car back this evening. Will you be able to?"

"Yes. He's coming over tomorrow morning after work. I don't want your Pinto in the driveway."

"I'll take it with me tonight. My Toyota will be ready tomorrow."

"I'm sorry, Douglas. I want you to know, I love you, regardless of what happens."

"I love you, too, baby. Together, we can win this battle. We'll discuss it more this evening."

FORTY-SIX

Douglas came over at 5:30 p.m.. He prayed, holding me in his arms after he entered the house. This is what he said: *"Oh, Jesus Christ, our Lord and Savior. I call on You this day to rebuke the hand of Satan from this relationship between Vanessa and me. You are greater than Satan. You have already conquered him on the cross. I realize we wrestle not against flesh and blood but principalities of wickedness. Let not Satan and his demons have dominion over us, but let Your blood that was shed for our transgressions cover us and defeat our foe. The enemy wants to separate what You have put together. I declare the victory in Jesus Christ name. Amen.*

I held Douglas close as he finished praying. He reached for my hand.

"Listen, baby. The Holy Spirit told me you're the only woman for me. If we break up, there's no one left for me to have. We have Jesus on our side. We can lick this. The reason Raymond can come back into your life is because of fornication. That's why I hate fornication! When you fornicate, you leave a part of yourself with your partner and he leaves a part of himself with you. There is a spiritual bond formed between the two of you. That's why God ordained sex for marriage, to nurture the bond. I know what's happening to you. Since you were abused coming up, you need a controlling man in your life. Raymond is that kind of man. I am not. He also is manipulative. You have to be careful, baby. He only wants you for sex and to take care of his children. You don't need him. He needs you."

I listened to Douglas, taking in every word. "I will still see him tomorrow morning. I want to see what he has up his sleeve."

"Be careful, baby. He's a conniving man. And whatever you do, don't let him touch you."

"I won't. You don't have to worry about that. I just want to talk to see what's on his mind."

"Baby, I love you, and I don't want anything to happen to you," he said, pulling me up to kiss me. We kissed and embraced for several minutes. "C'mon, lets go return this rental car. I don't want to keep you out too late."

I followed Douglas on I-285 West bound to Camp Creek Parkway. He stopped at a gas station close to the expressway. As we were getting ready to pull off, Douglas put the car in park and prayed. I saw the hurt come over him as he bowed his head. My heart ached, knowing I was breaking his. A lump came in my throat as I watched him pray.

"Dear Lord, help me ease his pain," I prayed. *"He doesn't deserve this from me. He has shown me kindness, and I am causing him pain."*

Douglas held his head up and drove from the station. I trailed behind him. We reached the car rental place ten minutes later. We went inside and I hugged him around his waist. He hugged me back as we waited for his transaction to be completed.

Douglas didn't come inside when we returned to my house. He said he had to go home and pray. I told him I would call him tomorrow after Raymond left. He kissed me good-bye, removed his things from my car, transferring them into the Pinto before he drove off.

Thursday morning, Raymond arrived at nine. He said he had to wrap up some things before he left. We talked in the living room.

"You don't know what I've been through these past few weeks. It feels good to be with you again," he said, getting up, coming up to the loveseat to pull me up. "I want to hold you in my arms again."

We embraced. I felt nothing for Raymond as he held me. It was at that moment, I knew all the love I had for him was gone.

"Let's go to the bedroom," he suggested when the embrace ended. "I've had a long night, I need to get some rest."

"We can go to sleep, but we can't have sex."

"Whatever you wish. I want you to know, I prayed that God would give you back to me even if you had been defiled. I know it's not right to pray selfish prayers. But I'm glad He answered it this time."

"I'm not defiled. I haven't had sex since the last time we had sex. I've repented of committing fornication."

"I told God I wanted you back, and I would do anything to keep you. I realized after I lost you, I must be doing something wrong because I keep losing my women."

"Well, He answered your prayer because I was gone. I was unofficially committed to someone else. We had planned to get married in May."

"That's behind us now. We're back together again. That's all that matters now. Let's go get some sleep. I'm really tired."

We went up the steps to my room. I took off my clothes and put on my pajamas. He slept in his T-shirt and underwear. He held me close to him the entire time we slept. Raymond slept like a baby, but I hardly closed my eyes. All I could think about was how I wanted to be with Douglas.

When the alarm went off, we got dressed so Raymond could pick up his kids on time. We were in the living room saying our good-byes when he said, "You have made me the happiest man on earth. I want my keys back," he said taking his door and car keys off his key ring and giving them to me.

I looked at the keys in my hand. I didn't want Raymond to have my keys again, but I didn't know how to tell him. Instead, I said, "I'll go get your keys. They're in my room." I went to my room and got two house keys and my extra car key. I thought about what Douglas said as I got the keys. He warned me, Raymond was manipulative. And indeed he was. That old serpent, the snake. "Here are your keys," I said, handing them to him.

"Thank you. I feel whole again," he said, placing them on his key ring.

I walked him to the door. He let himself out. I watched him as he left, closed the door and paged Douglas.

"Hello," I said, hoping it was Douglas answering my page.

"Hey, baby. What happened?" Douglas asked.

"You won't believe what happened. Raymond asked for my keys before he left. I didn't want to give them to him, but I did anyway. I see what you meant when you said he was manipulative. He made sure he was not leaving here without my keys. He didn't want what happened the last time to happen again."

"See, baby, I told you how he is. You have to get your keys back. No man should have the keys to your house if he's not married to you."

"I know I have to get my keys back. I just haven't figured out how. I need to get them back before he makes copies."

"We'll work something out. Look, baby, I sure would like to see you tonight."

"Tonight is his off night. He might come back to the house, unannounced. You can't come over here."

"I'll meet you someplace close to the house. Where would be a good place to meet?"

"What about in Pep Boys parking lot across from South Dekalb Mall?"

"What's a good time?"

"It's 5:37 now. What about 7:00? That will give me plenty of time to eat."

"I'll see you at 7:00."

"You know another thing I found out?"

"What?"

"I don't love him anymore. All the feelings I had for him are gone. I'm glad I met with him today. I'm glad I found out, I'm over him. It's you that I love."

"I love you, too. Baby, I'm at work. I'll see you at 7:00."

"Okay, good-bye."

The dial tone hummed in my ear. I laid the phone down in it's cradle and started cooking dinner. While I cooked I thought about being with Douglas. I became excited knowing we would be together soon.

At 6:55, I drove into the Pep Boys parking area and spotted Douglas's Toyota close to Block Buster Music. Parking beside him, I waited for him to get in. Hurriedly, he hopped from his car into mine after locking his door.

"I feel like a criminal," he said, getting into the passenger seat.

I laughed. "Do you want to drive? I don't know where to go."

"Drive from this spot. We'll change someplace else. Baby, you have to get your keys back soon. I can't do this again. I feel like I have committed a crime."

I drove down Chandler Road, turned right at Clifton Springs Road then left at Panthersville Road.

"I'll take it from here," Douglas volunteered.

I pulled over on the side of the road at Dekalb College. We got out to change seats. Douglas drove straight ahead, crossing River Road. "Where are we going?" I asked ready to reach a destination.

"Someplace where Raymond will never find us," he said, turning left. We drove down a street with very large homes. "I'm going to get us one of these," Douglas stated as we approached a large beige brick, two story house to our left.

It was a very nice house; one I would love to live in. Douglas kept driving until we reached the end of the cul-de-sac. He circled around and parked near a wooded area. It was dark and spooky.

"Is this spot all right?" Douglas asked, turning toward me.

"It's a little eerie. I hope no KKK people live on this street or we may be history."

"Don't worry, baby. I prayed before I turned on this street that no harm will come to us. We're protected by The Holy Spirit and angels."

"Good."

"Let's get out. I want to hold you in my arms."

Car lights flashed in our faces. "Wait-a-minute. Let this car pass before we get out." The car drove to the house behind us. As it parked, another set of lights came. This time it was a truck with two white men inside. They circled the cul-de-sac then stopped at our car. The passenger, a forty-something white man with a studded beard, greasy long brown hair and piercing eyes, looked at us with his arm hanging on the side of the truck. We all gazed at each other before they drove off.

"Baby, we can't do this anymore. We might get killed," Douglas said, turning to me.

"Those are my feelings exactly."

"C'mon, let's get out. It should be safe now," he instructed, opening his door.

We exited the car, going to the front. Douglas held me in his arms as I rested my head on his chest.

"Baby, we can't go on like this. You need to call the marriage counselors tomorrow. We need to get this ball rolling. I can't wait much longer. This whole thing with Raymond has really disturbed me. I don't want to lose you."

"You don't have to worry about losing me. I love you. It's over between Raymond and me. Tomorrow, I will get my keys back and call the counselors. This is the last time we have to sneak around like this."

"Have you figured out how to get your keys back?" Douglas asked, looking into my eyes.

"No. Not yet. Do you have any suggestions?"

"Be direct and ask him for them back. Tell him you don't love him anymore. It's that simple."

"Okay, that's what I'll do. I'll call you as soon as it's done."

"I love you, baby, and I want you to be my wife. I want to share my life with you and Righteous. I have so many plans for us. I can't wait to begin."

Douglas and I stayed in that spot until it was time for me to go to work. When our time expired, I drove him to his car where we exchanged our last kiss before we departed.

That night at work, I built up my courage to ask Raymond for my keys. It was the only thing to do. The more I thought about him having my keys, the madder I became. How dare he come back into my life after kicking me to the curb like I am nothing! I'll show him, in the morning, a side of Vanessa Lewis he's never seen!

FORTY-SEVEN

I went over to Mama's house when I got off work. It was our morning to get our hair done. We both got our hair pressed by Betty Manning every other Friday. We went to her house, near Perry Homes, after Mama shampooed my hair.

While driving on I-20 West, I told Mama, I was going to drop her off then go to Raymond's apartment, which was less than ten minutes away. I was breaking up with him for the last time and needed to get my keys back from him.

"Nessa, he has no business with your house keys. Don't be giving out your keys to no man," she scolded, smoking her cigarette. "What does Raymond have on you anyway? I never have seen what you see in him."

"Don't worry about Raymond. He's history as of today. It won't take me long to do what I have to do. I'll be back before Betty is ready to do my hair."

"Are you still seeing Douglas?" she asked, exhaling.

"Yes. He's good to me. We plan to get married in May."

"You're gonna forget about having more babies at your age, aren't you?"

"Mama, you might as well get a grip because I'm having my daughters after I get married."

"Nessa, I don't understand you anymore. You get crazier by the day. You ought to forget about having more babies and concentrate on raising the two you already have," she said, extinguishing her cigarette butt in the ashtray.

"Mama, you might as well get use to the idea of having more grandchildren because when I get married, I'll have my daughters."

"I'm sorry, I ever took you to see Madame Lee. Being foolish is one thing. But being mentally insane is something else. Do you really believe what she said will come true?"

"Yes, I do. Everything she told me has happened except for my daughters. She told me I would leave Carl and I did. She gave me six initials of men who would be important to me in my life. Douglas is the sixth initial. Whether you like it or not, I'm getting married soon and my daughters are coming. I never told you this, but I also saw an image of a baby and an image of me very pregnant."

"Now I know you have lost your mind! I should have taken you to Milledgeville," she said, lighting up another cigarette. "Look at me. I don't smoke like this until I'm around you. You make my nerves bad."

"What are you going to do when you have to keep my daughters?"

"Have a nervous breakdown."

We both laughed. Betty's house was five minutes away. I dropped Mama off then went to Raymond's. The closer I got to Raymond's apartment, the more vengeful I became. I kept saying, "Get behind me Satan, you, low down, dirty snake! You have deceived me for the last time! I am getting my keys back, this day! Then you and Raymond can both kiss my ass!"

Raymond's car was parked in his usual parking space. I adjusted Mama's yellow scarf around my head to hide my plaits. I got out, locked my door then walked briskly to his apartment. Knocking several times, I waited for someone to open the door.

Mrs. Simmons came to the door on one crutch. "Good morning, Mrs. Simmons," I greeted her as she opened the door.

"Good morning, Vanessa. C'mon in," she said, opening the door, stepping to the side.

I sat on the sofa, next to the door. Raymond was in the bathroom brushing his teeth. He stepped in the living room when he heard me come in.

"Hi," I said, smiling as if everything was honky dory. He smiled, showing all his teeth. I saw happiness written all over his face. He went back into the bathroom to finish brushing. When he left the bathroom and went into his room, I got up and went into his room too, closing the door behind me. I didn't want Mrs. Simmons to hear what I had to say. Raymond was sitting on his bed, putting on his sock when I entered the room.

"I was hoping you'd come by today," he said still smiling.

"I came by to get my keys back. It's over between us! When I went back to you, I hurt Douglas, who has been good to me. He was there for me when you kicked me to the curb like I was nothing!" I exclaimed, kicking my foot. "I loved you, Francine and Raymond Jr.!"

"You can have your keys back," he said, going to his dresser with tears in his eyes. He gave me my keys and I gave him his. "It's over, Raymond!" I shouted, clasping my keys.

"No! No, baby, no!" he said as he cried.

"I'm happy, Raymond! Douglas asked me to marry him and I will! I was with you for over a year and you NEVER asked me! Your loss is his gain!" I exclaimed, storming out the room, leaving him sobbing, sitting on his bed. I walked passed Mrs. Simmons, letting myself out the unlocked door.

On the way to Betty's I felt good. I had defeated old slew foot, Satan. I had my keys and life back. Now, I was free to be with Douglas.

Betty was still working on Mama's hair when I arrived. I told them what happened. Mama was happier than me.

"Now, you don't have to worry about raising his kids. You have enough on your hands trying to raise your own. You're finally getting some sense. I was beginning to wonder if you had any."

"Mama, I keep telling you, don't worry about me. Things have a way of straightening themselves out."

"I'm glad."

"Not all things straighten themselves out," Betty added. "Sometimes, you have to use some force." We all laughed while Betty finished Mama's hair.

I took Mama home before going to my house. The first thing I did when I got home was page Douglas. He called me right back.

"Hello," I said, picking up the phone.

"Hey, baby. Did you get your keys?"

"Yes! I have them in my hand."

"God is good."

"I told him it was over. That I was happy and you asked me to marry you. He started crying like a baby."

"You hurt him good. He couldn't do nothing but check into Heart-Break Hotel."

"I'm calling the marriage counselor today when I hang up from talking to you."

"That's good, baby. Tell me what they say when I come over tonight. By the way, I'll have your computer ready. I'll bring it tonight. I'll bring the keyboard, monitor, printer and fax machine, next Thursday."

"That sounds great. You'll put "Uncaged" on the Internet?"

"Yes, I'm working on it."

"You're wonderful!"

"Thanks, baby. So are you. I have a small favor to ask."

"What is it?"

"My hair is getting too long. I need you to cut it for me."

"I've never cut hair before."

"It's easy. I'll instruct you."

"Okay, if you don't mind me learning on your head, I'll cut it."

"We'll do that next Thursday, too. Tonight, I want to enjoy you before I go to reserves this weekend."

"Do you want me to cook something for us tonight?"

"No. I don't want you to work. I'll pick up some jerk chicken and bring it over."

"Great! I'll see you tonight. I can't wait to get off the phone to call the counselor."

"Don't let me stop you. I'll see you later."

We hung up then I dialed the counselor's number. She took my name and telephone number and asked for the same information for Douglas. She said someone should be calling us in two weeks. I asked how long the counseling sessions lasted? She said there will be three sessions over a three month period. We would attend one session a month that lasted approximately an hour.

That was perfect, I thought, as I hung up the phone. Our counseling sessions would be over in time for our May wedding. God is good!

When Douglas came over, that evening, it was as if we were on our honeymoon. We kissed most of the time. It was fantastic being together again at my house without Raymond hanging over our heads. We ate jerk chicken, drank coffee, talked, laughed and kissed. Since we wouldn't see each other again for almost a week, we cherished each moment we had together.

I didn't hear from Douglas again until Monday morning. He promised to call me everyday since he wouldn't have a chance to come over before Thursday evening. Wednesday when we talked, we could hardly wait for Thursday to arrive. He told me he had the rest of my components as he had promised. I told him I was nervous about cutting his hair.

Wednesday night at work, I saw Raymond who barely spoke as I walked by. I told Tia how he acted when I got back in the lab. She was sitting by the Coulter, answering her C.B.C.'s. "Tia, I saw Raymond in the hallway. He acted as if he didn't want to speak," I said, standing beside her.

"Men can't take rejection well. They can treat you anyway, but they can't take what they dish out," she said, fingering her keyboard.

"I'm glad he's out of my life. I'm happy with Douglas."

"Your happiness is important. I wouldn't let no man rob me of my happiness either."

"I'll be glad when I marry Douglas. I thought about my situation the other day. I felt like I was being pulled in two different directions when both Douglas and Raymond were in my life. Sort of like a human yo-yo—going back and forth. I also realized, I've been in relationships, non-stop, since I was thirteen years old. First there was John, then Carl, Zakee, Bryson, Herman, Raymond and Douglas. I've used up my six men, Madame Lee mentioned, counting Lawrence Chestnut, who helped me with "Uncaged".

"That's something."

"Now, I understand I will marry one of the six men Madame Lee gave me the initials of. After I get married, there will be no other man in my life because I will be married until death do us part."

"So, Douglas is the lucky one?" Tia asked, smiling.

"Yes, the others have been canceled out. He's the only one left."

"Oh, I almost forgot. Your son called while you were out. He said he was having car problems."

"Okay. I'll call him in the morning. He should be asleep."

"I know I will be invited to the wedding," Tia said, putting more samples on the Coulter.

"You and everybody else I know."

"Blood gas," Jenny said, putting a plastic bag with ice behind Tia.

"I'll talk to you later, Tia. You have to do your blood gas," I said as I walked away.

I called Douglas to wake him up at 5:30 a.m.. He said he'd be over at 6 o'clock with the rest of my computer and asked if I was still nervous about cutting his hair. He told me not to cook because he would pick something up.

At 7 a.m., I called Little Carl, but the phone was disconnected. If he was having car problems, how would they get to school? Little Carl was responsible for taking him and Carlos to school since they were not on the bus line. I knew that meant one thing. I had to drive to Clayton County when I got off work to make sure they got to school.

When I pulled up into their driveway, Little Carl's Toyota was gone. I felt relieved, knowing they were able to get to school. I knocked on the door just to be sure they weren't inside. They weren't. I then drove home with a peace of mind.

When I got home, I turned the phone off downstairs. I was tired and ready to get some sleep. The phone rang in my bedroom as I reached to turn it off. I hurried and answered it, thinking it was Douglas.

"Hello."

"Vanessa, it's me," Raymond said, crying.

"What's wrong with you?"

"You have to help me get through this," he said, crying louder.

"What are you talking about?"

"I know it's over between us, but I have to talk to you sometimes, just to get through this. I can't stop crying," he said, breaking down.

"Do you want me to come over there? I was getting ready to go to sleep, but I can come over if you want."

"Okay, if you don't mind."

"I'm on my way," I said, hanging up the phone. "Lord, what have I gotten myself into," I said aloud as I rushed out the door.

On the way to Raymond's I cried out to God. *"Lord, why is there always two men in my life? All I want is one good man. When I was thirteen, there was John and Carl. I married the wrong man the first time. I can't afford to make the same mistake again. Please, Lord, make it crystal clear which man you have chosen for me. I don't even know why I'm going to Raymond's apartment. If I had went straight home, I would have missed his call. All I want to do is get some sleep."*

Mrs. Simmons opened the door and pointed me to Raymond's room. I entered his room only to see a broken down shell of a man. He was crying like a baby, lying on his bed. I sat next to him. I guess Douglas was right. Raymond had checked into Heart-Break Hotel and couldn't check out.

"I don't want you to see me like this, but I can't stop crying," he said with snot coming from his nose.

I ran to the bathroom to get some tissue. "Take this," I said, handing him a large wad of tissue. He blew his nose with the tissue and wiped his eyes with his shirt.

"Last night, when you looked at me as if I was a total stranger, you hurt me so bad. I love you, Vanessa. I would have given my life for you," he said, blowing his nose again.

I ran to get more tissue. He needed more than I realized. When I came back, I handed him the tissue.

"Thank you," he said, blowing again, still crying. "I took the rest of this week and next week off because I can't function like this. The kids tried to help me, but all I do is cry. I told them they would have to go live with their mother because I can't take care of them like this," he said, crying his heart out.

His words cut through me like a knife. Raymond loved his children more than himself. For him to give them up because of me was more than I could take. He showed me then, in his weakest state, he loved me with his whole being. His love for me was greater than the love he had for himself and his children. It was at that point, I knew I had my man. Thank you, Jesus!

"Raymond, I had no idea how much you love me, until now," I said, holding him in my arms.

"No, Vanessa," he said, shrugging away. "I can't take advantage of you. I don't need your pity."

"I'm not offering you my pity, but my love. I realize now how much you love me. I want to show my love in return."

"You're committed to someone else," he said, blowing more snot from his nose.

"No, I'm not. There's no ring on my finger. All I wanted you to do was ask me to marry you. You never asked. You just teased me to death. You can ask me now," I said, looking into his eyes.

Blowing his nose again and wiping his eyes he said, "Will you marry me?"

"Yes. I will."

He held me in his arms and started crying again.

"It's okay, Raymond. We can get married today."

He looked at me in disbelief. "Are you sure?"

"Yes. Go get the ring from your closet."

"I don't have a ring."

You don't?" I thought about what Bryson said in the hallway. Here I was thinking, Raymond had a ring all this time.

"No."

"Well, get dressed. We have a lot to do."

"Can we get married in one day?"

"With Jesus, all things are possible. Let's give it a try."

"Okay. Let me get dressed. I've already showered," he said, perking up, kissing me on the cheek.

"I'll wait in the living room. It's improper to see the groom get dressed." I got up and left. He started getting ready. I prayed silently as I waited.

Dear Heavenly Father, if it is Your Will that we marry this day, make it possible for us to do so. If Raymond is not the right man for me, put a block in our path to prevent us from getting married. Only You know if he is right or wrong. I pray for Your blessings or intervention, whichever one applies. In Jesus name, I pray. Amen.

Raymond came out of his room, twenty minutes later, wearing a long sleeve white shirt, gray suit pants, his tan London Fog coat and matching brim. I had on navy blue pants, a blue and red shirt with sneakers.

"Let's go!" he said, smiling again.

We said good-bye to Mrs. Simmons as we left.

"You don't know how this makes me feel," he said, walking to the car. I thought I had lost you to another man and now you will be my wife. Several times last week, I almost killed myself, running stop signs. I couldn't concentrate on nothing but you."

We kissed as he opened my door. All the love I had for Raymond resurfaced. Indeed, he was my man. "You have me for the rest of your life, starting today."

"I will love and cherish you until the day I die," he said as he closed my door.

My watch said it was 9:30, we only had seven hours to do everything. Our first stop was Rich's at Cumberland Mall on Cobb Parkway. We went to the jewelry counter to purchase my ring after being stalled in heavy traffic for forty-five precious minutes. Carefully examining the selections in Raymond's price range, we decided on a gold wedding band with clusters of small diamonds on each side of a three-fourth karate stone.

Our second stop was Grady Hospital to get our blood tests. We reached Grady at 11:40 a.m.. Only four hours and fifty minutes remained—would that be enough time for the blood tests?

The blood test for men, in Georgia, is the RPR test for syphilis that takes less than ten minutes to perform. Women need the RPR test and the Rubella screen for German measles. The Rubella screen, depending on the methodology, could take anywhere from several minutes to several hours to perform. If it takes several hours, samples are run only once or twice a day. When I worked in Immunology, six years ago, we only had one morning run that started before 9 a.m..

We went to Immunology before we had our blood drawn. I told Robin, my former supervisor, my predicament. She informed me they had changed methodology since I left. The Rubella screens were now run on the Axsym and only took twenty minutes. They run specimens throughout the day as they receive them. With that information, Raymond and I went to the main lab to get our paperwork for our blood tests and marriage license certificate. Mazie Harris and Fern Ivey, the lab secretaries, prepared our necessary papers and instructed us to go to the Out Patient Lab to get our blood drawn.

After we got our blood drawn, we took our labeled tubes to the Immunology Lab and gave them to Robin. We also requested HIV tests to be done. They wouldn't be run until tomorrow which was all right since we didn't need the results for our marriage license.

By, now, it was 12:30 p.m.. Robin told us to come back in an hour. We decided to use the time to spread the news in Raymond's department. We also went to the chapel where we prayed silently holding hands.

At 1:30 sharp, we went back to the Immunology Lab. Our blood tests were ready, but we had to get our certificate signed by a pathologist. Robin informed us only one of the three pathologist, was available today and she didn't know if he was in the lab. She then went in the Blood Bank Lab for Dr. Silva. Thankfully, he was present and signed our certificate. We thanked him, Robin, her staff, and the lab secretaries before we left for the courthouse downtown.

The courthouse was a few minutes away. It took us until 2:25 to get inside because we couldn't find a parking space. Once inside, we asked the medal detector guards where to go get our marriage license. We went to the right place; paid our $35 fee; filled out papers; then got our license. After we got our license, we asked the clerk where to go to get married. She told us to come back tomorrow at 2:00 p.m. when the marriages are performed. We explained, we had to get married today, not tomorrow. She shook her head, letting us know it couldn't be done today.

Raymond and I looked at each other with dispair on our faces. "There's no one here who could marry us today?" I asked, turning back to the clerk.

"No. Not today. I'm sorry. Try again, tomorrow," she answered, preoccupied shuffling papers.

As we walked away, a crackling voice caught our attention, "Excuse me,"

"Yes?" we responded, dejectedly, almost in unison.

"Did I hear you say, you wanted to get married, today?" a male clerk asked.

"That's right, we did but...," exclaimed Raymond.

"I know someone who can marry you if he's still here."

"What?" we responded.

"His name is Gary McCauley. He's a minister...,"

"Where is he?" Raymond asked, grabbing my hand.

"Oh, yeah," the first clerk responded, "I forgot about him."

"Go to the library room downstairs to see if he's still here," the male clerk, instructed.

"Where is that?" I asked.

We followed the clerk's directions to the library room. Raymond asked an attendant if Gary McCauley was present. The attendant said no, but he knew where to find him if he had not gone home. He told us to wait on the side while he send someone to get him. We cuddled up on the wall while we waited.

Ten minutes later, a tall black man approached us and said he was Gary McCauley and asked if we wanted to get married.

We exclaimed, "Yes!"

He led the way to his office down a flight of stairs. After closing the door, he walked behind the desk, picked up a book then asked if we were ready for the ceremony. Reading our vows from his book, we repeated them as he instructed. Mr. McCauley asked Raymond if he had a ring when it was that time in the ceremony. Raymond took the ring from his pocket and slipped it on my finger.

"I now pronounce you, husband and wife," Mr. McCauley announced as the ring rested on my hand.

We then kissed as husband and wife.

"That's the longest kiss I've ever seen," Mr. McCauley stated, smiling at us.

"Mrs. Raymond Miller," Raymond said, kissing me again. "We did it! We got married in one day."

"Yes, we did, dear husband. God was with us every step of the way," I said, holding him tighter.

"I love you with all my heart, Mrs. Miller. You'll never regret marrying me," Raymond said, smiling with joy.

"I love you, too, Raymond. I know we'll be happy together."

"Let's go. We've accomplished what we came for."

"Okay."

"Thank you, Mr. McCauley," Raymond said, shaking his hand. "You've made me the happiest man on earth!"

"You're welcome. It's part of my job," he responded, shaking my hand, too.

"Thanks for everything," I said, still shaking his hand.

"Come on, Mrs. Miller. It's time to go home," Raymond instructed.

We left the small office and found our way to the front door passed the metal detector guards. It was 3 o'clock when we left the courthouse.

On the way home, I told Raymond, I had to call Douglas because we had a date at six. He understood. I paged Douglas when we entered the house. When the phone rang, I picked it up.

"Hello."

"Hey, baby. How you doing?" Douglas asked.

I took a deep breath and exhaled. "Douglas, I just got married." Silence filled the other end.

"How could you do that?" he asked with his voice cracking "Did you pray about it first?"

"Yes, I prayed, first."

"I can't believe you got married on me like that."

"I didn't plan it. We decided to get married today."

"I have to go. I can't talk no more," he said hanging up the phone.

I hung up the phone slowly. Raymond was by my side the whole time. I felt bad for Douglas. He did not deserve to be the one who got hurt. His pain was my only regret of marrying Raymond.

"I have to call Mama," I told Raymond. I dialed her number. "Mama, I'm married! I just got married today."

"You're kidding."

"No. I'm not."

"Nessa, you're kidding. You didn't get married today."

"Yes, I did. My husband is standing right beside me."

"Put him on the phone," she instructed.

Raymond took the phone. "Hello, Ma Grant. I'm your new son-in-law." He handed the phone back to me. "Your mother wants to talk to you."

"Nessa, is this some kind of joke? Raymond is your husband?"

"Yes, Mama. It's the truth."

"Wait until I tell your daddy."

"Mama, I have to go. I'll talk to you later."

"I hope you have some good news later."

"Bye, Mama."

"Bye."

Raymond, I have one more call to make. I want to call the job." I dialed the number.

"Emergency Clinic Lab. Abeba speaking. How may I help you?"

"Abeba. This is Vanessa. I just called to tell everybody, I got married today. I married Raymond Miller."

"All right. I'll tell everyone."

"Thank you. Good-bye."

Raymond held me close as I hung up the phone. We kissed a long passionate kiss. "I love you, Mrs. Raymond Miller," he said after the kiss.

"I love you, too, Mr. Miller, my husband. Wait-a-minute! I have some keys that belong to you," I said, pulling away to go up the steps.

He waited in the kitchen while I went to my room. I saw a piece of paper on my dresser and decided to write Raymond a few lines.

"Hurry up, Mrs. Miller! I want to pick the kids up early so we can get something to eat," he shouted after a few minutes.

"Okay, honey. I'm coming! I shouted back as I finished writing. I retrieved his keys and read the lines one more time.

Dearest Raymond, my husband and best friend.
I pray, our love will last forever and never end.
Although we didn't have a fancy wedding or go on a honeymoon.
This day, we were wed by a man of God in a small courthouse room.
My wedding ring is a symbol of our commitment and love,
to Jesus Christ and our Heavenly Father above.
I know I married the right man.
With that, I have a peace of mind.
Because you, my dear Raymond, are the bearer of the sign.

To be continued with...The Image: A Prophetic Birth.

Printed in the USA
CPSIA information can be obtained
at www.ICGtesting.com
LVHW081614311023
762279LV00005B/27